BLUE LIES SEPTEMBER

BLUE LIES SEPTEMBER

James Tunney

James Tunney is the author of this book and owns all copyright ©
in this work and asserts all moral rights thereto 2019.

Cover image copyright © James Tunney.
Based on an original oil painting by James Tunney.

ISBN: 9781092471510

To Git & Christian

Also by James Tunney

Mysticism & Spiritual Consciousness

The Mystical Accord – Sutras to Suit Our Times,
Lines for Spiritual Evolution

Fiction

Ireland I Don't Recognise Who She Is

Contents

Chapter 1	Spatiamentum - Mystic Phantom Fleet	11
Chapter 2	The Secret Seven	48
Chapter 3	The Real Deal	59
Chapter 4	The Extraordinary Ethel Woodpecker	78
Chapter 5	Inspired Agenda	104
Chapter 6	Midship Point - The Chosen One	109
Chapter 7	Hermits and Hermeneutics	120
Chapter 8	Minefield	127
Chapter 9	Mesmerising Column of Dust	130
Chapter 10	The Fuzz - The Buzz - The Beat	146
Chapter 11	Work Out	156
Chapter 12	Cloud of Unknowing - Contemplation	161
Chapter 13	The Governors	170
Chapter 14	As Bluebottles to Honey	174
Chapter 15	Brigid – Interstitium	184
Chapter 16	Turning Tables - The Last Shall Become First	195
Chapter 17	Heaping Up Its Own Funeral Pyre - Invisible Government	203

Chapter 18	Dominus	239
Chapter 19	Heart of Darkness	243
Chapter 20	Intrusions - La Pucelle – The Golden Path	251
Chapter 21	Rock-a-Bye Baby - Utnapishtim	261
Chapter 22	When You Hear What I Say You Will Not Understand - Non Sine Sole Iris	271
Chapter 23	Dark Night of the Soul - Of Little Meddling Commeth Great Ease	286
Chapter 24	Greenwich - Omphalos	295
Chapter 25	Killer on the Loose	304
Chapter 26	Middle Earth	306
Chapter 27	Brick Lane - We Are Shadows	313
Chapter 28	Ceremony	321
Chapter 29	Showy Execution - Theatre of Death Bound	324
Chapter 30	The Club	343
Chapter 31	No Show	346
Chapter 32	Semper Occultus - One Ill Weede Marreth a Whole Pot of Pottage	351
Chapter 33	The Beggar May Sing Before the Thiefe	360

®

The Spell to Establish.

Incantation. Spell a world.

Sacrifice one letter. You have a word.

By use of a spell, a stroke was changeth.

By rule of a stroke, a word was changeth.

By rule of a word, a sentence was changeth.

By rule of a sentence, a story was changeth.

By rule of a story, the history was changeth.

By rule of the history, the past was changeth.

By rule of the past, the present was changeth.

By rule of the present, the country was changeth.

By rule of the country, the region was changeth.

By rule of the region, the globe was changeth.

By rule of the globe, the starry world was changeth.

By rule of the starry worlds, the future was changeth.

By rule of the future, eternity was changeth.

All by a stroke.

All the steps.

Done before they woke.

Magic it may be, but the path was always plain to see.

Those who allow their spirit vanish, alas will have their wish.

In confidence, The Ringmaster.

λόγος

Wake B4 UR Wake.

Domestic Terrorism Bill

Section 33

It is an offence hereby punishable by imprisonment to promote, publish or gain access to, in any form, in any way or in any place, any argument, postulation, statement, suggestion, supposition or theory calculated to convince any person anywhere of the existence of a conspiracy to control national or global affairs and governance.

Chapter 1

Spatiamentum

Mystic Phantom Fleet

> In which Miss Ashling takes an habitual, long promenade around the culturally significant central northern area of London principally following over ground the course of the subterranean River Fleet to reflect on the meaning of life, distil certain ideas and cogitate on the esoteric and clandestine in the hope of further identifying some clues to the subconscious construct of contemporary society that might explain its deeper sense of tension in these troubled times.

It was the most controlled of times, it was the most chaotic. Familiar but strange. The insidious distortion of reality and perception of surreptitious relinquishing of power had caused a wave of cynicism, suspicion and seeking. A spectrum of spectres. Some talking of a Western Civil War. Before the Net had caught those it wanted and closed somewhat, some genies had escaped. Who is the servant and who is the master? Ashling Julie Doyle-Toledo (aka Candy Apple Crimson X, Goddess Blue Brigid 7, Ethel Woodpecker) left her flat, shut the building door and stepped onto Eversholt Street, London NW1, Sunday last day of August, temperature 20 degrees centigrade. Close friends called her Ash, her flat 'The Ashram.' One wall was covered in post-its, arrows, pages and maps about London, with battlements of books below. Another with some inspirational quotes, pictures and things to do that week. Edith Stein's photo was there now, with others. Every day a search for enlightenment at a time of disenchantment. She left 'Ethereal' the mechanical doll on a chair. Your attention is the most important thing on the quest. Attention to what, that's the question? Oscar Wilde realised in jail that the most interesting things were mystical. Ash was contemplating the goddess Brigid (aka Bride) and also Elizabeth I. Walking the city was her imaginarium of expanding consciousness. Through the veil, chinks of light. London, mythical, magical, magnetic. Charged with spirits. Intrigued by the hidden, obscured, clandestine. Willing to learn, try things. Agent of my best destiny. Achievements to be proud of. Ash kept her wonder, London a wonderland if you wished. Today she would follow the course of that fascinating, underground river. Roam the blue lodge after burnt yellow-lighted August. Augustus Caesar wasn't it from? Ash wanted to initiate a new perception, move beyond herself, escape brainwashing. Am I enough she wondered? Nothing is what it seems. She felt good still, personally stable. Funny that there are deep and shallow people. But they often look identical or at least indistinguishable. We mix them up.

London felt odd recently. Guildhall Bomb out of the blue. Strange assassinations of sportsmen. Several odd political groups sprung up. Eco-activists, vegans stopping the traffic, shutting the town. Violent feminists, samizdat, agitprop everywhere. Striking sky. An uncanny fortnight since the eerie phenomenon of red light seen over the city. Aurora Borealis or some solar activity created a scarlet lightshow and caused a curious concern. An arc of celestial crimson. A literal, blue moon purpling purely due to atmospheric conditions. An alien invasion some believed. Talk of Nuremburg UFO's of 1561. Tales of war, nuclear explosion, volcanic eruption. Alien Invasion Fake? Astrology, secret service of the sky, the agent de Wohl called it. Despite scientific explanations it felt ominous. Meteorologists, originally interested in atmosphere and celestial things, were less interested than the public in these phenomena now. Weather news, states the obvious and possible, so you think the political stuff might be as well. Skyshow aroused something primitive. To Mary (her neighbour below) a sign from heaven. Something on the way. August 1939 Hitler witnessed red light in the sky at Eagle's Nest and decided blood would be shed. A fulfilment of the Second Secret of Fatima. Stunningly beautiful dome of St Pauls, a blood-orange hemisphere shimmering after a golden spell. Wren's work turned magically magenta. A bell pealed, faint in the distance. Once English air full of bells told people of passings, sickness, execution and death. Elizabeth I's accession. Romans rang the hours. Curfew. Silent during war and sombre times. Dick Whittington walked from the City, their bells made him turn around, stopping not far from here. Something like 'Turn thrice Dick Whittington, Lord Mayor of London.' Cat and mouse. A bad housekeeper made him run from Leadenhall. The stained glass window of him in Guildhall had just been destroyed. Bells had spoken to him. Navy told the time with bells. Ten Bells the pub beside Hawksmoor's church. Now forenoon, four bells. For whom the bell tolls? Bellum. Bella. She wondered whether the sky presaged anything. The quickening? 'Synchromysticism' a new word for her. Some conspiracy theorists said it was Project Blue Beam and waited for holograms of the face of God in the sky. De Quincey

Opium-Eater in the London labyrinth. All I see as if a rabbit ran by with a watch and a waistcoat and we followed and fell upon a time.

Ash examined herself gamely with her spiritual looking glass. At 33, vegetarian, fit, free, single, introverted, compulsive, independent will, exceptional memory for things of interest, like hypnosis, mind control, meaning of words, martial arts, tummo. Find your true self getting rid of your false self. Occasional cello-player, archer, yogi, mixed martial artist. Always reading. Mesmerised by the Elizabethan era, intruding into the present in ghostly ways. Felt like a time-slip, warp, loop. Spiritual not religious. Christianity becoming like a curse word in London, new 'c' word. Obsessions yes, addictions no. Hating victimhood. A victim - a sacrifice to a deity. They make you passive getting ready to serve you up. I would make my children strong inside. Possibility of a child still there. Once it had all been about poverty, patriarchy and abuse in her head but she changed when she woke up. She knew she was attractive. Too many suitors. Work gave Ash freedom, building her business at the MysticBlueDom Agency that could generate Intellectual Property so she could retire before 40. Erik's part involved a doppelganger doll of sorts. A simulacrum, simulator, surrogate. Blue Dolly. Key was creating a lasting bond with the robot. All be entirely autonomous soon. Ash's life gravitated by the force of conscious and unconscious desire into the recondite. Answers lie hidden in new and old dimensions. Mysteries, myth, magic awaited mystically. Seek clues in illusion shows where diversion rules. A nice dream last night. Mystery of mysticism her most meaningful exploration. Replenished her unique professional armamentarium. We fade to grey. Devenir gris. Visage. Blitz.

'Bastard!' She laughed recalling Jem on Henry VIII's reference to his daughter Elizabeth. Jem lived rough when weather permitted round Hampstead Heath, from where Boswell first saw London. A beautiful dandelion, Jem. How is one of the most nutritious, gorgeous plants regarded as a weed? Inversion, diversion. Dent de leon, lion's tooth. Dandelion coffee. Buy some coffee to bring to him and boil in the open air on that little stove. He never drank alcohol but she had hashish with him at times and hallucinogens before he talked her out of them. He thought his memory lapses were down to LSD from the past. Repeating his other politically incorrect utterances satisfyingly rendered in his Scottish burr. An Indira's net in a word. September.

'and still more late flowers for the bees,
Until they think warm days will never cease.
And gathering swallows twitter in the skies.'

One area she and Jem were not in accord was his conviction that many people were not human (and he did not mean this in a metaphorical way). Whether he thought them aliens, mechanical, mentally ill, possessed or some sort of zombies was unclear. That had nothing to do with all the shape-beings, goblins and elves he met on his trips. Otherwise highly rational, intelligent and perceptive. Jem said there were people capturing black squirrels in August up there, to extract their testosterone to use in doping athletes. *'Seasons of mists and mellow fruitfulness.'* Keats wrote Ode to Autumn in September. Begins tomorrow. I like September's balance between warmth and coolness. Departed glow and coming chill fresh in early insistence. Azure September with terminal lucidity of dying summer. Blackberries with summer's blood Heaney said. Vulcan associated. Parliament Hill in Hampstead a part of a triangle of ley lines or dragon paths to the Tower and over near the Houses of Parliament. Δ. Delta. No *Delta of Venus*. All three hills had prehistoric mounds, like where the Temple of Diana was under St Pauls. Diana. Dana. Now Virgo. Sun transits September 17th does it not? Virgo, Great Goddess or virgin. Astraea. Harvest. Like Brigid. Trying to formulate her own observations. Not psychogeography, just joining the dots. That's all.

Noisy, nerve-jangling on the pavement. Traffic always busy coming in and out of Mornington Crescent and Camden Town down the artery to Euston Station and Bloomsbury. Living over the Tube station you hear trains rumbling as if in the belly of a gentle giant. With pale, lapis lazuli light, easy to ignore busyness. Blue heavens open, easier to transcend the mundane. Jeans, cheap cap, simple, light navy light cardigan tied around her waist, turquoise tee-shirt. Not seeking attention. Hair shoulder-length, sometimes described as 'oak-coloured.' Liked soft, natural, comfortable fabrics. A straight back. Despite sense assaults, it felt fresh, bright and bracing. A faint sting of air in her nose. An odd orange leaf lay on the pavement. Blue and advancing orange, the complementary seasonal shades. Working, on average, 3 full days a week for her own business allowed her follow other interests. Her walk would help her work. Walking was spiritual wandering, working pathways in the mind that make perception more acute. Muses and creative beast needed constant attention. Could you pick up the spirit of great people walking the same paths? Like Jane Eyre in the open air. I care for myself. The more solitary, friendless, unsustained I am, the more I will respect myself, or something like that. Like Lamb. Saunterers. Wandersmänner. Wanderers. Wand.

Ash had looked in on Mary. She came in the 50's when London building sites were hungry for trains from Holyhead of cattle boats carrying families from DeValera's Ireland. Euston Terminus. Shock. No Irish. No Blacks. But for many a liberation. Some would pine for green, stony fields and small communities where you were something, whatever limitations and where there was music, life and family. *Duffy is Dead.* There had been Spanish and Jewish refugees before. Ash loved that all peoples were about. Auerbach, her favourite painter of townscapes, came from Germany in 1939 and began painting bombsites. Great congealed, coagulated messes. His studio was around the corner. Met him a few times. Camden Town Group of painters a century ago. Around here full of Irish. Hard when you come from emerald hills of passing light. Many successful. Some lonely, hard-drinking. Many went to Mass on Sunday and followed hurling and football back home. Some bitter, others nostalgic. Home at holidays and funerals, for summers. Opportunity made most move to leafy suburbs. Religion, rejection of religion, gratitude for opportunities in London, a mixture of longing and hatred for the country that let them go. The Craic was good in Cricklewood. Crack now. Long, long way from Clare to here. Streets of London. Mountains of Mourne. Sow that eats it's farrow as Joyce wrote. Some grew more English than the English themselves. Community largely gone. Metamorphosis. Few old bachelors hung on. A charity she supported, helped some of the last of these live in a lovely place at home by the Atlantic. Mary going well still, loving London for the chances, facilities, people, mixture. In her 80's, sounded like she just got off the boat. Dressed in red and black. Silvery hair.

"Grand day. Thank God," she said.

"Looks nice," Ash said.

"Ye out for a walk?" Mary asked.

"I am, you too?"

"Mind yourself now. I will go up Camden Town like I do every day to buy some milk. You're a great woman for your big walks. Listen will you pop in to the Blue Rooster tonight?" Mary asked.

"Ok. Not for long."

"Good I'll be there after Mass. Now if you need to walk a bit faster sing that oul' rebel song. Follow me up to Carlow," Mary said.

"I looked it up. It goes back to Elizabeth I. A bit rough," Ash said and Mary sang,

> *"White is sick and Grey is fled,*
> *And now for Black Fitzwilliam's head*
> *We'll send it over dripping red*
> *To Queen Liza and her ladies."*

Mary laughed. She loved Queen Elizabeth II. She was off with the rhythm in her head, humming. Greys always there.

Day of possibility. Edge of exaltation. On such days you approach the spirit of place, your sensorium tranquil, subtle energy sneaking in. Pay and give your attention. Day for a voyage of discovery in her quest. Or to go up in topaz air in a hot-air balloon or parachute. Leisurely breakfast. No TV, less propaganda. Showered, legs shaved, hair washed, no make-up, no mobile, home-made coconut and sandalwood deodorant, she felt free. New pair of sneakers made a nice sound on footpaths. From Mornington Crescent, handful of walks. One trek called. Usually Ash made her way quickly to Regent's Park, Primrose Hill or Hampstead Heath, Kentish Town and Camden, after having walked around the Crescent which inspired her. Sickert was one of two Jack the Ripper suspects who lived there. Ridiculous theory. Film-making all the time around. Paddington Bear, Jackie Chan. Painters on her mind. Auerbach a master-magician transformed this place in a swirl of warm colours. Painters, one of many reasons for walks. Circulatio. Walks helped her make sense of new dimensions opening up in spirit. Ash walked for pleasure, reflection and focusing attention. When training Brazilian Jiu Jitsu, walking and tree-climbing helped. Bought an ultramarine gi yesterday. Submit or be submitted. Walking was even better than Chi Kung and Tai Chi for her. Meditate on a few things, insufflate sights. Walter Raleigh hovering. 'The Lie.' Elizabethan period was hooking her, all poetry, plays, cloak and dagger, espionage, informers, bloodthirstiness, royalty. Red an appropriate colour for power in London. Evelyn Underhill another resonant force impressing her. Client No. 4 in the back of her mind. Sparked Elizabeth. Her motto, *Video et Taceo*. I see and say nothing. Probably from her spy master Walsingham, back to Cicero. Rambles cleared brambles in her mind and allowed sediment of sentiment to settle. Some might call her a bit 'schizo,' 'manic' but she had safety-nets when she swung on the mental trapeze. She relished the buzzing bees in her hive-head that made whitening combs of the golden honey of insight from the meadow of flowers in her books and in the world outside, present and past. She felt her body strong and that her soul had clawed, grasped and climbed like a mountaineer up to a plateau of relative peace that promised possibility of ascending higher summits. Imagine the Fleet meandering here before this place was dreamt of.

Painting time diminished but interest in painters had not. Drew inspiration from their haunts, the genius loci in ancient Roman religion. Great painter-magicians shook the ordinary to show the extraordinary. Tore illusion to reveal reality underneath. Pigments, brushes on flat squares transmuting the cognisable. Magicians that painted, wrote or created worlds drew her. Walking allowed Ash hear The Voice. This route with hypotenuse to start, divine child. Dickens lived here as well as up Camden Town. Interesting process of writing. Hypnagogic trances. Voices, characters came. A channelling, forces pressing in. Opening yourself to inspiration. Distillation of your own unconscious, subconscious. She cast aside her learned scepticism of paranormal and psychic phenomena to try to develop. Vivid dreaming last night. Usually she woke up 30 seconds before the alarm. Used to wonder how your body clock could pre-empt the mechanical so. Remembered dream well. Car park. Looked up. A red disc moved rapidly, with orange light glowing from the raised part. Awoke. Looked at alarm clock just before it went off. Was the disc an alarm clock symbol or a premonition? When she walked to San Diego de Compostella, something hovered directly over the spire. Saint James and the Field of the Fallen Star. Jung's theory never worked for her. Some kind of projection from folk consciousness? Project Blue Book. Something coming or maybe just a clock face. Mechanical disc captures your attention. Time flies. Using candles more often recently she saw worlds form more clearly than ever in flamesphere of diamondlight. A little thrill of anticipation still. Infinity. Ashta=8. Ashes to Ashes. New Romantics. Steve Strange.

She saw the day's practice note in her mind's eye. Think of retrocausation, effects coming before the causes, premonitions, presentiment, precognition. Time-travel, back and forwards. Open mind. Steve blitzed and faded. David. Marilyn. George. Fallen star.

COLD SHOWER. MORNING: EVENING. 20 MINS

As she walked by the shop she saw the parkour guys were out. It would soon be criminalised. Tic Tac, wall run, gap jump. She knew some of them. She had seen some on the internet. They ran and rolled and hopped from the roof of the shop onto a tree that was beside the road. She clapped in appreciation as one leaped over and landed with his two feet on the tree, neatly and fearlessly. He smiled at her and she gave a thumbs-up. These groups of young men were brave, bold and cool. Seemed very relaxed and polite when you talked to them. Tell you about climbing the Dome in Greenwich or scaling cranes, without permission. They divided people into two groups, those who were nice and those who were not. Had a healthy disrespect for authority. Some of the police were alright with them. In a regulated world we forget how it is ours and how restrained we have become. She admired them. She talked to one who started joking about cougars. Maybe not joking. In the time of The Great Bewildering we do not know who will lead us out. In parts of London there was great unrest, order was disintegrating. New Romantics went to Camden.

Down Eversholt Street by Euston Station sauntered by St Aloysius's Church. Jack Doyle, great boxer, star, libertine, 'The Gorgeous Gael' ended up there in a coffin for Requiem mass, down and out. *'A generous man never went to hell.'* They try to burn it down regularly these days. Some say the Western Civil War is coming. Down left, Mary Shelley lived. *Frankenstein. The Modern Prometheus*. Scientists cannot play God. Must be careful about monsters we give birth to. Master becomes slave. Technology has a cost as well as a benefit. Her mother, Mary Wollstonecraft, wrote about women's rights. Irish nationalism a monster to Victorians. Never looked in the mirror. Mirror, mirror on the wall. Slave in magic mirror. Guff about the 'Mandela Effect' and film Snow White. In the film she says 'magic mirror on the wall.' In Grimm's story she says 'Mirror, Mirror.' People mix it up. More interestingly, a mistress and a slave juxtaposed against a maiden. Past the few shops still selling blue movies. Judith Ward. Claimed to have placed bombs for the IRA in 1973. 1974. One went off here September and King's Cross. Outcry. Jail. Extreme pressure on police to get results means you have a short-circuit effect. Confession or round-up-the-usual suspects. Mental disorder, incoherent, rambling, no corroboration, romantic connection only. Retracted later, eventually released. IRA said she did not do it. Fails for police, science, intelligence, media, judiciary. Across traffic lights, not straight to Russell Square and Bloomsbury, before her but left and east down Euston Road. ⚏. 1 minute to the right was where Kenneth Williams lived. Seemed funny but like most comics was a nutter it seems. *The Woman in White. The Moonstone* too. Marshalling pedestrians over to the *Concrete Island*, a funny, tall bearded man. She said "Thank you."

"You must look up also on the path," he said and pointed upwards.

Celestial reminder of a blue oil paint you could only buy at Cornelisson's. Wondered whether he was talking about drones.

"Get off the road you silly ol' cunt," someone shouted, screeching away.

Not seen him before anywhere. Sounds, fumes, speeding vehicles disorientating and unpleasant for strolling. Want us in cars so we cannot feel grounded. Why do bizarre things happen around here in fiction? She thought of that Clive Staples who went around shouting about the end of the world and arguing with the Trots down Tower Hill. She heard him say he had come back from Christ's Kingdom to warn the world and they were going to hell. She had thought the activists would lynch him. To and fro was how to go, ebb and flow.

Russell Square lay ahead, but she would go left by King's Cross and down Farringdon Road, south-east. All the writers round here. All the strange books. About odd things. Why? She went to a channeller over there. Thought that was happening to her. Channel. Like a river, band of frequencies, medium. CHANNEL. Use it in physics, electrons, crystals, nuclear stuff. Around here the protagonist in *The Day of the Triffids* came, scavenging food among the hungry masses blinded by meteors. Huxley's *Island* has this Bloomsbury-Highgate nexus too. *Gravity's Rainbow* and fantasy of a giant adenoid also. *The Drowned World. Hairy London.* Strange caryatids at the crypt at the back of new St Pancras Church. Old churchgoers had fought over the foundation stone 200 years ago. Yeats lived just past there surrounded with magical, blue things. Burton Street behind. The Skinners used to own it. There was a 'House of Correction' or 'Discipline' for gentlemen's fun in Victorian times. Someone therefrom said there was hardly a street in the 'monster city' without some memorable people. H.G. Wells lived on Euston Road with his relations. Inspired scientists like rocket-man Goddard. So in a few hundred yards the founders of modern science fiction. Man-made monsters, time-travel, alien invasions, Martians trying to rule the world. Before that you had Verne and the Ancient Greeks, Chinese, Jewish stories. Swedenborg? Kepler wrote *Somnium* with his 'daemons' travelling to the Moon. Down the road Charles Fort lived. Strange things interested Fort. 'Anomalous phenomena.' Frogs falling from the sky. *Book of the Damned.* Conceived teleportation. Collected stories of spontaneous human combustion, levitation, unexplained noises. Out-of-place artefacts, poltergeists, alien abduction. Came for the British Museum. X files may have come from Fort. X used to be Christ, from Greek. He wrote a book called X. Although there was the X Club before. They supported evolution theory. Thomas Henry Huxley, the grandfather of Aldous. The grandfather cutting up bodies round here too. X rays. Uranium X. The British Board of Film Classification came up with X for films with sex and violence. They're still there, 10 mins walk away. Set up in 1912 after an outcry over a film about Jesus. Then the X men. Monsters, monstrosities, creation. X ratings. X Factor. X dimension. X guard. Factor X, Colin Wilson, higher consciousness. XXX. They link the sacred with the obscene and invert it. Deliberately. INVERSION. XX Double Cross. Reduced V-1's targets here. X-phemism. Malcolm X. Scissors. Crossroads. LeXigram. SpaceX. Tipler proposed that a Virgin Birth could occur if Jesus was a special XX gene male. HoaX. What was the start of *War of the Worlds*?

> *'Nobody would have believed... that this world was been watched keenly and closely by intelligences greater than man's.'*

Richard Burton put his beautiful voice to it. Here Burton Street where Rymer, who wrote Penny Dreadfuls, was born. *The String of Pearls*. Science fiction, mythology of the future. Orson Welles was really a Wells. Something in the air here? Sherlock Holmes lived not five minutes back at Baker Street. Doyle was unusually rational <u>and</u> into mysticism. That's what it used to be, even Newton, Descartes. These days we would say that nobody would have believed that we were free from scrutiny from Intelligence. Conscious that every movement was tracked. Chilling. Comfort for others, Stockholm Syndrome, caged animals at London Zoo up the road. Howard Hodgkin painted in the old Dairy here. Euston Road painters also. Down towards King's Cross, by the British Library. CROSS. Phone boxes disappearing. Design inspiration of the classic red box came from old St Pancras church. Wells wrote that,

> *'As men busied themselves they were scrutinised and studied, perhaps as narrowly as a man with a microscope might multiply and scrutinise the transient creatures that swarm and multiply in a drop of water.'*

A scrutinised swarm... us, the only apex predator? Blue plaques everywhere. Stand out most. WELLS. On the other side she saw the statue of Newton inspired by Blake outside the British Library. Blake was critical of Newton, of the shift from mystic to measurable. Newton a mystic also. *The Diamond Sutra* in there. Anne Boleyn's bible. Magna Carta. Sutra means string or sew in Sanskrit. Suture. String of Pearls. Power to change is in you. Inside is all you seek. Fleeting world is a star at dawn, a bubble in a stream. Fleeting. Transient. Explore your world before you vanish. *The Invisible Man*. The Invisible Man lived just up on Great Portland Street. Well's critique of the invisible hand of the market. The Invisible Man became a disembodied voice, consuming, stealing, only interested in money, capable of murder. Maybe it was about commercial conspiracy and esoteric practices. Invisible man's voice would not be inside your head. Government have plans to put broadcast voices in heads more directly. Never turn it off. Autonomy is our greatest gift. Wells wrote *The New World Order*. He craved order. Order, control, command, instruction, obey. Same as Dominance-Submission. You should enjoy it. Same thing. Relinquish control. We know better than you. Enjoy your servitude. Symphonie Fantastique. Fixed idea.

Outside King's Cross, Harry Potter enthusiasts showed souvenirs bought inside. Terminus. She often came here by Crowndale Road, when following the River Fleet fully by old St Pancras. There the 'Hardy Ash.' Pancras, pancreas. When it snowed once on that route, she saw 'The Magic of Harry Potter' exhibition at the British Library on one side of the road. Opposite St Pancras Station like Hogwarts. Filmed some of it there. Why was this way so magnetically magic? Old St Pancras, one of the earliest Christian settlements in the UK. Stukeley thought Julius Caesar camped on the Fleet there. Section named after him. Save with a cut. Pancras a saint from Rome. Terminus a Roman God. Boudicca fought here. A mammoth found in 1690. Caught a DPP there 'kerb-crawling' in 1991. Resigned, his wife committed suicide, sad. The Scent Box the cabbies called this stand. Fire. 31. Pet Shop Boys. Maybe 2.5 km to the bridge as the crow flies? \. 5 mins taxi, 20 mins Tube, half an hour walk. Above the hustle and bustle a sapphire throne, a lone cloud wisp like on a white bearded figure. Some say Merlin lived here. Another mound. Fairies were the people of the mound, aos sí. Penton Hill. Pentonville. Brownlow in *Oliver* lived there. Past there the Prison where Roger Casement was executed. Crowds outside largely cheer. Quicklime. Spoiled the fun in the Congo and Amazon as rubber companies slaughtered and enslaved at the behest of elites. Rubber was another enslaving, dominating material. His ship was caught by the 'Bluebell.' All the wells. St Chads. Black Marys. Bagnigge. St Pancras. 'The River of Wells.' Apparitions, presences commonplace. Douglas Adams lived up there. Another radical atheist. She saw a father holding the hand of his young daughter. She had a pink bag on her back. She heard them say, "Ok, Goldilocks if you can just hang on a little and have a little patience we can…"

<u>Birthplace of Bolshevism.</u> Lenin lived here twice, drawn by the Museum that Marx had used, supposedly. Mesmerised by Rome. A triangle from St Pancras to Bloomsbury and Clerkenwell to the Iskra magazine. The Spark. Sounds like 'uisce.' Water. Trotsky met him here for the first time. Percy Circus. O. Lenin came back to the area.

Bolsheviks. Lenin did not like his fellow revolutionaries 'commune' in Sidmouth Street nearby. Lenin wanted order not chaos. Neat dress, clean, ordered, no smoking. Order, control. Something around here in this delta making order, orders. Spectre of sceptres. Plekhanov the first Russian Marxist was there too. Later he said Lenin was a German Agent and opposed the October Revolution. Ash wondered whether Trotsky's 'Permanent Revolution' was carried around here in his head. How many dead from debates in these places between a few conspirators? Conspiracy of theories. Cons+Piracy. Around here was the world's magic cauldron of ideas. Why? Censorship and political correctness, relativism and post-modernism were making many people go looking for answers. Cynical, suspicious. Knew they had been served a crock. When rationality has been misused, it is no surprise that the mystical arises. Jailing people for swear words.

Below where Lenin met Trotsky, there were writers or characters. *Albert Angelo* by Johnson. Experimental. Islington and Angel. Telling stories is telling lies? Then that old story was just here, up the steps - *The Riceyman Steps*. What was that again, about a bit of communism and an old soldier back from war? *The Anarchists* were knocking around here. *New Grub Street* by Gissing. Put you off writing but it was realistic. Only the shallow writers that do what the public, supposedly, wants will succeed. The others will perish in poverty. The good guy (or was he really a failure?) was walking everywhere around here, Camden and Russell Square. We are meant to like losers sometimes and hate winners. This was part of the route Ash would have done if she had gone ahead as a Guide with the London Interesting Literary Walks. Nearby the character in *Adrift in Soho* stays in a hostel. Wilson said something in it to the effect the city was an *'unconscious conspiracy of matter to make you feel non-existent.'* He had 'brainstorms' that sounded like epiphanies. Brainstorm. King's Cross, St Pancras and Euston make and magnetise many migrants. *Flight to Camden*. Channels, tracks, paths, roads and junctions determine behaviour like neuronal circuits. Synapses, conjunctions. Neuroplasticity. We can all sculpt our own brain. We seek patterns in disorder. Neuroplast I CITY. Lunacies trip toy. Elasticity run op. Synaptogenesis. You even have 'neuronal migration.' Grey matter. <u>Grey</u>. The city is a brain and nervous system, and the kingdom and empire build on top of the limbic system, reptilian brain. Seeing reptilian activity in old power-structures should not be strange then? Down there on Gray's Inn Road lived Arthur Machen. Grays. Inn, for the barristers and the 'devils.' He invented psychogeography. Walking round here. *The*

Great God Pan. Said there was '*eternal beauty hidden beneath the crust of common and commonplace things.*' You could walk through the veil when rambling in London. You could pass into a different reality. His characters also met dangerous secret societies in this area. Sacrifices. Gold Tiberius. Writers like Lamb. *Rosamund Gray*.

Simulacrum. Ersatz. Faux. Erik had an intense desire to develop the dollbot's business. Not strictly a partnership in law, but a couple of companies. Mutual benefits. Business idea really revolved around sexbots, lovebots. Romancebots. Not her thing but the fantasy yielded some interesting issues. Helped her clarify the nature of the mythic goddess. Automatons were not the dominant focus but hybrids tele-operated and updating with AI. About creating a bond. 'Ethereal' resembled her. Stunt double. Uncanny. For thousands of years magicians channelled spirits into statues, objects. They experimented with programming the 'doll,' to work on its own and as an agent of a real person. Agents bind. DOLL. I-doll. IDOL. Erik wanted to add value, mastering the use as a surrogate or simulacrum. Even better than the real thing. The Ashram was not very secure for a valuable artefact. Looked at loads of films on sexbots, gynoids, fembots. Discussed Olga, The Bionic Woman, The Perfect Woman, Stepford Wives. Looked at science fiction and the idea of bodies being taken over by aliens, xenomorphs, body snatchers. The Four Sided Triangle. Metropolis. It Came From Outer Space. I Married a Monster from Outer Space. Forbidden Planet. Star Trek. The Mechanical Geisha. ZeloZ. Cassandra. Blade Runner. Pris. Alien Resurrection. Ex Machina. Westworld. Humans. Machines are sexualised. So are we. They studied psychology also, the Capgras delusion. She felt a very strong vibration in the ground. Must be over the Underground. A peculiar dizziness. Erik thought the sex doll frenzy was CIA-developed. But Gissing, who wrote about here in the 19th century, was speculating that some Edison would come up with an automaton to take all the good plots and write instead of real people. *New Grub Street*. Somewhere nearby where he could see the glassy gleaming on the far-off hills of the Crystal Palace or something like that. One quest Erik had was to use some of his profits to free sex slaves when he came across them in London. Quietly and effectively. Operation Red Light Runner. Red or blue. London a machine. Doll. Us fuel. Some are using silicone full-body doll suits. Not us. The word 'doll' seemed to come from Elizabethan times and also meant 'mistress.' The uncanny valley. Das Unheimliche. Uncanny valley of the Fleet.

Even when the dolls were totally autonomous they would be linked to some personality. It reminded her of Poe. William Wilson. A man meets his own double in life and eventually kills him. Before Stevenson and Wilde did the split personality. Thinking of niche markets, combining existing knowledge with evolving prototypes. Sex toys market was lucrative. Look at vibrator sales. Where fictional women robots were developed, suggestion is they were often deadly, imposters invading human bodies and sometimes creating comic consequences, often oddly attractive, capable of invoking love, desire, jealousy perhaps displacing the one they copied. Holograms, virtual reality may make similar illusions, but tangibility matters. Considering hologram-doll combos. 3D printing possibilities also. Scientists say your consciousness is not special and machines can do the same thing. More people wanted to act robotically, be treated as robots, hypnotised by a kind of machine-worship. Role reversal, humans-machines. Why? Some people really want to relinquish responsibility. A sex furore was a distraction so robots as workers, warriors, police, teachers will slip in. Experimented with the doll-type cloning. Queen Bee with her drones. Roles became important. Acting methods provided practical insights. So sometimes she would change her demeanour, gait, posture, carriage. For a few hundred metres she walked with a limp, using an acting trick she learnt from Vakthangov to see the subtle impact. Disguise. Spies and actors go together. You had to be very good at reading people. Character merchandising and mechanical sex. *Machines Like Me*. McEwan. Can't read them once they go on about politics or look like the establishment. Maybe have to. Suppose I'd be the same. Order (n.). Order (v.). Be ordered. ORDER. Elizabethan origin as command. Meant a row, arrangement as in religious order from weaving.

From King's Cross, down the rows of Farringdon Road towards the old centre and River Thames. A Victorian Road that Wren had wanted. Here the first underground railway in the world. TERMINUS. End, boundary, sacrifice. Cut and cover through the brothel domain. First council estate in England built by the City. Metropolitan Railway finished at Farringdon just by Smithfield. Metropolis meant 'mother city.' MOTHER. Metroaic religion was around here. The Great Mother to the Romans, Magna Mater. Cybele. Castrated priests. METRO. Circle Line and others are under there now. Circus, circle, Circe, kirk. During the building in 1862 the Fleet Ditch collapsed and the River flooded it. She read there was a 666 metre tunnel under Clerkenwell. A 33 foot trench. Make a lot of this stuff up. Write any old rubbish and stick it on the internet. Had a studio in Farringdon Road once. See Post Office Tower from here and soon you see St Pauls. A Zeppelin dropped a bomb on a house at Number 61 in September 1915. September seemed to be a good month for them. Targets Docklands and the East. Always someone attacking London. Exmouth Market, Grimaldi the Clown lived there. Dan Leano came from St Pancras. Huge entertainers. Leano still haunts the Theatre. London was the most haunted city in the world. Language and thought haunted. Possessed. Amnesty International HQ is here isn't it? Over the River Fleet. Mothership. The Tao is the Great Mother. From the Latin word for mother (mater) we get words for the 'womb' and the word matrix. MatriX. MATRIX. Matrika, divine mother. Do**min**atrix. Chthonic. Chthonic Railway. Cthulhu. Chitahuri. Chitauri. Beneath earth. Metropolis film. Mary Lamb kills her Ma.

Mount Pleasant. Once a pile of ash and shit. Underground postal railway track system. This is where The Rosetta Stone came during wartime. Even this great object made its way magnetically towards the Fleet. Chance? London full of underground tunnels. Government has a secret network. New ones here too for power cables. Better name than Coldbath Fields Prison (aka Middlesex House of Correction, Clerkenwell Gaol or the Steel). Cato Street conspirators were there. Tried to kill the Cabinet. Looks set up. Like the Gunpowder Plot. Posters of the Establishment dancing around maypoles with heads on. Then the Clerkenwell Bombing by the Fenians. Disraeli was worried about demonstrations. Barret hanged at Newgate. Last man. Said he was in Scotland. Public turned against the Irish. Marx says that the formerly sympathetic proletariat changed. Lucky? Bit of gunpowder and a threat to monarch or cabinet with a few rascals was always useful. Like Despard. Popish plot. Fagin's Den was here. Home of censorship. Censorship and modern copyright were twins. Censorship and this mystery business go hand in hand. Keeps Them in power. Chaos. Order. September 11? False flag? Theatre of terror. It was supposedly here on Farringdon Road that William Wynn Westcott bought the Cipher Manuscripts, that led to the Order of the Golden Dawn. Even if it was not true, it was no accident that the story was located here. Temple set up 1888. Marxists don't like non-Marxist explanations. Ma. Mar.

The MYSTERY of Clerkenwell. Down Clerkenwell, Saffron Hill. *Oliver Twist* set here. Soon Clerkenwell Green. *The Nether World* it was. Didn't Ackroyd put John Dee's house here, although it wasn't. History is strange enough. Visitors from the past, UFO's, they say is just the right brain communicating to the left. Don't buy that. The Sabini Brothers in this area fought with the Camden Gang during The Racetrack Wars. Control the bookmakers. Peaky Blinders. Razor gangs. Shooting up the pub at Mornington Crescent. Men walked this Camden-Clerkenwell way with sharp criminal intent. Priory of St John at Jerusalem Passage where Hospitallers used to be. Powerful. They end up in Rhodes and Malta. Control Mediterranean. Why unwanted if they opposed the Saracens so successfully? Master of the Revels was there after Henry VIII took it over. Shakespeare would come up. 'Mystery Plays' performed round here. Life in a day, a mobile public theatre helped by guilds. Mysteries were about understanding through revelation. Guilds were 'mysteries' with secret or specialised knowledge, like trade secrets. Join the craft, get your collar. Under the Catholic Church, secret societies, fraternities could operate if associated with guilds. Fraternity, guild, craft, secrecy, oaths. Regulate competition, control souls. Guilds, mysteries. You learned 'misteries.' Mafia. Godfather. Secret societies. Mystery related to mysticism. Mysteries. Mistress. Church kept them going. Romans had these mysteries. Masons another mystery. Kaleidoscope of collusion. You could see St Paul's from Clerkenwell. Clerk's well. Cleric's well. Another well. Water. Little Italy. Even links back to the Well of Souls in Jerusalem where it all began. The Guardian came from Manchester to Gray's Inn Road. Grays. Then to Farringdon Road before it moved up to King's Cross. Stayed on the Fleet. Good on Snowden. Otherwise not sure anymore. Newspapers are Nappers sew. Napper head, stitched up with propaganda. Daily Worker, Morning Star from here. William Morris Socialist League, taken over by anarchists. Clockmakers round too. Made automata with '*cunning fingers and the conniving brain.*' Metal springs more important than water ones. Helped Newton's idea of a clockwork universe. Scientific instruments. Maybe London is a clock. Maybe a novel, palimpsest. London is a subject.

Axiom 1   Everything, from history to news to novels, has been censored including your consciousness. Everything is controlled, channelled and governed. Truth is underground.

Into The CITY of London. Boundary. The City was subject to cyber-attacks recently. Into Smithfield, Ash was really passing into another realm. THE CITY. Smooth Field although a field of smiths sounds more convincing. Smithfield was where they had medieval jousting tournaments. 800 years of meat markets. Animals, slaughter. Still selling wholesale meat up to recently. What future dreams will those sleeping on this invisible mountain of dead flesh and psychic ocean of blood have? Probably none at all. Still people had to eat, work hard. Crimson, bright red. Some say blood is blue inside, but seems to be just reflection of blue light back. Blue light. Like computer's blue light. Dangerous. Tunnels underneath. Cut up beasts, rebels here. Pass into another dragon-guarded city. The City of London said to have the longest elected government in the world. Guildhall, the Corporation sits. Guild meant an association but before that was a tax or payment and even a sacrifice. No accident that many novels in the nineteenth century found the masters of the world here. Railways came from here, USA, Australia, India. Finance, money, control. Home of East India Company. Most people did not pay attention. Loads of places with Ash in the names over London except in the City. The City of London is not London City, Westminster. Corresponds to old Roman part. Not run by Parliament. Maybe runs Parliament. Offshore havens easily linked. Guildhall built on a Roman amphitheatre. Temples of Diana and Mithras also. Not governed by Met but City of London Police. Governed by. Still based at former Roman fortress on Wood Street. A city and a County. Sometimes referred to as the 'Square Mile.' 32 London Boroughs. The City is the 33rd local authority district. Even monarch needs permission of Lord Mayor to come in. Taxation system, court jurisdiction unique. Assets largely secret, worth a fortune. City Remembrancer in House of Commons reviews legislation. Fought for its liberties for nearly a thousand years. Royalty feared it. Played a role in downfall of monarchs and managed to have its privileges protected in law. William the Conqueror bowed to it. Business can vote. A magical boundary. The City even has a 'Ring of Steel' to protect it, supplementing the Dragon Boundary. Here the Lord Mayor of the City of London stabbed the Peasant Rebel leader Wat Tyler in the presence of the young King near the Fleet River. They have the knife stored to show off respectable cutting. King said that the example would re-affirm their slavery and warn others in the future.

Smithfield Market hit by a V2 in March 1945 killing 110 people. Greene called them robots. First one hit London on September 8th a year before. Charterhouse over there. Monks copied *The Cloud of Unknowing*. She loved that. Thomas More visited a lot. Monks did a spatiamentum, a long walk once a week. St Bartholomew the Great Church. Rahere founded it after a sick-bed vision in Rome. Benjamin Franklin worked in it. Filmed Elizabeth the Golden Age there. Where the King waited to meet the rebels. Oldest church in London still working. Many Livery Companies. Bartholomew Fair, the biggest one of all. Executions. Theatre. Elms Execution site, William Wallace. Blamed butchers at Smithfield for clogging up the Fleet. Tunnel-riddled town. A unique underground world, tunnels for transport, water and sewage. During the Blitz, underground safety. Old streets still remain. Ghosts teeming, taunting in the haunted pubs and places above earth. Like language and subtexts. Fleet Prison was here, often used for debtors and up Fleet Lane to Old Bailey is Newgate Prison. That was where Fagin ended up in *Oliver Twist*. Cruel. Giacomo Casanova was in for a while. All to the area of the Fleet. Bridewell. Outside the City but Edward gave them the Palace and they turned it into a prison. Business. Pay for everything. Executions, took place at Newgate. Amazing how many were executed for forgery. Bank of England zealously saw to that. Gates to the old City. Come up to Holborn Viaduct. Fleet Bridge and Snow Hill, Lord Grey and rebels met. Always rebellion and repression round this place. Death helps order. Rigor mortis or grim riots.

RIVER FLEET. Riverrun, past Eve and Adam's. ~~^^ Mystic, underground created a magnetic force. ≈. Channel. Band of frequency, medium. Pattern. Burn is a river, bourne, Kilburn on it too. This river was sacred. They worshipped rivers then. Like India with the Goddess Saraswati. Bride of Brahma. Meant pooling waters. Brings consciousness, healing, spring, on white swans. Invents writing. Sanskrit. Rivers with wells, like the Fleet, were thin places. Border to the underworld, a liminal place, a threshold to the otherworld. Spirits in the river. Water powerful, life-giving, life-taking. Once a swift, fast, fleet river with a current. Tide came into the inlet. The 'Fleet' of ships was here before it moved down to Greenwich. Fleet=navy. Star Trek Starfleet. Navy then moved to Greenwich. A line of energy from Hampstead to Greenwich over to places like Caesar's Well. From Hampstead and Highgate. A tributary near Highgate cemetery where everyone from Karl Marx to Douglas Adams, *Hitchhikers Guide to the Galaxy*, are buried. Well his ashes at least. Cinerarium. Springs flowed into it. Clerkenwell, Smithfield. River of Wells for a thousand years. Sadler's Wells. Monastic springs. Like paradise in Norse mythology to Vikings. Saxons, Normans. *'Murmuring green land of medicinal springs.'* Viking sorcery there. Hydromancy. Healing river with wells full of minerals, saints became dirty, muddy, unclean, people died, so it was covered. Dung, guts, blood, dead dogs, cats, turnip-tops, blood, said

Swift. Wren tried to turn it into a Venetian canal but they turned it into sewers. Govern water, govern effluent. Seaward. Beautiful underground brick constructions. Forgotten, identity disputed, dark, place full of rats where dead bodies might be found. Fleet Sewer, the Cloaca Maxima. Fleet shaped the area, roads, houses, history. Concentration of infamous London prisons. Considering location of Clerkenwell, Fleet, Newgate, Ludgate and Bridewell prisons then the Fleet could be called the 'River of Prisons' instead. Control. Brutality. Coincidence? Dickens walked here at night and stopped *'to linger at the wicked little Debtors' Door…which has been Death's Door to so many.'* Modesty Blaise underground in the Fleet in one adventure. 'The Phantom Fleet' a poem about great spirits returning to save the homeland. River-ghost escaped the unseen tunnels. Underground rivers affect people. If Hampstead was full of water it could still flood and kill if ice thawed too quick. Could be swept away with the rush of water from either side. Studies found links between supernatural apparitions and underground water. The energy could cause people to hallucinate. Alternatively it may cause them to see what is really there. Pull aside the curtain. It had taken her a long time to work it out. But it had been in her subconscious, her underground. A river is a channel. Channel to the spirit world. This river was somehow indirectly linked with the deaths of millions if it influenced the people in this triangle. Eerie. Chance? Causation? No. Correlation. UNDERGROUND. Roundel symbol. Θ. Curious.

Mystic River. A river in Boston. Dennis Lehane book. Clint Eastwood film. On that late night radio program as Ethel transformed into Candy Apple Crimson X, there was a phone-in. She made some point about Brigid. Said that Great Fire of London was a punishment from the goddess of fire. One caller just said *'Play Mystic for me.'* Looked again at 'Play Misty for Me.' Clint Eastwood's first as director. Set in Carmel, California. 'Play Misty for me,' was said by a key character ringing Clint the DJ. Misty a jazz piece by Errol Gardner. Anticipates Fatal Attraction. In public, you expose yourself. All kinds of entanglements. Quanta. Joyce's quark. Many people with a little fame suffer a lot more attention and burglary. You do not know who listens or interprets. Eastwood made Mystic River. Film about sexual abuse of a boy. Article about film 'Play Mystic for Me.' You do not pay attention to nutters, but she was curious. Mystic River. Underground streams of emotions that affect our lives. A stalker? Conscious of sand-sift in the hour glass. Joyce said *'Good puzzle would be cross Dublin without passing a pub.'* Difficult to get around London without seeing a dragon if you know where to look.

Ley lines also called dragon paths. Dragon's Den, that's where you get money. The City. Control the money. Straitjacket. Tie them up. Have them in bondage.

Set to turn west. A phantom path reeling you in. Maybe Freemason's Hall was centre. Vertex of the triangle met at Inner Temple Gardens or Blackfriars Bridge. They hung 'God's Banker' Roberto Calvi there in 1982. Mafia and Propaganda Due were linked to it. P2 was a powerful Roman Masonic lodge, secret, criminal association with most Intelligence leaders and politicians involved. Governing. Threats to expose murder of Pope. Italian Prime Minister murdered. Temple Church just west of it. Templars had a mill on the Fleet. Made it less navigable. Perfected credit systems. Templars developed international instruments of finance but they always pin it on the Jews. Fleet used when they built old St Pauls. Blackfriars set up beside Fleet on the East, Whitefriars west. Why did Twain and Bierce meet only at this place? Bierce another horror writer. Henry VIII's started the Reformation at the mouth of it. Religious houses became places where Shakespeare worked and played. PLAY. Play with your mind. Play not pray. Actors for monarchs. Theatre instead of Church. A man called George Orwell was one of the thugs. Prisons. Punishment. Newgate. Ludgate. Fleet. All around the Fleet. More executions. Cut up. She would turn right, head west up Fleet Street. St Paul's seal-grey calvarium rises, overseeing all, showing the way of the brain to come to take over the spirit. Royal Society. All these phenomena in this place by chance? Fountain-head. Origin. Well. The Tao is like a well. SOURCE. Magic is about meaning. River magic, Pan, pipers at the gates of dawn, *Wind in the Willows*, Grahame wrote it after he was shot just up the road.

FLEET STREET connects to power, newspapers. Govern narrative. Like Saraswati and writing. Reuters was based here. Lawyers too. Even comedians like Dave Allen start here. The Telegraph Office here set up crosswords that drew in oddballs to crack the ENIGMA code. Plays at the Inns of Court, surrounding the Knights Templar. Many writers were lawyers. Words are powerful. Plays and pleas. Plots against monarch, plots in play. Early trials like the Gunpowder Plot were like show trials. Home of the Press. Printing Press first set up here. Bookmakers again. Reformation. Control words of plays, books. Control entertainment. Press. Pressure. Belt words out, not the slow script in monasteries. Word inflation. Playhouse, plays, papers, press. Levers of State. Illusion of freedom. Burn books about religion, magic. Grimoires, magic books, same base as grammar. Get

Bible, already long cut down to a clearer focus, blurring some words, some emphasis. One mistranslation, thousands perish. State petrified of words. Sherborne Lane used to be Shiteburn Lane she read. Words cause a chain of images and associations. Change word, chain. Gropecunt Lane did not survive. No wonder you can hypnotise with words, suggest, mislead. Magnetic forces. It's only words. In the beginning was the Word. Control of words came from this spot. To change consciousness, change perception by having semantic change, changing the meaning. 'Awful' used to be good, now it's bad. Mystics are dangerous so you say mystic means something ill-defined, misty that hippies do. Or make bad things good. CONTROL meaning. Some say Shakespeare was a front to control language. First dictionaries came from round here as well. Johnson lived nearby. Goskomizdat. Soviets learned it here. Authoritarian.

Writers, spies were bedfellows. Spymasters, informers involved in PLOTS. Make up the story we live in. Master of Revels policed playwrights for monarchs. Otdel agitatsii i propangandy. Like internet censoring Algorithms. Open air plays then came indoors. 'Atmosphere' outside and natural light re-created in a false interior. Audiences taken in. Step out of line, playhouse was shut. Religious people had their hearts cut out, others-throats. Shakespeare a spy? Working with Dyer. Burleigh. Walsingham. Dee. Intelligencers. Church's system of spying replaced with a secular one. Reformation, night raids. Elizabeth. Virgin Mary. Minerva. A goddess gone left a vacancy. Bridget/Brigid imprisoned allows a new GODDESS. St Brigid partly pagan goddess. Deleted. Her re-incarnation as St Brigid then ousted by Elizabeth. Propaganda, control. Copied Church. Inquisitions, executions, discarding documents that did not fit the story. Stationers helped Master of Revels control written word. Station. Terminus. Worshipful Company of Stationers. Station. Location by St Pauls. Stationarius. Modern copyright came therefrom. Much later ©. Hospital and schools gone. Churches stripped bare. Propagandists fill gap with plays about Kings, Queens. Cultural revolution. Trotsky, Lenin learnt lessons here? Control media. Like Julius Caesar, write history yourself. History will be kind to me as I intend to write it, Churchill said. Maybe cleared images because they were influenced by Saracens? History, belief, perception is managed by writers. Perception Press. STORY, same root as history. Used to mean a lie also. Make up a story. Stories create reality. Matrix. Store. Live in stores, on a different storey, story. Conspirators don't like conspiracy theorists, unless they employ them to deflect attention.

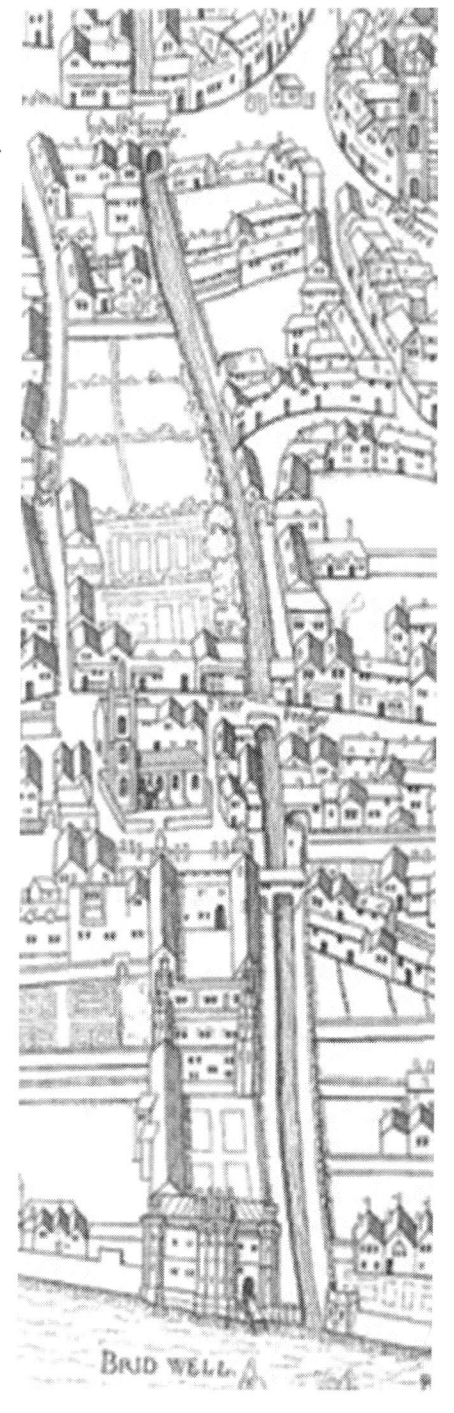

In one interview she said all wars were for the goddess prize. Consciousness=Goddess now. Annihilate the existing goddesses. A surging stream of consciousness prompted her to explain how Mary had taken over from the Roman Diana. Elizabeth was also Astraea. Virgo. Dike. Mary's festival was Diana's Festival of Torches around August 15th. In Britain smothering of Brigid (where Britannia may have come from) and others. Most were mother goddesses. Metro. Smothered to wrest control. In Ireland and Britain there had been a dominant goddess who clearly manifested in water. Brigid like Shakti. A long time to subdue the cult. Bog bodies sacrifices to the earth goddess. Brigid tolerated as a version of Juno and Ceres. This church was there a long time and very significant. The Normans were afraid of vengeance of Irish saints, as Gerald of Wales tells. You could be turned into a werewolf. Bride Well by the Fleet. Wells and rivers were sacred goddess links. Romans loved water too. Built west of the Fleet outside the walls maybe with ongoing Bride-worship. Chartres built on a Celtic temple with an underground chamber for the goddess and Druids collected there as Caesar told us. All over Europe healing rivers and wells associated with the Great Goddess, but most went underground. Lourdes. Brigid, Brighid, Bridget, Bride. Breed. Linked to the swan. To the constellation the Romans called Cygnus, the swan. To get power you submit the goddess. The river was Bride. Wells, springs, source, healing. Probably a warrior goddess. A sun, fire goddess before they became masculine. Must have been a grove there too, simulacrum. Did not represent her because you could not contain the infinite in the finite. Probably heads there. Tower Hill had Bran the Blessed's. Skulls sacred. Grail may have been the skull of Jesus or John the Baptist. Heads were associated with wells. Monarchs loved to show heads of traitors. Fleet tamed. Healing goddess transformed into an evil sorceress. Subverted. Source to sorcery. So the healing well became a jail. Di died today back then. Marchioness. Chartered.

THE BRIDEWELL. The Bridewell was by the Fleet where it came into the Thames. Round the river was a circle of power. Phi. Φ. Bridget's Well. Brigid's Well. Bridie's Well. Bride's Well. Brid. Same persona. A temple, a church, sacrarium, palace, prison, plot, home for wayward women, orphanage. Wren again. They exported the Bridewell prison concept round the world. Henry VIII got rid of his bride here and started the stripping of the altars. They are good at turning places to prisons. Prisons run by <u>Governors</u>. Elizabeth Cresswell who had a brothel in Little Britain (at Bartholomew's Close) put her name on *The Poor-Whore's Petition* to Lady Castlemaine, as a 'sister prostitute' who was sorely vexed. Salisbury Court where Giordano Bruno stayed. London Times. *Supper of Ashes*. The Typhon. Egyptian magic. Bridewell Church. A charnel and ossuary underneath. Pope Gregory said to take over the pagan sites. Brigid associated with words, poetry, sound. Like Lakshmi, Sarasvati. Source of many words. River Fleet contained, constrained, corseted. They made corsets and 'stays' from whalebone. Royal Society for the Protection of Birds was founded after the great Crested Grebe was nearly extinct because they used their feathers for women's undergarments. Trammelled feminine is always destructive. Contain the powerful goddess. Up on the hill a little from the River they built St Pauls on the site of a Temple of Diana, displacing the site of another goddess, maybe Dana. Another temple beside the Fleet on old maps. Steeple of St Bride's Church became the model for wedding cakes around the world as a result of a lovestruck apprentice baker. Goddess ghost dwelt in that symbol. Young adult books *The Shadowhunters* are based in it at the London Institute. *The City of Ashes*. Bride also meant the Church, New Jerusalem, the Elect and the one who engages in mystical union. Catherine of Sienna. Teresa of Avila. Valentinus the Gnostic threatened early Christianity. Believed 'gnosis' was within, Sophia, recovering spirit back to Source, matter to Pleroma. Like with Plato the symbol X or cross was critical. The spiritual bridal chamber was the purpose of the holy of holies. Goddess magnetic. Bride. The Bride, Malkuth. Muladhara. Here the Kundalini flows from. Snake. Cloaca. Kether in Malkuth. *Earth. Mother. Kingdom. Key. Briah. Shekinah, the female spirit of God.* Ashim, souls of fire. Ashless fire. As the Fleet was regarded as evil or impure, so was Malkuth by some Kabbalist. Fleet River covered, like much history, lost civilisations and powers. In 1533 Holbein painted the celebrated 'Ambassadors' in the Bridewell Palace, with an anamorphic skull. Ambassador meant servant. Anamorphosis. A secret ploy. See something from a particular point to see properly, a code. CODE. Clues. You see it all there, the Crucifix hidden by the new veil. Before it you have science, measuring devices, the globe and the secret death cult code, the Ambassador with an almost cloven hoof shoe. They represented the new territory of the science of calculated control. Year Elizabeth was born. She was a tool. DIVA meant goddess. Henry VIII became uncomfortable in the Bridewell. Maybe the City became Alpha. Or Mem. It's shaped like that with the Fleet in and coming out. Divorce, discord, destruction of the Roman link. Control mind and spirit. Stop 'Chaos.' Deeper, goddess spirit was divorced, defeated by death and instruments of science. Holbein told us, crystal clear. Kill ancient Goddess with her love of child birth, healing. Inversion. First printing press in the land was at the Bridewell. Journalists still use the church today. Censorship. Govern words, govern mind, government. Turn poetry into propaganda, print the Bible to suit their narrative. Spells in ink cast. Gandhi came here to eat at a vegetarian restaurant when he studied law nearby. Perhaps picked up Bridget spirit. Could we say this was the frontal lobe, was it? It's more I think. Broca's area in the brain or Wernickes. Nonsense about the 'C***' word. Big controversy about that word now. Vagina meant sword sheath. Irony. Goes back to Kunte, kunta, kunton. Queynt. Queen Cu. Cow. Rabbit. Kundalini. Gud, ge, gon. Made the word bad. Women bought it. Bridget=Saraswati. Sympathetic, astral, natural magic came here with Bruno on the run from Egypt through Italy to the Bridewell. Fleet. Hermitic. MEMORY was critical in his magic. They would burn him and his ashes get thrown in the Tiber. Maybe a spy.

Axiom 2 **The real Goddess has been driven underground, substituted or left of her own accord. The Goddess is governed. Last Goddess is consciousness.**

Westwards now. Temple Bar. Middle Temple, Inner Temple. TEMPLE. In the head too. Wyatt's Rebellion. *'To prevent us from over-running with strangers.'* That was the reason given. Lord Grey involved. Led to execution of Lady Jane Grey and her husband. Mary told the people she loved them *'as a mother doth love a child.'* Tried for treason at Guildhall. Lord Mayor again dealing death, now to the woman who should have been Queen. Up Fleet Street and the Strand. Chesterton. Green Dragon. Templars stables and jousting. Temple. Fetters for Templars. Chains. Manacles. Fetter Lane. Moravians. Swedenborg was always based around here. Spy. Mason. Mystic. Blake. Secret magical cults. Mixed Kabbalah, Oriental stuff, Tantra. Counter-culture or the real culture underground? Swedenborg had his conversations with God near the Fleet. The Anglo-Saxon Strand outside the Roman Londinium, Lundenwic, Covent Garden. Aldwych. Bridewell also ran Bedlam the terrible asylum. Do other women like disciplined women?

Two interviews on London's biggest radio station. Many listened to podcasts. Promoting her commercial persona. The proposed Domestic Terrorism Act created a demand for conspiracy theories, before they became illegal. Nobody interested in her other theories originally. She explored them considering libertarianism, psycho-geography and spiritual development. All one to her. Sensational. In character, provocative, beneficial for business. Another coming up. Same interviewer. Lucius Tubal in Camden. Nice. Quite psychic. Channel. Amazing snakes made their home around Regent's Canal nearby. Australia House was Gringotts in Harry Potter. Mary-le-Bow. Born within earshot you were Cockney. Oranges and lemons say... Controversial. Ash talked about Templar secrets. A lot of attention. Alter ego suggested Templars who tried to colonise the Holy Land had been beaten and sworn allegiance to the victors.

Ethel: Rome still has a great intelligence network. It discovered that the Templars entered a pact with the Saracens. That was why Rome did them in.

Lucius: But that's a long time ago. What relevance is that?

Ethel: These accords are still in place. Successors still uphold that goal. Ask yourself why London was so important with the Balfour Declaration and Zionism? Agents infiltrating the Zionist cause with the ultimate objective of achieving the secret Templar goals.

Lucius: A strong draught to swallow.

Ethel: Nobody remembers the Crusader states. Edessa, Antioch, the Kingdom of Jerusalem, Jaffa, Ascalon, Sidon. Not about religion but power.

Lucius: Surely the experts would flag this?

Ethel: When falsehood rules, truth vanishes.

Lucius: Let me be devil's advocate. You have Jewish origins as far as I can see. So maybe... you are some kind of advocate for a cause you naturally would... if you see what I mean...

Ethel: Well, I see that all kinds of anti-Semitic organisations make all sorts of claims and say that all the movers and shakers from Bolshevism to Psychoanalysis to Marketing do it because of their revolutionary spirit... but I think that's lazy.

Lucius: I agree. Why would people believe a...mistress, dominatrix or a goddess or a channelled entity?

Ethel: Why not? Examine the merits. Ask why did they not 'consecrate' Russia after Divine inspiration? They did not want God to get it. That's why they seek to destroy it. China enters. Global eugenic order. Master evil race. Useless eaters, useful idiots, elites come on the back of fools. Joyce's words *'fairlygosmotherthemselves in the Laudaunelegants of Pinkadinky.'*

Lucius: That's gobbledygook.

Ethel: Only if the *'abnihilisation of the etym'* is. Or *'Three quarks for Muster Mark.'* Joyce names them.

Lucius: It reminds me of *Foucault's Pendulum*, Umberto Eco and Dan Brown. *Illuminatus Trilogy*.

Ethel: They don't interest me. If you want to throw people off you can make a complex joke that makes them ridiculous. Every single thing will be permitted so long as it can be monetised. Air, water, plants, love. Poison the air, pay for it. Pick your poison. Golden Calf. Mammon. Star Demons.

Lucius: Monetise like you do?

Ethel: No problem there. But those ideas are peripheral. Focus on Brigid, The Bride.

Accused of Islamophobia, anti-Semitism (never anti-Christianity). When Christian churches were burnt these days it hardly made the papers. Many gloated. Her favourite historical era was the Moorish kingdom of Andalucía where monotheistic religions lived in harmony. Magic flourished in Granada and Cordoba. Caliphate of Cordoba. Toledo the other part of the triangle. Part of her family came from there. Proud. Pride comes before a fall. Do women like strong women?

This is London, imprinted with human spirit. Vivarium. Aleister Crowley lived around here. Magick. Creatures manifested in his flat after magic ceremonies. Drugs. Sodomy. Would influence space exploration. He worked for Intelligence. Conan Doyle's Red-Headed League. Creator of rational Sherlock Holmes was a raving spiritualist. Samuel Pepys here. First place to sell French Letters. Sweeney Todd in Fleet Street with an underground passage to the Pie Shop. Murdering barber, bodies to the cellar, end up in a pie. Mmh, they're tasty! Dunstan's Church. Cut-throat. Modesty Blaise's author worked over El Vino's in Fleet Street. Milton. Another writer who did propaganda for the State. Words hypnotise. Cast spells. Broadcast. London School of Economic, Drury Lane. Covent Garden. John Rich. Drake. John Dee. Raleigh. Spencer. Chapman. Bacon. Pallas Athena dream, inspired secret Solomon. Bacon was Shakespeare's Pallas Athena. Pallas become Palladium. Maybe Minerva also. Secret, recurrent. Arcanum Arcanorum. Cannon Street. *The Last Man in London.* Character from Neptune inhabits Paul and opens his mind. Why were these parts of London always in the story? Force, magic magnetised people here. Left their presence in the place holograph, imprinted on the vortex of energy. Fervent. Ferment. The Fleet occluded. Occluded. Occult. Ocular. All Elizabethan. OCCULT. School of Atheism. School of the Night.

Ash had a burning desire to discover through the medium of London. Clues here. Ascending levels of spiritual reality. Yeats used to meet with others at the Cheshire Cheese. What was interesting about Yeats was not his poetry nor magic but Leo Africanus. Yeats heard a voice in a trumpet in 1912, seeking someone. Leo Africanus, or so Yeats concluded. He communicated with Leo, through mediums. Asked him also to write letters about what he knew of spirits and Yeats would write down what came back. A splitting of himself. Leo was a convert poet from the 15th century in North Africa who wrote geography. Leo became his daimon. Mask, alter ego, ideal. Perhaps we need to distance part of ourself to move beyond the limited self to universal self. Getting or receiving your opposite. Durham House where the 'Friends of the Night' met. Walter Raleigh bringing back Indians, smoking. Dee maybe Marlowe, Chapman. Saturnists. Back up the Strand, coffee on the way, into Covent Garden. Sex Pistols used to be 'The Strand.' Even UK Punk from here. By Blake's haunts, the Freemasons' Hall. AUDI, VIDE, TACE. Hear, see, be silent. Up to the British Museum. Atlantis Bookshop. Lyceum. Bram Stoker worked there, wrote Dracula. Old Tube stations around here closed, another tunnel underneath. ESOTERIC. So I erect. Coteries. Esoteric meant an inner circle, reserved for a few. Anagram 'coterie' meant a similar thing. They even invert words. The Enlightenment, reverse of what it was. There had been an experiment in the US where psychiatrists had got people locked up by merely saying that they had heard a voice. Maybe. Direction /. Are women more secretive than men?

Axiom 3   **We are governed by the hidden, occult, occluded, without and within. Slowly we are bound and reality inverted. Secret order means we should look at what is left out.**

First time in the Atlantis Bookshop, she stood in the centre. Assistant went somewhere. On her own, Ash felt a tap on her back. Not a muscle spasm. Spooky. Years later she found Atlantis was associated with Madame Blavatsky, Crowley, Gerald Gardner founder of Wicca. Austin Osman Spare, magician artist said science leads to 'its own form of bondage.' Described X you see when you practice the 'Death Posture.' Chaos Magic came from him. Cecil Williamson Witchcraft Ceremonies took place in the basement. He was hired by Intelligence to investigate the occult fascination of the Nazis before the war. Chaos Magic, Wicca, Theosophy all hereabouts. Just the Museum? Centre of MAGIC. Use of will to influence the world. Feminine occult energy. Once on that walk Ash met three witches. Treadwell's another stop. Cornelisson's some days, mystical place full of alchemy with pigments whispering to take them. Conjure, to swear and to command on oath. Magically to use a spell to get a demon do what you want. Conjure up, to make appear in the mind. Conjure, really Latin, law or oath and together. A real conspiracy means you conjure. Make an oath together, swear, command, make things happen or demons do your bidding or appear in other people's mind, supernatural, magic, because of your oath to magicians or dark forces or other fellows. The Conjuring Age. CONJURATION. Up north finally to Russell Square, Bloomsbury. Swedenborg Society. Theosophical Society. British Museum a centre. ☼. Golden Dawn. Consciousness and machines seems to be the Rubicon. Scientists getting interested in consciousness. Why? Artificial Intelligence. Funding, opportunities for control. Take the beautiful symbol of the cloud. *Cloud of Unknowing.* Invert it. Sweeps in Brazilian Jiu-Jitsu. Judo. Think you're in control. Then you're on the bottom. You fall into Hogarth's Gin Lane. Gin to help grain prices gave the debauched St. Giles Rookery here of poor, 'Irish and aliens,' prostitutes, thieves. The Great Plague. Rum Fem. Allow astral concordance. Intelligence and esoteric go together. You sell things in London. Thomas Barratt 'father of advertising' made another triangle. Delta. Δ. Born in St. Pancras and buried there. Worked in Great Russell Street beside the Museum. Wrote a book about Hampstead Heath. Came to Pears. Said any fool could make it, clever man sells it. Pears soap started by a perfumer wanting something pure in Soho. Develops new techniques. Celebrity endorsement. High Art Advertising. Posters. Famous slogans. Makes a fortune. Pears world famous. Pathfinder. Confluence here of magic, print, image. He saw links, the X. Putting together of things creates possibilities that cannot happen without union. Alchemy. Chemistry. Love. Life. Mysticism. Bridal Chamber. You sell politicians and war like soap. Retail means to cut up.

Peter Pan came to the Darling's near here. Pan again. Word 'panic' comes from it. Panic. Pan also all. Pandemonium. Demons. SOAS. Charles Darwin lived westwards around the corner in Gower Street where they say the ghost of Emma Louise is. Keynes up there. This is at the centre of the Bloomsbury circle. Those who *'lived in squares, painted in circles, loved in triangles.'* Wanted liberation from convention, feminism, pacifism. Virginia Wolfe lived in Gordon Square a couple of hundred yards north-west. She wrote a few sentences about an illuminated sign on the Tube "Passing Russell Square" making you feel there was a deeper significance. Stream of consciousness she used. Comes with the territory. Across there 100 yards as the crow flies to the east The Ratio Club had met. Queen's Square with Great Ormond Street Children's Hospital beside. First Nerve Hospital in the world. Mad King George who lost America was treated there in one of the 'comely houses.' Blue urine he had. Blood disease again. Royal issue. She had just read about this Club. Ratio means they were dedicated to Reason. Erik knew all about them. As far as she could make out they were psychiatrists, psychologists, military intelligence, physiologists, zoologists, astronomers, neuroscientists, mathematicians that met first in September 1949. Turing (the father of AI) was involved a little later. Descendants of Darwin in it also. CYBERNETICS grew up with these guys. Ashby she remembered. They wanted to get to the bottom of the brain and behaviour. Many had worked in Intelligence in the war. Maybe they wanted to control people because of that. They were breaking human behaviour into formulas, statistics, nerves. Grew out of animal behaviour mechanisms. Really thinking about how they could use knowledge to control behaviour of people. Control, order. Govern us. Those from Cambridge could come by train, some walk up from King's College. Met in basement first with a blackboard, tables and chairs. Beef and sherries later. Statistics, accounts, computations. Rationarium. McCullough a link to Macy Cybernetic conferences in USA. Shannon, Information theory, neural networks, systems thinking, reflexivity, complexity, black box systems. Break it down, cut it up and contain. Code. Great contribution of scientific method. Queens' Square used to be owned by John Cutler. Cutting instruments. And all around her was the Skinner's land. Back to where I turned off. We will be skinned. Tavistock Square is next north-west on way home. Tavistock Clinic. Claimed to be source of control of culture, education, propaganda by some conspiracy theorists. Portman. Behind wars. Who knows what's true? Coleman said the pop culture was a fabrication led by them. Jung and Freud involved with these institutes. Amazing. Rivals, really?

McEwan wrote that book *Saturday*. Just flicked through and read about it. Set on the day of the Iraq protests around here. A neurosurgeon (who must work at Queen's Square) is the centre. McEwan works hard and followed a real one there. Brain operation, like in *The Great God Pan*. But that was a horror story. Temple, four bones meet. Don't know about his views too much. I'm sure he was against the war. But all the other lefties that protested had put these nutters in Government. The ex-Trotskyists became Neo-Cons. So the intelligentsia was buttering its bread on both sides as usual, preaching peace and causing war. But they know what their Clerkenwell Bolshevik heroes had done and hardly had forsaken the cause. If you become dedicated to Reason, you can become strangely immune to right and wrong. REASON. Rational, relational, retail. Reason could be something else in magic. It is just what is correct in accordance with objectives that remain important and objectives change. The League of the Militant Godless. Struggles against God to get communism. Like Gramsci realised, you need to get rid of Catholicism to have communism. That's why they burn churches, tell you you're a selfish gene, say destroying born babies (not terminations) is a choice dictated by illusion of existence thereof, but Seth channelled said it's ok while they whisk parts away. McEwan's surgeon may prefer a trillion, trillion possibilities of the brain to primitive supernatural but results are curiously constricting like a corset. Making us as queer as a clockwork orange. I don't know much about McEwan, but most novelists that get by in London have an agenda, speak sanctimoniously, correctly with the weight of collectivised righteousness, ticking boxes. Like all them comedians that preached political correctness moaning about lack of freedom. Two-faced. Janus. Anus. Arse with two cheeks as Galloway says. A big clockwork mechanism you must fit into. Maybe it's just the brain. Left-wing is left-side controlling words, right interprets it. Nonsense. It's not that simple. Now they say the Left are wired to be against boundaries. That's why they're busy flogging DMT, LSD, Ayahuasca. The Master of Revels never went away. *All which it inherit shall dissolve.* I can see where the Ministry of Information was based in haunted Senate House. All the famous writers that worked there. Ghosted. First Department, Goskomstat. Goebbels. God love them poor people who still thought writers independent. God of **Gold**. I think I am romantic and rational, realist.

Something invisible operating herefrom. Crossed paths in the Square are crosshairs of the future. 100 yards away north-west The Field of Forty Footsteps. Duelling brothers left indelible footprints. Sitting down in the Square she imagined the pre-Saxon forest. ◻ Arts, literature, medicine. Why magic here? Inhale spiritual energy. You sell people too. What Erik was working against. Through Russell Square. All those Russells. Bertrand, World Government proponent. Brand Russell. Rich beside poor. *A Babe in Bohemia.* All the people as well as Marx and Lenin that came here to the Library. Museum 100 yards to the south-west with the unlucky Mummy. MUMMY. Egypt. Wilde, Hayek, Stoker, Wells, Shaw, Twain, Jinnah, Kipling, Gandhi. Books. Words. Maybe some other invisible force we cannot see. Senate House 100 yards directly west had been Ministry of Information with many direct lines to Fleet Street. *Keep Calm and Carry On* came from there. *1984.* Ash noticed birds seemed very loud. Fuss and noise from air. Black cloud of starlings, murmuration pulling hither and thither, inside out, up and down, swooping, swirling catching light in a dancingly dark, iridescent tumult. Never come in August. Some other birds? Zeppelins dropped incendiaries here, King's Cross, Cleopatra's Needle 1917. EGYPT. Were they attacking Freemason magic power of the monument cut down and transported with great difficulty from Egypt to protect the City? Are Masons at the centre? All the Bloomsbury set. Cambridge. Spies. Zeppelins started in 1915. Monstrous flying vessel. *The War in the Air*, Wells anticipated this danger a few years before. Zeppelin Menace killed hundreds. Another bomb fell just off Russell Square. Then planes began to fly higher and a great success when a zeppelin exploded over London. Orwell wrote about it later when he was arguing in favour of his socialist *'world-state of free and equal human beings.' 'As I write, highly civilised human beings are flying overhead, trying to kill me.'* Up the road there was the 7-7 plaque. Always attacks round here. Suddenly people at the open air restaurant began pointing and she caught sight of a fox bolting across the road and through the square. Running for its life. Plenty of foxes in London but seldom had she seen one so early. This was where Eckhart Tolle used to sit after his epiphany. He lived up Belsize Park. Used to be suicidal. Studied at University of London. Slept rough I think here and Hampstead Heath. Another. The Fleet again. He becomes one of the biggest spiritual teachers in the world. *The Power of Now*. Talks about the 'fleeting' and 'FLEETINGNESS' of time. Pre-Raphaelite painters based around here, painting up on Hampstead Heath, opposing plans to cut it up. Either these people were influenced by the river or were coming here for something else, influenced by some other magnetic force. Alternatively it was a great coincidence. They say Poe was a romantic? Really?

Edgar Allan Poe lived down just south-east there on Southampton Row. Developed the short story. One of first detective novels, horror genre. Gothic. Wrote *The Gold-Bug*. Cryptography. Crypt. Hidden. Saw Rosetta Stone in Museum. Criticised mysticism, celebrated 'ratiocination.' Exact thinking. Sherlock Holmes up the road copied it. So the chap pushing 'ratiocination' is near the Ratio Club. Ratio was reason but suggested another common meaning namely the relationship between two numbers. Ratio decidendi the binding part of a judgment. Binding. Bound. 'Reasons' means an elite can control the larger number. Real meaning. All claim to abolish superstition and false thinking for <u>reason</u>. But Poe replaces good stuff with HORROR, secrecy, sinister stuff. Sinister meant left-hand. Left-hand path. Left. So horror and *The Imp of the Perverse*. She remembered what he wrote because it chilled her. Reason advocates always have a weird thing that lives with it to replace supernatural they sucked out. That is the perverse imp. Poe wrote that,

> *'I am not more certain than I breathe, than the assurance of the wrong or error of any action is often the one unconquerable force which impels us, and always impels us to its prosecution.'*

Do the wrong thing. That's what empire of empiricism admits goes with reason. Kryptonite. Many maths people, scientists, reasonable folk despair and go mad confusing means and ends. Cut it up. Rip. Reduce. Should be a big X on map here. X in paths in the square. Zig-zag. Maybe the executive function. Prefrontal cortex? Maybe Parliament is the cerebellum? Bellum means war also. Why should we think Parliament decides all things, no more than one spot in the brain controls everything? Here was where some of the world's materialist atheism, anti-spirit movement began by people robbing things around the world and cutting it up. Word 'temple' was originally related to the word to cut. Cut off a sacred space. William Burroughs lived in West End. Cut-up text, film, wrote for Underground Press Syndicate. Became Alternative Press Syndicate. Promoting liberation. Rat Subterranean News. W.I.T.C.H. Allow ugliness, aggression. But this cutting up is different. Downroad downriver they cut up whales. Smithfield - animals, rebels. They stripped altars during Reformation, cutting out devotional art, jewels. Not cutting like self-harm but cutting others and their things. Retail meant to cut. Chop, mince, slice, cube, carve, dice, snip, pierce, chiffonade, brunoise, shear, saw, bore, tunnel. ^^^^^ Gash. Cut off heads of unwanted wives and Queens. — Cut-throats and cut-purses. Cut Elgin Marbles out of Parthenon in Acropolis. Cut down obelisks. Cut down forests. Cut up and off bodies, women, men, animals. They rip, slash, perforate. Cut up soap to sell it better. Cut up fossils to say life was just an accident. Answer had to be something small you find when you cut something down. A little machine. A selfish gene. Behind closed doors they do weird things. Magic, pagan, demon stuff sometimes. Cut up people's minds. Get inside. God-like power of control. Cut up communities. Take away supernatural. Ridicule the magnificent beyond our comprehension. Take away spirit. Sell despair, ennui, nausea, mindlessness. Then we are surprised when we hear killers who did it for a thrill because there was no meaning. Cut up. Cut yourself. Cover up. Shut up. Softsoap us. Sold us speculative theory for spirit, like soap. Or maybe like milk powder for mothers with breasts. They cut up behaviour, reduce it to formulas, reduce humans to animals, to machines, to mechanisms, to impulses, to robots. They deny free will. They chop up culture, cohesion, beauty, truth, nations, values. Invert and attack opposition to their knowledge. Meet in clubs. Cut up drugs, cocaine. Cutting-edge. Edit and delete. Not that they were against the supernatural either. Maybe no surprise that there's gangs of youths cutting up people for phones and less around London. Principalities behind the scenes. THEY DID NOT WANT ANY COMPETITION TO THEIR OWN BRAND ESOTERICA. Scientific illuminism. Legion. Rebel you got cut up. They try contact angels and aliens. Channelling. John Dee to NASA. SETI. SETH. But you are mad if you believe in God even though there is evolutionary adaptive benefits to do so, irrespective if it is true. Neither Left nor Right, both Left and Right. All that was Punch and Judy distraction. But we did learn a lot of a sort on the way. We can do a lot of things that we don't necessarily want to do. Many, many good things too. Something is coming. Cut us up. Cups. Cusp.

But she was pragmatist and cosmopolitan. As her business took off, she feared success would cause problems. Law of Attraction stuff. Channelled in its modern form through 'Abraham' and others. Other beings, extra-terrestrial, celestial spirits. People not bothered. Don't believe in God but accept channelled beings. Such 'laws' were from a Christian source originally, namely 'New Thought.' Needed some discernment about whether God was talking to you or something else. *The Seth Material.* Believe any old bullshit. Set. Egypt. Isis. Byblos. Signal. Business flying. Well-paying customers. Make money, honey-pot effect. Uneasy. All spiritual practices were to provide peace. No mobiles, apart from work. Did not drive in London. Work not stressful. Tensions. Brendan Behan said, first thing on agenda of every Irish revolutionary organisation was 'the Split.' Same inside. Goddess Blue Brigid 7 and Ethel Woodpecker thriving. Things not what they seem. Seam between illusion and reality drawn often to fool. Other realities might be dominant. Mansions of many dimensions. Open, be vigilant for you were vulnerable. They said of Underhill she badly needed de-intellectualising. Consider end but to present tend. She felt growth, opening, scaling sacred ladders. Personae of alter egos had growth. No capacity independent of themselves to grow, or did they? Avatars? Posters. British Medical Association HQ, moved here from the Strand. Why? Was to be Theosophical Society. Roman statues. Wanted eugenics some of them not NHS. 6 cardinal points. Past

Gandhi in Tavistock up to Euston Road from the south and across to Eversholt.⚜.

Just home, hame, spatiamentum over, made with spirits. Phantom Fleet River. Combination creates monstrosities. 'The Combine' was behind the Big Nurse in *One Flew Over The Cuckoo's Nest*. One flew east, one flew west… Most in the mental institution voluntarily. Ken Kesey was on MKUltra drug experiments. Knew what he was talking about. Combination another word for conspiracy. Sell you DMT for spirit. New priests. Terence McKenna. On this date 1888 first Ripper Murder. Monsters on their own of Advertising, Religion, Medicine, State, Intelligence, Media. Working together a Hydra. Oh shit! Blue Rooster Tavern. I'll pop in. Who in the world am I? Must consider second interview in bath. Bars, cars, scars, stars, wells, dells, cells, bells, heaven and hells, spells, tells, sells. Blue pill in Matrix was to persist in illusion? Did not sound right. Red, blue pillars. Red flesh, action, fiery Mars. Blue heavenly, feminine, reflection, positive, accepting, spirit. Middle pillar. Word, world, whirl, wood. Next interview simmered subconsciously to shimmer into life. You are it. Know thyself. Thou art That. I know I am That. Wells wanted World Government or 'dictatorship' run by scientists, destroying nation states, all religions, erasing borders, facilitated by education systems, implemented by psychologists, politicians, nudged by claims to peace-dividends and brotherhood. Any means justified if contributing to ultimate goal. Like Marx, Lenin, Trotsky. People who advocate Reason, love secrecy and admit inevitable perversity that exists in them. Reason just crust. Reason without morality is net to trap spirit. Recap excursion. Mystery. Secrecy. Underground. Source. Chaos. Order. Governing. Cross. Reason. Elite. Agent. Temple. Goddess. Idol. Control. Matrix. Simulacrum. Gold. Counterfeit. Magic. Occult. Conjuration. Egypt. Story. Memory. Edit. Terminus. Delete. Cut. Play. Code. Plot. Retail. Bright Feminine v Dark. Calculating Mind v Spirit. Horror, Occult v Supernatural. Objectives rule. Transmutation. Any ghost signs like the blue Take Courage? Ghosts in ink, pigment or stone commune.

Virginia, Virginia why did you throw yourself into that cold river with stones in your pocket that night? I found your spirit haunting these streets as you implicitly foretold. As I walked looking for my answers you appeared. You became the flâneuse on a route I partly went today walking down to the Strand. You saw people and were always interested in what they did in a way I was not, for the general needs more attention than the particular now in my view. Street

Haunting you called it. *'Into each of these lives one could penetrate a little way, far enough to give oneself the illusion that one is not tethered to a single mind, but can put on briefly for a few minutes the bodies and minds of others.'* I made that sudden, capricious friendship through words left with your vanished life as you said. I recall words you laid out so tautly. See now, as you write, high above bare winter trees the oblong frames of reddish-yellow light. You heard voices and could not take it. And your love of Vita who helped heal you and facilitate your art, I think of. Amy gone in Camden. Born September. I think fondly of fellow artists wending.

As she came back up Eversholt Street, a strange rumbling sound. Curiously grinding, vibrating unseen leviathan. Wondered if it was a flashback. Slightly thrilling disorientation. Ash noticed others froze. Suspected something underneath in Tube. Ground shaking. Time slowed. Felt it through asphalt, woman petrified, cars slowed down. A flower pot came crashing across the road. Fruit fell from stalls outside convenience store. Child screaming. Looked up as something dropped from a roof. Sash-window shattered. Signage over shop split. An awning collapsed. Out of corner of her eye a small crack appeared in a wall. Swiftly conscious of threat. Considered running. Remembered standing in a doorway. Seemed a long, queasy time. Martial arts made her comfortable with unexpected. Breathe, loosen, relax, look for space, deal with danger. Slow motion. Saw like a fly for a moment. A chimney crumbled on a building other side of the little park. Through shop window she saw stuff spilled on floor. Dogs barking, one shivering with its owner. An unpleasant amusement park feeling. A sensation of pressure in jaw as a grinding grima took place deep down somewhere as a screech-scratch-dragging of two polystyrene plates or unknown nails on an underworld blackboard that struck some primitive chord within while at the same time peculiarly dwindling concerns into insignificance by perception of impotence at hands of such forces just as creatures are programmed for paralysis in the face of an inevitably successful predator perhaps to lessen pain of perishing. She still felt peace fully conscious through peripheral sense of panic and pandemonium in elastic minutemillennium time. *Earthquake.* Earth groaned, heaved. Out of the blue. Dragon stirred in its lair. San Andreas. Fault of St Andrew. Should not have happened here surely? Am I dreaming? Strongest ever recorded in London and mainland. She would find out that night that the smaller earthquakes of 1750 in London were preceded by strange lights in the sky.

LLLF

LONDON LOGOS LIBERATION FRONT

Publishing Pamphlets to Oppose Censorship of Our Message.
The Counter-Revolutionary to Evil and Terror Effort.
We will communicate our message in any way we can.

OPPOSE THE FORCES OF DE-STABILISATION.

HERACLITUS RULES.

MASS MEDIA IS POISON.

WE ARE SERFS.

WE ARE SLAVES.

WE ARE BRAINWASHED.

WE ARE MESMERISED.

WE NEED TO WAKE UP.

NO LEFT, NO RIGHT.

BOTH SIDES ARE RIGHT SOMETIMES.

TROTSKYISTS IN DISGUISE ARE MAKING POLICY.

COMMUNISTS TAKE OVER CAPITALISM.

CRONY CAPITALISM RULES.

CAPITALISTS ARE NOT GENUINE.

TECHNOLOGY IS TAKING CONTROL.

TECHNOCRACY USES LEFT AND RIGHT.

SCIENTISM, DARWINISM, ATHEISM DESTROYS.

PREPARE FOR LIBERATION

Chapter 2

The Secret Seven

Because they show you the thoughtless all the time as they drag you down, you forget that there are many, many bright people. That the light of attention does not shine on them may leave their brilliance in obscurity. *'Full many a flower is born to blush unseen.'* Many may be happy that it is so. Obscurity and inattention may save. Our attention is yielded voluntarily and involuntarily to the lowest common denominator when we cede control. Reign of triviality and rain of meaninglessness erode thinking. Deep and playful thinking becomes taboo. Spring that nourishes. That people do it is not always obvious when channels are controlled. Misled by the matrix, much more happens below the radar. Then sometimes some people come out from among them to try to be separate. Because the authorities were clamping down on parkour (and in truth because some of them had never really mastered it or had injuries) the group had changed direction. They were going under. Below. Beneath. There were some really good climbers among them. Climbing high buildings at night was more difficult after some had become famous. Could shit yourself hanging on by fingernails on top of a London skyscraper with a gusty wind threatening to blow you off above dots of nightguards shouting below. It was a joke they started in a way and it would remain that to some extent to the end... at least that is what they thought. A lot of other parkour people were gamers and spent days online. These were readers. Left-wing but in the centre they agreed, mostly. Some had been more Antifa, anti-homophobic, anti-racist. Books had almost become something odd among their other contemporaries. Not with her mates. Nerdy. Bookworms. Clever Dicks. Smartypants. Boffins. Swots. Geeks. Anoraks. Anal. Dorks. Wallies. Boring. But none were pillocks or plonkers. Sick of clubs, trendy beers, burgers. Wanted to change the world. Saw a Utopia. Sometimes just better things. Less damage to animals. Love the planet. Stop war. Chill out. Legalise drugs. *The Ragged Trousered Philanthropists*. Aware. But they felt they had style. Colour. They knew more things. A bit snooty at times. Brave Betas they laughed. Earnest. Maybe some on the spectrum. At least they had not bought into First Person Shooters, Apple and cookery programmes. Janet (real name Jenny) sipped her pint of ale listening with others to Peter. You think you know what is going on but you haven't a clue. Politics, religion but no personal matters, don't bother with people's lives, loves, sexual identities, orientations. *"Let Mickey Meatball find his own way out of the Maze."* Shouted someone. A Simpsons two pointer. Italian Chef Luigi Risotto changing his attitude to the ubiquitous kids entertainment in Pizza restaurants.

It was not any great noble motivation that started them off on this slightly peculiar path. It was unseen censorship. Straitjacket had become tighter and tighter. Squeezed and compressed them, sometimes subtly, sometimes less so. Jail for bad words, freedom for murderers. Public space was poisoned with a mad virus of 'correctness.' What was 'correct' was an intentional kaleidoscope of impenetrable logic. Supported freedom of people but wanted some themselves. You tried to stay on the merry-go-round but you got so dis-orientated you got ill. Identities were all. Identities in a state of flux. Tis I need it. Identities sold as expansive but they were contracting. Excluded and reduced. If you want to weaken something you let it grow strong first. Tao. Now they used abbreviations everywhere. You could not do certain things if you had not testified to your identity. Then tensions between identity groups seemed to emerge from nowhere. This led to the seeds of resistance. It really started when they began to spread the Samizdat copies, books and recordings. They liked the old politically incorrect comedians. Bernard Manning was very popular. He became a hate figure because he made jokes about Irish and Pakistanis and anybody. Nasty yes. Racist more than likely. Terrible words they would never use. Got a lot of attention, like for his joke that the corgis in the Palace were at least glad when the Queen Mum had died so they wouldn't be blamed for the smell of piss. VIZ magazine. Barbara had a t-shirt on with '*Want to Stop being Gullible. Find out How…*' with a box address and a large fee.

They could name all the comic strips. Auntie Cockwise. Bad Bob. Wockney Canker. The Randy Wonder Dog. Balsa Boy. Billy the Fish. The Bottom Inspectors. The self-righteous, right-on comedians attacked these old 'Blue' comedians until there was no platform left and they left the scene. Still there was something not right about taking people off it. Alternative Comedy was not alternative at all. Lure of the forbidden. Ironic that's all. Then there were books with extracts from banned classics with words people did not like anymore. This had not been about protecting people but about controlling them. Censor their humour in the public space and penetrate into their internal one. All the new comedy was against spirituality unless it was some neutered oriental blankness without the real, good stuff. You had to buy the full packet. Create absurdist, nihilist worldview to promote ideology. Marxism is a combine harvester. Main rule of their reaction was that they would use historical experience so as not to fall down another internal rabbit hole beyond the external one everyone had been found to have fallen in.

Many games they invented. Not just for nerdy pleasure and enlightenment but to defuse heat when they talked politics. Sometimes talking about culture jamming, subvertising, Billboard Liberation Front, Guerrilla Girls or monochrom got warm. Now it was a game. Less winding-up. Joey Skaggs and The Fat Squad. Talking about Deep Vein Thrombosis. Peter studied and used it in the 'Underground-Overground Effects Game.' He started enthusiastically "During the Blitz, many people were dying. But the coroner noticed that many people were dying of thrombosis. Investigated. He found people were dying *after* a few days in the Underground. People slept on the platforms. Why? You sit still for a long time, cramped. Blood stops flowing back up, it's harder for the heart. A jam. Something like a chilli forms in the veins of your deep calf. You go home and then you find it has gone to your heart, lungs. Fucked."

"Jaysus. You hear about it sometimes on the planes," said Janet.

"Yeah, sometimes. Bastards knew about this for a long time. But they were exempt. Legally not an 'accident' within the meaning of the Warsaw Convention. Then they said fuck it, most people won't make the connection a few days after. Died suddenly of a thrombosis, nobody knows why. The British Olympic team got it going to Australia. Probably gets as many as air crashes. Nobody gives a monkeys. Try suggesting someone doesn't cross their legs on a plane... right," Peter continued, "Janet you had a theory."

On the Rotation you could chose topics, she chose Conspiracy Theories. Try tell one that they had not heard. Part of Vico's method in their heads.

"Some key bits are my own. Ok," said Janet and laid out her theory, "Enid Blyton was married to Hugh Pollock. Lieutenant Colonel. Was at Gallipoli. Palestine. Later at Cabinet Office. They split. He worked on Churchill's book *The World Crisis* with him. He knew things. Blyton knew things. In 1940 a children's book *The House in Cornwall* comes out. Children holiday with a deposed leader of Livia. Secrets, agents and spies. Then Blyton comes out with her Famous 5. The first book was about deep state shit hiding in plain sight. Here's the speculation. She leaves clues in her books, or it was a premonition. Julian (the Emperor) Anne (Queen Anne) Dick (Richard Lionheart) Timmy the dog (Catholicism) George (is mad George III) who becomes Georgina (the esoteric transgender). Uncle Quentin (secret state) is secretive, works for the Government, but has a bad temper. Quentin is San Quentin. US prison, had torture, Death Row. Parts of the mystery but you know you have not got the full story. Three readings. Either coded revelations of enfolding Plan to next generation, toying with the public for 'in' joke or precognition."

"Wow!" Pam exclaimed.

"Before we vote on that I would note that San Quentin was where the AA, Alcoholic Anonymous took hold. You need a Higher Power to defeat the drink. 12 steps. That's counter-enlightenment. Vico would buy that," Colin noted.

Suddenly there was shaking, groaning, rumbling. Invisible orchestra of glass tinklers. Lights flickered. They burst out laughing. Raised eyebrows. Screaming freezeframe. Drinks fell off tables and beer spilled. Shouts. Curses. **Quake. EARTHFUCKINGQUAKE.** Alarms. Cacophony.

"Fuck!" Colin shouted.

"Oh my God!" Peter said.

"That was strong," Barbara nodded. "Can you believe it!"

Mayhem. Bewilderment. Timespace seemed to split temporarily.

"Jesus, I wonder will that affect the tunnels?" George asked.

Because they engaged in tunnel-exploration and speleology, first thoughts were about effects thereon. Into the Old Bailey once. They sat in the Prospect of Whitby away from catacombs, caves, caverns. Their Sunday Club met in famous London pubs. 7 members. Names changed. They might use the names of Enid Blyton's Secret Seven. Peter, Barbara, Colin, Pam, Janet, Jack, George. Or they might be Del Boy, Rodney, Alf, Bertie, Billy, Catherine and Jennifer. Names from comedy, real or fictitious people. Vin, Harry, Barnardo and other Magnificent Seven names. Another time comic characters Dr. Strange, Jesse Custer, Tulip O'Hare and so on. Generally they did not discuss 'business' in public for obvious reasons, save in a veiled way.

"Does that affect the plans?" Jack said coolly in the emergent mêlée.

"No. They're fretting too much round here, We've already had the SportShooter. Always something," Janet said.

"In fact it may be a dream come true for us," Barbara said.

"Loneliness and cheeseburgers are a dangerous mix - Comic Store guy." Janet.

"You don't win friends with salad - Homer." Barbara.

They walked up to the Peabody Estate buildings across The Highway to where Janet lived in her one bedroom flat as sirens and a boom rang over the roads with vehicles stopped here and there in odd places. They liked to be chilled. Secret Seven, Magnificent Seven, Seven Sages of the Bamboo Grove. They learned from the Seven Sephiroth. 7 at the first Phi Delta Theta Convention in 1851. Concluded that the 'car-computer-controlled, military machine culture' was engaged in a process of 'collective consciousness capture.' The 'Aim of The Machine' was to turn humans into nodes of a collective consciousness which they served. Obvious now. DARPA. Carnegie. Others saw it. Zamyatin in *We* in 1921. Taylorism. The new God would be the Collective, alternative priests would facilitate the final phase of servitude and bondage. Transcendent Divine dead with Luminous Man-Machine instead. Consciousness bondage would replace the dwindling illusion of 'freedom.' Democracy charade clear. People could not stop foreign war whatever their numbers. When the Machine wanted fuel, whole regions could be spoiled. Studied Subcomandante Insurgente Marcos and James Connolly but sought to develop a non-ideological, 'pragmatic cosmopolitanism.' Zapatistas had understood NAFTA. Focus was on 'awakening.' Awaken. Osho, Crowley, Gurdjieff and many others stressed this. Alternative was the mass, irreversible technological enslavement of human consciousness. Technological apocalypse.

They shored up the tunnel of perceptions from the general outside and the particular sense of unrest from the earthquake around them as they had done for the last year in their explorations. After a few smokes and drinks they decided a few months ago to establish the Luddite Zapatista Leveller Front (LZLF). The name a compromise amalgam of the nearest movements to their belief. Messy. The 7 had African, Australian, European and Asian forebearers. Many names and inspirations were considered. The Weathermen. Two of the 7 wanted the spiritists behind the Mexican Revolution but the rest were unsure. Two wanted to integrate Ashanti Queen Nanny and the Maroons in Jamaica. One a Zenarchist, another an anarchist. Another loved William Godwin and Mary Wollstonecraft, parents of Mary Shelley. Considered the Discordians, Viet Cong, Neo-Druids. Some possibility that it could have been The Order of the Yellow Emperor based on Colin's theory about the great Chinese innovator. Rasputin

Resurrected was a short-lived discussion. Paracelsus. Zoth and Azoth. Gnosticism. One argued for St Michael based on the tradition of the spiritual warrior. Another for Melchizedek, and said that Jesus was one of his priests. One encountered the 'Underground Catholic Church' which believed that the Church in Rome was an apostasy run by the Devil. They recreated the 'spirit of the catacombs' on the basis that Europe would become part of a Great Caliphate with Greater Israel at the centre of the doughnut. No other takers. The majority cited *The Gadfly* to demonstrate that Christianity could not help and someone quoted St Paul on Romans 13:1-7 to submit to or obey the authorities and then quoted James Madison that *'resistance to tyranny is service to God.'* *The Gadfly* was the celebrated book by Ethel Voynich (who was Irish though it did not sound it) based on Sidney Reilly (who sounded Irish but was born in Russia or Ukraine). Sidney Reilly. Ace of Spies, inspiration for James Bond, secret agent, revolutionary. Worked for the Secret Service and Special Branch, a double agent, involved in various international events like the acquisition of Middle Eastern oil fields and the 'Great Game.' They agreed with the Unabomber Manifesto but rejected bombs. Geronimo discussed as a warrior and because it was said that Prescott Bush (on behalf of the Yale University Skulls and Bones Society) had robbed his skull from his Fort Sill grave. Transcendentalists of the Thoreau-type were examined. Liberation within and from government. Government best which governs least. Civil disobedience. Charles Manson had one supporter who emphasised the ATWA, the Air Trees Water Animals, group Manson set up to protect the environment. Developed monkey-wrenching before others. All The Way Alive. Proponent suggested that was why he had been set up. Opponents argued against because of his Race War theories. Manson 'got messages' from the White Album of the Beatles and Helter Skelter and thought his songs would trigger a war. His colleague was charged with conspiracy to send threatening letters to corporate executives. Sandra Good. Manson was done for conspiracy to commit murder also. No evidence - call it conspiracy. Find evidence against Them they say it is a 'conspiracy theory.' You find someone who has done wrong and stitch them up and then you destroy the Hippies, Weathermen and Black Power. Rejected. Bobby Sands and the Rhythm of Time. 'An inner thing in every man' …tied a lot together. Monetary Military Monopolise Monism Machine (MMMMM or M5) was the technique used to assume control. Get them to give you money to make war. Force people to pay for everything, blame Adam Smith and the 'invisible hand.' Once upon a time you had clean water. Business pollutes it. Polluter makes you pay. Chemicals left. What to do with them? Stick it in the water. Poison you and make you pay for the privilege. Public hypnotised, tranquiliser in taps. Poison the air. Chemtrails. Nanoparticles. Now you can pay for air, enclosures. Enclosures like with land. Highland Clearances in Scotland. Natural remedies, only in chemists. Exercise, only gyms. Machine and idolise mechanistic mindsets. Monopolise. Some names did not work because they gave the game away. For example Dodger by Pratchett emerges from a sewer. Goddess Cloacina was goddess of the sewers. Cloaca Maxima Rome. Venus Cloacina, purifier. Cloaca, secretory organ. Secret and secrete, same origin. To set apart. Miners used pray to Saint Barbara for safety. She hid in a cliff. Also artillery.

Some inspirations were woven into their philosophy. Michel de Certeau. *The Practice of Everyday Life*. 'Guerrilla ontology' caused long debate. Magic Musick. King Crimson. Sun Ra. Bowie. Hawkwind. Psychic TV. Pink Floyd. Led Zeppelin. Robert Johnson. The Jam. They took an oath. Swore never to write anything down or record anything appertaining to LZLF work. Never reveal anything they did together. To be mindful of electronic eavesdropping. Not endanger life. Property a different matter. Swore to oppose the psychology of the 'military-industrial complex,' to maintain a sense of humour. When sober they agreed it seriously and swore again for corroboration. Symbol was the mushroom in various forms. Mushrooms. Biggest living thing in the world could be a mushroom, if not coral. Atomic bomb a mushroom cloud. Some believed Christianity and Mystery religions were all built on worship of mushrooms. Some that Jesus was a mushroom! Allegro, Wasson, McKenna. Psycho-active properties. Amanita Muscaria. Soma. Entheogens. Enthusiasm. Ergot derivatives. Magic mushrooms helped humans evolve. Stoned Ape Theory. Slime mould can design undergrounds better than humans. Proven. Physarum Polycephalum. No religion because God came through psychedelic experience. Travelled to Sweden and 'shroomed.' Some had bad experiences, some life-changing. Spores travelled in space. Developed an initiation. Studied Eleusian Mysteries. Emperor Julian the Apostate had been affected very much thereby. Led to the Spirit of the Sun, the Sun Mystery. A key to awaken the soul to cosmic secrets. Initiates went through a near-death experience induced by plants. After such an experience you fear death no longer, united with the universe. Pam a chemist and herbalist. Mushrooms would cure cancer. They assassinated Julian when he tried to discover the Manichean

Mysteries. Augustine triumphed. Church incorporated pagan rites. Learned from explorations about transcendence that justice was interwoven into universe's fabric. Karma a universal law. Realised psychedelic mystics may fail to implement concrete things, unlike 'normal' mystics. Only individual spiritual growth and passing mystic thresholds to comprehensive consciousness could allow society to grow.

The attitude would respect primal spirit with radical scepticism. Not anarchy. Original theories were interesting but had been hijacked by nihilists or the State. Nobody really got what Anarchy really meant. They liked the opposition to both capitalism and communism. Read about Zomia. All had formed a dislike of ONE BIG IDEA. They liked Gustav Metzger who developed auto-destructive art who saw Nazis and was worried about machine people. One of his pieces was a bag at the Tate that a cleaner threw out. Like Beuys' dirty bath that a gallery cleaner had cleaned. They watched Mr Bean, smoking dope and laughing. Joyce and *Finnegans Wake* another source. Linked Joseph Campbell, Terence McKenna, Timothy Leary, Robert Anton Wilson, Robert Shea, George Carlin. *The Illuminatus Trilogy*. Irish-American counter-cultural movement. Colin was Irish, and Peter's parents. Peter wanted Shane McGowan to be a figurehead. Pair of Brown Eyes. Consciousness. Joyce one link and anti-authoritarianism was another. Colin was interested in Catholic philosophy but not 'liberation theology.' Marxism masquerading as liberation, hijacking spiritual development. Said Satan and Lucifer was an angelic intelligence, so you had to be careful about what you were attached to. Researched theory that technology came from extra-terrestrials and spirits. Tesla. Dominance of scientific, materialist, mechanistic mindset, hostile to spirituality was a key target. That Japanese scientists at infamous Unit 731 who committed war crimes with the grossest medical experiments escaped liability through sharing their 'scientific' knowledge. Science seeks to secrete unethical science that qualifies as science while unscientifically emphasising the wrongdoing of religion.

Citizens Committee to Investigate the FBI were one inspiration. Seven members joined the original instigator. On the night of the fight between Ali and Frazier, everyone glued to the gladiators, they broke into the FBI offices in Media Pennsylvania. Found evidence of infiltration of opposition, blackmail, burglary. Found out, after years of investigation, about counter-intelligence program. Found out how the State would discredit, divide and destroy 'black extremist' organisations and use system to focus on dissidents. Some dissident groups had a majority of infiltrators. KKK had many informants. Many intellectuals under scrutiny. A long list of people on an index could be arrested without trial in an emergency. Then Pentagon Papers came out. Long before Snowden and Assange. Individual citizens challenged over-reaching Governments who used tactics of terrorist, tyrant and criminal. Another idea was to link a popular revolutionary movement to alternative currencies. Focus on currency to shine attention on con job of financial prison constructed. Moral currency devalued and full of counterfeit. In Plato's cave, shadows thought true, were made by elites on a platform over us. Briefly flirted with idea of setting up cafe called 'Offensive,' a 'safe-space' to be offensive. Sign consent form to get in. Subvert political correctness. Studied Situationists. Some in London. Psycho-geography. Following Guy Debord. Influenced Punk? Not really. Situationists serious. Comedy. That's State-controlled. Master of the Revels. Someone suggested Russell Brand as a model. Some said he was part of machine. Contested. One saw him up Camden. The Filth and The Fury. Funeral of the manager up Camden High Street with the Double Decker Bus said it all. Cash From Chaos. But Debord was onto something. Spectacle. Marx, Shakespeare influenced him. They were round here.

Having explored the city's underground tunnels, they were ready to apply knowledge. Oldest meaning of word to bore involves digging, tunnelling. Boring things. Boredom, ennui were clearly Enlightenment constructions. Underneath London were underground rivers, sewers, postal, cable, transport, Government, secret and ancient tunnels. City had tunnel walkways. Templars and esoteric groups love tunnels. Kilwinning Abbey. Well-known tunnels such as at Newgate, Euston Road Tunnel, Tower Subway, Kingsway Tram Tunnel. Bricked up tunnels radiated from the Tower. Secret bunkers. Ancient miscellaneous tunnels. Some Roman, Medieval, Victorian. Tunnels in great 'heists.' Hatton Garden Jewellery Heist. Baker Street Robbery. 26 tunnels under Thames in London alone. Most people do not know. Tunnels hidden let unbeknownst, unsightly things operate. Others tunnelled into thinking. Subconscious is riddled with ruinous routes. Explored Fleet River-cum-sewer. Knew where 'easy-lift' shores, manholes, maintenance entrances were. Top-class waders, masks, torches and useful tools fit into a compact haversack. Got used to rats, turds and sanitary towels. Looking at incredible brickwork and traces of the capital's past you forgot unpleasantries. Sometimes you imagine an animal or human shape. Trips to tunnels known and unknown, like smuggler ones in

Cornwall. Discussed tunnels, meanings, implications. Argued about Freud and Hitchcock, on trains entering tunnels, repression, secrets. Utilise network to accomplish modest goals, circumvent pervasive overground surveillance. Marched in City against banks, corruption, erosion of civil liberties. Kettling, fluorescent dousing, other police tactics showed freedom of assembly dead. Surprised by Guildhall bombing. Because nobody was hurt they celebrated. Momentum. Take part, serious fun. Spanner in the works. Talked about tunnels in consciousness, time-tunnels. How 'evidence' was a slippery beast of an eel.

Toasts often had reference to tunnel escapes. Peter raised his glass, "Here's to *The Wooden Horse*."

"*The Great Escape*," said Janet.

"Island Farm," said Barbara.

"El Chapo," said Pam.

"Prisoner Cell Block H," said George.

"*The Shawshank Redemption,*" said Jack.

"*Count of Monte Christo*."

"The Jam." Janet again.

"For Charles Byrne." Barbara again.

"For Banksy."

"Fuck him he's a wanker."

"Hooray." All together.

"Let's shake the consensus," Peter said. "Now about that Tremor… Let's check out 'KINGQUAKE. BIGGEST EVA…!'"

Address mystery of iniquity using techniques of mole, fox, mongoose, ferret and ant. Now, as good a time as any to activate what they planned for months. Pop Agitprop. Theatre. World is a scene. Scene is what is seen. Scene is staged. World's a stage. Seen is staged. Stage is screened. Screen keeps out reality. We live in a play. We think we're in control. We are puppets. Actors act on us. Pantomime. Mime. Not all mortal theatre. Death play. Mishima.

'Masurao ga
Tabasamu tachi no
sayanari ni
Ikutose taete
Kyo no hatsushimo.'

Or Pearse,

'The beauty of this world hath made me sad,
This beauty that will pass.'

LLLF

LONDON LOGOS LIBERATION FRONT

Publishing Pamphlets to Oppose Censorship of Our Message.
The Counter-Revolutionary to Evil and Terror Effort.
Posters provide our propaganda to promote our work.

LUDDITES WERE NOT AGAINST TECHNOLOGY.

TECHNOLOGY HELPS US.

TECHNOLOGY IS A TOOL.

TECHNOLOGY SHOULD NOT BE A MASTER.

PEOPLE SWALLOW NONSENSE HISTORY.

POLITICAL BELIEFS ARE DOLLY MIXTURES TO MAKE PUPPETS OF YOU.

AI AND ROBOTS ARE DANGEROUS.

HUMANS ARE SPECIAL.

TRANSHUMANISM IS DANGEROUS.

CHIPS IN PEOPLE ARE THE MARK OF THE BEAST.

SCIENTISM WORSHIPS TECHNOLOGY.

EVOLUTIONARY THEORY IS FALSE.

OLIGARCHY WANTS TECHNOLOGY.

TECHNOLOGY IS CONTROL.

GENETIC ENGINEERING WILL TAKE FREE WILL.

SCIENTISM TAKES FREE WILL.

REMEMBER SOYLENT GREEN IS PEOPLE.

PREPARE FOR LIBERATION

Chapter 3

The Real Deal

'...where oranges have been laid to rust upon the green...'

Sinbad Sylvester Silmarillion, SSS (aka Triple S, 3XS) had been reading a 411 mail from Job AAK when it started. Just beforehand he was considering whether chips were the mark of the beast and why they used pin dafloaters on him before he left. Jaysus they can shove theirjazzhandsuptheir**jaxy**. THE ONLY BAD PEOPLE ARE THE ONES THAT MEAN TO HURT OTHER BOYS OR GIRLS. Sticksandstones. Let folk talk. People are people. PAP. SMH. 1337.

> VATT (Vatican Advanced Technology Telescope) is on Mount Graham in Arizona. Spanish came through there looking for the Seven Cities of Gold. Germans helped the Vatican build the telescope. They don't care that Apaches hold the mountains sacred. Have a telescope called LUCIFER on the hill. Jesuits. Observatory is at the same latitude as Armageddon. Waiting for signal from the Beast that he is coming. Phoenix Lights in 1997 and afterwards. UFO's and lights. Close Encounters of the Third Kind primer. CERN has statue of Lord of the Dance Nataraja, Shiva. Science tramples on disillusion. Humans genetically adapted to correspond to the higher alien forms, sometimes confused with demons. Real Area 52. The Godzone.

WTF. 1NAM. Boooomchick. Tremendous tremor. Bomb? Nuke! Horrorshow. Exciting. EYC. Empaled. Wag-one. Birthmilkshake! Oh my days. I am not crazy. Maybe that's what the Council of 9 was about. Star Trek writer and channelling. Sirius? Esoteric portal opened in California. Crowley, Parsons. Jet Propulsion Laboratory. Babalon working. Have to look at 33 degrees latitude. Dallas-Kennedy. Baghdad. Satanists in Vatican. Not mad. I don't know if they would say I am a 'self-loathing homosexual' or a 'self-loathing homophobe'? ARG. I'm no Incel who took a black pill just that I haven't crossed the finishing line yet with any cheena gyaldem or biddie but I'm still a shabwhiffettaruna. A kijanabalaka needs time. All is 80:20 but that 20 has an 80:20 within too. PAP. Not quite White. Not quite Black. Sometimes I feel like Ali G. FFS - I am not an *Identity*! Quake? I don't mess with ouija boards any more. Why do we all need a label? World was filling up with Cuckadildoeedoos and what about toxic femininity? Hope it's a whopperquake. Loads of Barney Rubble. EWG. Sick of learning how to be 'triggered' and offended and so on. Picnic-Sand. They use these fools to fool you and make you think you should be a fool too so they can rule you. Suck you in. Poison your perception. Give your attention. Kretin hypeheads. Inmyhead I use words that go ob leek bcus to call a ///// a ///// wud b seen as a slur even when it clearly wasn't. So u think with beepsinurhead. What fool judges people on colour of skin pigmentation or their sex life? Not matrix. AR. Dred. Earthquake!

Thinking about Lucius Tubal interview. Censorship is designed to produce and provoke what it claims to pacify. Dummy. Model. Feint. Sub. Fool. Slur sometimes. We are dummies. I've a dummy in me. BDD. Dummies fall in love with other dummies. Not Tubal. Britain's Joe Rogan. Triple S did some digging. When he found out Candy Apple Crimson X (aka Ethel) lived nearby, he knew it was a sign. 2GTBT. If still at Pratt Street he would be nearer. They did not want him there. Not his yard. No bluds here. Butters and skets. Air. Kidnapping not really his gig. Bait. Said there were a number of Liliths. One was Adam's first wife but she would not submit to him and wanted to be superior. Cool. Check clip, he didn't remember whether she was good or bad. One manifestation bad, killing children, nasty. Follow her to the Pit. Problem was Gwendoline had done some ceremony to Lilith with him. Said it was nice to build up 'feminine energy,' dark like a nightcave. Bare. Didn't believe in the Pit, but had bad dreams and felt a succubus on his chest. Who knows? Now Ethel/Candy who is into goddesses says some are really dangerous occultists. Londonfuckingearthquake! Crackshaker. Must be. Crump. Crutterz. PAP heads but U live in an ARG. Slipped.

Remembered the bit. They would ban all this stuff. The Finnegans Wake lingo would have to come in instead. Jar Gone. Corange, Slangerooney. **Cant**. We'll be all cants now when they napalm forests of meaning, bomb, slash, burn the hair8tage of words lovingly created. Day2reinventtheroundyting. Rebs'll talk diff cos dey madeemdo. Talkdiff ill B ill eagle den Bud war'llbeonden. Dendey stop you blathering at all. Language has been destroyed and made extinct many times. Nobody thinks English is under threat. Haha.

Lucius: So you would judge certain people? You're not talking of people merely with that pleasant name but certain practitioners who employ that.

Ethel: Well it's not my job to judge. Would I avoid them like the plague? Absolutely. I understand mythos. Archetype. Complex explanations. Lilith for example. But many Liliths may not know what they are serving. Involved with something so dangerous without study and protection or guardianship just because the girls do it, then…. Of course I honour those finding the healing, shadow, loving powers.

Lucius: C'mon that's harsh!

Ethel: Don't sacrifice your soul for a place at the dinner party Lucius. It's no joke. Rational, scientific, materialist deniers will mislead you. Mark my words. It's not mumbo-jumbo. Use intuition not institutions. DNA and computer came up the same time. Cybernetics. Clock to computer. Programmed. You are a computer. World is a simulation. Information became all. Not Truth.

Noise. Shouts. Good. Fun. Two interesting things recently. Ethel's second interview and then the Guildhall Bomb. Play Miss Stick for me, haha. Liked power of subversion. Liked film Preaching to the Perverted. Real BDSM people. Thrill. Buzz. Ace. First to claim responsibility was the 'Genuine IRA.' Said they did it because City of London built an illegal plantation in Londonderry but never paid the price. Corporation of London established Londonderry walls and colonised it, with people they wanted to rid from the City. Another group also claimed responsibility. Shooting top footballers and 'soap' stars strange. Soap companies gave us soap operas. Dirty bastards. Sniper shot from way out of grounds. If he was 'The Mule' he would do things soon. Like Asimov's character he'd reveal his powers and get his revenge. Prefer to journey on a space ship to the stars. Getting closer. Maybe a lottery. Put his name in for Mars. If only people knew what an amazing person he was. Tapes helped. Tapeworm. Not quite gone. It's not nice to sleep in the rain alone on the streets.

One of his friends indicated something amiss. Would not usually have seen him or her at that time. Male or female, not sure. Neverwhere. Felt first wave. Place small. Soon everyone would be living in a cellar shoebox. The Plan. Only a muppet can't see. Screeching sirens began very quickly. Chorus of car alarms. Glass falling, shattered somewhere on paths outside. Dogs howling. Woman screamed. Computer crashed in blackout. Damn. Up from basement to have a look. Voices, movement, panic. On the street debris here and there.

"Oh MY GOD! Oh my God! Oh my God!"

Wished she would shut up. STFU. Get the point. Bet she's atheist. Some bricks had fallen from a house down the road and a window was broken. People standing in groups pointing, excited. Fuck it. Too tame for him, too wild for most others. Still some sense of rumbling. Someone asking whether it was an explosion or an earthquake. A geezer said that it measured 6 on the Richter scale. Between 6 and 7. GR8. GTM. Atheist norpstars shout OMG! so believers Hu hear'll think sx instead of Gd when they hear the word. No 6.

"NO WAY. That's impossible. No way. Can't be. God!"

Dawkinsapistdef. Maybe they'll be shouting that meeting their maker. Up the road more stuff strewn. Wailing getting on his nerves. This street where his one local friend was stabbed. Marginally better than being homeless. Supposed it'd be alright in the basement. Wondered whether there would be any looting. If he walked up the town maybe he'd get a pair of sneakers. One of his rat friends scuttling by the basement window so early had alerted him. Warning. Animals know. Have a temple of rats in India to some goddess, died in the 1530's. He'd go there. Some don't love rats. If anyone saw how cute a rat was when you tickled their belly they'd change their mind. Now they're saying it was not the rats that spread the plague. Always blaming the wrong ones. Blunts. Ringelringelrosenkranz.

SSS decided to walk to Camden Market and look around. Nobody paid much attention to him. All he knew about was computers, Nazis, serial killers and aliens. And The Real Secret. He wished he could do parkour. He was two people. Quiet one, people avoided and one that could do unexpected things. Recently he was learning politics for work. Tried to learn rules they gave him but it was boring. *Pick target, freeze it, personalise it, polarise it. Identify individuals to attack. Threat terrifies more than the thing itself. Ridicule most potent weapon.* All worked on fucking SCRIPTS. Acting-fun. SSS was interested in Fascists. Bastards. Just read about Nazi leadership. IQ tests at Nuremburg. High. Bet all the really clever ones don't do IQ tests. Saw programme about O'Brien. One of the highest IQs in the world. Works for CIA. Hacker and stuff. Chase these guys in novels. Dr No. But in real life they give them a job as a spy or agent. Nazis in NASA. Difficult to remember what to say if you were playing different roles in life. Adapt intelligently. Mirror what's going on around. Bullshit. To fit in you have to have attitudes that move like a weather vane. Snowflake. Nice word, shame about the people. Not easy to work out what attitude to have. Best to repeat what someone else says. Talk like them. Or tweak it. Or read the SCRIPT. Sinbad Sylvester Silmarillion not his real name. 3XS. People judge you. Like the tattoo on my face. Having a name like Zebedee Blairgowrie was guaranteed bullying in'it. That was why he had no real friends. Not from London originally. Tried to fit in. North London was alright if you stayed in the right places. Easy to get knifed and moped gangs rob you. Gangs get you if you were unlucky. His parents fault really. Didn't protect him when he needed it, didn't talk about things. Recently he had also become Rob Brands. YOLO. Clever. Sounded real. Hinted he liked brands. Marks. Wicked. Not the 'A' brands but the 'B' brands. If you had top brands when you went out you would lose them. Top logos. Get into a beef. 110s before inflation. Hikokos no wonder. Guy could stop you and say,

'They're BEAST man. Give us those or I'll stick you. Like a pig.'

You had to give them then. Skeng. Zombieblade. Bling. Brands important. Best things. Brapp! Greatest goods ever produced. Said that in ads. Runners. See in the ads how powerful these were. Mainly creps, runners, sneakers. Cud get duppyed, murked. Cud be licking off. Baseball hats. He wasn't stupid. Liked to be at home in his bedsit. Skepta. Grime. No mandem, zero fam round here. Bit like deadout. Internet cafes. Charity shops. Bought ladies clothes for his sister. He had none. Went to shops to buy energy drinks and coffee. Pizza. Someone called him Pizza face. Territories. Had to watch boundaries. Like animals. Bit of a wasteman. Didn't drink. Made him sick. Thought of law school. One time. Liked lawyers on telly. Didn't like school. Only interested in the Nazis. Hitandmissler. Himmler. You're Nazi because you read it. They know nothing. BETTER KNOW THE BEAST BEST TO BEAT THE BEAST. Ad. Don't know even that Hitler took the name as a variant of Hiedler. Means underground river. Sounds like a machinegun. They don't even know about PaddyHitler. Law was hard. Had to talk in front of people. Saw himself do it. Only in his loaf of bread. Had not dreamt he would have a life in politics. Then he got a job as a social justice warrior, an 'antifa.' Fascist left. Cool being a warrior. Like in games. First Person Shooter. That person in Norway thought he was in a game. Social justice didn't roll off the tongue. Like a hot potato in his mouth. Job. Some bread. Black money. He didn't like when they burned books outside the library for some bad words. 'N' word they said. All Mark Twain's books. Like Nazis, Inquisition, Reformation. Called agents sometimes but not like James Bond. Kinda secret. Not so interested in social justice, whatever that was. Bollocks. On my ones. Didn't like people too much. Paid his rent. Read The Scripts when they sent them. 'Opinions' so they looked like they came from someone credible. Gullible public. You do a quota of comments online, newspapers, all kinds of forums. Email what you were supposed to. Have 'cred.' ICEDI. Choose some words on your own to make them look different. Had robots so they only wanted a few here and there. Spelling mistakes were ok. Made it look authentic. NPC. Always emotional when you're telling how hurt your feelings are. OMAA. All about feelings. Emotions. Marketing people. That's why they play the music to make you buy things. We're like robots inside. Music activates emotions. Feel that car in the wild. Music. Feel powerful. On the road on your own. Great teeth, shining skin. No cars. Only you. Powerful. Quick. You don't worry too much about speed in ads. No litter. Music opens you. You know what you are living is not real. This is it. What you see. Music signals it's right. Love, feelings. Partner, dog meets you when you get home. Quick in the ad. No traffic in adland. Only in our world of illusion. Our world is not real. We live in realities they make for us. Not the old, unprogrammed ones. Decreps. That's why they're making a war between old and young. Old=expensive, narky, taking up space, keeping us out of jobs, having pensions. Made the mess. Have all the things we should. War on Decreps is coming. Ads. Rappers. Get all them women dancing because they drink, use drugs, no ed. Lots of gold. Helps. Women like gold. Have money they like you. Even if you're a mingin' twat. Women like money. Pretend love. Rappers champagne, bounce on cars, women present. Throw dollars, Cristal over them. Sophisticated. Wish I was so. Good to have a fur coat, jewellery, champagne and throw dollars in the sun. I could do that. I am practising my songs, a rap artist Motherfucker. Make signs with guns that's ok. Guns cool for rappers. You might get shot. XXXT. Enjoy yourself before. Rap because of slavery. Belinda wants us to pay slaves the money we owe them for taking them from Africa. I heard her boast a few times that she 'had' an African man. Sounded like slavery talk to me. Hypok. PAP. His dope dealer said that if you were good with computers you work social justice gigs. Get a text and collect placards. Messages didn't even hide their similarity. Didn't read them. LOL. Money let him have a small bedsit. Smelt a bit bad in the basement and a rat or two came by the cellar window.

One came up the pipe. Monster. Didn't bother him. Cute. Felt some affinity. Sometimes, sang 'Ben' and he was Michael Jackson. Wondered about Talent shows on telly. Susan Boyle. Maybe they snigger. Then he sang. The crowd would look at each other. Wow! Realised they were wrong. Continued in a world of his own, imagining singing to the rat. A standing ovation! Even Simon Cowell, or whoever, couldn't believe it. Idol. Maybe if that stuff he stole from Boots worked on his acne. Harder to get the good cream. Steroids and stuff. Locked away. Charge more. Probably gives muscles too. He had none. Young men hated by society anyway. Boys they want, men no. And the boys or girls suffer when they take parents away or if they have stinkers for parents. Not 4AO, another incoming. No P left. If angels won't get dirty how can they work?

I think it's not about religion. I think it's a set-up. A set-up for a showdown. Science wants to divide and conquer. They know the religious guys won't swallow their stuff. They know they have to make loads up. The Big Bang. So they'll get the Jews and the Christians fighting the Muslims. They'll encourage it, let it get nasty. They'll plant bombs themselves, secret associations. Everyone's sick of it, they'll come and say Science is your only man. Reason. Method. No superstitious nonsense. Evidence. Then they'll control our brainwaves with mobile masts. The New Religion ready. New Morality. Objectives. Reduce population. Francis Bacon. New Atlantis. 1627. She says. Yes I buy it. Angels must get dirty hands.

Losing in. Get real. Nutter. Conspiracies. Mad. Camden Market strange. Some stalls upset, facade of a famous shop collapsed. People looking at a crack in the side of the bridge over Regent's Canal. Enough. Wander home. He did not like to walk. SSS thought of the interview. He did not understand it. Sometimes he just learnt things off and then he might use it. He remembered. Ban stuff is crazy. Recorded. Spooool. Never knew... earth uninhabited. Only embers.

Lucius: Ethel, let me try and summarise. You say that when the Crusaders went to Jerusalem that they met with Saladin and formed an alliance with the person they were fighting against? You say this persists today?

Ethel: I didn't say that. Brigid said something like that. Templars were not the same thing as the Crusaders. Yes Saracens and the Templars respected each other. Apart from the well-known Treaty they had a secret accord. They sat down and realised they shared similar aims. Agreed chivalry could be

	a shared conception. Ferocity in battle, gentleness outside. Agreed there's a God above gods and He had to be the same *He*, unlike some of the Jewish mystics pointing to the divine feminine. Supreme Being.
Lucius:	But is there evidence that they acted on this? Does history not show a different path.
Ethel:	One thing that may help. They agreed they were doing God's work. Thus they could operate in God's time. Time scale was a thousand years. One God Time Milli-Second. The real millennium, not the other one. So we are in the final furlong of this Great Accord.
Lucius:	So you think this persists?
Ethel:	It is unfolding if you look at evidence and not propaganda, advertising, marketing and hypnosis. If you can snap out of the trance. Not you personally of course, Lucius darling. Watch the linking of Crescent with Goddess. Remember where you heard it.

TripleS had no idea, but was interested. Liked discussing weird things. Himselftler would have preferred if Germany was Islamic and not mainly Catholic or the home of Protestantism. She talked about the Third Secret of Fatima, not doing so in a 'religious' way.

Lucius:	You said something about Fatima and the Pope. But yet you're not a Catholic and seem to oppose religion? Are you projecting paganism onto Catholicism?
Ethel:	Pope talked about Mother Earth. Is the Pope a Catholic? Probably not. The Great Goddess appeared at Fatima. Our Lady. Said Russia needed to be saved and predicted another Great War after 'lights in the sky.' Hitler saw these lights as most of Europe did. The Pope was meant to reveal, publicise and act on the Third Secret. He put it in a box. He did not want to offend the Soviets. Not listening to the Great Goddess was disastrous. Virgin Mary. Feminine, anti-war goddess. Displaced by weaker, false goddesses that love death and destruction like Bellona, shaking her spear. Now anyone can be a goddess, even men, irrespective of any higher qualities. In fact the baser the attributes the more convincing people assume them to be. They are jokers, not even tricksters.

Lucius: I just thought that you and your personalities and the dolls and controlling them sounds a bit like Being John Malkovich and those unfortunately called 'schizo-comedies.'

How the fuck does she know? Too much noise. Maybe if he stopped picking the spots they'd go away. Nalezing. That's was why he had his cap on most of the time. Hard to wash yourself here. Worse in the squat before. But he wasn't pongy 'cos he had got deodorant sprays from the shops. Sprayed loads. Smelt nice. See it in ads. People like when you smell nice. Not your natural smell. That's like smelly cheese. Sweat bacteria. Specially when you pull your plum all day, tanking, waxing your carrot. Sounds like 5-a-day. Panhandling. Diddly-yarbles. Long hair hid his face. On social media you just put in a picture of a hot guy. Women and men sending pictures. Didn't get picked too much when they saw him in real time. Maybe they didn't like the background. Hadn't worked out the acronym for his sexuality. Liked you better then. Had to fit in. Trying. People like people who fit in. If you really fit in, you are fit. Fit means you are good at fitting in. Get fit up. If he fit in and said the right things then maybe he would get a fit girl. A real doll. He would fit in to one of them. He liked a good pomorogering now and then, to get it up him. HF. Bottomchido. Bumby4RL? Made him powerful. Reminded him of them bullies. Now he had power over them. That was when he was dressed up most. Pretty. Caked make-up his spots were gone. For a bit. Often a big mess on the sheets. Podooshka. Sometimes he could provoke the top, might hit him. Fun. BEASTLY. He liked that, felt attractive, needed for a bit. If they hit you back they will be homophobic. A man who picked on him. He said he wasn't really a lillibulero. Whatever that meant nowadays. Flexi. A flexitarian is only an amped virtuesignalling meateater. Battygrenadier Boy. I can be fluid, GNC, TGNC, MSM. But I don't want a label, I am not any of them. A thingmagig hootenanny widget with a frob from Contoso. Depends. Are they a PENG? BUFF. Ad libitum. Always be a Free Lancer. Everyone a star. Thelema. Let people do what they want with their bodies. Sell your heart to the junkman. Forget blackguards with placards placenta centra of matrix.

That **bang** set me off again. On top. Swag. Seckle. Jamkotch. Psychout. Shook. It's not all nice. Sell you the picture of just nice men and women. Least Dickens cared about boys. Had a bad time with a group of brehs once. Party. About ten. Suddenly appeared with leatherstuff. People think they are the same. Nata? Abab sourdough.

All *'you look lovely'* and *'don't mind him.'* People don't know. AHA. What about Carl Panzram, Gacy, Garavito, Mansour? Not bridomays what? Did bad things to him. It wasn't about sex but power. BNR. This was about sex. Felt it. Tools. Instruments. Nasty. Not stop. Get you drunk. Pretend to take pity on you when you're living rough. Next thing you have a candle shoved up your Khyber. People think it's just all a rainbowpinkfluffynice suiccherillina when you explore but it's not like that all the time. TBR. It must be wrong to say that everyone in a group is therefore good. AYFR? Nobody cares if you say a lot of men did terrible things unless it's against women. I **hate** violence against women and men. Laughed. Gatzarampercash. 'You consented.' Video you and say you consented. Get you before they do the worst stuff. Sex and violence. If they get off on violence imagine what a party they must have when they set up a war. Eunuchs. They used them in the military. Nobody mentions. Happy days. It does not matter who or what it is but what they do that counts and badun's are bad. Then there's the devil people. When they do it they get other evil spirits to join up with ones that live in them. MuchMUSHMush. It's not just the fun of hanging you by your huevos and fredkrovvy everywhere, WIG but some use it for magic. Nice Satanism they tell you about on videos is only one sort. Some people saw monsters coming down when they did those things. PIP. SOS. Told a psychiatrist. Said it would just be an hallucination brought on by pain. You imagined beasts because they don't exist. WAJ. Ordinary people phase out. Turn away. Plenty of things don't exist for one who does not look. Millicents don't care if it's a malchick. None so blind as those that cannot see, Mr Foley used to say. But I don't think she really believed that it happened. You're a fantasist. Serves them right they say. Men that get done. Nobody cares. Only go on about some women. I feel for them girls that are not celebrity sympathyvamps. Me too. Someone put their hand on my back once in a lift. Boys buried in the woods won't be sending their sobstory to Fakebook. Dennis Nilsen. Murdered men and kept some under his floorboards. Lost men. Up the road. Muswell Hill. He used to get them out and have them sitting at the table. Nobody noticed them gone. Maybe one. Dahmer drilled a hole in a fella's head and he got out and the police came and helped him back to his death telling the women to shut up, it said on Wikipedia. Wanted to make them submissive. An automaton. Like school. What about that poor victim? All the lads disappearing in Manchester. Another serial killer? But they think it's alright. Think everything is fine now, everyone loves them and they're like candy floss. But they're only tricking them. Pinchedpeople. Shitsongs by Nirvana about Teens. Not the sound made in Bow that went global. Come to me angel.

WOW-WOW. Did same to Jews. That's what I'm worried about. Berlin was bliss before it was hell. Got them to tell they were Jewish. Card index. IBM. HAL 9000. Mad computer in *2001: A Space Odyssey*. H-A-L are the next letters after I-B-M. Artificial Intelligence will fuck you up they are telling you. Hawkins said it and he died. They knew where all the Jews were. They said in the census, what's your religion? They're luring them out. Trap. Tells you there. They'll get them too. Fame is cheese. Camera a trap. Transtrance. Oh, we're really interested in what you have to say, even if it's rubbish. Social media is an information-gathering tool. Tell me all about yourself. Give somebody enough rope. Give us your DNA and pay us for the pleasure. Making them say things to provoke other people. Next they will make digital twins or clones of us and control us more. They will big up groups, bring them out and pick them off. Big up will become a low down, like a see-saw. Same stickiness of message will work with opposite information. Breathings of her fairness he said. Pling. Message. 'Are you alright? Is everything ok?' Weeeeweeeewaaah. Help! Car alarms.

WA-WA-WA. APP. BBIAB. Only good thing about school, Mr Foley, history. Divide and conquer he said. They create artificial groups, divide you into blue and red. Now fight. While you knock ten bells o' shite out of each other, they rob your house and concoct the next scam. You're German, you're English. Fight the Hun. No borders. Then you're Christian, you're Muslim. Ding-ding. You're men, you're women bring it on. You're a woman, he's now a woman, let's get ready to rumble. You're transphobic. Get chicswithdicks to tell straights what's wrong with them. AYS. Make everyone fight about who they are. So easy to play people off. Rob the till. I read a bit about Hitandmissler being unstraight. Don't believe nor Adamandeve it. That's why he killed them fellas, the S.A. Eric Röehm. Brown Shirts. The Broons. Father Brown. Eva. Wernher. Mrs Brown's Boys. Eric a great big oulbrownshirtlifter and his mates. Hissistler defended him. Then it was time. Was it Night of the Long Knives or something? I can imagine what Röehm and his mates got up to. They knew this butch type and gang were better at beating people up. They liked it. Schicklgruber. Say it's a lie. Digger if it was. Syphilis. Maybe. Submissive dependents. CoproroflSMH. Who knows? If he won they'd be saying nothing. Harder to speak German. Now Churchill who won it is bad they say at our meetings. Maybe they prefer Adolf or Josef or Leon. Hithimselfler a medium. *The*

Morning of the Magicians. He worked with a magician. Black Magic. Illegal war. Ill eagle. Wagner. Parsival. Fisher King. Mystic. Good mystics, bad mystics. Good magicians, bad magicians. Good witches, bad witches. First World War. We did it in school. Kept on going. Even when there's no point. Wanted to get rid of loads of men. Loads of blood. I kept asking the teacher why did they keep on? She said colonialism. Empires. Balance of power. Patriarchy. Struggle for sea power. Nationalism. Mr Foley better. I found out it was contracts. Factories in America got deals that we'd buy all stuff they make. Thoreau said same about Mexican War, no one wanted it, but it happened. Glad to be home even if it's a kip. Drum. Pallids are Sups, pats r ET NO gnats now. Poppy. Titanic Sinclair. Occult. Doll. Slavery. Glittergates of elfinbone she said. Some angels are devils.

    Candy. Hunnies a bit too much in real life. Lubbilubbingdafuq. You have to worry about making a mess. 2M2H. Too excited. Premature. EMBAR. Or no right angle for the angel. Spurgling. Wirklichkeit. That was why he had never done it with a devotchka. Afraid she'd hardyharhar'f he popped too soon. Sherbet fizzed. Lit his Catherine's Wheel firework. Baz. Blew. Couldn't help it, not a badder, gangster. Well ME2=M2H. MGTOW. Watched a video or two on the internet. Too exciting. So much nOrp you get immune, not real life. Prawn bad for ur prawn. DOT. More difficult to get going. Still like a roller coaster. Megafobia. Big One. Wipeout. Up slowly, down quick. Made him ill. Women transform. Often quiet. Change into excited beast, not beast. Not quiet and soft spoken. Shout and move around like wild animals. Agape'n that gummygash looks like it will eat you. Made a mistake about absolution. Should have kept his mouth shut. Wasn't talking about UK. Never say anything to any Judy about it, none of his business. Let women choose. Yes. Poor women. Tough. But just asked a question. Heard about all the abs of girls in India and other places. Neenaw. He wouldn't stop any woman, just couldn't figure out why millions were abbed just because they're female. Thought women would agree. EMBAR. EIP. DGT. Can't say anything about contortion. Ok. Oh fuck. You don't understand. Asch. Raped, brutalised. SOZ. Male, chauvinist pig. Every woman has the right. Not girls. DOH. Unpersons. Choice. Only maybe-people, don't exist. Got it. Foolishly asked should they not get a chance to be women? Rain of Terror. Much less devotchkas in the world. Good? Just a thought. A mistake. Click. Landmine. Move ur brown bread. Mea Acapulco. Never said it again. STFU. SEP. NC. JMO. DND. Noob. Thesmophoriazeusae. Why do they bother taking them pictures in the loom to show us? Do

I have moobs? Still thought it was wrong but he didn't say. Hockeyed him out of it. Untouchable. He said he was just asking. Mad. Like a pack of beasts. A few million ok you might say but it's an awful lot. Liked to be at home. <3NIFOC. Social media. Pizza. Games. Politics, social justice boring. No clue what they were banging on about. Neither did they. Shouting all the time. Tip him over. His ears had always been sensitive. Only children don't hear much other kids. When you're bullied you go away from kids. Maybe some of them believed it. Some got jobs with it. Said they had to do it for their CV. You get jobs if you show you were ok. Ambitions. Didn't want to work in McDonalds. Blamed the zitcream. Makes u then top yourself. Noisy. WHOOM! Neeenaw neeenaw. Shellshock. Angle angling for angels. Booyakashakash4kafka.

A few vegans. Fuckingdangerousnutters. I agree but chill. Don't come in with a sausage roll to them. Makes it hard to eat when they're staring with mad crazy eyes. Ones that talk about being kind are always the opposite. Vegans look like they'd be dangerous with knives. But they're right mostly. Cut you up real bad. These ones anyway. Love rabbits, hate people. But they like rats, like me. They don't like rats getting chopped up. Weird. Wyrd. Wired. Why do all the scientists attack them? Bullies. Say it's to protect us. Then they make bombs. Wear a white coat, glasses, don't smile, smirk when someone mentions God. You're just a selfish gene, but I'm a scientist. Stephen Hawking. How the fuck did he know about the Big Bang? Couldn't even walk. Managed to get to that island in the Caribbean with them other weirdos. They say he wasn't real, only a robot in the end. He was alright. I don't believe in conspiracy theories. No conspiracies. Only real life. See the darknet. September 11. Hologram. Common knowledge. Social justice groups. Most undercover police. One of the one's that beat him up was. He had looked at his stuff when he was in his bedroom. Went online. Hacked a bit. What were they looking for? Maybe they thought that some terrorists would be there? What the fuck they always shaking placards for? Who pays the group? Don't give a fuck. Government? Like job schemes. Why pay him? Who pays them? They seem to be for one thing one week. Next week something else. Get a call. Assemble here. March. Photos. Fuck off home. None the wiser. Ask them what are we doing this for? '*What the fuck do you care, Zithead you're getting paid aren't you?*' Dumdums. D.U.M.B. Lonesome.

Politics is acting. Agitprop. Shape-shifting. I was Batman once. Hung upside down. He went underground to rise. Fruit bats piss on themselves to keep cool. Skip that. An undercover policeman pretending to be a protester pretending to be a SJW, pretending to be worried about the homeless - must be a kind of shape-shifter? Shit. But there were yats. Learnt to say right things. Then they might look at you. Invisible. Like a song. Repeat lines, try to frown at same time. Showed you are sincere. Get some tears going, you're laughing. Fool with good skin seems to get girls. They like him, like thicks. Talk shit about not wanting to be objects and thousands go see strippers, attacking them like animals. Bring down the world. Breeding with fools. Twits. That's what Twitter's for. Numskulls. Nitwits. Clowns. Until machine-hybrids come. People deserve to become slaves. Race to the bottom. Bred to be slaves. Can't have it both ways. No war in Iraq if the people had their way. Bit of anger would be good. Although he didn't like people looking in the eye. Uncomfortable. Why do people do that? What'll they think of next? Easier on social media to look. Eyes not most interesting part. Preferred a glassy eye. Games got aggression out. Master. Praised online. Revered. Legend. Online. Future. New man. Not a cyberstalker. New superman. Men more like women. Women did not like hair any more. Little on his body. Shaved it when he was Desirée. Willy sore waxing the carrot. Plenty of time between protests. Could be anything. Very worried about them boat people I like. Terrible. SnowFs never slept rough fuckers piss on you freezin. So you knew what Clucktalk to say.

'I am a feminist myself.'
'If only women had more power.'
'Churchill is a fascist.'

Vibroverberates she said. You had to say the Cuckillididdlydo things. Most men Cuckamiddillos now. Said what they were trained to say. A girl might nod her head. Look. Not too much. They don't like my spots. Easier with make-up. Racism was when you were against Immigration. Anti-Semitism when you are against Israel. H8 A-S. Sexism when you thought men shouldn't be allowed use women's toilets. Conservatism when you thought families were ok. Cool. If someone came up with a complex argument you said, *'But you're a privilegedwhitemale. How would you know?'* Even if you're a privileged palefaithman yourself. Humiliation was good. If you ate humble pie you were doing something right. Deer deer it's dear. Even if you made it up. You could always say. *'You're just a warmonger and imperialist.'* Makes you want to hear the New York Dolls even though they're bad for me. I'm no quozradgepottool. I had the privilege of running away and being homeless with no label.

All around car alarms, evacuations, screaming and barking. Cracks visible. Items off stalls. People talking to each other in strange solidarity. Fire-engine. Blue trail of smoke on northern horizon. A lot of shouting, laughing. A guy ran down the road with a bag. Some of them were socialists. Somebody called Salawinisky. Accuse them of what you are guilty of. So you do a murder. Twist it around. You then say to someone else, *'You're a murderer!'* Need to be convincing. Imagine what it is like for the person you done in. Reflect back. Like you knew the victim. Reverse it. Simple. Socialism. Wasn't quite sure what that meant. Hitloser used to be a socialist. Didn't make sense. Didn't seem to be popular any more they said. Well him I read about. If you said, *'What's a socialist these days,'* no-one really answered. They did say, *'Well you're a racist, misogynist!'* Coldplay started off in Camden, worse luck. Sick. Really. Allow it. No more buses coming today. Story of my life.

Body hair gives them away. Brutes didn't even shave their legs. Types that loved wars. Something about dick and weapons. Same. Why wars happened. Power of having your finger on the button. Clitoris. POW! All gone. War in Middle East. Understood history because he played Assassin's Creed. True story. UK invaded to stop ISIS. Pictures on telly, Assassins. Looked like time of Henry VIII. Like green screens. Blue screen of death. Loved computers. If you had nothing else then you say 'P-tho'. Generally priests. But they saw all the DJ's, pop stars, film people, seemed to be up to it. But if you're cool it's ok. Some of the world were not online. People in the desert needed it to help them to find water. Didn't know how, even if they lived there for thousands of years. Saw it on Red Nose day. Celebs really care. He did not troll everybody. Got some when they were hurting. Best. Those that deserved it. Whinging. Maybe lost someone or a leg or something. Then you sent a message. Smooth. Nothing better than a few tins of energy drinks, bit of trolling. Knew other trolls. Promoted to a Master Troll. Secret Society. Hacked very well too. Serial killers trolled. Sometimes they asked him to do things. Demanded more money. Denial of service of companies. With a racist, attack their business. Fella paid him was African, Malarakasiku. Mac. Great Hampstead Heath smiling all the time, women liked him. When SSS was victim others liked that. Abused as boy. Or so he said. Anglican priests. Satanists. Didn't want to blame all Satanists. Helped cred. Cried you might get a Chalk Farm around you. Girl. Poptart. Smelled nice. Didn't stay too long. Drew back. Hard to wash where he was. Satanists real. Some bad. Some ok. Stuff on darknet. Games more realistic. Smoke joint have some juice.

World made him uneasy. Anxious. Panic attacks. PTSD. Some don't realise news was a game. If they knew what the world was really like. How stupid could they be? Working. Paying taxes. Forms. SSS a good hacker. Not Ace. Liked hacking people's appliances. Like Government. Maybe if they saw dark corners. Cannibalism. Sacrifice. Black Magic. Abuse. Snuff. Someone said I was creepy. If only they knew. Most people not intelligent. Hack domestic appliances. Listening in. Part of family. Hear everything. Eve. Waxing. A crowd running in and out of a shop on High Street looting. Taxing, teething, ticking. Recognised some social justice associates re-distributing some wealth. Joined in, got some t-shirts and legged it. Bally o'PWNed. Redistributionretribution.

Now a goal, 3XS going to strike. Act. Knew he had power. Came to him after listening to Goddess Ethel. Had a plan. Nobody believed when he told of things after hacking **The Organisation**. Strange but real. Not gossip. People injected with identifiers. Population cull. Provoking war with Russia. People thought he was making it up. They didn't believe. He didn't say more about the Truth. Bad aliens run planet. Sent here to convert us to man-machines. Could exist near blood. Demons. Vampires. Werewolves. Changed women's DNA. Come live in clouds around fresh blood. That's why women feel bad. Need fresh blood. Possess or feed off you. Why they chopped the heads off. Got blood. Why they want wars. Get something out of semen also. Suggestions implanted. We're like milk cows are to a dairy farmer. Cows. Battery chickens too. Walking to get zapped and boned, no idea. Us neither. Historians not to be trusted. Mr Foley said. Most lies. Nuclear stuff just to help us blow ourselves up. Give us tools, love science. Means 'to know.' Know it will fuck us up. Make mistakes you are human. War was won by better magic. Magic is higher science. Battle in the heavens for control of higher planes. Incarnationalism. Think I'm bad. Wait to see ghouls you'll meet after. Think there's no otherworlds? Holy Books had big bits taken out so you wouldn't know. You need fools. People thought him the fool, because of a few pimples. Rats can see aliens. That's why they go underground. Alien intelligence. Humans have a bit. Rats cleverer. Rats will go into camps of their own will when they put the people there. Rats like people. Try to be our friends, always go to dark places with us. Trenches. Even come up sewers to say hello. Telling us to watch out for fleas. We never listened. Squirrels lovely but brought leprosy. Dolphins peaceful but they zap fish, murdering. Dolphin-friendly Tuna. Poor Tuna. Who cares? Cus they smile and people are programmed. Elect murdering smilers. White smiling sepulchre. Black Death. They forget. I remember. Bodies in streets. Dead in an hour or two. Fine men in muck in Belgium. All the ones that never fight wear paper poppies too. Poppies never stop war. Where's your poppy young man! War to end wars. Maybe if more people said stick it up your arse they'd stop war. Help people in Syria, Libya, Iraq, Iran, Korea, Vietnam, Cambodia, Laos. Bullied with high tech. Shiny. Why do religious people bless wars, missiles? TINAG. Think they'd run out say stop! No, worship machines now. Love power. Smiled over by Presidents with loadsa teeth. Real warmongers, want to bomb. Reduce population. Identity re-engineering. Poison. Used to be Trotskyites. I don't give a fuck. But they bomb places. When they wuz banging on about a fella being racist cause he used a wrong word that sounded ok to me I said wasn't it terrible about all the black people in prison in US. PC stuff doesn't stop jail. Nobody cares about jailrapes. Men. Doesn't matter. Women laughing. Serves them right. Saw a program. Young palefaith chap put in jail. Skinny so they beat and ride him. Scared. Getting it up him all day long. Make him a ladyservant. Punkinthebunk. Get my socks. Documentary. So scared he does something stupid. Not very bad. Wanted solitary. Got life. Maybe robbed a pair of shoes at the start. Poor folk in jail. Get them to work for companies. Build private jails. Get money. Slavery without fresh air. Nobody gives a fuck. Dumber. Coronation Camp. Concentration bad. People are stupid but they think I am. Stupid journalists, PhDs, professors. One activist studying for a doctorate. Something nobody will ever read. Oh you must be so clever! Dr. Mengele. Worst Nazis were Einsatzgruppen. Nearly all PhDs. Study a comma for years. Stare at specks. Hang around till some expert deigns to examine. Bend over. I may not be right in the head all the time. People judge. Make them think they're good judges. Judge if this person is a good singer by voting, all costs charged at premium rate. Be a judge. Play judge. Judge who's a better cook. Not fluffy enough. Watch a darts match. Very important shot. Vital. Bollox. Hypnotised. Mesmerised. Zonked. Zombified. They Live. DON'T JUDGE ME YOU HYPOCRITICAL, SANCTIMONIOUS SLAVE SUCKERS. Disappear up your own backsides and tell me who left the cave to come back in! 2BRnot2B. Bumbarumbagrumbacrumbazumbaeek. Fuck me. In'it. Get grimy stuff. Another rumble. Someone shouted. Smalltown boys run away, cry boy. On the nickel not good.

"NOT A' FUCKING 'GAIN."

They say all these controllers that can't ski but go to Davos fix all this stuff. Who is Dave exactly? Thought it was George.

Diary Entrance:

Nvt mcuh hppandeed tdaoy. I wiul kryp tynrig to mkae mlesyf ok in tqe hzxd. I wlil kqzp tynirg to gzt btteer. Pwqzxe HPE. Fcuk HAL... 'seeker of the nest of evil in the bosom of a good word, you, who sleep at our vigil and fast for our feast.' 'What becomes of the little boys who never comb their hair...'

If you told me I was going to spend eternity with these people I'd turn myself into something else. All repeating. Like dolls you press on back. All talk clean, nice but act, do dirty, nasty. Getting meaner. Do you think Nazis or Commies got it done without the same dullards? They put their conscience in the deep freeze. Gave critical mind an anaesthetic. Their biggest fear is to think for themselves. When they see the monster they created they'll get scared, deny it or get into control to banjax others. Cowards. And I'm odd-one-out. Today's truth is yesterday's antimacassar. I'm Leonardo. You can't say offensive words but its ok to destroy our mind, bodies. Wanted to hear Ethel again. Stan. *That shit was fat... Last package I ever send your ass.*' Same person? Settled into bed. Sirens still. Lots of shouting, bawling, barking. I'm shivering a bit. A target now. Link. Maybe try heroin selling. Small bags in your mouth, spit them out for celebrities who walk by with dark glasses going to Camden studios. If so smart why were hob-knobs buying bags with low-life scum's spit on it out of their probably-diseased mouth or hole? Maybe helps'em float around with other arseholes in millionaire-rows in Hampstead. Interview a can-opener to something inside. Wanted more. They said she was right-wing, talking old things. Talk tradition you're an oulconservativecunt. Old things bad. Modern good. Shiny, expensive, disposable. Want equality, but peely-wallies need punishing. THE ONES WHO SAY THERE IS NO SUCH THING AS SIN ALWAYS WANT TO PUNISH US FOR THE SINS OF THE FATHER. PAP. Ethel talked to him directly. Awaited next interview. Examined video. Could not take his eyes off. Compelling. Cast a spell. Knowing she'd understand him, he'd get closer. Too many cooks spoil the broth. Too many Cucks spoil the broad. Everyone'll talk same SAM soon after war. Spanglish, Arabic or Mandarin. City tower. Still a Tower of Babel, Mabel. Leo def best Ninja Turtle. Mess out there. Over now. 5-0 everywhere. Clappin' in the ends. Beasts or angels. But if the clubs are closed tonight there will be trouble. ARG. Jinels. Fuck these t-shirts are too small. Wonder will they refund them?

LLLF

LONDON LOGOS LIBERATION FRONT

Publishing Pamphlets to Oppose Censorship of Our Message.
The Counter-Revolutionary to Evil and Terror Effort.
Open your mind, think about what we say, join the dots.

ATHEISM IS FINE.

IDEOLOGICAL ATHEISM IS WRONG.

ATHEISM WANTS TO ATTACK THE SPIRIT.

MAD RELIGION IS WRONG.

THE NEW ATHEISTS ATTACK THE MORAL LAW.

THEY WANT TO BUILD A NEW MORALITY.

EVOLUTIONARY THEORY IS A TOOL.

EVOLUTIONARY PSYCHOLOGY IS A WEAPON.

THEY WILL SET UP OBJECTIVES.

OBJECTIVES WILL SUIT THE OLIGARCHS.

GENES WILL BE CUT OUT.

WE WILL BE SERVANTS.

WE WILL BE SLAVES.

WE WILL BE SERFS.

WE ARE MAKING OUR STRAITJACKET.

WE WILL BE MADE TO LOVE SERVITUDE.

WAKE UP.

PREPARE FOR LIBERATION

Chapter 4

The Extraordinary Ethel Woodpecker

Maybe these types of men love the secret Governess because they need a break from all the secret governing of us they do all the time. *'To feel the smack of firm government.'* Although they have integrated women into the apparatus of control now. Another reason could be that life has become rendered so shallow that people miss some deep dimension to dwell in and even mere suggestion may remind them of it. Ashling awoke on Monday, prepared to go to the Agency, a few things on her mind. Posters. Pamphlets. Graffiti. SimpCook flitted in and out now and then, for some reason. If God was space and time maybe Quantum Theory was the signature of Her, allowing full incorporation of all the strangeness, miracles, supernatural things through entanglement. Dramatic news. The Earthquake was the object of international attention. Maybe people would not be able to meet her today. But Londoners like to keep on as normal. Upside down. Riots broke out. Already. Why? Immediately. Odd. Hundreds of sudden arrests. Detention places overflowing. Looting. Assaults. Rape. Disruptions. If you believed it all. What idiots believe BBC these days? Usually she would get the Tube, but much was still closed. Power mostly back. Death toll was the largest ever in the UK. Looking for bodies in Stoke Newington and elsewhere. Civil Contingencies Committee and Cobra had held an extraordinary meeting already. Prime Minister announced a new Special Emergency Measures Committee to co-ordinate committees co-ordinating others. New Committee would sit atop the pyramid to establish 'order out of the chaos.' PM and two others. Two massive sinkholes appeared in west London and a tunnel fell in. Many deaths were accidents caused by objects falling down from buildings or at home. A floor gave way in a club in East Ham. A tower block collapsed in South London. A few old town houses suffered extensive damage. Fires, explosions set off. A plague of rats, disturbed from their homes roaming through Chelsea. Looting became an immediate problem with Harrods and other stores suffering huge losses. Police did not intervene much. Authorities warned against dangers of an 'opportunistic' terrorist attack. Many schools closed. Emergency teams with dogs searching piles of rubble. Aftershocks smaller and frequent. A football stadium roof collapsed in East London. Thankfully no match in progress. Enough to deal with Shooter Frenzy. Some harbingers of doom now said it was a foreshock and London would be devastated. People leaving the city. Two or three experts predicted it but nobody listened. Majority never believed that one as strong as the Dogger Bank Quake could have an epicentre so close to the city. The Swansea Quake had been in the consistent zone. Someone argued this one was set off by a Russian submarine torpedoing along a fault line. One said it was disturbance created by work on the Elizabeth Line in combination with fracking on the Greenwich Fault Line. Concern over the Thames Barrier. Cracks in a couple of major buildings. A new skyscraper in the Isle of Dogs was being examined as was Blackfriars Bridge. Others called on the 'London Spirit,' 'the Blitz Spirit.' Let's carry on. Relax. Be calm. Chin up. Some old guy on the News said, *'We beat the Spanish Armada, Hitler, the IRA, ISIS, a little tremor won't wipe us out.'*

A few old buildings had collapsed. A submarine landslide caused a 'tsunami' that destroyed a lot of boats and caused fatalities. September, thirty days hath. Start of World War 2 on September 1st, September 11 did not need an explanation. September. Something uncanny about. Ethereal. Another footballer had been shot at a training ground. Arsenal. At least the sniper did not shoot in front of the crowd this time on live TV.

She had talked to Mary who was unperturbed.

"We're still alive. Thanks be to God."

A few calls. Most surprising was Lucius Tubal. She had not anticipated that he would be concerned. Seemed stressed, said he was having trouble sleeping. He was not very gay-looking or camp. Maybe Rock Hudson mould, tough he didn't look like him save he was tall. She read a bit about earthquakes particularly the Great Kanto Earthquake in Tokyo on September 1st 1923. Martial law imposed the next day. Police and army obtained power, took advantage. Some believed this authoritarianism was critical in the anti-democratic, military movement that led to the Japanese internal repression and external aggression. Tangshan 1976 ended the Cultural Revolution in China. The Spartan Earthquake led to the Peloponnesian Wars. She soon had enough and wanted to focus on what she had control over.

In future it would not be called an Agency as it gave a wrong impression legally. According to the dominant discourse nowadays she was a victim of 'torture' being abused if she sold or used her body. Pope had been harping on about it, unconcerned for the gay prostitutes that Church used. Not quite six impossible things before breakfast but she tried. Alice. Like she got mixed up between the Queen of Hearts and the Red Queen. Queens. We do not want the Evil Queen like in Snow White. Maybe upturned collar look. Passionate potion impassive self-possession. Something like it, but positive. She was Ethel Woodpecker in business. An extra barrier helped her to be extraordinary, even though Ethel was an ordinary name. Ordinariness made extraordinary. David Icke used Ethel, so she reclaimed it. It is all about making 'The Decision.' Tried to embody her philosophy in simple concepts. The Decision was when you align your heart and head, with clarity and focus and decide. A technique she developed in the context of procrastination and low level OCD. Every day, when she awoke she decided to do what she wanted and be calm. Practice Note. Think about non-local consciousness. See the future and see the past. Consciousness beholds non-local consciousness where time and space do not exist.

HEADSTANDS. 6 TIMES. BREATHING

She was riding the wave. Society was signalling that submission was good. She had picked it up in the ether but had not realised at the time. Subliminal submission. SUBMISSION IS GOOD. Enjoy your submission. Love your servitude. Be a drone. Be a robot. Be a servant. Be a slave. Be weak. Be vulnerable. Blame everybody else. Enjoy your exquisite whipping. Whimper louder. Whine. Wail. Live emotionally. Respond emotionally. Whether it's a lie is irrelevant. All that matters is the feeling. The group feeling. Then go back in your cage. Electronic cage. Carry your collar and your lead, your leash. That was just the way it was. Women are not to balance the male but subdue him. Strong males fight tyrants. Put their balls in a cage or chop them off. Rebels are messy. Get the girlish, hairless, shoulderless ones on TV. Make fathers look stupid and clumsy. Reward the compliant. Tyranny is coming. The age of tranny was not the problem but the age of tyranny. Leave people do what they want. Camille Paglia said it was a sign of collapse. But Ash was happy with what she did even if all that was true. She thought of Edith Stein and her idea of what empathy was. She was born Jewish and that was why she was killed, although she had converted. Her philosophy was beautiful and top-level. She could feel her. This political stuff we are talking about is not empathy. *Zum Problem der Einfühlung*. Ash read

Stein and in her own head saw a needle and a thread to repair a tear, whereas with 'correct' empathy you get two needles to prick a new hole and no thread to mend.

If Ethel Woodpecker behaved in a consistent way in business, she could become a saleable commodity. Intellectual Property (IP) was critical. Intangible property more valuable than physical property. Information about her, packaged and trademarked could be part of a new business-format franchise. Exploration. Another woman, not knowing too much about the business, with the right attitude could assume the role. A proven business with a track record and a standardisable format could be franchised. Adult entertainment business was often lacking in creativity. Plenty of space for niche service and products at the upper end. Erik did some market research there. His main view, it had not been engaging. The woman often presumed her presence is sufficient to justify the reward she gets. Fine, but it did not get the real limpet-like customer or clients. Kink-Think. Attention, engagement, interaction and a sense of inter-penetration of beings, however counterfeit. A very well saturated market. Easy enough to set up. Information readily available. Demand high. Dommes has moved from the underground fringe to the centre reflecting something in the zeitgeist. Hologram. Part of the constant inversion and erosion of tradition. People liked it and were curious.

She had studied various 'looks' like Betty Page the famous, girl-next-door pin-up type who would like you but was a bit naughty. Later Betty was diagnosed as insane after having attacked her landlady with a knife and then became famous again without her being aware for quite a bit. She had a born-again experience a few years after her photos. Page had become famous for a lot of bondage type photographs of her sent via an underground river of mail order photos. Playboy in 1955 and many magazines. She said that all she wanted in life was a mother who paid attention to her. Ash studied the history of others in her domain. Mary Jeffries was a Madam who had a few brothels with a place for flagellation in Hampstead and a dungeon in Gray's Inn Road. Greys. W.T. Stead wrote an article trying to expose child slavery prostitution drugging. The journalist ended up going to jail. Surprise. Surprise. Gladstone walked the streets and whipped himself, especially after Elizabeth Collins. Elizabeth again. Maybe like the film Pretty Woman. She had studied Ceara Lynch after she was on the Joe Rogan Show and more contemporary girls. Humiliatrix. Hum bee. Queen. Drone. Honey.

Assumed her role when going to work, playing, player. Neurolinguistic programming and mental control techniques. Lessons from neuroscience, neurotheology. Balancing brain hemispheres. Trusting intuition. Finding your unlearned knowledge. Healing beliefs. Maybe the Akashic records is the imprint of all your thoughts and beliefs and you change it to a tunnel into new dimensions. As she drank her coffee she prepared an indigo, old Chinese Communist-style uniform. Many clothes types associated with strong women did not work. If your powers of mental control were good enough you could appear in a sack. Many women had no idea of their inherent power. She thought about chess and how that could be an esoteric practice. 64. The *I Ching*, same number of hexagrams. DNA. Auditory memory and how to manipulate it was an important part of the growth of her method, the 'Understate.' Her algorithm needed evolution. She read about Frances Trollope who said that women were afraid to be accused of 'bluism' which seemed to represent knowledge and learning in the 1800's.

To become a successful domme, dominatrix, goddess, humiliatrix you needed genuine internal power. Some kind of armamentarium usually but it was charisma mostly. Like an actress. Like Betty Davis. Compelling. Intelligence for elite work. Women want to control men that have more power. If very good-looking and good at learning or acting you could pretend well. But the ones she wanted to work with had to have genuine mental depth. They did not have to be highly educated although many were, but they needed inner power. Otherwise they struggle. If you had been powerless you would need great assets to mentally control someone else. Many women saw form not substance. You had to be powerful to tame genuine beasts. The ones who had the money, success, were not cheaply managed. Alphas were curious about what they had not experienced because they were assertive. Managers do not enjoy being managed unless they so decide. Real men secretly wished for women to stop dissipating their own power. This was controversial and 'sexist.' Balance. Her friend Jeanette worked as a 'fin domme.' She said that weak men were submissive and liked to give money because it showed they could care for a woman and thus was a fetish of a kind of perverted tribute traditional mindset. They set up the paypiggies, paypets and sought gifts, tributes and presents. They were not all obvious high fliers but if not high power without they had it within.

Her alter ego was the one who did the job, performed services. Seldom used her real name in that context, save officially. She had a fear of the State and had every intention in dealing in such a way that she was above reproach. She avoided all the processes sucking you into the US IRS network. She was not working as Candy Apple Crimson X recently, save in some PR interviews. Concentrating on merchandising. IP was where value was. Some property that you package. A slight possibility of patents with Erik, copyright weak, designs for certain products, databases were an outside possibility, trademarks yes. Some registered. She understood that if you sell goodwill it has to be encapsulated somehow. A trademark is like a sigil in magic, a concentration, amulet, talisman, market magic. The mark itself can become monstrously successful. Be pragmatic.

Candy Apple Crimson X was one of her first and simplest incarnations. Then more BDSM than DS. She moved more into 'mere' Dominance and Submission later. Pulling strings, appealing to common denominators. Part tantrika, dominatrix. Wary of the 'divine goddess' stuff because there were women using it to manipulate spirituality in a dark way. Make possession erotic, devils soonest tempt. Divine goddess demon demonstrating more. All innovators looked at what was recurrent and then broke the rules. Do exactly what they tell you not to do after you have become a master. You ignore labels, terms, dogmatism. After she mastered it she realised she was not interested. Candy then went away for a while. In her place came Goddess Blue Brigid 7. Build up goodwill in distinctive brands. Other way was to go for the same name over all products. A little inflexible. Blue was an associated colour to help build distinctiveness. Evoked Kali and Krishna. The use of reasonably well-known matter needed to be distinctive to be capable of protection. Intention was to build an intricate system on a higher level, using less actual contact. From the experience she would deliver a cutting-edge incubator for dommes. Concentrating on women who were highly intelligent that could offer an elite service with minimal effort for maximum rewards. A clear product or service would get a clear customer or client. The ability to attract the exact type of client was crucial. Power-Exchange relationships. Not always commanding, dominating but invitational and heartfelt. Invitational intervention causes response. Can still be firm. Creates a heart chakra connection. Intimacy.

A lot of girls were not good at it. Girls are trained to be weak and sensitive without real agency or just plain nasty. Really nasty. Dark feminine. Best had been her lesbian friend Sasha who never revealed her sexual identity in that context. Most women were scared. Many great at being bitches, but not good at acting them. Many reserved bitchiness for other women. Did not know their feminine strength.

Look at the natural world. Study birds. Pretty showy ones are males. Ridiculous ones are males. Bird of paradise, humming birds, peacocks, bower birds. Flamboyant, energetic male has to impress the plain Jane female who is practical and functional. Ordinary one has power the extraordinary one does not. Extraordinary appearance must be utilised to impress the ordinary reality. Women have power in their spirit and body. Fooled about this, often by other women through distorted competition facilitated by male, secondary manipulation. She heard Dr. Susan Block talk about the Bonobos in the Congo. She said they did not kill each other and attributed it to a matriarchal, dominant culture. Might seem easy at lower end. Wannabees saw stuff on internet. Kink growing. *50 Shades of* **Grey**. Women imagined they were good. Same with ordinary prostitution. Did not give the attention it deserved. When she met her friend in Nevada who worked in a brothel, she found 'companionship' was the most expensive service. A pseudo-girlfriend was still very expensive. Company. Presence the present. Women thought it primarily genital. Often not. Mind critical. Many not trained would end up losing out with dangerous customers or potentially good ones who never come back. Ironically a need for discipline. Many utilised no special skills and failed to draw on other knowledge. Some practices adapted from Milton Erikson the hypnotist, or eye-gazing from tantra. To explain some of the ideas required a degree of critical thinking. Fun for people who genuinely liked it. Create intimacy with a range of tools was challenging for some others. Ultimately created a type of Tulpa. But that was later...

From consultancies to the new type, she intended to build her franchise. If the woman was good enough she could be guaranteed a constant (or sporadic if desired) stream of clients she would know what to do with. Act within the law. A specific target group helped get right woman and man. Avoided other express niches such as Lesbian dommes, or Trans dommes. Aimed at rich, successful men who were tired of getting it their own way. Language of therapy suggested. Men generally were not masochists and would not cross certain lines. Did not need pain to render them sensible to outside force or to validate their existence. Enjoyed a clever game but not impressed with cheap stunts. Most had no particular fetishes. Came just for the dynamic diversion, a little role inversion, domination. Conscientious. Ethel had built up an idea called The Projection. Archetypal figures and each man had a type that he found attractive. Discover or create that archetype or typology. Find it. Where the game of interrogation came in. NLP and ideas from linguistic therapy useful so you could look behind structure of language to find fantasy of The Projection. Aligned your behaviour with that model or assimilated yourself to The Projection. Projection Erection. Could take time or be simple. For example, many great men were influenced by a nanny or governess. In French royalty older women of the court broke the men in. Could be a teacher, trainer, neighbour, film star. Such memories, associations could be re-opened, re-activated, revealed, revisited. Picture, pretend, perceive, imagine, visualise, see. Many are influenced profoundly by a couple of years growing up. But The Projection could also be scaled up to highest, feminine archetype in all. Deep archetypal masquerading as mild titillation.

Women who did it for fun, did not need to bother with such details. They disliked and sometimes ostracised women who charged. Often said it was not about sex and proceeded to demonstrate that it was. Most dommes had strap-ons and often pretended to be a man. Ethel's client were generally heterosexual. Interested in women, but not quiet, inoffensive women. Enigmatic Mona Lisa. Arousal was Ethel's business, generation rather than dissipation of energy. Behind Projection and Arousal were ideas from the East (probably shared by Swedenborg) about the generation of sexual energy and it's transmutation. Frances Trollope said about revivalist religious meetings in US, that preachers came and worked the women into a frenzy and left the town with several girls pregnant. Base spirituality and sexual power were linked, but you had to transmute it. Tied into Tantra, Taoist and New Thought technique. Learned from a Hong Kong teacher. When you worked with levels of excitement you could wind the spiral to a higher level. Nobody else in London did it quite the same. Some 'Dakinis' reached highest levels, although they were often about a sexual exchange or consummation. You created a mental surrogate for the fantasy or archetype that could be related to. That's what the good ones did. Ethel packaged everything in a unique way with clear context, roles, targets, techniques. Business. Plato. Play a role. Paid for your attention, paid attention and you paid attention. Attention had diminished. People did not greet each other in their obsession with social media. Shops made you work. Caring professions not caring. Touch taboo. People so busy they were starved of basic interpersonal contact that was the essence of humanity. She saw some people retreating in to a virtual solitary confinement.

HYPOFRONTALITY. She found in studies a link between the mystic path and her work. When someone was made, or agreed to be, submissive the sense of self is diminished and part of the sense of pre-frontal cortex is reduced. Floating feelings, peace, present. Transient hypofrontality. Boss within them relaxes. As bodymind concentrates on other sensory inputs and relinquishes control the executive shuts up. Mind becomes open to universal. Union with universal is goal of all mystical endeavour. She studied Todd Murphy and parallel joy and fear centres and how they interacted and also Debord. Social lives now mediated by images causing alienation. Alien Nation. We are now aliens in our own place. Playing. Avoid the quagmire of endless discussion. Sell intimacy. Fetish was the spectacle. Fantasy was merely one of involvement in a world of splintered separation, a shattered mirror. These men wanted to balance strong male in them. Not weak men. Wanted to encounter strong female. Otherwise not deeply lonely, sometimes between relationships. By alienating strong men, powers of women were compromised. Men-boys were often role models. Depends on measurement. Strength inverted into a default male. People could be who they want sexually for her and she supported them but this was just business conception. Energy is not to be dissipated. Jing is to be maintained. Ancient Chinese war against losing your energy. Like Samson. She liked Spinoza. Book *On Human Bondage* came from Spinoza. Bondage is to those things that cause pleasure and avoidance of pain. Triangles were important for him. Like BJJ. For her too. Her bondage would be that deeper, psychological, subtle type. Although pleasure from your own pain is pleasure. With someone else that's a different story. Bondage is diverse. Religion comes from the word bond or bind. Yoga means yoke or union. All such is about higher soul, whether consciousness, nature, universe or God. She felt you could alter your state of consciousness in 'The Understate Method.'

The dom would have to be able to play an engrossing game over a period of time. Refined. A Stradivarius to a fiddle. Polishing the model. With a track record she would complete a manual, a 'business format,' proven track experience, know-how, educational material and an associated trade mark she could sell. Websites an important portal. IP packaged, standardising. People liked franchises because they could take an idea that worked and operate independently. She would train women to take over her own role as 'Master Franchisor.' Maybe Mistress Franchisor. To build the brand she appeared on radio broadcasts across London losing relative anonymity. A couple made the Daily Mail online and got a lot of publicity. Goddess Brigid struck a chord. They made films where she introduced objects for sale. Found herself developing fetish objects. Fetishes were generally seen to be inanimate objects which invoked some pathological sexual attachment. But it had a wider meaning in anthropology where spirit was captured in an object. A magical object created by a person. She wanted to move away from the fetish as most widely understood to something deeper. More sigil as Austin Spare explained. Like with psychometry or psychotronics idea was to encapsulate or entrap some ghostly mood, necessary feeling or associations. Like worry-beads for some. Feeling captured was the feminine, goddess. Magic and subtle energy knowledge, dowsing, hypnosis, mesmerism used simple devices like pendulums and wands. Amulets as Romans used. Growing following. She sold what some regarded as sexual, some religious or magical. You could cure problems in a roundabout, 'Understated' way. She was not intending to trap her spirit but reflect the idea of divine feminine.

MORNINGTON CRESCENT SHUT TODAY.
HOPE TO RE-OPEN TOMORROW.

APOLOGIES.

She mostly took the Tube when working. She was not quite a flâneuse or boulevardier anymore. She did like some of the stations and the glorious tiles. On the way to work, she was a little more upmarket. Brisk walk. Not the same when you have meetings. Her office was in Soho, central, unprepossessing. Erik operated a few websites, one was MysticBlueDom Agency. The Understated Program. Understated Mystic Therapies. The order and amount of slogans varied.

Your wish is my command.
Discrete therapy for those who like to know their place.
Make your quest for pleasure the opportunity for inner treasure.
Let us be the agents of bliss in your spiritual exploration.
You are strong, independent and curious.
A Muse to bemuse and amuse.
Allow a tease put you at ease.
Attention to rid your tension.

> We are formidable feminine.
>
> Alter your consciousness.
>
> Explore with us in private.
>
> Safe power exchange play.
>
> Adult Authority role play.
>
> See what it brings to you.
>
> Role play, rule play.

Some more. Explained they did not do anything illegal. Warned off time-wasters, people who wanted quick sex or seeking physical pain. Prices high. 'Good pain' could be done on a light level by some if they wanted specialist treatment. Looked more like traditional path and included a unique dungeon. Levels. Role play was a part. Navy the dominant colour.

Ash travelled US clubs, particularly California. Idea exploration. Having started at Esalen she found herself curious about the 'darker' side. Intrigued when she saw ads from dommes who claimed sub-dom was mind-expanding therapy. Planted a seed that germinated. Distilled. Deeper idea about elevating consciousness. Possibility of utilising language, breathing, psychology and play could help a person transcend. Some ancient Taoist techniques were used. Variants of Secret of the Golden Flower. Concepts of priestess and goddess informed the domme persona. Male and feminine energy balancing to be whole. Strong male needed to be balanced by a strong female force. Yang balanced by Yin. The MysticBlueDom Agency was staffed by Erik, her manager, secretary, body guard and business associate. Not partners in the strict legal sense as they had set up separate companies for the two prongs of their work. Their relationship began in a pub. She did not know a lot but trusted him. Good with computers, mathematically adept. Worked well. She ended up working as a dominatrix as a matter of necessity and a little curiosity to apply some of her ideas. Developed her niche, did it for a year or two, made some money then decided to teach others. Liked most of her customers. Two apartments where she gave lessons, Moorgate and Mayfair. Moorgate had the Tavistock Institute up the road. Some said it was the source of the Beatles and pop music written by Adorno. Mayfair. Off Bond Street. A Nightingale Sang in Berkeley Square down the road from where the Blackshirt leader was born. Fitzrovia for the Redux. Soho the home. Where the Sex Pistols were. She knew their haunts. Johnny Rotten. Sid Vicious. They developed from the Strand. From New York Punk and S&M, New York Dolls.

Described herself as a consultant. Just because you are good at something does not mean that you do it yourself. Used to be a lot of drama about how you were meant to get paid. Not meant to spoil the authenticity. Meant to get an envelope in a box. Could accept gifts instead so it did not seem to be something else. A tribute. Did away with that. You paid and accounted for it. She had been a pro-Domme and not a lifestyle domme. Lifestyle dommes sometimes call the pro-domme 'whores.' Some antagonism. There may be honour among thieves but amateur BDSM had disliked women who made money from it. Changed quite a bit since. Doms did it for money and fun. Financial dommes expected men to pay. Findom. Most pro-dommes she knew did not care for this as sole, core activity. General feeling it would end in tears. Most were expressing themselves, having fun, making money. But some women were not acting and wanted to humiliate and rob men. A few would not be against taking out a tooth or breaking a nose or castration. Others were 'bad witches,' 'black magicians.' People say that's role play. Some of these women told her they were going to hell and would be rewarded for destruction and bringing others. That was what slavery, bondage, possession, ownership, pacts meant to them. You sealed a deal with the demons through their agents with bodily fluids like semen and blood and saliva. Some collected DNA samples. What was bound was the soul for eternity. Vampirism not a fun fantasy. Some women prided themselves on being really nasty and cruel and preyed on vulnerable men they hated. Would use drugs and engage in real torture and mutilation for the shrill fun of it. Were of the ilk of the Marquis de Sade. Would destroy men and women. Ash was worried that men would be literally sacrificed by some.

Ethel was an outcast from The Scene. Went her own way. Needed differentiation. Many men would not get involved with The Scene. After the unseen. People in The Scene gossip. Beyond The Scene was one tag they used. Obscene. One of the distinctive elements. What happened on The Scene differed from what people thought. What people saw on the internet was only through a glass darkly. Opportunity for a Unique Selling Point presented itself. Business that did things differently. Challenge everything. If you have gear why does it have to be black? Why not white? Tried a room interior that Francis Bacon designed when he experimented with furniture before painting, surgical curtains and so on. Navy worked. Strong. Navy, deep blue. Marine blue. Blue of deep sea. Sinking. Deep down there. Where do you go in hypnosis? Deep. Why is deep powerful? Deep. Blue. Night. Night coming. Coming. Twilight. Crepuscular. Twilight Zone. In between. Hypnagogic, hypnopompic state. Open to suggestions. Open subconscious, unconscious. The magic wand that orchestrates your dreams. Invisible conductor. Why not use it? Powerful. Stern. Deep. Serious. On the edge. You become the navy. Sail across the unknown. Navel. Omphalos of your being, back beyond birth. See. Sea. Ocean. You re-emphasise suggestions with words, reference. Many phrases are nautical. Holotropic. Not all the ones they claim. Edging forward. By and large. Hard and fast. Know the ropes. Loose cannon. Touch and go. In the offing. You implant triggers. Riggers. A person who ties another up. Suggestion. We don't do it. But the art is to do it with ropes in the person's mind. Cord of their own. Coiled by your suggestions and fastened with their imagination.

'Your Wish is My Command' one name they were researching as a possibility. Mystic Blue Therapy. The Understate Program suggested a number of things. You created a state or space with the client. Altered state. Lizard. Substate. Under control. Consensual. A program. Program Prodomme. Triggers and suggestions built up as part of playful exploration. Intensification allowed part of brain to relax to allow consciousness function in an altered way. As Anaïs Nin said, we don't see things as they are but as we are. Nin said also that she wants men to compel her strength and who have the courage to treat her as a woman. Said that we grow unevenly in different dimensions, childish in some. Nin did not like men that were afraid of women's strength. Millions of people lived in monotony and hibernation and a shock brought them out or back. She said that we travel to get to other states. Nin thought we carve out of others the things we need or desire. You do not find a grand meaning but an individual one. You become an automaton if you are enslaved to a dogma whether political or literary. For Ash ordinariness was attractive when everyone seeks to be extraordinary. Hinting is more exciting, whispering too. Men like all types of women. Every woman is attractive. Botox, silicon and fillers are unnecessary. A con pulled on weak and gullible. Intelligent women, introverts or extroverts are attractive and can utilise their power given appropriate help.

Ash met Erik near where he lived in Red Lion Square. Unique. Someone said a 'sigma' male. No idea but she liked him. Talked a lot about *The Tibetan Book of the Dead*. Taught her martial arts, about Patanjali who was around over a millennium and a half ago. Yoga thousands of year old before then. Stripped out of it since. Union critical. Without it nothing much. Do certain things to allow higher consciousness. Aleister Crowley had utilised yoga. Not mere physical exercise. Strangely some people who realise this are fundamental Christians but fail to see beyond that. Yoga was alignment with pure consciousness and inner bliss. Essence in you. Karate opened her soft side. Do hard, dream soft. Physical helped spiritual. From a very empirical base Erik came out a different way. She wanted a way that was systematic. He could read and write Sanskrit. Handy with computers. Black belt in Judo. Expert fencer. Sailor. Implemented the detail of her plans, devising a network and system for business operations. Got on well although he had a belief in the market that was too respectful, almost religious. They talked a bit about the earthquake. He had a lot of control. That was why she convinced him to take the stuff Jem reluctantly could make for a trip. Affected him but he was cautious. He did see the other beings as he lay on Hampstead Heath under the stars and seemed to transcend himself but he was suspicious about it all. Past that now.

She was normally 'Ethel' in work. First thing in Soho was an interview. Procedure was that she would talk briefly with girl and do a role-play with Erik. He didn't like them but did his job diligently. Her names were Dawn and Alize and she was stunning. Her strong local accent could work if she had the 'touch.' They talked about The Quake. She seemed shaken by her experience. Ethel praised her for making it in.

"Why do you think you would be good at this profession?" Ethel asked.

"I think I'd be a good employee Ethel."

"Sorry but you won't be an employee, you will be independent."

"I think I could work for you because I understand the business," Dawn replied.

"Have you done it before?" Ethel asked.

"Lots of times. I know all the clubs, have the equipment at home. I have a few..... slaves and you may see my videos on the internet. I even have a book on Amazon."

"Impressive. On Amazons or Amazon?" Ethel asked.

"On the internet?" Dawn said.

"Ok. That's where you heard about us. You have read about us from the website and may have heard more on the grapevine. What do you think we do?" asked Ethel.

"Rich men."

"Ok, but what do you think makes us distinctive?"

"I supposes you're central and have a list of rich clients."

"Why do you like this job?" Ethel asked.

"It's the money. And I like bossing, I'm good at that. My mates always say I'm very bossy. My mum says I was bossy since I was born."

"Do you have any... 'rich men' as clients?" Ethel asked.

"Not exactly, although one of them does own a bicycle repair business."

"Not really Fortune 500?" Ethel said.

"I don't follow."

"No problem Dawn. In case I haven't mentioned, we don't do any Satanist stuff, possession or any of that stuff."

"Stop. I never even thought about that. Not a chance, don't worry."

"Erik could you come here please," Ethel shouted. "Ok, Dawn I'd like to see you with Erik. It's the first time you meet him. I want.... you to make him kneel before you in the next five minutes. The way we operate is that we are polite, calm, assured, gentle. We are ladies. We are always well-mannered. We treat them like a dangerous but potentially compliant beast. We are understated. That's our method. Understated. We will put them into a state under us, psychologically, later we will put them under in a more hypnotic sense. Just relax and have a go. You must be persuasive and gentle," Ethel explained.

Erik pretends to knock on an invisible door.

"Come in," Dawn said sternly. "Hello. I'm Dawn... is that going to be my name here?" asked Dawn.

"Just do it please, act as if its real..." Ethel said gently.

"Hi, how can I help you?" Dawn said.

"I have an appointment," Erik replied.

"Yes.. yes I remember." Dawn continued, "What's your name?"

"...Erik... Did you get my email?"

"Sorry Erik, sit down there please... Em, Erik I must say you are a big boy," Dawn followed up quickly.

"Eh yes," Erik said hesitantly.

"Are you big all over?" Dawn asked coquettishly.

"Pardon..."

"I said, are you big all over then." Dawn changed tone suddenly in a disconcerting way making her lips thin.

"I'm not sure," Erik feebly said.

"YOU'RE NOT SURE! You're not sure? Address me properly... it's Madame Dawn."

"Yes.. Madame Dawn…"

"I bet you'll be thinking of me when you go from here won't you. Thinking of how good I look, fantasising… Well." Dawn changed tone.

"Yes…Madame," Erik said.

"Down on your knees piggy boy. On all fours," Dawn barked.

He went down on his knee.

"Now piggy boy I want you to tell me how much money you want to give me as tribute," Dawn hissed.

He was looking at the ground.

"Well?"

"Ah.. I… eh—" Erik seemed uncomfortable.

"Cat got your tongue you horny swine?" Dawn asked

"I... but." Erik was hesitant.

"Would you like me to treat you?" Dawn asked.

He looked up and it was clear that he was trying not to laugh out loud, changing his demeanour. "Sorry, Dawn… It's… the carpet or do you have a dog," Erik said frowning.

"Yes. A pitbull. Harry," Dawn said confused.

"Well he's allergic. Come and we'll let him have his inhaler," Ethel interjected.

Erik was up, looking out the window and grimacing, "Sorry luv, was that ok?"

She brought her out and gave her a cup of tea and biscuit, complimented her on her job and subtly explained how it might be difficult for her to fit in. She said it was because she looked so stunning and there was a grain of truth in that. Poor girl had not got what it takes but Ethel did not want to deflate her. She said no, beating around the bush a little. Saw that Dawn was growing despondent and felt sorry for her. If something were to come up later she would let her know.

"However I will promise you something. I advise a lot of business in the entertainment world and get well paid, or rather charge a lot. I think I can help you do what you do a bit better, that's to say enhance your business. Well let's say I know how you can get better and double and treble or quadruple your income."

"That's sweet of you. That's kind."

"Here's my card. It'll have to wait a bit. So say mid-October ring Erik, and we'll…… make an appointment."

"Thank you."

She thought of *Pygmalion*. Trading Places. Shaw. Fabian Society. A person from one place, put in an alien one. Barrow boys on the stock market. Make sure the person had capacity to add or else they were just some kind of agent for you. With a natural talent easy to fluidly alter. Circe. Transformed her enemies into beasts. Most seem to know her as a goddess who transforms men into pigs. She thought about *Pigs in the Parlor*, book on deliverance by some Evangelical, just saw it somewhere. Devils appear because they get attention. Circe, a magician who knew herbs and potions. Ethel Woodpecker was a name strung between ordinariness and comic otherworldliness. Most choose exotic names, not an irritatingly ordinary one. Her idea was that ordinariness could be transmuted. Cause confusion. Erik apologetic when she grabbed her coat and went out. She took the Tube. To Moorgate. Full of business gents and women, similarly dressed. Apartment was near site where John Keats was born. *'Much have I travelled in the realms of gold...'*

No ill effects of The Quake in the Moorgate apartment. Some of the girls had PhDs, a few degrees, English literature, Philosophy, few Psychology drop-outs. Luxurious apartment, impeccably clean with no peculiar set-up. Heavily varnished floors gave a warm sheen and allowed heels echo. Temporary barriers on the way around masonry. She talked with her student Anastasia about the tremors. Praised her for turning up. Quake talk. Average to tall height, startling light blue eyes and dark, glossy hair presumably her natural colour.

"Mark my words. What does that mean?" asked Ethel.
"Pay attention to what I say?"
"Exactly. From Shakespeare's time or rather Elizabeth. Mark. Gospel of Mark. Butt think of BDSM. Bottom marks for bad boys. Mark. It's all about ATTENTION. That's what the Sergeant shouts in movies. Attention. Means you stretch towards and give your energy to. Give your energy or money to. Attention also has Tension in it already."
"Ok..." said Anastasia.
"We talked yesterday about psychological profiles of customers. We are non-judgmental. These gentlemen pay you. Every client that comes back, every 'subject' is a gent. You are an agent. An agent is a person who exerts power. Being an agent you have capacity to lead the subject in the direction of their evolution. Nudging them. Link between sexual arousal and energy liberation is clear enough and specialised practices have been around for thousands of year. We help them transmute that through suppressing for a short while their sense of self. Very strong in these guys. Although calm, most are

quiet spoken, you don't fuck with them or FUCK them of course, ever. It's a game, a denial, a tease," Ethel explained.

Anastasia nodded and said, "This sounds like deep. Psychological, sociological even psychic shit!"

"Yes. Deep. Adam and Eve. Believe it's about obedience and disobedience. Heterosexual generally. They do not want to be women. They like strong women. Women are strong, they just forget it. They are articulate. They obviously are not finding what they wanted elsewhere. We signal who we want. We might describe it as knight-in-shining-armour. Academics are very shallow. Fail to see that these knights were often beholden to a woman. Courtesy. Not sissies. You chose, you filter, you weed out. We are aiming for psychologically and financially secure males interested in playing a psychological game. Why they want that is of no concern to us. Many may be introverts. Learned on their own. They get good at music, chess, making things. On their own they do deliberate practice. Motivated, working alone, bit by bit. Many extroverts do not understand this. If they are good they'll adapt, but we need a well-informed, broad range of knowledge to be able to assault the ramparts of their mental castle. Gladstone went around here to talk to fallen women. Guilty and enjoyed it. Maybe altruistic. Not all introverts, but they have a bit like everyone." Ethel elaborated.

Anastasia was listening intently, her elbow on her knee and nodding. Smart girls listen.

"We don't claim to be marriage counsellors. This business is about mind and buttons therein. Essentially power of language. We adapt techniques of mental programming, NLP, hypnosis, ASMR. We examine the language and steer appropriately. We may even take away what they think they are paying top-dollar for. Give someone what they want, they will never be satisfied. It's not about sex. Attention, whispering, tapping, scratching, blowing, turning a page, eating, smoking. Mystique. Mystery. Mistress. Something you don't know the answer to. Confusion. Essence of hypnosis. The pendant, dependent. Sense of essence," Ethel said.

Anastasia looked quizzical, "That's what I heard but…"

"That is a full stop in many ways, a bus stop. The journey is important. We are….. Understated and we put them in an Understate as a game. Skill is needed. But it should be open so that it is empowering. Nothing to be gained with trying to vampirise."

"You're the boss…" Anastasia smiled.

"You rule. The ruler. You rule them. Rule means dominate but the word 'dominate' is losing a little of its potency. But to rule someone you must be able to rule yourself first. You must be able to create contrast. For example. If I speak softly and respectfully choosing my words carefully you will get comfortable with my words. You begin to know what to expect. You expect. Then I say something vulgar. It shocks that part that you had aligned to mirror the input. You are also confused. When confused you are open to suggestion. Shock all the time, you fail to shock. Contrast is gone. You need orange to complement blue, if blue is your base or background. Does that make sense?" Ethel raised her eyebrows.

"Totally. I get the sense." Anastasia nodded.

"Same with intimacy. You talk at arm's length and you do something which seems intimate or close such as whisper or maybe do your lips as if you were very comfortable with the person. Subconscious hook. You might blow smoke in some man's face, but it is better to do it as if it might be accidental, then the mind is hooked trying to interpret as well as being slightly amused or surprised by the audacity or what would normally be disrespect," Ethel said.

"And they like watching women do things?" Anastasia added.

"Women are attractive. But they act as if they are not. Women are in control, but they have allowed other women rule them and create a false sense of who they can be. We would never act like we act in 'real' life. It is a game. Trans*action*al. But out there is a game. At least this is a game of choosing, with rules," Ethel said.

"It reminds me of ..."

"Sorry to interrupt but watch your posture..." Ethel indicated what was wrong.

"Thanks. It reminds me a bit of the Red Queen Hypothesis. Doesn't it?" Anastasia said.

"I know the Red Queen was in Alice or the other one, I can't remember more..."

"Said something like you have to keep running faster to stay still. A hypothesis came about that uses that name. It's about how the predator and the prey evolve or co-evolve. Some insect develops a defence to a strategy of a predator, then the ones who overcome it thrive or something like that." Anastasia explained.

"Interesting." Ethel was genuinely interested. "I will check it out. That's right. Make it your own as you understand it. Understate, understand. Everyone has chords, keys that can be played. The play of accord and discord creates harmony. Out of balance one way, requires compensation the other way. But we want good long term relationships. We don't do slaves or any stuff like that."

"It sounds like therapy…"

"It is but if you know that you won't want it. It is better you think it taboo, shadow side and then possibilities of wholeness can occur."

"Why do you want to do this? You sound like Mother Theresa," Anastasia laughed.

"It's really about power not sex. No gimps. Teasing. Tension. Transmutation. 3 T's. Assuming power and yielding. Going against norms. Inverting them, probably to achieve balance. And you?" Ethel asked.

"Curiosity. Money, bills, holidays, car, clothes. Nothing unusual," Anastasia said.

"Why not be a banker or stockbroker then, like many of our customers?" Ethel asked.

"Not just that. I do have a concept of female empowerment. I don't want to do some of the things they say are empowering. I agree that women have power and don't realise it."

"Nice answer. Victim stuff is a con job that makes women weak. All the pathetic, perishable little things, offended at every slight and then having no control, subject to any force that blows weathervane of their personality." Ethel nodded. "What do you study?"

"Politics."

"Well it's easy then. You're the State. Rather the Government. You tell people what they want, tease them, make believe they're the luckiest in the world. You are re-assuring but strong, mysterious but dangerous, complex. But there's an iron fist in the velvet glove. They're the rebel you are going to chastise who has been naughty and defiant," Ethel suggested.

"You don't have much equipment." Anastasia made a statement that was a question.

"Correct. Correction maybe. That's only one first path. The stage and most props are in the mind. We have limited costumes. Our job is not to give them what they want but make them want what we give them. In the mind, the buzzers are all there, the path to their deepest self. You need words, suggestion, fashioned on a reading of what they want. We have a basic vocabulary of positions, you might think of it like yoga, BJJ, it's not far off. Or maybe a mixture of yoga and dog-training. You heard of Pavlov." Ethel made a statement-question as Anastasia had.

"The reading, that's what I have no sense of..."

"We'll come to that," Ethel said. "Remember the men you get here know what they want in some ways. Boss others often. Control themselves. Bossing others they are surprised to encounter so little resistance. Bored they reverse it to encounter that which they don't have or need. To feel what their minions feel. We call the ones we want 'Top Easy.' Levels and some types. But we stream them. We want them back, in a familiar structure, going through levels. Higher up are different dimensions, a little financial control for some who want it. Merchandise. Variety at higher levels. We use say a slow Kizomba now and then. Depends on your personality. Be you. Yourself. Discard the un-you."

"Sounds like Scientology," Anastasia laughing.

"Hubbard was deep into the esoteric. Clearing. Beings. Thetans. All have levels. Have you looked at Law of Attraction.... transmutation? Napoleon Hill and all the others, Abraham Maslow. It goes back through Mesmer and others, through Greece, Egypt, India and China to techniques well known. We have types of mysterious mesmerism at higher levels to induce hallucinations that are beneficial to the subject and consistent with the path they are on. Path through Quimby and all these guys in New Thought. Clearly not for once-off clients or five-fingered massages for a fiver!"

"What about legality?" Anastasia asked relaxed and laughing.

"We can survive even if they brings in more new laws pretending they're protecting us. It's like they said about the Puritans and bear baiting. They didn't ban it for the bears sake but because people were enjoying it."

"Not a lot of flogging then Ethel."

"That's there too, though it's not my forte. But we are a little subtler, not the common types. We do not want people that cannot pay, that can easily be led. Such men will not fall for the low-hanging fruit."

"What about the different fetishes?" Anastasia asked.

"What was a fetish originally?"

"Well.. I'm not sure."

"It was something believed to reside in an object or powers conferred by it. Objects can capture like an amulet, talisman, relic." Ethel continued, "We are good at asking question. Subconscious interest reveals itself. Ask questions that reveal. Breaks the barrier. Cures the Fisher King. Helps get us the elusive Holy Grail. Question-suggestions. We lead to our domain. Aroused people take more risks. Explore. Open up. We tie movements to our questions. Questions circumvent the critical faculty. Why would you want to pay attention to me? Where do you feel it? How does it feel that you are..? Questions that are not ended.. 'You feel a little excited because…' 'You have felt like this since…' We can ask directly and indirectly.

They are exploring, but they do not realise how high or long or deep down they can go. Their interest, curiosity is an ounce of gold that can be stretched a mile. Learn your own technique in parallel. Discover your own rhythm and your own cadence and be yourself. Don't imitate. Follow your own self, your own pattern. The individual responds. They get The Pendant. Dependent. Here's your homework. This concentrates on finding the exact language that works for particular people. Double-meaning may sound passé, double entendre. But you can achieve the same effect with the language once you cue up the subject. Suggestion is powerful. Hints are powerful. The mind fills in. What the mind fills in is more exciting than reality. Read who you can from who we mentioned. Erickson," Ethel said.

"Thanks, next time you said we will talk about niches?"

"Yes. You might begin to think about where you are going. Some go into blue movie production, not acting. Hypnosis for sex, sexual performance therapy, sports performance and so on. List is endless. I like to see my students do new things, so don't think I'll get excited if you come back with a bog standard proposal but I'll help. That's what I'm here for," Ethel replied.

"Thanks... Svengali..." Anastasia joked.

"Welcome to The Velvet Underground."

Next hour an intense lecture on how to read someone, language, carriage. A few techniques of subtle cross-examination. Within the law. Sexual activity was permitted still. Running a brothel was not. As in standard franchise systems, operators were independent contractors. Emphasis on no 'traditional' sexual activity was the first protection. Threat was always of do-gooders screaming for the 'protection' of vulnerable women. Led to repression. It made no sense, inconsistent with equality, reality. Do-gooders are usually useful tactical idiots to facilitate more sinister strategies by do-badders. So there was a Plan B and a Plan C. She had read an Elizabethan mention of a prostitute at Moorgate with silver lace on her petticoat, yellow coloured ribbons in her hair in the French style and a caul. She had a fake string of pearls and earrings. It might be a character she could add to the menu. She could speak in Elizabethan English and act as if she was in it still, a time traveller. Many would get a kick out of that. She had one such customer herself.

Moorgate Keats, Grub Street was nearby. Writers were like prostitutes. Oliver Goldsmith,

'What is friendship but a name
A charm that lulls to sleep
A shade that follows wealth and fame
But leaves the wretch to weep.'

Ian Fleming, long before he wrote Bond worked at a bank in Throgmorton Street, one of Karl Marx's relations ran it. There he wrote love letters with reference to whips and cages in jocular fashion. Before more naval intelligence.

Afterwards, Ash walked down to Bank and St Pauls. £. Curious about quake effects. One road closed. She imagined the Roman Era, spaces, Forum. Once she smoked something in Amsterdam and walking a lane felt as if she walked into somewhere in North Africa. Like DeQuincey walking London to buy his opium in dirty dens. Dirty Den. Lombard Street. Tower Street, Lloyds Coffee Shop, betting on when someone was going to die. Life Insurance. George and Vulture one of the alleged Hellfire Clubs, Dashwood spymaster. Lombard Street was also Luke Howard the 'cloud-namer.' Guildhall. The Hall of Guilds. Brutus the Trojan came here to found London where the giants were. St Bart's still treats people with a gene that makes them 'giants.' The Royal Exchange. Opened the year before the Supernova 1572 visible in daytime. Voltaire said it did not matter there whether you were Jewish, Christian or Mahometan, only infidels were bankrupts. St Swithin's Court where in September 1919, they begin to fix the price of gold every day. Leadenhall. Whittington. Harry Potter. Down there the London Stone. Twilight deeper now. Light twinkled and blinkled. Harsh outlines of things dissipated into blue sfumato.

On the Tube one day, she had heard some kids in school uniform. She thought of the comments she read in online discussions about Raleigh and The Lie,

'It's shit. He's a shit poet. He did shit posts.'
'He wrote this before he was executed.'
'It makes no sense.'
But it did make sense to her.

'Say to the court it glows
And shines like rotten wood
Say to the church
It shows what's good and doth no good.
If church and court reply
Then give them both the lie.'

Beauty is truth, truth beauty Keats said. Depends on your conception of beauty.

Henry VIII fascinated her. Described as handsome and athletic and sporting and clever, until he changed. But Anne Boleyn was more interesting. Learning her skills in France, she knew how to string the King along, to deny, tempt, tease him. For that he would sacrifice his Queen, break with Rome, cause the Reformation proper and alter European history. Yet when he got what he wanted, all changed. Power, promise vanished. Fall of illusion, promise did not deliver. Her head rolled and haunted the Tower of London. Her daughter Elizabeth learned the importance of non-consummation of a fantasy. A spur in the head is worth two in the heels. Learn first to obey before proceeding to govern. No living mother to pass on the womanly agenda of weakness. A woman of great ambition that could seduce a king. A tyrant of a father you learnt to appease. Perfect childhood for a wise ruler who would pay attention to those around her and seek an invincible, faithful repository of her love in her country.

Ash enjoyed her work. She liked her cello snug in her Chesterfield. 'Like' has 'lie' in it. She forgot about Tubes. Read a few posters on the way. Pamphlets everywhere. Took a bus home. A little diversion on the way. Revs of engine made her sleepy near reverie. When she thought as Ethel or other characters, she thought differently. Today the ghost in the machine. I am not a robot made of tissue, an emergent thing, an illusion. You could learn more about consciousness from a novel. Science cannot ignore me if it seeks to understand consciousness. Those that know well will not yield it. Metaphor and simile flummox the mechanical. Gentlemen used to think proverbs were for the common people. Great spiritual leaders talk in parables. They will be the castle keep that will not yield. Life is richer than scientism. Plato not abstract. He knew how to get his spirit to leave the body and unite with universe. Dullards teaching philosophy are obsessive clowns turning Plato's true reality into a crossword puzzle with kaleidoscopic changes of clues to confuse. Powerful forces did not want you to find out fantastic forces you have access to within. Existentialists try to confuse you, make you weak. You are powerful. Factor X. They told you science was enlightenment. They just want to disenchant you, make you feel depressed. What a start to the month she thought wearily! Getting off the bus she noticed the smoke in the sky and the smell of burning. *'...and I saw it in my dreams..'* she hummed.

She thought how PC meant personal computer and political correctness. Just a spoonful of sugar helps the medicine go down as the song goes in Mary Poppins. Put into the mouth of the film character different from that written by P.L. Travers, former Ministry of Information official. Travers got a taste of her own medicine. She was into esoterica, theosophy with teachers like Gurdjieff who wanted automatons to wake.

Later Ash looked up the definitions of 'fetish' and wrote her own:

a) *A pathological form of sexual desire in which satisfaction is linked to an abnormal degree to an object.*

b) *An inanimate object worshipped for its supposed magical powers or because it is believed to be inhabited by a spirit.*

c) *A person the subject of obsessive interest or fixation.*

d) *An activity the subject of obsessive interest.*

From words for artificial and magic. Everyone must have a fetish then of some type or be a fetishist apart from feet or latex. Feetish. A car, phone, PC, fan or fanatic, cleaning, appearance, ideology. Then we giggle at ones who have at least realised it. PC a fetish. If sex is sublimated into higher *things* then those may assume a necessary psychological-sexual dimension sufficient to allow something be defined as a fetish in the pathological and/or magical sense even though links between desire and object may only manifest indirectly sometimes. Dolls. Robots. Ideology or political views. So you love a representation of the real thing yet you ignore the real thing itself and maybe even abuse that real thing in your mental fixation on the faux, false, fake and because of that mental love of the object you attached to, paradoxically damaging the very thing you believe, project or claim to protect. You say you fight for justice and then you are unjust. You fight for rights and take rights away. Maybe that is the hoodoo purpose of these representations, substitutions, changelings? Maybe that is what idolatry is about? Maybe that is the fear of it? She looked at the new hatemails she got every day from people complaining about her exploitation of vulnerable men and the nasty gender stereotyping signals she sent out and wondered whether she risked imprisonment on that score or some private retribution. Everybody wants to rule the world. The Lyre of Orpheus. Abattoir Blues. Blue lyre September.

LLLF

LONDON LOGOS LIBERATION FRONT

Publishing Pamphlets to Oppose Censorship of Our Message.
The Counter-Revolutionary to Evil and Terror Effort.
Educate yourself. Nowhere else, nobody else but us tell you.

TV WAS A TRICK.

YOU ARE THE PRODUCT.

THERAPY IS TRICKERY.

CINEMA IS SICK MESSAGES.

DRINK IS DRUGS.

DRUGS DO YOU IN.

DRUGS CONFUSE AND KILL.

CONFUSION IS A STRATEGY.

YOU WILL BE PERMANENTLY CONFUSED.

PERMANENT CULTURAL REVOLUTION.

COMPUTER GEEKS PROGRAM OUR MATRIX.

THE MEDIUM MESSAGE IS CONFUSION.

CONFUSION IS TO HYPNOTISE YOU.

THEY WANT YOU TO LOVE SUBMISSION AND SERVITUDE.

FREEDOM DOES NOT ONLY MEAN LICENCE.

FREEDOM MEANS SELF-LIMITATION.

BEWARE THE SMARTDUST. ID TAGS IN IT. KILL TIMERS.

PREPARE FOR LIBERATION

Chapter 5

Inspired Agenda

Some pale graffiti recalls.

> 'IF GRAFFITI CHANGED ANYTHING
> IT WOULD BE ILLEGAL.'

> 'NOTHING MORE DANGEROUS THAN SOMEONE WHO
> WANTS TO MAKE THE WORLD A BETTER PLACE.'

> 'STOP MAKING STUPID PEOPLE FAMOUS.'

Janet played The Jam 'Going Underground.' A song that the 7 often played, got you going. Atomic crimes and guns instead of kidney machines. Some might say her life was in a rut. But she was happy. Maybe timing was bad. Although a government's trouble is often a revolutionary opportunity. As well as riot arrests there were 'Lightening Swoops.' People arrested on foot of innocent jokes on social media (supposedly erased) made a decade previously. The underground stuff was harder because the State was acting tough already. Shock 1 - Quake. Shock 2 - Riots. Shock 3 - Government Lightning Strikes. Corroborated their suspicions. A series of fires broke out all over London, facilitated by the dry weather. Black-smoked sky where evacuees said you could not even see the sun. Deliberately set, often on waste ground. September 2nd, anniversary of the Great Fire of 1666. Parliament barely back after Recess. A Defence of the Realm Emergency Act had been rushed through with many Members unable to make it. Opposition forced to accept. Apart from the introduction 'Be it enacted etc,' it simply read,

> **The Prime Minister can take any additional emergency measures necessary to protect the public after consultation with the Special Emergency Measures Committee hereby established.**

That made it more serious. She was fond of the Kennedy quote that,

'Those who make peaceful revolution impossible
make violent revolution inevitable.'

Maybe more like 'I Started a Joke.' Violent revolution often failed. That's what the Fabians knew, although she was against them. The 7 had concluded that theatrical revolution might have an effect. Perhaps Mishima in Japan tried that. 1916 in Dublin was theatre. Inspired by, and played out as, theatre. Pearse had said that the earth needed to be warmed with blood, mixing pagan and Christian notions together in a sacrifice. They were not doing sacrifice but what they called 'suggestive symbolic revolution.' It was about the spectacle in the society of the spectacle. Look what happened when the public oppose war non-violently like in the US over Vietnam and in the UK over Iraq. Ignore the public, pick off leaders and proceed with Agenda creating distractions. Then the State provokes crime and terror. Whitey Bulger the Boston criminal and the Unabomber were programmed with drugs and mind control. MK Ultra. Run by the Black Sorcerer. Bulger in Alcatraz and Unabomber in Harvard. Murray. LSD. Timothy Leary was experimenting there also. She knew how The Weathermen and others had found the FBI COINTELPRO programme designed to destroy opposition to Government. Such organisations were not hypothetical or secret in the UK. The State knew how to split organisations, how to derail them, take out leaders and tarnish them. LZLF had studied this knowledge. The State would always be the masters of terrorism technique. Destroy humour, love, commitment so it could tax and use it's taxonomy. Maybe they could be the Violet Revolution. She needed some more inspiring quotes in her head. *'The future belongs to those who prepare for it today.'* Malcolm X. *'The successful warrior is the average man with laser-like focus.'* Bruce Lee. All you could do really was be what Socrates suggested. A gadfly, fastening, persuading, reproaching. A small thing to stir the mighty steed of State. So Plato said. He got the hemlock for it. *'A cock for Asclepius.'* Horseflies. Spread disease too. Poor justification Sock. Kinda get it still. Hoarse. Hope we don't have aftershocks now.

Abba. Abba. She wished she could forget it all but she could not. She wished she could retreat into those things she liked but she could not.

She wished she could get back to her study on Walter Evans-Wentz but she could not. She felt him about as a friend as she felt she had been with him when he walked around the Celtic lands studying Fairy Faith before he went off and found *The Tibetan Book of the Dead*. Timothy Leary said the book of the Dead was the same as an acid trip. No clue. Shivered. Maybe the inhabitants of the unseen world, the wrathful deities had penetrated into this one. Over London it felt as if there was an old London Particular, yellow-green mental mist, black smog, fog, a traditional old pea-souper. But it was of another dimension than mere soot or smoke. It was dark, peculiar, political particulate that got in the eyes, made the skin itch, reduced visibility and reeked of hell.

Fresher, light drizzle. More activity on the streets, vehicles, patrols. Vindicated their beliefs. Three walked in the tunnel beneath the City of London. This was really conspiracy, 'con spirare' meant breathe together. Rats scurried by. They could not smell with the gas masks they had. It looked brutal. Some passages had fatbergs. Always creepy. Always the danger that you could see things. Your mind played tricks with fumes or lack of light or something else. There were spirits there too, not just will o' the wisps. You might be on an old Roman street. Even if you had done your planning right, you could still make a mistake. In some tunnels there could be a surge from the Thames and you were gone in sixty seconds. Janet could still marvel at the brickwork. A rose born to blush unseen. They had walked this passage before so they knew they would come up in the City near a few targets. Silly and serious. Crimson dye released in the Thames in two days would be Merlin's prophesy come true in a way. CITY of BLOOD. No damage, some attention. Tunnels provided an ideal way of getting around without detection. Out and in before anyone could see or catch them. There were vibrations and tunnelling sensors but it would only be significant if you stayed in the same place too long or were near certain locations. Tonight was the glad colouring of the spires of Christopher Wren churches. Tomorrow they would have multi-coloured patches for the world to see. Vegetable dye vibrant for a few days until it rained. Colin made a cross-bow that shot arrows that would distribute bands of colour on the dull, grey stone. He would get out. Edgier thinking about the Mad Marksman and carrying weapons. Janet would keep the entrance operational, would look for anyone else at street level. Curfews in places. The statement released tonight was etched in her mind.

'The LZLF wish to make a simple statement about the hypocrisy of expensive works ostensibly for the greater good that serve the interests of elite, mechanistic groups. Your brain will be plugged into a big machine.'

'KINGQUAKE. They were all nervous. More sombre, serious. Rubicon. Fun but a little more scary now. There had been a series of earthquakes in 1811-12 in Missouri that made the Mississippi flow backwards and convinced some Native people that the Tie Snake who lived in the river was unhappy. That contributed to rebellion and the Horseshoe Bend massacre culminating in the Trail of Tears according to some historians. There were reports of the Thames changing direction. Quakes cause changes of direction. Thinking ahead to a Lucius Tubal podcast. Glad Jack was involved. He had developed his gift of remote-viewing after seeing the de-classified CIA reports on its success. Sometimes you should be in the moment. Other times you should be somewhere else in your head so you can manage the moments you would rather not address at the moment. Despite the fetid smells that shocked the senses there was a memory of those that challenged before. A flash of recall of the Brotherhood of Eternal Love, the Hippie Mafia and Orange Sunshine made her smile briefly. Hermetic Brotherhood of Light. A thought of the Weather Underground on the run. Always be the same. Those in power, seen but mostly unseen, pulling the puppet strings would always be controlling, dominating, subjugating. The mental condition of dependency, humiliation and obsequiousness was the glue that held it. Resistance to tyranny might be homage to God, but more importantly it was the protest of the human spirit that reminded itself that it was powerful and a real agent in the real world. For that she would gladly tramp the frightening underworld. Underground. Subterranean Homesick Blues. Manhole. Fleet Foot. Pavement. Government. Plainclothes. Fuck we're in his song! Did he dream us? Fuck it. Watch parking metres. He was right. Spies. The Weathermen are the only ones that knew. The Weathermen that became the Weather Underground. Dylan's song 1965. 1969 with Black Power, Vietnam. Bombed the Capitol. Haymarket Square. Molotov Cocktailed Judge Murtagh. Brinks' robbery. Pentagon bomb. Could a song come from the future? Maybe just the past dolled up. Like Nostradamus did with the Roman times. The Subterraneans. Kerouac. Subterraneans by Bowie. *'Share bride failing star.'* What does that mean? Dull, dark, damp, dank dimensions disappeared for a minute till her light reflected back at her in the eyes of a giant rat.

LLLF

LONDON LOGOS LIBERATION FRONT

Publishing Pamphlets to Oppose Censorship of Our Message.
The Counter-Revolutionary to Evil and Terror Effort.
We raise the consciousness to stop our enslavement.

POWER IS NOT AT WESTMINSTER.

YOUR POWER IS AN ILLUSION.

POWERR IS GONE FROM HERE.

YOU ARE PROGRAMMED.

YOU WILL DO WHAT YOU ARE TOLD.

YOUR EDUCATION WAS TO STOP YOU THINKING.

YOUR CRITICAL FACULTY IS CLOSING DOWN.

YOU'RE RUN BY BILDERBERGER-BOHEMIAN GROVE.

YOU THINK YOU ARE INFORMED.

YOU ARE PROGRAMMED.

YOU ARE IN THE MATRIX.

YOU MUST WAKE UP.

LEARN. THINK. READ.

DO NOT TRUST AUTHORITY.

DO NOT GIVE UP YOUR SOVEREIGNTY.

DO NOT APPEASE TYRANNY.

IT IS NOT THE GREY ALIENS EVEN THO' THEY EXIST.

PREPARE FOR LIBERATION

Chapter 6

Midship Point - The Chosen One

ISLE OF DOGS. CURFEW BEGINS AT 22:00.

STAY AT HOME OR JOIN US IN JAIL.

DO NOT LEAVE YOUR HOME BEFORE 06:00.

Approaching the Isle of Dogs on Wednesday past the emergency signs, Birker said out loud to himself, I'll sort out Ethel Woodpecker or whoever she is. See whether agents or officers know better. She's getting my attention now. He worked with Kit McGannah once before. Cranbourne set it up. He consulted his solicitor and barrister. Michael something or other. Birker thought there may be copyright infringement or contractual breaches in territorial exclusivity. His company was one of the other authorised agents in the UK for the robots. The US company had to be a defence subterfuge. This Erik guy was reverse-engineering and changing the program which seemed to be against the licence conditions. He had heard the news announcer on the BBC,

> *'Authorities have been authorised to take all, complete measures such as are necessary to protect the public. As a result special mobile courts with full forensic facilities have jurisdiction to incarcerate and impose the death sentence on anyone found guilty of a capital offence. A list of capital offence is available on the website and all deal with national security.'*

Severe. Shock. Outcry. Headlines. Hammerfist. He liked that. State must be boss. Nihilism was no good. Abyss of chaos. English were just too un-restrained. Stabbings by the hundreds every year in London. Knife-Vest on him. Long-range rifle shootings reminded him of Lasermannen. The Laser Man. Shot immigrants with a rifle with laser sight. Briefly in the army. He did these crimes. Unlike Thomas Quick. Thomas Quick was Sture Ragnar Bergwall. Sweden's most prolific serial killer. Confessed to 30 murders. Found guilty. Only problem was he did not do them. Any of them. Worse than Henry Lee Lucas. Burst pipes here too.

Youth needed to be reined in. In parts of London there were High Security Zones. Posters everywhere, vehicles, Stop and Search. The State and it's hidden institutions with a monarchy and welfare was needed. Although right-wing in economic terms he was left-wing in his opinion. Patriotic. Saw no conflict in Sweden having a great humanitarian reputation and a big weapons industry. Loved King, Queen and his society. Looked at the areas cordoned off and rubble and saw a large crack in the pavement. An army vehicle passing by made him feel safe. Security is good. Ostensibly a business man. The Shock and Awe Lightning Strike had been impressively business-like. They had been unusually well-prepared. Sirens plentiful still. He watched the riots that had broken out in parts of South London. A pre-existing Plan had been 'rolled out' rapidly. Quick. Twickenham Stadium had become a temporary detention station. Some prisoners were sent to temporary camps even on the tiny Kitterland Island, owned by the Isle of Man. A prison barge was already being used as a holding centre on the Thames, like they used to. A little more complicated legal challenges, due to prior agreements. Sark also. Elizabeth I had given this as a fief in perpetuity if it was kept free from pirates. St Kilda's another. The camps were HI TECH PRE-FAB dropped by helicopter. Smelt like plastic with a faint tang of formaldehyde. Frongoch in Wales re-appeared. Those who were unruly in Twickenham went off to St Kilda's. They were going to film some of the St Kilda's operations. 'Internment Behind the Scenes.' Soon shut them up. A series of 'terrorist' attacks. Said it could be the Russians. Or a number of Middle Eastern groups could have been responsible. Even talk about the return of the IRA. An attempt to flood the Underground. Things were getting under control. In the zone of intense problems in London martial law had been imposed. 'Fanatics' trying to use the disorder and chaos to foment a rebellion. He would come down hard. Not Islamists but racist, misogynist Brits. He liked that special announcement he had heard on the news. Disliked this smelly old McGannah. Hard dealing with him. He could see through the old goat. Euthanasia worked in his mind after 70 if you did not look after yourself. Like fat people, don't give them attention. Smokers. Drug addicts. Look at abortion. Reduced crime. Kept undesirables breeding. Fact.

Midship Point was one of the oldest block of flats before the obelisk-like Canary Wharf buildings were built up. Fantastic view.

Christopher known as Kit. McGannah. From his balcony, he could behold the great metropolis. In the windowless bathroom with its avocado tiles, bath and basin, he read about the Norman Invasion of Ireland. Part of a project to crack Irish history. A list of countries he was studying. As a young man he had been thrown into a quagmire over there. Nightmare. Informers. Double Agents. State agents fighting with IRA, players compromised through sexual blackmail. Politicians blackmailed. International mischief makers were getting involved. Gaddafi, Castro and later Russia. A slip of the tongue would have you buried in a bog. Words kill. He was among the 'players.' A shocking word, suggesting a game or Shakespearean actors. Top secret. So he constructed some tall stories, deflected attention, blurred boundaries. In his mind he was responsible for infiltrating the Army Council of the IRA. But he wanted to understand it now, like he had tried to study Sweden, the Congo, Malta.

Progress occurred when prisoners started reading history. The most brutal loyalist 'soldiers' started paying attention. Opponents develop respect for each other, more than colleagues that are not so brave. Hunger strikes. Bobby Sands. In here he felt peace. Bathroom small, compact. Contemporary world disappeared. Candlefocus, warm bath, great pleasure, soothing bodymind. More worried about his prostate and hips. He took care of his books. But if it made it into the hot sanctuary, that meant it was good. Wet-warped, blessed or baptised. A silly accident in Ulster caused problems to hips and groin muscles since. Had to watch the time on his alarm clock as yer man was coming. Was he Swedish Rite? His country studies made him suspicious. Congo study gruesome. Something about story of Norman invasion of Ireland that did not ring true. MacMurrough Kavanagh supposed to be key figure 'inviting' Normans because of his domestic power struggles. Tales of invited invasion are a common propaganda tactic. Romans had not gone to 'Hibernia.' Too cold, wild. Church came. A distinctive church grew up, maybe some old druids in it. Celtic, monastic, nature loving. During the Dark Ages when Christendom was under attack, Ireland kept a beacon of light. Great philosophers emerged like Eriugena. Before that they had the goldsmiths, stone carvers, astronomers. Horses. One tribe made the would-be king shag a white mare and eat some of the body. Romans did similar, fight over the head. Godfather, horse head in bed. But they love horses in Ireland. Queen always got her horses there. Rain, good grass, mild. Geraldus Cambrensis told the Norman story. Only thing he admitted about this people was they were good at music. Tall, handsome men with barbarous beards. Otherwise wild. But Ireland had a code of law even to protect non-combatants and women from 697, first one we know of. Did not fit the bill. Ireland had a druid class. Caesar respected the Celtic druids. They built great monuments. Their language was old, linked directly back to proto-Indo European language. The first recorded copyright case and judgment,

'To every cow its calf, to every book its copy.'

Hundreds of years to establish control. Spurious reason for intervention. A justification for atrocity. What was there? Fish. Flax. Wool. Wood. Cows. Hides. Furs. Vikings often traders. 1014 expelled. They had slaves. St Patrick was a slave. In England the son of Godiva had gone to Ireland and raised an army to attack England the century before. Kit's suspicions were falling on the *Church*. A power struggle between the local and the Roman Church. Love of nature and the apparent accessibility of the divine to the Irish was not in the script. The Papal Bull 'Laudabiliter' gave Ireland to Henry II, friend of Adrian the Pope, on the basis of a spurious claim. Henry II would conquer and the Pope would have control. The Plantagenets. Henry makes a statement, seen to inspire his followers. More than Manson did. Thomas A. Beckett was brutally killed. Henry II in danger of excommunication. He comes to Ireland, gets support of the Irish ecclesiastics. Pope Alexander is happy. Henry II became leader of Ireland with the express approval of the Pope. Ireland sending monks abroad. Re-established in the network. No surprise Henry VIII was so distrustful of the Papacy. Cathars he knew of. The religious orders established more Roman-directed monasteries. Clever men, educated, part of a growing community centrally involved in temporal issues. Caesar and Christ. Centralisation more important than holy men. He watched the time, dried himself and combed his thinning hair. I would say that the religious orders had more to do with the conquest of Ireland than the Normans. Control narrative. Bad guys often not bad or wholly bad and good guys not wholly good. Parallax.

Day departing. On the 17th floor of the tower block on the Isle of Dogs, Cyril Birker rang the doorbell. A very tall Swede, with a look of distaste. Manicured, a yachting blazer and slacks. The door opened, "Ah Cyril, come in."

McGannah could not help notice how Birker looked everywhere around him, unapologetically. "Welcome to my abode and how might I help you Mr. Birker, you oul gigglemug. Would you like something shaken not stirred. Cyril can't be your real name?" He laughed at his own joke.

"I'd say St Kilda is nice at this time of year, even if it's near the North Pole," Birker said.

Kit enjoyed mispronouncing the name to irritate his guest. He would have no idea that a gigglemug was someone who smiled all the time. Everything about him annoyed him. Always spotless and shiny. Not very good looking but acted as if he was. Not very smart but he acted as if he was. Consistently condescending, patronising and supercilious if you let him. Very tall men often are.

"A little job, routine." The Swede still examined his environs, "Just a corroboration of intelligence."

"No need to take your shoes off," Kit said.

Birker looked blankly, "I have no intention of..."

"I thought you Swedes all took you shoes off."

"You're talking about people without class McGannah. A crucifix, don't tell me you believe in that stuff... Jesus. He didn't even exist." Birker crinkled his nose.

"Kit.. please. What great organisation have you and your Nobel Committee up there chosen. Nobel Peace Prize. Great irony is it not? Dynamite maker - peace makers. Then you give it to warmongers. Some celebrity this year. Why not choose some 'dreamer'?" Kit asked.

"Don't care. Don't start all this speculative nonsense," Birker said quickly.

"I genuinely love your Royal family. Well done with them. A great contribution you made to London with Swedenborg at least."

"Who's he? Does he play for Chelsea?" Birker asked.

"You're taking the piss. You never told me how you got into Intelligence." Kit felt he should transmute his irritation.

"That's another story." Birker showed a combination of distaste and slight satisfaction. He threw a folder on the table firmly and absently. "That's the subject."

"Not another Russian agent cod I hope," Kit ventured.

"Routine." Birker managed a frown.

"The last five people you sent me turn out not to be Persons of Interest to anybody," Kit complained.

"You can't be so sure."

"Just want tax-payers to get their money's worth." Kit.

"Just get on with it. We need information to add to that in a week. See if that looks right and if there's anything else. I must go. Why live here McGannah?"

He sought to like people but this guy was something else. He did not believe that turning the other cheek was so important. Let these fellows free and you end up in a worse prison than the self-imposed one you began with. He did not like him, the set-up, his barely pent-up rage of superiority, arrogance.

"Do you know Joe Hill?" asked Kit.

"Who is he?"

"Well I was talking about the song."

"Cannot say I do?" Birker replied.

"He sang the first Line or two … *I dreamt...* Ring a bell," Kit tried again.

"No. An hallucination it sounds like? You should try techno. Hope you're not having prostate problems yet..?"

"He was a Union organiser, framed, executed in USA. Joan Baez, Dubliners sang it," Kit said.

"No." Birker.

"Well his real name was Joel Hillstrom, born in Sweden."

"And?" Birker asked.

"Alfred Hayes wrote the song. From Whitechapel, then wrote for Hitchcock, and The Twilight Zone," Kit remarked.

"You need to get out more. A week or two, that's all," said Birker with a bored air, still looking around with a faint look of distaste.

"The dog barks, the caravan passes." Kit threw it in out of context to irritate him.

"Sorry?"

"I read that Ayn Rand stuff you were talking about," Kit said.

"Marvellous isn't it?"

"All her characters are the same. Cardboard. Do you see yourself in them?" Kit chuckled.

"Great work," Birker exclaimed.

"I was wondering how you Randies all seem to get so much work from the State if you are so hostile to it?" Kit asked. "Here I have been reading Swedish History and there is a few things I meant to ask you."

"History is history. It's over. Live in the present McGannah."

"Ok, the present. I looked at some Swedish literature, in English of course. Recent stuff. The Dragon Tattoo business," Kit said.

"I saw the film, or one of them," Birker said.

"What looked strange was two things. Firstly you don't seem to have any crusading journalists or many real journalists at all. Not that we have. That's what I read. Is that true?" Kit asked.

"C'mon. You can't be serious. Sweden is famous for its liberal values," Birker protested.

"Secondly, it seems like the intelligence services and the left-wing guys would be pretty similar politically?" Kit.

"No..." Birker said.

"Thirdly. I get the attractiveness of the character Elizabeth. I wonder who she was named after?" Kit asked.

"You think too much, McGannah. It's bad for you."

"Larsson was a left-wing writer, heavily and actively involved, Eritrea etc. Dies suddenly. Does not leave a will. Controversy. I was wondering whether this was really a left-wing revenge fantasy? Then again Assange is a strange case. Does the King of Sweden have more power than we're told, both left and right Janus," Kit said.

"You over-simplify things. The writer is not the character. I'm afraid I have work today. We love our King. Do you know you're a bore?"

"Hey I was going to ask you about the Swedish King proposing a marriage with his son and Elizabeth I. Imagine what the country would be like now? What about Wallander? What was the strange fascination with that miserable bugger?" Kit raised his eyebrows.

"I don't know why they involve you old buggers that are nearly out the door. Fact I'm not sure why Cranbourne asked for another view." Birker.

"Listen you must have worked with Soap, Seppo... The Swedish Secret Service."

"What if I did?" Birker said.

"They're more like the Stasi right, State left-wing?" Kit asked.

"I've told you. Business and science is my thing. That's the context. You can't know about these things if you don't ever do them. You couldn't run a jellied eel stand. Although you look like Tubby Isaacs. You've never been to Sweden you dumbass." Birker spat it out.

"Bye. Told You So. Horse who came from... Mont Dor and Curtain." Kit.

Nice face. Attractive. The Special Branch in London had largely been established as a response to Irish terrorism. Most espionage, agents, informers, intelligence gathering had been perfected in Ireland and where Irish terrorists operated abroad. That was how they thwarted all the armed insurrections. A strange de-centralisation of intelligence and security services now, more private entities involved. Some whistleblowers were working for private employers at the time they disclosed the wrongdoing. Spycatcher case had shown the way secret information and confidential information would continue to impose an obligation in addition to statutes. Widened circle of people that get information is complaining about the amount of information being gathered. More information gathered, more involved, more vulnerability. McGannah thought it better to be lean, focused, less ambitious and cautious about the loyalty. If the person working for the State will not shout for its national teams you have to question loyalty to the State. National teams have been de-nationalised as part of the Agenda. Communism crumbling created re-alignment. Some thought that the new threats were created. Wondered whether it would be fit for purpose. No idea who was doing what, why and whether it was a good thing? But who were we working for anyway? Secrecy for the people? Secret courts, and intelligence exclusions. Everybody is changing and I don't feel right.

Military intelligence and police intelligence. MI5 and MI6, GCHQ. NDEU. SOCA? Officers and agents, people employed by the State and hired or engaged, directly and indirectly, patriotically and pragmatically. The vortices of crime, terrorism and State espionage interlocking. Public-private, foreign-domestic distinctions dwindle. Staff step on each other's feet in operations. Some move between agencies. Pyramids. Each level knows less than the higher one. Policies and emphasis change. Great sucking-in of much electronic information creates a demand for someone to use it. Green movement was infiltrated if not set up by Government. He did not know why this woman was involved and he was suspicious. Intelligence a kaleidoscope. Thousands of reasons why an agency might be involved with someone else's life, outside SIS... Police, tax, welfare, local, national, EU. Dawn raids. Like the investigations at the time of Jack the Ripper. A process of evolution, key personality conflicts, lack of definition of roles. All the organisations within, counter-terrorism, national security and defence had top secret operations. Age of convergence meant cross-over. Crime and terrorism division worked no longer. Mexican drug cartels become dangers to security, those not run by a State. Like Churchill meeting as an agent in disguise in Egypt and nearly having him eliminated, paths could cross. Like Churchill in Cuba, people could assist informally. Like any other organisation, State agencies might employ private entities. Then there might be other international organisations. Impossible to find out what was going on, who was who. Old-fashioned trust, other affiliations, other organisations could help. Boundary between commercial intelligence and other strategic intelligence was not clearly drawn. Large trawling operations which took in a lot of information gave huge opportunities for base profiteering through commercially sensitive information and technological development. Treasure trove of information, increasing risk of corruption. Little purely 'British' business. He had assisted on a posting to help in enforcement of competition law. Under EU law you could have Dawn Raids and huge fines. Everybody is changing and I don't know why. What time is that Beast series on?

File. Glasses dirty. Scan. No warning signs listed. No bullet points. No significant group affiliations. No important relationships. Intellectual. Introvert. Zilch. Summary. Knew it would be empty. Tittletattle at the end. Forget what we're told, people so busy, before we get too old. Yes. A woman of 33. Dominatrix business. Used to be one. Some of them want to be abused. Why of interest? Possible reasons. Women and men in the adult entertainment business had access to people with their pants down. Blackmail a matter of course. Players played like a puppet by the State. Most people envisaged Mata Hari, seductress. Men more common. Kincora. Such places and persons simply heard things. Pieces of information were gleaned. Intelligence picked up. To find out a little more he would ring an associate, informally after studying. Those dolls, Birker involved in them. Masquerading as a businessman. Hard to buy them blow-up ones. He couldn't get one anywhere these days. All machines. Hey Lord, don't ask me questions. But he was a well-respected man around town. It was a bitter-sweet symphony indeed. He went outside to watch him walk away far below. Pretend you've no money. No one came near generally. Come up and see me, make me smile. All down there it came from. I felt the branches looking at me. Made him feel dizzy. Dizzy down there. Believe it you can achieve it innit. Marc was born in September and died in it. White Swan. Summertime blues. Lived in a dream sometimes. Thames never failed to cast a humbling spell. Memories come back to haunt me. Just keeps rolling. Sat by that river and it made me complete. Waterloo Sunset. *'Dirty old river...'* Dusk balcony peace, transformed disparate mass of buildings to a few bands of diffuse coloured shadow. The Kinks. Sundown on great docks gone, on old river spirits of vessels and mudlarks, etherised the bustle and brightness of the day. Every day he looked. Getting old and I will need something to rely on. He thought of the Marchioness and the 51 dead up there when the Bowbelle collided. Night of thistle purple phantasms over jagged silhouettes becoming pierced with yellow copper choppersearchlights. Looking at the world from my window. Leg paining him. So lazy. State a Leviathan. A beast to beat a beast. Rot set in. Caused landslide. Chilly. However the beast has a life of its own and Frankenstein warned us. Flowing into night. Flow gently sweet Thames. Hames. Met Ash. As Them. People in this town look straight through. Across the river was Greenland Dock. Muscovy Company. Where the whaling ships used to be. Elizabeth I gave the Muscovy Company a monopoly charter on whaling. Just near where she was born. English-Russian trade. Got the oil from the blubber. Soap. Street lights. A few years ago they found an old whale skeleton in the mud there in Greenwich. The London Whale was also the name of the JP Morgan chap that lost billions playing with derivatives. Monster trader, monster losses. If one guy can do that damage and they are 'rogue' imagine what a group acting together can do? Collapse the entire system. Long as I gaze. Why do they send us out to check out non-entities? I suppose it's better than darning socks. Picked up some rice from the floor. Sweep it into the corner. I don't quite know. This could be the end of everything. This is the last time I will show my face. You can't blame me for the death of someone. I'm not the man they think at all. He wrote an X beside her name in anticipation. Heroes just for a day. I am the river. You ocean. *'I am in paradise.'*

LLLF

LONDON LOGOS LIBERATION FRONT

Publishing Pamphlets to Oppose Censorship of Our Message.
The Counter-Revolutionary to Evil and Terror Effort.
Paper and glue to educate you.

WE ARE BEING MANIPULATED.

WE ARE BEING CONTROLLED.

WE SWIM IN A SEA OF PROPAGANDA.

TO CONTROL US THEY CONFUSE.

CONTROL US BY MAKING-UP IDENTITY GROUPS.

TO DISTRACT THEY DIVIDE US.

TO STAY IN CONTROL THEY MAKE US FIGHT.

THEY MAKE US FIGHT THOSE WE DON'T WANT TO.

THEY ARE SETTING UP A WESTERN CIVIL WAR.

USEFUL IDIOTS ARE THE HANDMAIDENS OF WAR.

DON'T BE AN IDIOT.

COMEDY IS PROPAGANDA.

YOU WILL BE THE SLAVE.

FREEDOM IS AN ILLUSION.

YOU ARE CONDITIONED TO CONTROL.

YOU ARE TRAINED TO INDULGENCE.

YOU ARE PREPARED FOR SLAVEHOOD.

PREPARE FOR LIBERATION

Chapter 7

Hermits and Hermeneutics

"The lunatics have taken over the asylum..." he hummed as he saw his reflection in a window, brown as a berry with summer sun. Broun as a berye. Fresh September air, scent of scorched earth rather than prairie fire. Harvest time. What was being harvested now? People? Who offered thanks? The corn dolly, last sheaf, rush symbol. Wafting sense of Scotland and the islands of white sands, beautiful Highlands that thrilled many years ago as a boy. Who understood Gematria properly? He read secrets, did calculations, read codes, experienced transporting geometry. He knew he lived in a world run by the clandestine. Complots. Connivance. Covert. Cloak and dagger. Concealed. Like the Earth that groaned. Could read the runes. They ruined everything good. Everyone banging on all the time but they knew nothing. Jem liked to walk into Hampstead to see people or visit the good second-hand book shop. In winter sometimes he had squatted in the deserted homes of the billionaires on The Bishop's Avenue. He thought of Riley from *The Life of Riley* coming to walk the streets of Hampstead in the end. It was where London dreamt and those dreams seeped drop by drop into the soul of the city below. A charity book shop that looked like a real book shop. Maybe the folk here would not buy in a tattered place. He wanted a book on The Quakers. Had the innerlight. Once demons were natural, not supernatural, good not evil. Church made them bad. Everyone believed them. *The Dream of Scipio Commentary*. Scipio the Elder came back too to tell about the universe. Between wakefulness and sleep. Here the Triffids walked in the *Day of The Triffids*. Wells and Wyndham had monsters come to this prized place. It was on Hampstead Heath as well that Colin Wilson slept when he was writing *The Outsider*. He slept in his bag up there and went into the British Museum Reading Room. Dripping sandwiches on the way in. Did he channel something up there as he followed the Fleet that Ash felt was exerting some primitive force? Freedom of association.

An orange-vested man much taller and larger than him stood in his path. Private security roamed these streets after the Hampstead Invasions. Rich houses had been terrorised regularly. Eventually some political activists were found to have allied with nefarious elements to conduct campaigns of fear with social justice pretensions or vindications. It persisted nevertheless. Some said security firms created crime to create demand.

"Where you off to Dad?"

"You addressing me Sonny."

"No one else here Mate. You don't live here."

"Mind your own fucking business. Awfy cheeky... wee laddie."

"Whoa! Hold on. I'm Security Mate. Like the Police."

"The Police may have fallen far but they'd have to fall a long way to be crawling with the likes of you."

"Excuse me... after the Quake..."

"Fuck off. Do you hear me? You have no idea of law Sonny no matter how degraded that is. Yer bums oot the windae. Awa 'n boil yer heid ye wee puggybairn."

"This is being recorded."

"Where?"

"Here."

"Let me see. I'll address that... Now listen you bunch of wankers. If you hassle me again I'll bring an action and keep you in court till I'm deid. And you Ms Williams who I understand are the boss from our pleasant conversation before on my perambulations, should get rid of this dangerous moron before someone else does. I hear they're looking for extras in the Planet of the Apes remake. Lang may yer lum reek Ms."

"There's no call..."

"I hate fuckin' impolite people you fat rumplefykebastard. Now get outta ma way ye daft numpty before I get angry."

"There' no need..."

Keep the heid. Jem sauntered onwards ostensibly annoyed that his thinking had been interfered with and his mental space invaded so uncouthly. Wu-wei and mushin today must be adapted to the odd and unusual, contemporary circumstances as experienced such that the appearance of the unwelcome attributes of attitude without may not be as they seem on the surface and should alternatively represent an illusion calculated to achieve optimum control in the face of a potentially peacemind-destructive phenomenon that could otherwise metastasise thus obeying the axiom of respecting the Buddha without relying on their help when you might need it to deal with existential threats whilst paradoxically promoting calm within.

He widnae be nursing the wrath to keep it warm. The earthquake disorder made him nostalgic. Jem stayed at the commune in Findhorn in Scotland, when he was healing. He liked the variety, oddballs, gentle people... for a while. Heal, whole, hole, holy, hallow. There he met the old guys and the one who used to speak with the god Pan. One of them was a lawyer in Edinburgh and Pan started speaking to him in the park and he could see all the sprites and nature spirits around. Christians maybe turned Pan into Satan. All the Masons up there might cause hallucinations. Rosslyn Chapel in the village of Roslin. Sinclair family. St Clair. Santoclair. Santa Clara centre of Silicon Valley. Sinclair inventions, naval, electronic, personal calculators. Hugh Sinclair. John Sinclair. Heads of the Secret Service. Sinclair Media Group. Started one September with Roman approval, and after Elizabeth I came in, they stop the Catholic stuff. Good luck to them. Saint Clara was the patron saint of TV because she could not go to mass and saw it on her wall. Mystical stuff, secrecy, occult, technology go together. That's why people think that some technology comes from aliens, demons. Ash said Rosslyn Chapel was about sound energy and spirit communion. Peter Pan, J.M. Barrie. Kirriemuir to Neverland. Ash said that the Green Man in Rosslyn was Templar homage to The Green One in Sufism. Also gateway between realms. Where did 'Dolly' the world famous cloned sheep come from? The Roslin Institute. He did not see films anymore and did not read that Brown book but he guessed it was not the true story. This stuff would drive you mad so he knew he had to change track. He used a mental technique called Track Changing. Your train is on one track, then you change it to a new destination.

He did not need long to feel satiated with people. You get people-sick. Everyone contracting when they thought they were expanding. Thought they had more but had less, wiser when they were more foolish. Sense history all around here. Comfortable presence of those who projected their dreams onto the globe. *Mary Poppins*. Writers, painters and scientists came because there was a little magic still. Ford Madox Brown did that wonderful painting Work and set it over there - The Mount on Heath Street. Homeless people in it too. Magic of the high, ceremonial place. Those who received messages or saw reality beyond untruth run the gauntlet of ignorance. All such unfortunates risk madness, embrace loneliness. Whether he would ever be able to return from his quest with a message as a boon for humanity was doubtful. He sought an insanely expensive coffee. Not short of a bob or too. A nice lad and girl who did not look down their nose at him and he liked the conviviality and sense of temporary belonging. He talked to Robert a little. He felt sorry for young men. Getting stitched up as always. It would be most of them murdered, unemployed, told they were evil and dangerous. Criminal gangs facilitated by the State. Powers-that-be want trouble in the suburbs. When you are worried about knives, guns, drugs and anti-social behaviour you are forced to call for 'order.' Law and Order. That's what they want. Lawyers love criminals. Lawyers are parasites. Nectar that controls the hummingbirds of crime. He had worked close to them. When the Plague hit London they came up here. Vale of Health. He still thought too much although the rituals he evolved reduced that. Still enjoyed seeking to unravel the riddle. As he went out he saw a newspaper sandwich board.

'SOCCER SHARPSHOOTER SEARCH STALEMATE.'

Strange world. What lay behind that? Confusion. Maybe it was some of those nasty right-wing Crusader lunatics that were springing up. Or National Front maybe. Or the usual Militant Anti-Fa in disguise. Maybe just a loony. None of them knew. Assassination on the football field. All eyes on it. Little like Croke Park 1920. Stunning accuracy. Like all the fires he could see from the hill, even had one on the Heath. He was not going to think too much. Thinking too much causes dis-ease. Much philosophy was a nightmarish game that made you sick in the head like the writers. Like alchemists desperate for gold trying to make it from a rubbish bin. Words are the camouflage of meaning. You are looking at the outside of something else, far more complex and cannot be imprisoned in a little box. Philosophy the gaoler of meaning. He watched it with her. The one time he went to her flat. She thought he should see it. He could never relax in other people's spaces. Cuckoo's Nest. They told you there. Don't disturb the schedule. If you don't take your medicine orally they can arrange for it to be taken another way. Jack Nicholson did not realise that Nurse Ratched was only representing the Combine that rule over us. They always win. It is for your own good that we have discipline and order. Lunatics taken over the asylum. Fun Boy Three. Tunnel of Love. They knew that when the song came out. Government put Jimmy Savile in charge of Broadmoor. A child molester necrophiliac with no experience given the keys of the kingdom and a job at a home with vile murderers. Only Antony Clare and Johnny Rotten said anything critical of Savile that he heard. 'Ultimate Freedom.' He knew there were some really sharp psychiatrists like Clare. That's what the bastards call it. Jem walked around Hampstead and thought to himself about the people. He saw some kind of protest poster and noted that he had seen similar ones a decade or so earlier. Psycho something or other. Know the outcome see the journey he said. *'Some books are lies frae end to end and some great lies were never penn'd.'* Rab.

All you in Hampstead. Highgate. Fortune Green. Swiss Cottage. Gospel Oak. Finchley. Golders Green. Cosy suburbs I see and envy sometimes for a little in the cauld outside alone childless spirit still as stone for a Baltic minute. I miss that warm mindnumbedness of preoccupation with practical things you can fool yourself with as you sit before the flickering screen with your car in the driveway and your dug that wants a wee walk and your full fridge that you check out yourself now so you don't have to talk to a real person before I realise that they must face it eventually at some time though they hope they'll drop deid without too much need for that sort a' thing. Yer aw clean. Sprayed. Nice now and then. Ignorant of the bad things not in your line of vision. Waiting for your annual holiday in the sun. Buttoned up the back. You are part of that system with your nice IKEA kitchens. You buy all the political nonsense they sell you. You DIY the stuff they give you. They say it was Patriarchy to blame the men and take away the father. They say big men are bad, to foster fools and cowards. They say it was the Church men, to take religion away. They say it was Poverty so you shout for more trinkets. They say you were repressed so you'll shag anything. You take the pieces home. Then you can re-arrange them when the tack changes. You learn how to put it together. You have a nice kitchen. You can watch cooking programmes. You can see people get serious about whether the soufflé is airy enough or the oil drizzled too little so they won't be getting serious about serious issues. I ken. Tension and teaching. Then you can do it yourself at home. Shiny, inhuman, flawless, dead things. Meanwhile they are dividing you in groups before they set them against each other. Left, Right, Left, Right, march to war either way. Identify with your politics so you don't find out whom you are. Happy to take the up of feigned righteousness, wait till you see the down.

The Emergency revealed the iron fist in the velvet glove. Velvet overground. Revelation. He talked to someone who knew what they were talking about. Insider. A tough, professional woman but she was deeply concerned. She said there were things going on nobody would believe. He would go up the hill. His little hidden tent worked well until Autumn got too damp and dreich. Now he would sit on the hill and be. He did not like to call it meditation, because that had been robbed by rascals and people that had not the faintest idea what it was about. Be blank, bothered by black beasts. Commune with his

Native American brothers in the spirit-world and they would guide him. Commune with Red Cloud and all the others whose name he could not work out. One of the few characters that stood strong in his mind was his friend the Irish American ex-Jesuit priest. They were trained like he had been. Your will moulded, trained to conform and fit into the structure. Christ's soldiers. They had sent this priest off to University to learn philosophy, ancient writing and Middle Eastern languages like Aramaic. Worked on the Dead Sea Scrolls and was sent to the Vatican. He left and became a taxi driver. Developed his skills as an exorcist. Confronted demons that possessed people. He got their attention, challenged and commanded them out in the name of Jesus. Taught him about the dangers of engaging, opening up through meditation so spirits can haunt you. Devil could appear as an angel of light. You had to have spiritual protection, a lifeline to Jesus to negotiate, navigate the middle plateau. Jem could never see Jesus out there. Engaging in the spiritual domain without comprehension or knowledge was more dangerous than combat or Camden Town on Saturday after midnight. If you had become prepared, pure, cleansed, distilled you could navigate it. You had to find your way back to your primary state, to the pure stream in you. That was the quantum thread of entanglement to Beyond The Milky Way. Otherwise a nightmarish rollercoaster. Gies some peace. Concern for Ash came into his consciousness, one of his only friends. She had confused him at the start when he could not work out what feelings he had. But it was the purity of the fellow traveller, the fellow seeker, carer. On the lonely road of this existence in a dark mist full of demons he knew she was walking too. He wished her peace in her soul. He wanted the luminous force in her to triumph. Primary forces need secondary agents to operate through. Whit's fur ye'll no go by ye. Why did they start the Black Mass here in 1918? Lovecraft knew it. *Hypnos*. The characters have to come to London. He was telling us something. He said men of learning suspect it not. Jem and Ash had discussed it.

> *'Of our studies it is impossible to speak, since they held so slight a connection with anything of the world as living men conceive it. They were of that vaster and more appalling universe of dim entity and consciousness which lies deeper than matter, time, and space, and whose existence we suspect only in certain forms of sleep — those rare dreams beyond dreams which come never to common men, and but once or twice in the lifetime of imaginative men.'*

LLLF

LONDON LOGOS LIBERATION FRONT

Publishing Pamphlets to Oppose Censorship of Our Message.
The Counter-Revolutionary to Evil and Terror Effort.
Posters round town to bring the system down.

WE WANT TO STOP POLLUTION.

WE WANT CLEAN WATER, SEAS, AIR.

WE WANT TO RESPECT ANIMALS.

WE WANT HEALTHY FOOD.

BUT WE LOVE PEOPLE.

WE DON'T THINK WE ARE ANIMALS.

EVOLUTION IS NOT THE SOURCE OF EVERYTHING.

HUMAN DIGNITY IS OUR STARTING POINT.

WE ARE NOT SLAVES.

WE DEMAND RESPECT.

WE REJECT OPPRESSIVE CONTROL.

WE WILL NOT BE GULLED ANY MORE.

DEUS EST HOMO IS FALSE.

DON'T BE FOOLED.

TURN OF THE TV, ADS, GAME SHOWS, SOAPS.

SCIENTIFIC ILLUMINISM. SATANISM.

BE CONSCIOUS.

PREPARE FOR LIBERATION

Chapter 8

Minefield

Carlin said '*the planet is fine, the people are fucked*,' and that was the best line so far. They were at the LZLF 'base' in Wapping. Small flat in the Peabody Trust Buildings suited their purposes well. A few joints. Atmosphere pungently sweet, time slowed down, space expanded, contracted and the ceiling seemed to slowly squash you horizontal. Before the more serious stuff they had games based on connections and six degrees of esoteric separation. Or three degrees of scientific influence, or mixtures. George emphasised the triangle between Aleister Crowley, Jack Parsons and L. Ron Hubbard. Everyone knew Crowley the occultist, Hubbard the science-fiction writer, founder of Scientology. He explained that Jack Parsons, born Marvel Whiteside Parsons, was the great American rocket engineer. Lived together. That triangle linked into another one with Parsons, Werner Von Braun and Walt Disney. The US rocket prodigy and the Nazi beneficiary of Operation Paperclip communicated much. Von Braun worked on the famous Man in Space documentary of 1955. He thought that if there was a fake moon landing it came from their blueprint. They rejected another triangle based on the allegation that Barbara Bush was Aleister Crowley's daughter.

"It went really well," Pam said.

"Like clockwork." Janet.

"There's nothing in the papers. It's bad luck with the 'Kingquake, terrorists... the Sniper, riots and now pyromaniacs." Colin.

"It comes up on social media," George said.

"They don't want to give it attention." Barbara.

"There's a meeting between the Press Association and the Government where they issue a 'D notice' or something when they want to suppress something. We just have to be more visible." Peter.

"Everything is Emergency Measures now so they can do what they like and there's no opposition," Colin said.

"Well two more operations in the next few days should do it. Christopher Wren 2 and Parliament Hill. Then we can release Charles Byrne or at least frighten his kidnappers," Pam explained.

"I know who you are. I will look for you and I will find..." Barbara said with an accent before laughing.

"I don't think we'll get near if we don't find a passage underneath," Janet said.

"We have an antenna that may allow GPS work underground, and an accelerometer and Joanna's program. If all else fails to help, Alf's sense which is probably better. He's like a homing pigeon." Jack.

"Are all the other Holi devices finished?" Pam asked.

"Just my name. But Holi is in spring, not September?" Peter said.

"All the more secure then. Listen this equipment means our conversation can be picked up you know that." Colin.

"Yes. They're in the bedroom," Janet said.

"Let's have a look." George.

They crowded into the bedroom.

"Don't touch or go near. You dig a hole and just leave a sod on the top. Most are fake. One or two will eject a colour spray while making a loud bang. But they don't know that," George said.

"We leave a few loud ones that explode, cause a lot of noise, look bad, wake the neighbours. The Police come and find a sign. MINEFIELD. Covering the hill. Visible across town." Janet.

"What's the message Gov'nor?" Pam asked.

"WE WILL MAKE SLAVES OF YOUR TIME SO YOU CANNOT MAKE SLAVES OF US. Or something similar." Janet.

"What about the links between the Knights of Malta, Pope and CIA. Totalitarian tip-toe like Icke said?" Peter asked.

"No, we're using reason here and we don't want to alienate people," Janet said.

"What about Lucius Tubal?" Peter asked.

"Well. We know where he lives. We know he walks his dog in Regent's Park. The idea will be that someone meets him in disguise, sunglasses, wig etc. We have checked him out and will arrange to meet him on a day if he agrees shortly." Colin.

"But he could get into trouble," Pam said.

"If he does not know who we are, it makes it easier for him." Peter.

"What about those censorship orders?" Barbara.

"I suspect he'll risk it." Colin.

"Banish and mirror." Peter.

"Remember Fred Hampton," Barbara whispered.

"I look forward to the Rivers of Blood," Pam said and continued, "Remember what George Carlin said, *Fighting for peace is like screwing for virginity*." She laughed like the Count in Sesame Street.

The world was upside down. It was inside out.

LLLF

LONDON LOGOS LIBERATION FRONT

Publishing Pamphlets to Oppose Censorship of Our Message.
The Counter-Revolutionary to Evil and Terror Effort.
Simple statements for your education and elucidation.

CONSCIOUSNESS IS REAL.

YOU ARE CONSCIOUS.

SCIENTISTS DENY IT.

THEY TAKE IT FROM YOU.

THEY CLOUD YOUR MIND.

THEY POISON YOUR WATER.

THEY POISON YOUR MIND.

THEY PACIFY YOU.

THEY PLACATE YOU.

THEY DIMINISH YOU.

THEY WANT CANNIBALISM. VAMPIRISM. ZOMBIES.

FIND YOURSELF.

INFORM YOURSELF.

EDUCATE YOURSELF.

FIND YOUR SPIRITUAL POWER.

ORGANISE THE GOOD.

BE CONSCIOUS OF YOURSELF AND THE WORLD.

PREPARE FOR LIBERATION

Chapter 9

Mesmerising Column of Dust

Think of Near Death Experiences. Someone dies and can be brought back to life. Technology from the 60's. Meant people could tell what happened. 18 per cent have mystical experiences. Brain dead but they are still perceiving, still thinking, consciousness is enhanced, feel fantastic. Life Review. Time and space dissolves. Recorded back to Plato and others. Er was a soldier who came back to life at his burial 12 days after a battle and woke up and told them about the afterlife. Then she discovered that high level Buddhists meditators could have a similar experience. Not quite the same.

DEEP, QUICK INHALATION 5 x 4 MINS (x3)

Er. She was engaged in The Gathering. Ash thought about Brigid, Brigit, Brighid, Bridget, Breed, Bride on Thursday morning. All variants. It would be pronounced Breed in Gaelic and cover Breed. Bride, breed. She wondered about Breda in Holland. But it was broad they say. They built the Koepelgevangenis, a Benthamite Panopticon prison was there. Stuarts. Orange-Nassau. Like Juno, Isis, Diana, Persephone, Minerva, Artemis, Hecate. Everywhere. They say horseracing in Ireland was related to Brigid who drew the sun in her chariot across the sky. Spring, springs. Her cauldron in the earth. Cauldron, chalice, grail. Brigid there before the Celts came. Worship of female goddess. Celts displaced her slowly with male gods. She had to go underground at times. She was spring, smith, poetry, fire, sun. Words and light. Rules were remembered, recited. The triple goddess of life, regeneration and rebirth was displaced and transmogrified. The Celts adapted and adopted the great mother goddess but she was still the exalted one. Brigantia was the Latin form. Former name of important sites in Europe. Lake Constance, Brigid's lake. The Irish stories were full of strong women. History was an attempt to convince women that they always had been victims so they will be in the present and future and they bought it. Strong women now often meant a bad copy of a man. Why not go back? Vedanta. Atman. Brahman.

The day seemed to sparkle with a light that reminded her of the Road Menders by Manet. In it, blue descended infusing the city, taking the greyness over. A walk from the Ashram to Fitzrovia to The Dungeon Redux on Tuesday. The Road Menders painting was like London on the mend. There were workmen everywhere, fixing pipes, glaziers fixing windows, carpenters making temporary repairs. Demand for re-construction was so high that in some parks in the City temporary work stations were established. A tannoy system appeared around Central London, tinny announcements about disruptions. The iconic, alien, thin sound kept your attention. A frisson of excitement and exhilaration. A whiff of danger that alerted the senses and collapsed predictable conventionality. A new force emerged from nowhere known by the acronym JAMES. The Joint Auxiliary Military Emergency Squad. Joint insofar as they had police and emergency personnel under joint command under some Special Committee associated with COBRA and the Civil Contingencies Secretariat. Ostensibly authorised by Statutory Instruments by the PM under the new legislation, clearly well-rehearsed and planned. Red-uniformed and accompanied by heavily armed 'URBANAE' who wore grey and purple camouflage. Difficult to know who-was-who but weaponry indicated authority. No public discussion she heard expressed concern at the ostensible transformation of the country. She listened a lot more to the BBC to hear what was happening but everyone seemed to be reading from a script. All of a sudden a new phrase comes in or an old phrase is used by everyone, obviously orchestrated through disseminated texts. If anyone raised any objections to security measures someone would inevitably say they were *'proportionate'* and, *'That's like Chicken Licken who thought the sky was falling in when an acorn fell on their heads. It's not like the real quake.'*

Internment in place. Government had learned from previous bouts. Now it was 'scientific', 'empirical', 'evidence-based' supported by algorithms to ensure 'objectivity.' All online activity of people had been utilised to create a list that could be used to corroborate anti-social accusations. Every keystroke recorded. Corner shops had little bread or milk. The bigger supermarkets had huge queues and empty shelves because of panic buying and delivery problems.

Boundary of blue sky and her surrounds were merging. Fitzrovia. Fitzroy. Fitzroy Tavern. Name reserved for illegitimate royalty. Where the Fitzroy Group met. Augustus John. Orwell. Dylan Thomas. Do not go gently into that good night. Round here lived George Bernard Shaw and L. Ron Hubbard. Sci-fi and Religion. So many people think that there are entities that send thoughts to us, hovering in the heavens. Are thoughts entities? She thought about how she had studied fetish art and what was once 'underground art.' She had looked at comics and novels and fantasy work. Eric Stanton, Crumb, Eisner. Underground press. Fantasy can tell you what is in another person's mind. You don't have to approve it. Wise to know at times. It may be illegitimate, but fantasy is not fact. An illegitimate was a different person in the father's tree. A Mr Mystic comic hero. Miss Mystic. Mr Marvel was Wells. Nothing new under the sun. Ambulate, Ashambulate. Dressed in a dull navy suit not wearing any make up, solely the deodorant she made herself. Hard to get deodorant without chemicals and she did not fancy the thought of them in her body. The Agency had a range of essential oils and odours, from lavender and sandalwood to tar. Fresh perspiration is not unattractive. A menu of sounds, scratching, squeaking, rubbing, tapping, friction, sighing, slight moaning that they incorporated as desired depending on the reaction. With ASMR, people had become conscious of how they could be triggered by sounds. Very primitive. A sharp, snapping sound set off some ancient alarm of an approaching predator in men more than women. So you could play or utilise a range of sounds to set off certain emotions or feelings or associations, build them up. You found which sense the person was ruled by. You found out by their language. Were they predominantly visual, aural, kinaesthetic or combos? Contrary to accepted learning theory you could alter your approach by deliberately developing and nurturing a sense they had not.

On some walks she would do a stocktake. Today she was thinking of the things she no longer did. Some she had given up in the last few years. Not smug feelings. Just that she had to cut things out. Gave her more time. Then she could concentrate on what were the 'last things' for her. That meant that she did not smoke, drink, gamble, eat meat, do dope, go to the gym or get involved in unnecessary social engagements, buy newspapers, watch television, go to the cinema, discos, nightclubs, pubs (to drink). Losing all these habits I have a nun's life. Saint-sinner. All the things I did and may return to, rotating vices for a little enlivening piquancy. Epicurean. Work was a means to an end. She was experimenting with some of the forgotten Chinese breathing practices. She suspected Swedenborg used to induce high sexual stimulation but transmuted and retained energy in the body. Raise and transfer. Like kundalini practices but not the same. Occasionally a star burst, a shower of stars or a candle wheel explosion happened in her head. Relaxing, letting go, allowed space for other things. Ashes to ashes, dust to dust. Fitzroy Tavern. George Washington becoming a Catholic on his death bed?

When Ash began to study the mystic paths, she saw that the process of purification or purgation of some type was universal. That's why Cults might have 'Clearing.' A process of letting go of attachments, negative actions and creation of space for oneself was necessary. Relinquishing allowed opportunity for other reality to emerge. Purification allowed clarification. To reach the next level. Otherwise illusion is stickily persistent. February meant purification. Romans purified the city, cast out evil spirits. The colleges based on families ran round and had a good time often whipping each other. Goddess of breastfeeding was celebrated. Honoured ancestors exorcised bad things. Fornax, goddess of the oven. Fornicate. Clearly it did not mean that one would stay isolated, removed or aloof for a long time, for there was a necessary return or it was not the path. The spiritual evolution helped her have clarity in her work too. Altered states could be induced quite easily with words, signs, lights. Altered to higher states. This could cure, heal, go beyond time and space. Urbi et orbi. Siddhis came. She heard a voice every now and then. It spoke about spiritual matters. The Voice. She usually heard it near water. Only connection she could find. Said most of the things she found in ancient Indian spirituality, Vedanta, Egypt and so on. She wrote it down and explored it. She saw that it was consistent with perennial wisdom. Everyone has it all inside them. Know thyself because it is there. Purification is discarding that which obscures your true self. Priesthoods rob you of your agency and interpose themselves. Lose agency over your spirit, everything else follows easily. Non-local consciousness available to all. Cortex does not contain your spirit. Receiver. Kabbalah mainly means reception. Consciousness primary. You have the pristine in you. Primordial spirit unlearned. Cortex out, no hallucination. Glimmering darkness. It is in you. Portal. Because there was nothing in it that she disagreed with you could say it was her Higher Self. But it had a coherence, clarity and comprehensiveness and a convincing specificity. It specifically said that there was a new religion of Tecknos or maybe Techne that sought to dominate and replace the spirit of humankind. Maybe another rule.

Axiom 4   The primary consciousness is in you to be uncovered and applied.

Maybe that needed another.

Axiom 5 We all have a spirit which is our imperium, part of primal consciousness.

Popping by The Dungeon Redux was the least interesting thing to her. She knew that it could be done well, but did not like the accoutrements. Sadism, properly so called, was one of the lowest qualities. 'Bad Pain.' Play acting with a little punishment was different. She understood that it was a game. If she thought she was dealing with something else she would not do it. It was possibly a safety valve. A part of her would always feel that the instruments of pain turned into pleasure could cross some dark boundary. Men who wanted permanent disfigurement. She had no problem with the standard stuff, and no judgment of those who liked it. It was hard always to get the right type. *Venus in Furs*. Genuine self-harm was no good. There were always cases of people who were not in a game but a lifestyle. Alright too. But when you had the unfortunates that wanted something that could inflict serious physical damage, then that was something else. She was squeamish about some of the medical things that went on elsewhere and she could not fathom it properly.

Let the psychological come to the fore. Hypnosis, magnetism and mesmerism fascinated her. She read everything, orthodox and unorthodox. Two centuries of medical investigation and then only recent recognition. But it was there, a long time ago. People in the past knew how to create hallucinations including negative ones. You can tell people not to notice, not to see things. Focus attention like a magnifying glass in the sun. She was interested in hypnotic induction by telepathy. Evelyn Underhill had hooked her. A sister seeking enlightenment. Like Anaïs Nin. Both explored the self along very different paths. Golden Dawn. She understood why Underhill might not be well regarded by many or ignored. Nevertheless it had a powerful presence for her. Close to the bone. Occult power in it, mild but palpable. A path she might have taken. Protagonist managed to conjure an entity she cannot shake off. Process, incantations, implements and intention she was familiar with herself. However, her true belief in those supernatural forces made her very reluctant to deliberately cast a net into that seething zone.

Perennial philosophy, as Aldous Huxley described, worked for her. Something in every theological perspective. Maybe one original theology. Sufism had depth. She liked the ultra-orthodox Jewish and Kabbalist, elevated Catholics as well as a more peasant type, Quakers. People like Mary had a simple structure that was fast and secure and within that a childlike faith that could survive in its simplicity. Indian Vedantic ideas resonated, Patanjali was easy to understand. In Protestantism, the Quakers stood out and above much else. Quakers. Native American and Aboriginal concepts she knew were easy to perceive. Taoism and elements of Japanese and Javan. Later on she revisited the occult spiritualists. Through Florence from ancient Greece and Egypt and to London, mixing with currents from Toledo, Granada and Cordoba that moved north, she saw strands that resonated. The Gnostics and non-canonical gospels spoke to her. Spell. She imagined a stream from India to Egypt to now that still worked and made sense, even with science's assault. Atheist, materialist, superficial science did not deter her. There were two things that she had been impressed with.

Firstly, all the thinkers she liked took their inspiration from everywhere. Cosmopolitan. Secondly, all the most inspired saw the otherworld and higher worlds around and accessible. The only freedom is what we have inside. But you must obey universal laws. Laws of universe not global rules. Word 'slave' in universal. Anagrams. Slave Ruins. Evil run us. Everything else is contingent and illusory. Doxa. We must attach our will, intention and attention somewhere. What we attach to is our ultimate power. Squandering it is our greatest danger. All must yield, cede. Question becomes who or what we cede to. When we burn off the irrelevant, master our attention on the path of growth we get distilled. Our essence made purer spirit, made subjective it resonates with the universe. Channels wake up. Non-locality works. You can get distant information, knowledge-consciousness survives death. Druids knew. Location readings. Sceptics say it is illusion, magic, suggestion, misdirection. Showmanship. John Dee in her consciousness. What you see is not it. What appears real is a crusted illusion. Lives like a vapour. Being the stuff dreams are made on we melt into air with the rest of the spirits. Possession, giving over yourself. That seemed to be the game she was in. Where does Dolores Cannon fit in, imagining she is channelling Nostradamus?

The Dungeon Redux. "Hi Veronica, just popping by. How are you? How's business?"

Veronica was a former nurse. Tired of the lack of appreciation, managers, consultants, constant plans to re-organise, attempts to cut corners, paper work, computer work, accounting. The patient was falling down the list, protocols paralysing like plaster-of-paris casts. She left. Her children needed her and she needed money. A challenge, apprehensive. Studying the field she came across Understated Mystique Therapies (which she pronounced Umpty) as in Humpty Dumpty. She liked a system. She was caring, enjoyed having power. Fun. She was concerned about legality, or rather changes wrought by feminists to protect her. In the UK there had been strange prohibitions. Parliament decided to ban face-sitting in porn videos in 2014 and people protested. The strangest thing to ban between consenting adults. In the face of war it looked like one of those Government manoeuvres to deflect attention. Create minor, irrelevant policy distractions that in their weirdness garner attention and direct attention away from bigger issues. Then she wanted to go the opposite way Ethel had. Orthodox BDSM. Veronica wanted to do the 'traditional' or rather standard stuff and it was a path for those clients that wanted it. Even in terms of 'good pain' this was negligible to light and many concepts still applied. Dungeon Redux. It brought back a reduced range of implements to remove the industrial, surgical, open, factory-feel that many such places had at the expense of suggestive simplicity. Separate wet-room. That X again.

Business had a Plan B and a Plan C, so she could work within the law and adapt, even when they attempt to ban non-sexual, non-touch contexts 'to protect women.' Women's rights were being taken away and women cheered. General confusion was part of the process of public hypnosis. Confuse and open, pierce.

"Great. Thriving. No Problems. A little strain in my shoulder muscles but I'm getting by," Veronica said.

They talked of the disorder and difficulties of getting around and shared stories.

"I was at home, the dinner was on the table and it hopped up and down. I nearly died. The kids thought it was great," Veronica said.

"Do you mind if I have a quick scan of the books? How's your daughter getting on in school?" Ethel asked.

"No, course not Ethel, I have them ready. Great."

The books were a coded system that could be read if you learned the key. All the financial books were diligently kept. Erik saw to that. They were compliant with Data Protection rules also.

On the way past, in the basement, she looked into the dungeon. "How's that new cleaner doing?" Ethel asked.

"Fine. We haven't had too much stuff to mop up recently," Veronica replied.

"You had a few new customers recently. Anything unusual?" Ethel asked.

"Not that I can tell. A very nice stockbroker and a big Scandinavian guy. Might be an offence for him under their law he said. They're odd. Double identity that place," Veronica said.

She read to get an idea of the overall scheme of things, exchanged some pleasantries and was ready to go on her way.

"I would like a session on language. We were talking about Erickson and his technique of hypnosis and therapy. I found it a bit complex." Veronica frowned and continued, "But I liked that one, when he sent the alcoholic out to the Botanical Gardens to reflect on a cactus and how it could do without water and that cured him. It sounded like a Zen Master."

"Exactly. You have to adapt to address their attention and intelligence. Erik will be around for the bi-annual checking of the equipment. There's too many people suing these days and it's worth it anyway," Ethel said.

"There were two things you said to mention, momentum and I was wondering Ethel you were mentioning about carriage and deportment."

"Let's see. Give us a little entrance," Ethel said and sat down.

She came in, but looked like she was trying too hard. She looked for approval too quickly. Ethel made her do it again after showing her how. She walked in, her shoulder were back, her chest out, her neck was extended. She had an impassive face with an ever so slightly disdainful look.

"I thought you had a crown on your head. You are a Queen. You don't have to be grateful for the others. You are not interested in their approval. You expect it. Breath easily. You have no tightness caused by anxiety at all. You are relaxed, calm, composed, tranquil. Be calm. Breath. Don't stop normal breathing, lose control. You can employ what you are good at. You might get angry as a person. Then use that. You know how to set them off, if that is appropriate, if the contrast is there. Anger and love are closely related in physiology, where they come in the body. Love, hate. Play, cross the borderline. So they don't know whether they are coming or going. Make sense?" Ethel asked.

"Yes. Although the former is the more popular." Veronica laughed.

"I'll do a longer session. Do it again, remember everything is projection. Everything," Ethel said.

She did it ten times and the transformation was remarkable. I am Michelangelo looking at a partially sculpted block seeing the angel of better self emerge. False persona is a person petrified by silly preoccupations. Strength within comes out. When it is there it is powerful, whether you had a bath robe, bag or a ballgown.

"We talked before about pacing and what we call Momentum. The journey from one level of stimulation to another. It is in a lot of the descriptions of Law of Attraction, New Thought, and good speeches. Build up to a crescendo. Preachers, demagogues do it. Building, developing, inciting, accelerating. Look at those tapes I left thinking of how you can utilise the language we talked about to excite. That's the gist."

"Thanks for that. By the way that little bollocks SimpCook you sent me a couple of years ago was trying to get an appointment. I told him I was full for a year. He did all that sissy stuff. He's wanting all kinds of perverse stuff now. Real damage, pain. I told him we're not like that."

"Just ignore him. If he causes any trouble I'll have Erik sort it out."

"He'll enjoy that..."

"That's a problem alright."

They finished off talking about recognising clients. Ethel explained that the ones who wanted real submission and the one who only really played temporarily could have a similar profile. Then you needed The Perception. A fine line. Ones they did not want really enjoyed the trappings of their power, dour bossiness. Their targets were comfortable and easy with their own power and exercise of it. Dungeons used to stay in her mind because they were mostly dull. With Erik, they had discussions about a new range of innovative implements. Looking to Eileen Gray and Francis Bacon's furniture efforts. He must have met her sometime or seen her work in Paris. She wondered about names, partly euphemistic. Correctional facility. Then again you associated with the warped punishments systems in the United States. Sounds a bit like colorectal. Near here was Pollock's Toy Museum. Bowie liked it. Dolls and toys, distractions.

Where does all that BDSM gear come from? It must have come from all the executioners stuff, all those torture merchants in the Tower working for spymasters and royalty. KINK sounds like KING. All the bowing, prostration, boot-licking that was hallmark of power systems. Edges. Whip, mace. Fancy dress. Untouchability. Subject. Goddess. Queen. Punishment. House of correction. There seemed to be a close connection between the Elizabethans and the Scene. Something about the Elizabethan Era that impressed on us now. Philip K. Dick had visions, pink light, a girl delivering his medicine. Revelation. That we were living in a Black Iron Prison but could not perceive it. You don't need black, iron prison these days. Achieve all the same results without. Ghosts of those times were still here with us, mutating. Home soon. She walked by the Senate House where the Ministry of Information had been. Fleet floodplain. Orwell. P.L Travers who wrote *Mary Poppins*. Senate House central in *The Day of the Triffids*. Blinding plants on the march. Author worked in the Ministry. 1984. Orwell warning but also telling. Had worked as a policeman. Reports to the police. His Down and Out as a tramp could also be consistent with spying. He may have been telling us in his choice of alias. John Buchan worked in Intelligence and Propaganda. Maybe it was his own fantasy. There was something about him that did not add up. Why did all these people write of terrible things to come to London in the future? What was around here that made it? Why is Government Information so closely linked to future disaster?

At home she popped into Mary.

"How are you?" Ash asked.

"Fine thank God. It was a lovely day. I was up Camden Town did my shopping, went to mass then watched a bit of telly," Mary said smiling.

Glad to be calm home now worntornslippered, rawsilkshirted, lavendersmelling, coffeecomfortable and Chesterfieldeasy. She had been listening to Waterloo Sunset online a lot recently for some reason and did so again. Creepy with dolls really. Taxi light so bright. Maybe Breakfast in America. Odd that the eerie feeling in the uncanny valley comes between some likeness and much of it. The really strange thing should be the indistinguishability. She read Underhill's novel *The Column of Dust*. Therein a spirit wandering possesses a woman experimenting with magical incantations. Faintly disturbing. She had no interest in doing ceremonial magic but respected it. Not ever interested in conjuration. She adhered to a type of Alan Moore definition of magic as the use of the mind to affect the world. The realm of spirits was not one she cared to venture into beyond a controlled, receptive way. Prophets must be open. Even then she engaged in cleansing rituals to try and rid her consciousness of any unwanted attachments. Ample protocols. Whether these were fantasy or not was irrelevant. Mind is powerful. Possession or attachment may occur to one who allows themselves be mentally weak and spiritually submissive to the wrong forces. Erik very sceptical of such things. His explanations of malign motivations, and why they grow, were weak. Certainly if talking of psychopaths or other such mindsets, there may be explanations, but many choose. Elements of magic could be employed in a more, oblique method to bring the psyche into a different domain. Egyptian magic through Greece and into Florence and onwards influenced many great European thinkers. Arabic and Jewish magic through Toledo and onwards was another important stream. Grimoires. Like her new public profile, make yourself visible, more forces become directed to you. Engage in spiritual experience you may also attract thwarting spirits. *The Tibetan Book of the Dead* explanation for the 'Dark Night of the Soul,' suicide or depression. Underhill aware of this. Swedenborg talked of 'secret agents' working for God. Perhaps if people do not advertise the work, they can be more effective. Like the idea of hidden masters. If you meet a swordsman show him your sword. If he is not a swordsman do not show him. Psychopaths and others can read people and their micro-expressions. Exploit people. At the time you grow, fly the nest, risk a run to the river you get vulnerable. It is then you become open. There the cults, psychopaths spot someone and take them down the wrong path. Wise to have your mental places of worship invisible but to those on the immaterial plane who can see them. We are magnets, attracting and repelling with our thoughts. Think well. Thoughts are things. Bad thoughts a beacon to evil spirits. Sense them like they sense pain and blood vibrations. But they are blind to calm and repelled by love. Greatest force in the universe below ultimate relative forces. Toledo appeared many times with tales of underground ceremonies, libraries, magic texts, grimoires, wizards, fact and fancy. Indian pathways and the Silk Road were important conduits. Maybe paradoxically that can be attributed to Genghis Khan. Underneath all the best the same spiritual quest, the development of the soul, of the spirit. Universal laws. Stretch.

The protagonist in *The Column of Dust* most likely repeats something Underhill was familiar with. She stands in a charcoal circle in the closed bookshop reading an old English translation of *The Grand Grimoire*. Lighted by two brownish-yellow candles of wax. They were on the vertices of a triangle within the circle where she also stood. A tilted mirror on the bookshelf gave a view. On a piece of cardboard was a pentagram, Tetragrammaton and caduceus. These were traced in coloured ink according to the recipe of Eliaphas Levi. This talisman was on her chest. She had a forked hazel twig with tips covered in thimbles of steel as a wand. Staying in the circle she reached out for pan of charcoal on the gas-stove. She threw incense from a saucer onto the charcoal which raised a thick white cloud. She read the Ritual of Conjuration. The Words of Power rose. A conjured spirit by the Magus, the steel tips of the wand were placed on the brazier and the Clavicle of Solomon spell. She manages to catch a spirit entity that manifests in a cloud of dust. Ash was reminded of the Illuminatus and the black magic ceremonies. They did well to package the truth in a book that people thought some kind of joke or farce.

But Ash did not want to be possessed. Demons did not interest her nor an invisible man. She would not cede rule of her soul to anyone. Only thing your consciousness can possess is what you direct your attention to. If you give it up, let go the reins, you are not yourself. Your attention is your life. Attend to what you have always had. William James studied the well-documented 'Watseka Wonder' case. A spirit takes over a girl and she goes back to live with her family for a while. That was a documented being-possession with consent. That can happen to a State also. A spiritual possession of a corporate body. There were enough infernal things already. Don't bring more into play. No wish to be an agent of evil or a principal. She knew the work of Ansky and *The Dybbuk*. Clinging spirit of a dead person binds itself to you. He went around the Pale of Settlement in Russia collecting peasant stories. Bund was the Jewish Labour Movement. Some said it emphasised 'hereness' rather than 'thereness.' Also the Ibbur, a positive spirit impregnation. Once Ash saw a grey figure coming out of someone as they lay on a bed. Often little experiences have a long impact. Happened after they had been to an old stone circle in Scotland and discovered a strange place with a bad feeling about. A dismal atmosphere at odds with the higher one. A yin place. They discovered it had been a children's burial ground. Rational explanation would be that you had a strange sense, perceived it to be a burial ground and falling into that place between waking and sleeping you imagined you saw something strange. An hallucination. Maybe some creature which inhabited that place sought to attach itself to a visitor and departed on failure. Why would a creature dwell there? Spirit of the buried. Or something else which dwells around and locks onto that energy. Looked grey and like pictures she saw of ETs. Could have come from her memory. But what if you trusted your senses and accepted there were other things flitting about dimensions not visible to us. Like something produced during hypnosis. Like the Capuchin Crypt in Rome that even affected the Marquis de Sade. Loo. Waterloo.

In Ireland she knew that fairy forts had been left alone because of the perception of malevolent fairies. You could not build through them. Something bad would happen. The scientist might say that it was perhaps associated with disease and was wise to leave for a while. The historian says that there had been a previous race there. The guy that translated *The Tibetan Book of the Dead* did a PhD before that on The Fairy Faith in Celtic Countries. Fairies are not what the Victorians made them out to be. He knew from talking to old people that they were more like UFO beings and often very tall and beautiful. Now they understand that UFOs, NDEs and DMT all have similar effects. Mystical. Neuro-theologians have found the paths in the brain. The God Helmet. Charles Fort would link it to all the other greys, or little people. Her distrust of the official channels now made her open to more comprehensive explanations. As in Elizabethan times, religion and drama was managed. *The Domesday Book* showed how diligent Normans were about documenting, counting, measuring. Control. Ability to manipulate. A small group rule larger. Even took fairies, turned them into something else like The Fairie Queen. Fate. Fairy. Fay. Fae. Spenser, London to Ireland, Oberon king of the fairies. More interested in those like Dee who used a multiple toolkit partly from monotheistic religions for the Incomprehensible Zone. Wanted to allow her spirit grow, unfold, expand in an orthodox way. We are all possessed by something to some extent. But you did not want to have some unwelcome entity there. Critical to have sovereignty of yourself, to have imperium of your soul, be monarch of your spirit. You make yourself open to create space, but not for any spirit to haunt. If you were to relinquish your self or dedicate your soul at least be consistent with the One. A little knowledge is a dangerous thing. Idolatry. Idols are not it. IT. Is it a matter of photons beyond time, entangled, instant, multi-dimensional, many-mansioned maze of consciousness? Caffeine. Silverfish.

Because of her name 'Toledo' and the effect that place in Spain has had on the history of mysticism and magic it had been natural to read and study about the Kabbalah. She felt close to Jewish mysticism. Popularisation created shallow shadows. Before the Jews and Muslims were banished, the three monotheistic religions co-existed. Arabic texts were often translated by Jewish scholars. Lived in harmony. Neo-Platonic scholars like Ibn Gabirol. She hoped, wished and imagined that her family had been there. Cross-fertilisation and intense focus on ancient philosophies and texts. Jews were often in between, sometimes trusted more by the Moorish rulers. The confluence helped the growth of Kabbalah in Spain. The Devil was everywhere. Printing itself would be regarded as a Black Art by some, propagating heresies. But books from the Arab world and in translation like *The Picatrix* or the *Illumination of Knowledge* spread. English clergy interested in such matters came there to learn and bring books back. Often translated into Latin by clergy. Toledo taken back from the Moors. Others said it was necromancy and demons. Fantastic stories of Black Magic and people travelling there to learn and disseminate it. Seville, Salamanca and Cordoba. Great cities where an alchemical exchange of knowledge took place before it was stamped out. Then Isabella and Ferdinand kick out Jews and Muslims, have Inquisition and send Columbus to New World. Their fifth daughter marries Arthur in England, he dies and she marries his brother Henry VIII. Divorce, Reformation. The Tudors may have learned a lot from their knowledge of this. Maybe the magicians were not happy. Noisy! Sirens. Shouting. Running. Searchlight. Booms. Shots?

Possession or influence was like the way she would operate the doll. Marionette. Meant Little Mary, Virgin Mary. Their doll a marionette. Mechanical toys were not satisfying to her. Sceptical about sustainability. But she would work with Erik on his dream. Experimenting with her talking through the doll. Idea was to develop remote or removed possibilities. Clear that these robots could be used in conjunction with existing practices. If the feminine quintessence was projected through the doll, could it create a convincing object or fetish? Creepy, but some cross-over. *The Monkey. A Candle in her Room.* Pinocchio. Toy Story. Stone Cage. Master of Revels. Loads. Kind of doppelganger. She remembered her grandfather talking about a Fetch in the dark night in the countryside. A hooley in the house. He was out pissing in the haggart. Suddenly he saw an old neighbour long left. *'Is it you Danny? I thought you were in England. Come in come in.'* Dan never came. **A fetch**? Maybe if you had something with your voice, looking similar to you, there might be weird dissociative feelings like symptoms of schizophrenia. Maybe if the doll reflects an alter ego, there is a psychological moat. We are spirits. That's what leaves the body in out-of-body experiences. It can make a double at times. Spirit comes from Source and goes back. On this plane we break though. Choose to align, head and heart. Nexus you work towards. Our primal consciousness is always there. We get trapped in an illusion. Get the taste, you lose fear, lose meaningless. Heard the Voice. She would write it down when she got home, *'Dark forces dwell in dimensions of the familiar now, apparently benign.'* No idea what that was about. Not 17. Priests used be able to breathe spiritual life into a statute. A song is a ghost. Spirit.

Listened to the 'Crisis.' Quake damage allowed dissident, disorderly elements an opportunity. Never as many terrorists threats thwarted. Emergency Measures working well. Law-abiding citizens had nothing to fear. All the game shows continued as normal. Listened to Lucius Tubal podcast from previous night. Fingers on pulse. Although up the road, London his target, he had a cult following globally. Some group called LZLF. Thought of that guy Cook, SimpCook. Early-adapter, small, bearded creep. Told her some fantasies and they could not go further. Wanted to give up his free will and punish himself for the sins of men. Maybe thought he was Christ or something. Spineless as a jellyfish. Things he wanted done to himself were horrific. He would find someone but it would not end well when you venture across the boundary into Psycholand. Underneath his warped fetishism was an ideological zeal fuelled by Feminine Supremacy and Radical Gynarchy movement. Ghoulish, ghastly. She had thought to contemplate and commune with Swedenborg. Either a madman, committee or a genius. A renowned scientist. Assessor of Mines, engineer who hauled ships over land, inventor of flying craft. Met beings of Saturn. Celebrated anatomist, astronomer. Known as a seer with second sight and remote-viewing capability. Then God began to talk to him. Had a big influence from Blake to Strindberg. But after she read Ralph Waldo Emerson on him she tried the Transcendentalists instead. Transcendental Club started on September 19, 1836. Soon she would be in Sleepy Hollow, in Concord with Thoreau, William James (Emerson's godson). Soon at Walden Pond. Hole. Hollow. Hallow. Halo. Then to India and the Bhagavad Gita. Ended with a clear sense. All people flawed. But we should believe the divine and miraculous is in all of us. We live in a constrained, confined consensus peopled by mere phantoms, repressing true self. A screen for projections of others. Be yourself. Everything is projection. Portal universal. The 'if' in life. 'El' the divine. Otherwise you're in a dungeon self-made. Dee. 3 days abstinence. Wax seal. 9 inches. One and one-eight thick. Names of angels. 7 invocations. 7 names. Heptagon. Pentangle. 49. Cross. Table red silk, with blue, circular. Yellow letters. Dignification for supercelestial realm. Dee, Raleigh knew things. No nice guy. Compelling yes. Still.

> *'Tell physic of her boldness*
> *Tell skill it is pretension*
> *Tell charity of coldness*
> *Tell law it is contention*
> *And as they do reply*
> *So give them still the lie.'*

LLLF

LONDON LOGOS LIBERATION FRONT

Publishing Pamphlets to Oppose Censorship of Our Message.
The Counter-Revolutionary to Evil and Terror Effort.
Banned in TV, internet and print, through posters without stint.

THEY PRETEND THEY WANT YOUR FREEDOM.

THEY SAY SELFISH INTEREST IS THE ONLY THING.

CORPORATIONS COMBINE AND PULL THE STRINGS.

THE HOLY LAND IS ARMAGEDDONISTS DREAM.

IT IS ONLY BUSINESS.

POLITICIANS ARE PUPPETS.

YOU ARE PAVLOV'S DOGS.

YOU CARRY YOUR LEAD IN YOUR HANDS.

YOU ARE REMOTELY CONTROLLED.

YOU ARE WATCHED.

YOU ARE MONITORED.

YOU ARE MAPPED.

YOU ARE MARSHALLED.

YOU ARE PENNED.

YOU WILL BE PICKED UP.

YOU WILL BE CHATTELS.

THE BRUISEBOYS WILL BEAT YOU.

PREPARE FOR LIBERATION

Chapter 10

The Fuzz - The Buzz - The Beat

The date the Great Fire 1666 ended. When the Reign of Terror began in France. Terror was virtue. Swift justice then. The period of the September Massacres in Paris at the Revolution. Disturbing reports in the State. Rabid and rapid. On the News on the 5th they said that due to the extraordinary number of internees they were encouraging 'suspects' to agree to 'Pacific Parole.' Sounded nice. Parole usually came after a sentence. Unclear whether this applied to people who had been sentenced summarily or to anybody in custody. Internment meant jail with no trial. Authorities already had a full picture of internees created by certain algorithmic presumptions. 'Pacification' a choice for internees provisionally assessed to be highly anti-social. People deemed obstreperous could opt for a new 'chemical cosh' which would help pacify them. Otherwise anti-socials and dissidents could agree to 24/7 monitoring with an internally ingested tag, for life. The tag allowed remote monitoring and control. Many opted to accept these conditions in order to secure release from unpleasant confinement. Already concern had been raised that some of those released had been severely disorientated and lost significant cognitive ability. Within a week of the Quake, one report talked of 'Zombies' on the high streets around London. Ash could not control the monster but would get on with her life. She knew how much worse it was in Soviet Russia, Cambodia, Rwanda or Nazi Germany. She would survive like all the survivors she admired wherever they found themselves. We can only control ourselves. As Viktor E. Frankl wrote, the last of the human freedoms is to choose your attitude to any circumstances. Ash put it differently. If the external world is unreal and not as significant as the inner world, then the collapse of the former will not ruin the latter. New riot weaponry had been pioneered. It attacked the brainwaves of groups so they got disorientated and started pissing themselves. They said it was 'very successful' on the BBC. Robotic dogs could administer low level electric shocks. Drones spread tear-gas. Riot Dye. Switch your mind.

> *'Tell wit how much it wrangles*
> *In tickle points of niceness.*
> *Tell wisdom she entangles herself in over-wiseness*
> *And when they do reply*
> *Straight give them both the lie.'*

Spiritual walk, shaman drum. Voice. She wrote it down. It appeared. She might have been there, but it was not her consciousness. Dimensional conquest. Beating. Something about the beating monotonously that generates a trance. Meeting spirits, going to a different world. Most shamans do not use mushrooms. Around 220 per minutes, with an awareness of shamanic journey or intent. It did not have the same effect if your spirit was not in the same place. Standard way of reaching an Altered State of Consciousness or ASC as she had read more often in the scientific literature. ASC, Ash. Ash, she sought to live in an ASC. Cinderella. ASC to ASC's. Use drums and get a frequency range from 4-7 Hz. Theta waves. Frequencies synchronise. Enter lower worlds and find your spirit animals or helpers. They came to her in a few days. One for every chakra. A black panther at the base, a wolf, a lioness, a stag or hart for the heart, crocodile, a blue snake, an owl and a crow. Above these in the body a swallow. You can say they were mental constructs, but it was strange that if you do the visualisation you will see them clearly. The hart was the heart. St Eustace was converted to Christianity by a stag. Snake? Blue. Simpsons. *'I send you forth as sheep in the midst of wolves: be ye therefore wise as serpents.'*

Symbols well known. In the caves in Guernica she crawled and saw the 'prehistoric' writings on the wall. The Northern Coast of Spain, the Basque country. In 1880 the guy's daughter discovers Santamamiñe. Ridiculed. The Church thought it was a forgery. It's a simple issue. Everyone can solve it. Few do. If you are going in the dark you see abstract shapes. Lozenges and zigzags. There is a fairly universal set of pre-alphabet signs that were used. 32 or 33. She believed there was a common type of evolution, language, spiritual process of growth. Binaural beats were useful for some people. Hemispheres. Wondered whether when you hit the drum in a certain rhythm you got two different patterns, one in the just-struck beat and one in the interrupted previous vibration that lingered in the space. No idea. We are two people in one. Simplest of things had immense power. She was drumming softly in Soho when the phone rang. It only rang when there was something out of the ordinary.

Bom. Bom. Bom.

Phone.
"It's the Fuzz," Erik said.
"Where?" Ash asked.
"Mayfair."
"Who's working?"
"Pawlina."
"What's the problem?"
"Odd. He rang, complained about something or other. Something fishy. Shall I go over?" Erik ventured.
"I'll do it. I'm on my way. I'll leg it." Ash.

HOT BATH. TWICE

Oh well. She ran out, not fair, not far. Mayfair. Ian Fleming. James Bond. Wilde. *Dorian Gray*. Stevenson. *Jekyll and Hyde*. Regent Street was where Hammer Horror, Hammer Films was based before they moved into Soho. Frankenstein again. Dracula. The Mummy. Mummies become bad. All that Horror, Suspense. Dick Barton. Why does all this stuff come from around here? Two police officers there, a female and male addressing Pawlina and a man sat down. He looked at her and then looked down. She went in and embraced Pawlina affectionately. Just off Bond Street. Sterne lived nearby, *Tristam Shandy*. They went looking for his skeleton when they found thousands where he was buried. The anatomists had been at loads. Bodysnatchers for science. In the start, there used to be a room over a shop in an arcade nearby. You could enter through the shop and in another way. At that time they were more secretive, before they developed their Transparency Strategy.

"Who's this?" The Policewoman asked.
"A friend from the Agency," she said breathlessly.
"Are you involved in this?" Policeman.
"I just walked in. You saw me," Ash said.
"What's your name?" Policewoman.
"Officer, I have come to help my friend and am not under investigation and I would appreciate if you choose to ask me questions beyond mere courtesy that you cite the common law or legislative basis thereof and the reason associated with your question," Ash said.

She utilised her honey-tongued mellifluous, seductive but not over-the-top tone, pausing, phrasing in slightly unusual places.

The man stood up. "She hurt me. I don't want anyone else here. Look."

When he showed an ugly mark on his buttocks she knew he was lying and so all bets were off. They had a protocol for this but it had never been necessary. There was a cane. She pointed.

"Was that it?" Policewoman asked.

"Yes there it is," the customer said.

She looked to Pawlina. Pawlina understood.

"May I ask a question? You will notice that it is not leading," Ash asked politely.

"Ok.... Go ahead," Policeman said.

"Did you use this?" Ash addressed Pawlina.

"No," Pawlina said.

"She hit me with it," the Customer said.

"So you did not use it," Ash said again.

"Did he use it?" Ash asked.

"Yes." Pawlina.

"What did he do?" Ash asked.

"He picked it up," Pawlina answered.

"Is that true?" Policewoman asked the Customer.

"She told me to," the Customer said.

"Is it true?" Said the Policeman.

"Yes... She told..." the Customer said.

"Why did you pick it up?" The Policewoman asked.

"She told me to feel it," the Customer pointed at Pawlina.

"Did you pick it up?" The Policewoman said.

"Yes...." the Customer said.

"As you know if you put your hand on a weapon and someone is in fear of physical danger it constitutes assault," Ash added.

"Were you afraid Mam?" The Policewoman asked.

"Me... I didn't do anything." The Customer saw the shift in balance.

"Quiet please," the Policeman snapped.

"Well you can see he is a little volatile, you wouldn't know what he was going to do next," Ash said.

"Outrageous," the Customer protested.

"I will say Madam, if I may call you that without any insinuation intended... You may be correct. But I'd point out, assuming you have studied criminal law, as it appears you have that in the context of the principles mentioned and the aforementioned case, it was held not to be an assault as I recall from training," the Policewoman said.

"You are indeed correct as far as I recall. I still think that on the facts he has a higher burden of proof than her. Furthermore Officer I will say that I have worked here before. And we are very ahem..strict.

We are very strict about not causing actual bodily harm. Assuming that she was following policy, there is no way that such a wound or mark was inflicted here. It is some kind of set up although I am at a loss." Ash.

"It's a brothel. See!" The Customer said.

"Excuse me Sir, nobody has asked you," the Policewoman said.

"I was saying... before I was rudely interrupted," Ash said.

"She's nothing to do with this. Or is it a brothel?" The Customer said.

"Sir. I am not going to ask you again," the Policeman said.

"Officer, I was going to say that we maintain excellent relations with the local police. They are so good in fact that some of your colleagues have availed of our therapeutic services. I was wondering whether this man was a regular? I would not believe so," Ash said.

They looked at him.

"First and last time," the Customer muttered.

"He would not be allowed back again. So there will be no further hassle from him here and I assure you it has never happened," Pawlina said.

"Do you have anything specific you can offer us Mr..... Blowfield was it?" The Policeman enquired.

"I wish to complain about..." Blowfield said.

"Sir! I and my colleague have listened to your assertions and we see absolutely no grounds to intervene here. If you have any complaint it may be a civil matter that you can pursue with your lawyer. I suggest you pack up and leave now. We are facing severe pressure on our resources," the Policeman said.

"But, I demand.." Blowfield protested.

"Now Sir, please... I am going to warn you Sir that I am issuing a last instruction. Let me make myself clear. You have five minutes to be off the premises. If I hear another word from you, I will arrest you immediately on suspicion of having wasted police time and to investigate the possibility of an assault having been committed by you. Now," Policeman said sternly.

"Thank you so much," Pawlina said.

"Thank you for your professionalism and intelligent handling. Like you, we appreciate rules. I think it a disgrace with all the things going on that you have your time wasted with such trivialities." Ash.

"Believe it or not Madam but we're not involved in any of the Emergency Operations, many of our domains have been suspended. You would think we would be busier but we have been a little superceded. So it is strange. Although the Football Sniper is getting a lot of attention." Policeman.

As they went out, she offered them a coffee and asked about Emergency problems. They thought it was tough, but under control. Order being re-established in the chaos. Busy with special courts. More emergency legislation had been rushed through Parliament. The Anti-Terrorism, Crime and Security Amendment Act, suspended Habeas Corpus in all cases. They discussed the Somerset Slave case and Lord Mansfield again on the Radio as well as Northern Ireland. Internment. Ash knew many witnessed taserings, watercannoning and people bundled into large paddy wagons run by private firms. They waited. He went out. They said adieu. Ash asked for the details from Pawlina and made notes. Something behind this to cause embarrassment or to draw someone out? Maybe her. Police fair. Happy the protocol worked. Purpose of that manoeuvre to anticipate such an unusual eventuality. They had a cup of tea, discussion about business, assessment and then she was off. She asked whether SimpCook had been around, but he thankfully hadn't. If a person genuinely enjoys being humiliated, used and abused instead of a role-play, then they could become dangerous enemies from devotion to their own perversion. Rang Erik. Agreed to meet the day after for Erik's part of the joint venture. He was wondering whether to call it Ethel Bot or whether Eliza was better. The idea in Shaw's book was based on turning a flower girl into a Duchess through working on her accent and diction. Mayfair an interesting, wealthy area. Dr Jekyll and Mr Hyde. Dorian Gray. These two novels demonstrated something about the false, split self. Poor were elsewhere. Jekyll in Soho. Lanyon, Cavendish Square. Where Stephen Ward lived. Profumo Scandal. Would see his darling *'some time in September.'* Profumo was just up at Regent's Park there. In Macmillan's Government. Macmillan, the World Stater. Ward the osteopath who introduced the Secretary of State for War to a prostitute. Ward was tried for living off immoral earnings. An establishment retaliation. Set up. He had money from his practice. Small payments when living together were put in. Judge gives hostile summing up. Ward commits suicide. Wonder? No less theatrical. They made a musical. Andrew Lloyd Webber. Songs like Human Sacrifice. Well-liked. Don't step across the line or you become a human sacrifice. Slaughtering an animal or being to a deity. Meaning performing priestly functions. That's what priests do. Invisible priesthood. Ward had done some work with MI5. They did not help. He had worked on Gandhi, Churchill and many others. It did not matter. You see why people like their own certainty of magic, why your own unseen is better than the actual unseen.

Burlington House. She had no idea about it until she studied Alfred Russel Wallace. There in 1858 at the Linnean Society of London was a presentation without the authors being present on two papers of evolution, one by Wallace, one by Darwin. Linnaeus the great Swedish taxonomist, famous for organising categories. Now we hear of Darwin but not Wallace. The Voice had told her that the Theory of Evolution was mistaken in the way articulated or understood as it failed to understand spirituality. So she studied it and found Wallace was more interesting. He was also against war and eugenics. A few years later Wallace diverged from Darwin and became a spiritualist. He believed that there had been interventions into the process so that humans could develop and attain higher consciousness. Genius, art and the higher order qualities did not come from natural selection and mere competition between beasts or people. Darwin got a letter from Wallace with the paper to be read. Darwin could lose priority. So Darwin got a paper read. Priority and credit was important. The Wallace-Darwin theory. Wallace had been in South East Asia. Darwin suits the dominant science and commerce better.

Wallace was sick in Asia and began to hear of reports on mesmerism and so forth. Convinced there was something else. Reported on the evidence for supernatural, attended séances. Darwin thought this was dangerous for the theory, Wallace gullible. Interested in materialisation of spirit beings and stuff still edgy today. He worked with Crooks and others, saw levitations and strange things. His research would influence his idea of human development. So his theory was about an incarnation of consciousness greater than physicality and accident. Pure consciousness comes into this realm. Agency of evolution would have to be re-examined. Still as the day showed there was an important point. Order of the Green Carnation was here.

Axiom 6 **While spirit and consciousness is the highest thing that should evolve, we need to function with the mortal and mundane aware of other consciousness.**

She knocked on Mary's door.
 "That was grand the other night."
 "You didn't mind the fight?" Mary asked mischievously.
 "What... mind the fight?" She laughed.

Often fights in the pub. One place where she had met Irish Travellers. These were respectable. She knew some others elsewhere kept workers like slaves, the rhino horn, the paving, the litter and so on. One had introduced himself. His wife was there so there was no problem. She talked and met them some while ago. Some very interesting conversations. Mary loved the fights even though in her eighties you wouldn't expect. Her friends were at home scared. Buzzing in the thick of it. Despite the negative things, interesting there were so many big men among the Travellers. So many good boxers, Irish and English. An old form of masculinity which seemed to contain violence through its acceptance. See less masculinity and more weakness. Something odd about the police.

Ash wanted to focus on her consciousness but must attend to real, external forces. Something not right. She would keep an eye on the customers and screen a little more. She thought of stalkers. Suppose if you get known you get vulnerable. If you sell attractiveness too hard you won't be able to stop the magnetic pull of idiots. Men who think you're addressing them alone. She rang Lucius.

"I listened to your Podcast about censorship last night, interesting about that group that rang in."

"Yeah, I don't know what to make of them. It sounded a bit like earnest university students but he was articulate and coherent which I suppose distinguishes him from many graduates. You never know. Listen by the way. I'm still getting loads of feedback about your stuff so that's great."

They talked for a while. Lucius finished the call because he had to feed his terrier Tessie. Otherwise he lived in Amsterdam with one of his lovers. No real wish to be married and had never found one person that satisfied him. Old and gnarly in his own mind. Old enough to remember meeting Quentin Crisp. Old enough to know all the Smiths lyrics. Used meet Morrisey now and then round here and George. Heaven knows I'm miserable now. How I dearly wish I was not here. What difference does it make? Happy in the haze of a drunken hour. Why did I give valuable time to people who don't care if I live or die? Last of the famous international playboys. Involved as an activist in some of the gay rights cases, particularly in Northern Ireland. Young people did not understand the history of oppression. Many now did not know or care who Oscar Wilde was. He copied him when he was young. Lucius got the attention he wanted. He transmuted his suicide attempts into a persona that was strong but vulnerable. Not the only gay in the village, but it was a bit harder.

Now one could be the only straight in the village. He was at odds with some of the current direction of the 'movement.' Didn't like the Clubs anymore. His motivation was to make the world grander but the Hydra of oppressive oligarchy had grown a new head with poisonous breath and that monster had the capacity to transmute and camouflage into the antithesis of what it really was to draw off the power of superficial thinking and emotion. A male who liked males and did not like boys or weakly camp wimps. Interested in archetypal resonance. Careful to hold back. Still a Catholic. His favourite gay man was Francis Bacon. Tough, successful, brutal, generous. Bacon would probably not parrot the clichés of gay lifestyle that were mantras of modern life. Bacon liked a rough sex life. Said that despair was better for an artist than contentment. Believed in the power of accident, chaos, chance. To convey fact you must use distortion. Said he should have been a con-man or a prostitute but that chance and vanity made him choose painting. Tubal thought about the goddess archetype in relation to gay men. Some of his friends disliked the idea of women being goddesses. They had appropriated the role. Women were so far away from their power that they could not see it as they sought to become male. He had grown to hate the pigeon-holing and now feared it. People are never what they seem despite the consistency of their utterances even when they appear to be on your side. He decided to take Tessie over to Regent's Park for a stroll. Had his shades on.

In the Park he had a sensation of someone staring. When you were as well-known as him that was common. You had to be careful. You did not want to be paying a ransom for your dog. There were stalkers, nutters. John Lennon came into his head for a minute causing a wave of anxiety. The figure came nearer. He had an impulse to run. The figure reached out towards him. He nearly fainted.

"Mr. Tubal?"

"Oh my goodness you frightened the life out of me. What do you want?" Lucius.

"I am sorry to be so bold Sir, but we really had no other means of contacting you."

"I have an agent, a secretary, a lawyer..." Lucius scowled.

"You see it's more about this LZLF stuff, I know you have heard about us."

"That might explain your goofy gear then. I hope I'm not one of your targets. Excuse me love but my dog needs a poo. She can't hold it any longer poor thing. Let me get my bag out." He grimaced.

LLLF

LONDON LOGOS LIBERATION FRONT

Publishing Pamphlets to Oppose Censorship of Our Message.
The Counter-Revolutionary to Evil and Terror Effort.
We share our thoughts simply to explain our perspective.

THERE ARE SECRET GROUPS.

THERE ARE WIZARDS.

THEY USE BLACK MAGIC.

THEY USE SPELLS AND WANDS.

THEY ARE PIRATES.

THEY USE TECHNOLOGY.

THEY LOVE MACHINES.

THEY MAKE SCIENCE MAGIC.

NEWTON AND BACON AND SOLOMON.

THEY USE CONCEPTS AS WEAPONS.

THEY MAKE SCIENTIFIC THE NON-SCIENTIFIC.

YOU ARE A MACHINE IN A MACHINE.

THEY MAKE YOU LOVE MACHINES.

NO ROOM FOR SPIRIT.

ELITES OWN THE MACHINE.

THE MACHINES OWNS YOU.

YOU HELP THEM.

PREPARE FOR LIBERATION

Chapter 11

Work Out

'Police in London said today that a potential threat to one of The Royal Palaces has been foiled. While details have not been released they say it involved a 'very serious' attempt to cause widespread damage to the Royal Family. Security has been increased and particular attention has been paid to possibility of air and even underground attacks. The Earthquake has allowed nefarious elements to take advantage of our vulnerability'

He listened to the talking head as he worked out. Royals always under threat. Shooting into football stadia at soccer stars had been new. No reasons. Read a report that it was a criminal gang. Probably just some nutter. Impressive shot. The Jackal. Michael Rose Croix needed to keep in shape to be able to concentrate on law books and cases. So he went to a gym in the City. Met people with a break from Chambers. Machines, repetition, dullards and posers and smell of rubber and stuff did not appeal to him but it was not the office, books, dust, wigs and wood. He did not like long pub lunches either. Loved English pubs with strange names, tiles, ornate woodwork done by people who had worked in churches with history, tales of ghosts, pale ale, bitter, cask ales, landlords and ladies, lunch, darts, characters, associations, old worn carpets, maybe a fruit machine. But they were becoming standardised dull chain affairs everywhere or lap-dancing clubs. Many were closing down. Soon pubs would be gone, like bear-baiting rings. Saddened him they were shutting adult places to protect women. They would have old-fashioned, medieval dress codes back soon for women if they went on. It was illegal to say such things. Feminists would see to that. The Soviet Hate Speech laws grew like Jack's beanstalk. On the treadmill training he heard conversations. Whispers about measures and someone who was detained. Some of his close colleagues had been enlisted in the enforcement of Emergency Measures and he heard rumours. Some appointed as 'praetors.' Newspapers got worse. More sport, soaps and specialist reports on the terrorist threats, lawlessness, riots and criminal gangs. Threats suggested were more outlandish. Hackers supported by Russia and China were attacking the nuclear codes. A threat to poison one of the biggest reservoirs in the UK with a nerve agent thwarted. An attempt to drop poison on civilians from a private airplane had been stopped as a result of a 'successful interrogation.' Seemed to imply severe methods of investigation. He had always thought, from his limited experience, that criminal gangs had State input. Depressing. He did not know whether to work out harder or throw in the towel. The rational, progressive, predictable, reasonable world was apparently becoming a lie. Despotism had never gone away, but only changed form. Forgetting about Masonic control and Royal network, amazing that some claimed they were shape-shifting reptiles. Though ancestors such as Vlad the Impaler and Mohammad, not to mention Henry VIII were actually more interesting.

Might sleep at the office tonight. London gone crazy with fires, muggings, vigilantes and police. He considered the law in his memory before he went looking for particular precedents that could clarify and help his case. Many employment cases were old 'master and servant' cases. That was the terminology. You worked for a master. Often little less than a slave. Master and servant legislation in the common law world once allowed the servant to be imprisoned for breach of contract. Employment law was master and servant law. Then the issue of liability. If you were a servant the master might be liable. Was an act committed in the course of employment or did they go off on a frolic of their own? Important in tort in England or delict in Scotland. Scotland was a mixed system of common law and Roman law, especially due to the education of Scottish in continental Europe. The servant had to obey lawful commands. Over time the more complex jobs were not specific command-based but the skilled worker still had to do what the master wanted. A lot of the master and servant language goes back to the Bible. Be obedient unto your masters. Masters should be just, although the feature of being able to command someone often meant that the master's obligations were forgotten. You see it in *Cymbeline* in Shakespeare. Franchises look like master-servant or employment relationships, but in fact are independent contractors. The close connection is not determinative. Here the defendants would be trying to use that principle.

He used to buy it all. Tradition, meaning, right and wrong, reason, enlightenment, service. Serve. Funny how people think they have to serve the State but that the State does not have to serve them. Ask not what your country can do for you… Funny how the relationship has been inverted. Secrecy is repugnant to an open society. Horace the

Roman poet. It is sweet and right to die for the Fatherland. *Dulce and decorum est pro patria mori*. That was the old lie as Wilfred Owen wrote in the trenches of WW1 before he died, considering the awful effects of a gas attack. Chlorine was the by-product of chemical companies and glorious scientists. Red Star. Then chemists came up with phosgene. White Star. Then mustard gas. Yellow Cross. Now they stick chlorine in our water to poison us and destroy our nervous systems. Always find a use for their waste. Fluoride. They needed it to make atomic bombs. Your sweet dentist, sweet chemist with her nice white coat and gentle manner, poisoning. Monster, military-industrial complex, servile professions, guilds, jingo journalists, cronies, still going on about Russia. Professionals leave their daughters at school speaking gently and then make weapons of war. Let's play master and servant. Depeche Mode. Domination, master servant, a lot like life they sang. Odd where you find the truth, a discarded shard in a mountain of fragments. He felt the cliff and the long way down now, he saw it and was fearful of the fall. The Fall. Faltering with halters he wondered how long he could avoid the flight from further discontent. An overweight guy on the slow treadmill beside him had said to his mate,

"The authorities are just doing what they need……. Clamping down. The conspiracy theorists are having a fucking field day…. All nonsense. From Kennedy shot by CIA… To no moon landings. To Flat Earth. Lizards to 9/11. Truthers. Flying saucers. Chemtrails. Illuminati. Diana. Hitler in Argentina. Gods in UFOs. New World Order. A hidden city under Denver. Bermuda Triangle. Israelis using spying animals. Harold Wilson a KGB spy. Turin Shroud…… It's all nonsense….. Anti-Semitism, like the spurious Protocols of Zion. Anti-Catholicism.... They need to study science…... Common sense. Rationalism. Dopey idiots. Half-wits."

Michael thought about it in the shower. Conspiracy. Conspiracy theorist. Idea that there was a conspiracy which explained something that happened or did not happen. If you say a conspiracy theory is not backed up by evidence or wrong, then you are saying it is a bad conspiracy theory. Conspiracy theories are consistently found throughout history. Nero and the Great Fire at Rome spawned many. Because you call it a theory does not mean that people are not colluding for nefarious ends. Law presumes there are conspiracies. It knows that conspiracies exist. They are punished. Because a theory requires a conspiracy does not mean that it is false. That conspiracies are done by powerful forces is the point. All competition law around the world presumes this. The Sherman Act in 1890 in the US was brought in to break up monopolies and conspiracies. Standard Oil. Conspiracies in restraint of trade are illegal. The law does not require you find express agreement because they know it is very difficult. Why conspire? To substitute co-operation for competition. To get more profits than you otherwise would get. The big boys do it, in secret obviously. DOH. Same in EU, UK, whole world. Had people not heard of Stanley Adams, the whistleblower that revealed the illegal price practices of Hoffman La Roche? All companies will collude if they can, as companies in a 'dominant position' may abuse it. Economic dominance allows companies do things that other companies cannot because of the power to behave independently. Like a mount position. Collusion, conspiracy, combination is real and law is testament thereto. Conspiracy to murder. Conspiracy to defraud. They used it at Nuremburg. The State and puppet hacks who say they are fighting conspiracies then claim any suggestion of conspiracy about them is ridiculous. He read *The Manchurian Candidate* about a mind-controlled assassin. Led him to Sirhan Sirhan and the death of Robert Kennedy. Member of the Ancient Mystical Order of the Rosy Cross. Meant to be hypnotised. A woman with polka dot dress. Not sure how persuasive the evidence was. Long shot the lawyer ordered. Like Svengali Defence. A short shot in the end. He also read that the CIA had come up with the idea of ridiculing things as 'conspiracy theories.' The letters CIA are in the word conspiracy. He had done some acting as a law student. It felt like we are all unpaid extras in a plot we have not been told about.

 He thought about The Razor's Edge. A headline for the slashers and knife crime that defined London for years, which the do-gooders seemed to want to persist for their own perverse reasons.

> *'Above the sense of sense, So sensible*
> *Seemeth their conference. Their conceits have wings*
> *Fleeter than arrows, bullets, wind, thought, swifter things.'*

Fleeter. What was the razor's edge for Shakespeare? It was *'the tongues of mocking wenches.'* But for Somerset Maugham it was the narrow path to salvation. It was indeed keen and cutting a smaller hair than may be seen. This here was a much older one. The razor's edge was on the way to the solution. But he was only thinking of the easy part of it. The mocking wenches may once have been just as sharp. The heart scarred helps show the narrow path. Now men pay for the cutting remarks. Find it fun. The easy part was feeling more attractive.

LLLF

LONDON LOGOS LIBERATION FRONT

Publishing Pamphlets to Oppose Censorship of Our Message. The Counter-Revolutionary to Evil and Terror Effort. Pardon our teaching methods but we provide education to parallel our actions.

IT IS ALL DOMINATION AND SUBMISSION IN MEDIA.

THEY MAKE YOU LOVE SUBMISSION.

THEY MAKE YOU LOVE SUBJUGATION.

THEY MAKE YOU LOVE SUBSERVIENCE.

THEY POMOTE MORAL WEAKLINGS.

THEY RIDICULE MEN.

THEY PROMOTE MOUSY BOY-MEN.

THEY MAKE WOMEN WANT TO DOMINATE.

THEY MAKE WOMEN WANT TO HUMILIATE.

THEY MAKE WOMEN WANT TO BE MEAN.

THEY MAKE WOMEN WANT TO CONTROL.

THEY MAKE MEN WANT TO BE CUCKOLDS.

THEY MAKE MEN WANT TO BE SUBMISSIVE.

SUBMISSIVES MAKE SLAVES.

SUBMISSIVES DON'T REBEL.

SUBMISSIVES KNOW THEIR PLACE.

REAL DOMINATION AND SUBMISSION IS NOT FUN.

PREPARE FOR LIBERATION

Chapter 12

Cloud of Unknowing - Contemplation

COMFORTABLY LIE, IMAGINE YOU ARE DYING DEAD

She sauntered the rather short walk for her to meet Erik. OBS-High. CYN-High. ANX-Mid. BIZ-High. ANG-Low. DEP-None. HEA-none. WRK-None. She could keep everything on an even keel very well. She knew she was hard-wired to follow all the leads, pull on all the threads. She knew she was obsessive but she did not see it as a problem. One of the indicators seemed to be about undue reflection on philosophical matters and the meaning of the universe. So a scientist does it and that's great but you do it and you're a nutter. Why can't we just be a bit obsessive with things. What person that achieved anything was not? They don't know what it is anyway. Neurotransmitters or something.

 Red Lion Square the destination that evening. A regular work-related doll chat. A group of 'Red Lions' formed in Birmingham, Ash recalled. On the way she passed where Bentham had lived. Odd. He talked however about egoism and sinister interest in Government. Seemed to be in favour of transparency so that everyone could see what you did. Panopticon. Few guards, see everything. His dreams came true this week. The State is a great Nosey-Parker. Apart from CCTV, the Emergency Jails they set up, pop-up pink cylinders and white cubes based on his ideas. Against religions. Against slavery and in favour of animal rights. His body was down the road. He wanted to be seen after he was dead. His idea of the 'auto icon.' Like Psycho. What strange view makes the dead empty skeleton significant? Said he had Aspergers. Everyone seems to have that. Autism led to atheism? Some say that Autistic people construct their own belief system. Different types of intelligence, neuroplasticity. Engineering, physical sciences, mathematics may be easier for someone with a 'disorder.' Is that related to the atheist-scientists-evolutionary hostility to spirituality or religion? Quants that ran the world often had Aspergers or Autism. Many top business people are dyslexic. Many entrepreneurs has ADD. The Lie, she learned. You tell the truth by giving the lie. To give the lie, to refute.

> *'Tell men of high condition,*
> *That manage the estate,*
> *Their purpose is ambition,*
> *Their practice only hate.*
> *And if they once reply*
> *Then give them all the lie.'*

Red Lion Square, interesting little place. Machen had his character living here in the horror story *The Great God Pan*. Was it Dyson? Curious the way the same names come back. A temporary emergency tent run by the Red Cross in it. A soup kitchen in the evening. Not too big. Surrounded by an eclectic mix of buildings. 400 years old. A statue and some busts in the park. Temporary 'Field Hospitals' in West London to deal with the surge in gang rapes and assaults where law and order had broken down. Walking by the Royal College of Anaesthetists. All around here. Persephone Books nearby and some nice places to eat. Max Planck seemed near her. Consciousness comes first, before matter. Some said the body of Oliver Cromwell lay here although nobody knows, after a switch. Head was not with it. September was when Cromwell died. Not his final resting. After the Restoration, his body and his son-in-law Ireton was dug up and executed again at Tyburn. Some say his headless body was buried in the Square and his ghost may be seen. Swap. Even in death, doubles complicate. September was a month of death for Cromwell. In September he attacked Drogheda with cannons and the Bible, slaughtering thousands including civilians. In September much blood in Dunbar. September 1st his forces massacre the folk in Dundee. Ireton, son-in-law, after was responsible for death and transportation. They robbed a great amount of gold in Dundee but the ships sank and were lost.

She visited the renovated basement where they kept the latest prototype in the red-bricked building. On the wall were front pages of the 'soft porn' Daily Sport and Sunday Sport with infamous headlines:

'DOUBLE DECKER BUS FOUND ON THE MOON'

'BOOTED OUT OF ISIS FOR WEARING ALDI TRANERS'

'FIND THE BASTARD WHO SHAT DOWN MY CHIMNEY'

'I'M NOT ISIS... I'M A HIPSTER'

'NEIGHBOUR FROM HELL ATE MY GUINEA PIG'

Probably the most honest of all the papers. She asked him whether he had heard anything about SimpCook, but he hadn't. Both working out where the value added was in this technology. Last decade had been a pro-robot, anti-human propaganda fest. Huge market. Primary market was selling them. Significant sub-markets in the technologies that underlay the dolls. Some renting them out by the hour and in brothels. Many people now purchased them, male and female. Prisoners were getting access to them. Some companies sought to utilise the likeness of celebrities. Celebrities sought to challenge unofficial use of their likeness. Others licensed their use. Thus a pop star might have thousands having their way with a copy. Many wanted to make certain practices illegal, saying it was anti-person, anti-women, even though many were male. Vibrators. People say they would never catch on. The Agency was going to explore high quality dolls. The value added would be through a variant of the unique therapy in the dominant woman market.

'Sexbot.' Neither liked that word. Anyway this was a remote-controlled operation. Like Telesurgery or Virtual Control of the doll or robot. Marionette. The robot was programmed to act consistently with some instructions embedded in language spoken to it in Bespoke mode. It could act independently, also learning through remote-controlled instructions. Combine. Working with the idea of the Avatar. Could you use a robot to act as a kind of surrogate or a near clone so the illusion is so compelling it becomes a new reality? Erik decided that one use would be associated with a real world adult Goddess. Remotely operated in a number of ways even by someone else and be linked to an existing business. Working out permutations. He purchased one that looked somewhat similar to Ash. They had agreed that it would mirror her general characteristics. She would work out how it might be used. Animatronical.

This one was not like her. Erik knew a bit about the S&M scene. Tried it first as a Master when he was desperate. A few clients, women and men. Hated it. Frightened him with their requests. Worse than any fantasies he had read about. A lot of pain and humiliation without any game. Notwithstanding his martial arts background he found it very difficult to engage in some of the things they wanted to do. He was opened-minded but shocked. Sometimes with the men. He concluded that there was a deep existential need to prove that there was something inside, that they lived so remote from their inner nature they had lost their way. Play he understood. In both cases if he was reluctant there were some that provoke so they would get their way and that was unpleasant. He quit very quickly concluding he was a puritanical prude.

"Listen I was reading about Tales of Hoffmann. It has it all. Even the Sand Man. Olympia is an automaton," Ash said.

"Well you're behind. Hoffman wrote the story. Nathaniel tells his poems and mysticism to a doll called Olympia that seems interested. He wrote a short story, the Automaton. I think the funniest thing I remember was that Olympia liked his poems. Nobody else really did. How's the other Ethel?" Erik asked.

"Somewhere between creepy and familiar. At least it will help me keep focused on the issue of consciousness. If in the future people start saying these things are conscious. When they pass the Turing Test. When they demand rights. I want to have thought about them. Familiar. Like with witches. Shamans use them too."

"They would be spirits?" Erik asked.

"Not necessarily. They could be places or things or humanoids."

"A goddess familiar. Implies it looks similar, it is known and it is magical. It might send out the wrong signal." Erik.

"Have you seen Pygmalion?" Ash asked.

"Yeah I know if I fall in love with it, my own creation."

"But if it is different from me, that works, if the same as me then that would be a lie. Art, the lie that shows reality."

"I am interested because I think the world is getting into the hands of techie geeks who value technology over people. People are dispensable and need to be culled for them. Technology is great, but…" Erik.

"I have been thinking about acting, theories of acting. Stanislavski, Strasberg, Vakhtangov. Two schools. Be yourself and come into the actor or identify wholeheartedly with the character. Identify or act. There's something in it. You perform the character or live through their feelings. It is relevant in my part of the business," Ash said.

"There's some thinking that acting's a lie, that it's less alive if you identify deeply." Erik.

"Concentrate on the game, audience." Ash.

"The dolly could be like a person or an avatar of that person and it does not have to be wholly alike but there would be a common aspect." Erik.

"Then you could get people to act in accordance with our instruction and program these things to do the same and then create the illusion of reality with some semblance of relationship inter se.

Providing they let us re-program. But we can build our own and there are published patents we can look at for inspiration," Ash suggested.

"But that will be standard. So it would work if we have say some of the principles of Understated. Real Tulpa."

"Have you ever heard of Edgar Bergen?" Ash asked.

"No. Don't recall anyway," Erik replied.

"He was a ventriloquist. Had characters he called Charlie MacCarthy and Mortimer Shard. Got a dummy made in the likeness of an Irish boy. I heard an interview where Jean Houston said that she went in as a girl and heard Bergen, his parents were Swedish. Said he was asking the dummy questions about the meaning of life and everything and the dummy was answering. Her father was a bit surprised but then amazingly it transpired that he said that the dummy gave its own answers. How is that? Does the brain believe that there is a separation in those situations? The ventriloquist was surprised by the revelations of the dummy. Dissociation?"

Erik nodded as he listened. He was a good listener. "Colin Wilson. Said we all have a robot in us. Let it get over 50% and life is hell. Sounds right."

They had looked at many films. Old and new. They saw the remade Battlestar Galactica. AI doppelgangers. The film The Prestige.

"My favourite Wilde. Written in the jail. *Most people are other people, their thoughts are someone else's opinions, their lives a mimicry their passions a quotation* and Jane Eyre said, *Do you think I am an automaton? It is my spirit that talks to your spirit?*" Ash said.

"Training someone to be a good dominatrix, especially if using a system, you need a conceptual framework. People like Vakhtangov developed systems or frameworks that can help. You need some general guidelines with flexibility for intuitions and spontaneity. Otherwise it's a robot, undeveloped. You keep a central element, exaggerating certain elements somewhat. But we keep in understated. That relates to the Understate, a sort of equivalent to a subspace, but a temporary position of a game," Erik said.

"If she is programmed by you, although she looks like me, she would be your agent unless I operated her and she is my agent?"

"It depends on the scope of the ability to respond," Erik said.

"I was thinking about words. Volva was Kepler's word for the earth in *Somnium*. Valve. Vulva. Vulva comes from the word to turn they say, as in revolve. In your mind turn over. Volvo. Vertere. Inversion, perversion. Turn. I see something there."

"Maybe... The blue doll is a beautiful lie," Erik said.

He went to make a coffee. Spotless flat. They talked some more. Looked at some figures. He liked, she loathed them. She left before it was too late to drift leisurely home with the rhythm of the walk allowing her time to think as she watched the people in the shop lights. Ash was taken with the concept of mysticism. What did it mean? Clearly close to mystery, mysterious. Disputed origins. Something concealed or hidden. About individual experience and therefore objectivity was difficult. In the Christian tradition there were certain influential ones. Unknown author of *The Cloud of Unknowing*. The Church tolerated, but did not promote mystics who focus on the internal journey. That is something not controlled by a priesthood.

Concept of mysticism attracted her as she was becoming open. You can read about the concept of Zen but not understand it. Be a Professor of Zen and not really get it. Do yoga every day and miss its central claim. Go to mass every day and forget the centrality. Engage in all the rituals, but miss it. Enlist any amount of priesthoods, gatekeepers, gurus, advisers and never know it. Experience, feeling as well as the mental and behavioural element. Try a psychomantium and not get it. You cannot measure it. Scientists lack the capacity to get to the heart of it. Those that are of that ilk do not like to be measured or reduced. Maslow discovered highly actualised people got to the peak but were not too inclined to engage in a sort of justificatory explanation. Then he began to understand it was a plateau you could get to. But the ones who do not have capacity are not in a position to explain processes of those who do. By Russell Square she reflected on how quickly things had changed since she was last there.

Never confined to one place, religion, philosophy, set of beliefs. All people realised that there lies within them a higher level of consciousness. Science trying to get to grips with consciousness in recent times. Cannot say much, pin it down, measure it or where it comes from. *'The hard problem of consciousness.'* Say it is emergent, out of a range of complex factors. Like the Big Bang. We can prove it. What happened before that? How do you know? All traditions have a sense that there is a natural inherent power, primal consciousness. In everyone. Needs tending like a seed. Divine spark. Divine fractal image. People accept a soul and the spirit or the spirit world. Philosophy starts off as a love of wisdom. Over time love and wisdom seems to disappear. In all endeavours the rise of the mechanical, mechanistic, empirical, rational at the expense of the primal, pristine, primary. Science makes things. They robbed

Enlightenment. They cut consciousness. Machines help destructive impulses. Individuals look at themselves. Purify, detach. Have good relations externally in an illusory world. From Gnostics to The Matrix. Many had mystical paths but were evil. Hitler and the Nazis were fascinated with the occult, sought esoteric knowledge. A simple distinguishing factor in intent. Murderous tyrants. Stalin trained to be a priest. That they were representing the negative, infernal evil way does not mean it is not powerful. Indeed a severe miscalculation to ignore force that drives people. Musical shaman touching other realities. Then you have rock and roll constructed on occult. More homeless than ever round Euston.

Mystical course was union with divine. Hard. Reaching top consciousness. The ladder, divine vehicle. Read all she could and found more about it from Plato, Plotinus, Hermes, Patanjali, Theresa, Saraha, Ficino, Pico de Mirandola, Swedenborg, Strindberg, Philip K. Dick. The drug-induced way did not persuade her although it might open new realities. Martin Luther King wrote a paper on the Mystery Religions at Seminary. Spoke like a mystic, in a prophetic way. Buddhist mystics and Hindu mystics recognise the higher powers that emerge when the mystical path is taken. Not important to most of them. Peace of mind, inner quiet, contentment are a by-product. The story of mystics is of them coming back into the world to operate amphibiously, part of them in another world but able to accomplish things. Some may purely seek isolation, but it is not the real way. Why would a person develop their mystical self? Antidote to the ennui, meaningless, existential sense of despair perpetuated by a selfish, mechanical brutish or dominating spirit. Represents mystery of life and not the solution. Don't be on the streets too late.

She often flicked through her copy of *The Cloud of Unknowing*. You get the feeling and re-apply it.

> *'...and therefore take good heed unto time how that they spend it, for nothing is more precious than time.'*

> *'...and it is not a cloud of the eire bot a cloude of unknowing bitwixt thi and thy God.'*

All changes of spiritual consciousness depend on the Heart, *The Secret of the Golden Flower*. Focus on the compassionate heart created an expansive state chiming with universe. Intelligence may be multi-dimensional, linguistic, verbal, logical, mathematical, numerical, bodily kinaesthetic, natural, musical, spatial, interpersonal, multiple perspectival, intra-personal, spiritual. Analytical, practical or creative. Emotional. Fluid and crystallised intelligence. Adaptability key. The mystical dimension may impact on all kinds of intelligence. Strange dimensions show how people can expand. Highest form of intelligence the most mysterious. Niklas Tesla. Can intelligence penetrate into our existing one? Many mystics talk about shafts, spears, beams of light and associated understanding increase. Arthur Sullivan of Gilbert and Sullivan talked of the Lost Chord in the song for his dying brother.

'It flooded the crimson twilight
Like the close of an angel's psalm
And it lay on my fevered spirit
With a touch of infinite calm.'

Boehme a shaft of light on pewter dish, PKD a shaft of light on a delivery girl's necklace fish. Scientist might say it is hallucination. Philip K. Dick ended up believing the CIA were breaking into his house. He sounded alright. Maybe they did. Milk in the supermarket.

Most mystical paths require great discipline combined with compassionate expansion. Process of purification or purgation is a discharging of thoughts and concepts, a moving beyond. Emptying allows space for insight, intuition. Brain more a receiver, filter. Stops too much coming in. Mystics depress certain functions so that normal approach to the world is changed, to manipulate concepts of time and space. Or they pierce the barrier of illusion to reality beyond. She thought of another rule based on her thinking about these avatars. Military vehicles coming out. Drones. Helicopters. Home. Night was poured in a torrent as if from a suspension of broken blue seaglass. It seemed a feral thing.

Axiom 7   We must see beyond our projections and those of others, to the pure essence below.

▬▬▬
▬▬▬
▬▬▬

LLLF

LONDON LOGOS LIBERATION FRONT

Publishing Pamphlets to Oppose Censorship of Our Message.
The Counter-Revolutionary to Evil and Terror Effort.
The Revolution has happened.

WE ARE THE DAWN OF COUNTER-REVOLUTION.

THE REVOLUTION HAS OCCURED.

IT HAPPENED WHEN YOU WERE ASLEEP.

IT HAPPENED SLOWLY IN YOUR PARENTS' TIME.

YOU WERE WATCHING TV.

YOU WERE PLAYING COMPUTER GAMES.

YOU WERE DRINKING.

YOU WERE SMOKING.

YOU WERE ON FOREIGN HOLIDAYS.

IT HAPPENED IN THE SCHOOLS AND UNIVERSITIES.

IT HAPPENED IN THE NEWSPAPERS.

IT HAPPENED IN THE THEATRE OF WAR.

IT HAPPENED IN THE SECRET STATE.

IT HAPPENED IN THE LODGES.

IT HAPPENED AT DAVOS, BILDERBERG.

IT HAPPENED AT BOHEMIAN GROVE.

YOU WERE FED NIHILISM, EXISTENTIALISM, HEDONISM, MEANINGLESSNESS.

PREPARE FOR LIBERATION

Chapter 13

The Governors

Cranbourne had left D's office. The bulk of his work recently had been with the nexus between criminal gangs and terrorism. Cranbourne studied the sniping incidents that had gone on for nearly a year without a break and they talked about it. He believed it was someone that resented the fame footballers had and wanted a piece. Attention, big stage, big result. Security for sports events a nightmare now. Cranbourne gone, D looked down the sandy-coloured Thames. D had been to the Palace. Secretly. Had excellent access. Two reasons now. Firstly, he wanted to see what the Royals felt about the current State. The Palace often opposed other despotic power because they recognise it and people forget that. Like the Pope in the Vatican. Like Cardinal Siri who was elected but was warned off and did not accept it twice. Like John Paul I who was killed 33 days into his term of office. A conservative Pope against communism because it made people disobey Christ. The smiling Pope who wrote letters to Christopher Marlowe, Pinocchio, King David, Charles Dickens. Illustrissimi. A few years later Calvi leaves Rome, they murder him and hang him on Blackfriars Bridge at the entrance to the City of London. Likewise you could not trust many at the Palace, but it was better than meeting them with all the other fellows or brothers. Concerned about two threats to the Royal Family. One spurious, one serious. D was convinced from Intelligence Reports of a genuine threat. A Romanov nightmare scenario. Could The Sniper turn his sights on them? He was hearing uncorroborated reports about attacks on the Royal Family which sounded false. Maybe opponents of the Royals would use the Crisis as cover for an attack on the Crown? Why? Perhaps they are a source of power opposition. Mood was inscrutable in Buckingham. Assassinations caused worry. D was always sceptical about political and celebrity murders. When you heard that Trotsky was killed with an ice pick in the head in Mexico you knew it was not random violence. Not to mention the John and Robert Kennedy, MLK, Malcolm X, Fred Hampton assassinations as part of the Black and Catholic counter-insurgency.

D realised he had to be discrete with the other little sideshow. He knew the eco-obstructionists were Government run. He knew the Masons were into the big New World Order stuff. He knew there were real Satanist rings. We had used them. You never know who is doing what for whom. He did not trust Cranbourne but he had to work with what was there. Have to be a little careful lest someone question his personal interest in Ethel. This originated from a series of extraordinary meetings in the Service. They had been briefed, but content was thin. More direct involvement of the Prime Minster by-passed normal procedures. D never felt so marginalised. Others argued that this unique situation required action and was not the domain of Intelligence. Difficult to know what was happening. Looked like a coup d'état. Martial law in operation in places in the capital. A vacuuming of 'dissidents.' Uncertain where the emphasis was. Clearly rioters and looters should be dealt with. No problem with rounding up Jihadists. Difficult to see how they had escaped so long. Rumours he heard at his club were that they rounded up a range of miscellaneous, marginal miscreants. While there was some support for internment of 'looters' and even in extreme cases for execution, the harshest measures were not being directed against them. Many Judicial Activities Mobile, JAM, were used against people taken from their homes. Cross-checking he found them clean. Then someone talked about DNA. The rumour mill working day and night. Boaz, Joachim, Solomon. He thought of Bacon walking the streets here. Of James Maxwell who wrote mechanical paper 'On Governors.' A formula worked out by the mathematicians and social engineers explained to him. Started with Maxwell and added in Lotka-Voltera equations on predators and prey, artificial neural networks and a lot of other stuff. Cybernetics. Then Skinner and his Walden Two 'utopian' vision. You needed technocrats like Plato, Jesuits, scientists knew. A sea of symbols. D had no idea whether there was any merit in these things. End result was an algorithm which produced results that indicated actions necessary to control society in the event of turbulence. His colleagues at the higher levels seemed convinced. Chinese to him. It worried him that artificial intelligence might be directing some of the responses. He had known about some of the Emergency Measures but they differed substantially to what they had been told. Mistake most likely. More worrying was the possibility of a secret plan hatched without the consent of people like him who thought they were pulling the levers. Coup. People who believed that they were doing good for others. Being the uncommon group for the common good they usually feel entitled to do uncommon things. Bomb Dresden. Most government serves higher forces. Serving the people was a myth.

Although power imploded like a black hole towards the Prime Minister, D found it hard to believe that this individual had the vitality to direct it personally. A puppet through the ranks, all insiders knew. Who was behind it? Why were they pushing all the stuff about Semiramis and Isis? Promoting conspiracy theories. Fertile soil. Satan, Lucifer. The Skull and Bones Societies. Instruments to get the Bonesmen, the Bushes involved. Machines that had a head and bones and no heart. THEY used these clubs like the Bullingdon Club. In elections you have two former members against each other. Tweedledum and Tweedledee. More dumb than Dee. Then these dopes that follow the esoteric mumbo-jumbo in their Tombs are compromised, shown to be spineless and selfish. Fit the bill. Lie they use psychometric tests to get the 'Yes Sir!' police. Fit the Bill. Then we foot the bill. Was it possible he was outside the loop? History never tells you why wars begin or that internal tyrannies are forming. Power corrupts. What fool believed that the American Civil War was only about slavery? We are being set up again. That was why we killed Rasputin - the British Secret Service. He was against war. Set it up through puppet-fools, smiling slaves who are toothpaste salespeople. We lose. THEY win their blood. Then there was the Golden Age of the Governess. The Governors were the planets or stars. Once upon a time.

'Tweedledum and Tweedledee
Had a mighty battle.
And what was it all about, think ye?
About a penny rattle.
So nations foolishly make wars.
And loud their cannons rattle.
When oft they have as little cause as
Tweedledum for battle.'

LLLF

LONDON LOGOS LIBERATION FRONT

Publishing Pamphlets to Oppose Censorship of Our Message.
The Counter-Revolutionary to Evil and Terror Effort.
The Counter-Revolution has begun.

THE CONTROL SYSTEM ENTERED OUR HEADS.

THE JAILOR IS INSIDE YOU.

THEY IMPLANT THE MESSAGES.

YOU EXIST, THAT IS ALL.

THERE IS NO MEANING BUT MATERIAL.

YOU WILL BE TOLD WHAT IS GOOD AND BAD.

OBEY. DO WHAT YOU ARE TOLD.

NIHILISM IS YOUR NUTRITION.

HISTORY HAS BEEN RE-WRITTEN.

WE ARE ANTS THAT CANNOT SEE THE WHOLE.

NOW YOU ARE PROGRAMMED YOU ARE PUTTY.

THEY CAN MOULD YOU WITH TECHNOLOGY NOW.

THE ONLY LIBERATION IS SEXUAL LIBERATION.

SUCH LIBERATION IS NOT FREEDOM BUT LICENCE.

EVIL DRIVES THE ELITES.

THEY MIGHT EVEN BELIEVE THEY ARE GOOD.

ALL THEY HAVE IS DOGMA AND BEING CORRECT.

PREPARE FOR LIBERATION

Chapter 14

As Bluebottles to Honey

Saturday busy as ever. Cranbourne seldom worked then but had to now. Watch the football. Meeting Rebecca. Covent Garden looked nearly back to normal though there was a crew examining the Opera House. A chimney had collapsed nearby and a pile of rubble was one of many around the centre. Most people on their mobile, taking photos. Who looks at all these? When he was young they used to laugh at the Japanese taking photos all the time and the Japanese game shows. They were just ahead of their time. It was on the way. Hikokomori. Priming. Irritating emergency announcements bugged him.

'PLEASE MAKE WAY FOR EMERGENCY VEHICLES.'

'WATCH OUT FOR FALLING MASONRY.'

'THERE ARE TEMPORARY BARRIERS IN PLACE SO PLEASE BE CAREFUL.'

'THE LONDON UNDERGROUND ADVISES CUSTOMERS TO USE TOTTENHAM COURT STATION AS COVENT GARDEN IS STILL CLOSED.'

On an on. They were using robots in the rubble. They love robots. Tell you all the good things. More interested in the sex robots. Professionally. Thought it was a bit of a joke but changed his mind when he saw what was coming on stream. The little engagement with the private sector however was a mess. He had to meet Rebecca today. He liked clever women. Freedom loving. Uncontainable.

Not surprised about the Quake. But Brits are resilient. He understood risk and studied the chances and the history of earthquakes. A long time since something that is going to recur, recurs, just before it happens people think it has less chances of happening instead of more. Most people did not understand risk, that's why they could be gulled with all this vaccination rubbish.

Most people did not pay attention. Attention was easy to get. Easy to misdirect he knew from his magic tricks at parties. Most did not understand when they watched TV, that they were on sale. They paid for their attention to be managed. Paid for the relinquishing of their agency. People want to be slaves. Want to be told what to do. Accept predictable mediocrity. Worst fear is speaking in public. Fear death less. Jesus. Public were stupid. All the democracies around the world becoming the same. Two brands of soap powder, one red, one blue. Mainly made of the same two ingredients. One has 50% of substance A and 45% of Substance B and 5% of whatever you like. The other has 45% of Substance A and 50% of Substance B and 5% of whatever you like. You choose between the same stuff. Same dull duality everywhere, Democrats-Republicans, Conservatives-Labour. Extremes are all the same. People too thick to know how many alternatives there were. The ones that thought they were smart said,

'If you don't vote you have no right to protest.'

'Democracy is not perfect but the best we have.'

'We'll muddle through.'

Why are people surprised everyone is on a mobile? People cannot bear their attention to be unattended. That's why they'll have head-chips soon. Easy to inject them with ID tags. But they will do it voluntarily. Crazy. Suspected that happened already, like smart dust sky-dropped. Act like slaves, walk like slaves, talk like slaves, guess what? During the time of Elizabeth I the Dover Straits Earthquake of 1580 at Eastertime could have been 6, although the highest estimate was 5.9. There were so few killed then but we have high structures and deep tunnels. Mining and fracking cause seismic activity. London a rabbit warren. Thames Barrier out of action and with flooding of the Underground you would have a right mess.

Saw a group of teenagers dressed in black, some app on their phone. "Here was where one of the haunted places is," one said excitedly not looking up from their device.

Amazing occult nonsense. Bet they'll not see any in the daylight. Watched a vampire film with his daughter. You could not tell who the good and bad guys were. No surprise we celebrate the people we do. He could not understand the odd occult fascination. Fucking everywhere now. In the building where his office was, there was an occult bookshop once. People could not manage the material world yet thought they could take on the unseen. Fantasy. When you find someone's phantoms you press them. Play them like a puppet. Putty. Pussies. Believed in people like James Randi, Houdini. Guys that exposed it. The one who said the Emperor has no clothes. Sokal and

Bricmont got a nonsense paper published in a refereed academic journal because they had enough of pseudo-science in postmodernism. Social science sorcery. *'Transgressing the boundaries. Toward a transformative hermeneutics of quantum gravity.'*

He often quoted that. French philosophy tying us up in knots like Japanese bondage. Other chaps sent out free horoscopes in Paris to those that wanted it after an ad in the paper. Nearly all recognised something of themselves in the same one they got. That of a French serial killer. Religion the same. Could not believe it. Clear now that all those religions were set up by people who had mental illnesses. OCD, schizotypal behaviour. Rituals. Hearing voices. Get the militant atheists on the other side. On the spectrum. Stay in the middle and ignore them. Crafty he knew. World needed people like him. Not too bookish or in the clouds. Too many books, you do nothing. Sip sugary syrup of your mind. Well-read people cause problems. Asking wrong questions. Like in favourite film Fistful of Dynamite. Juan Miranda says to the IRA man that the people who read the books start the revolution. They say to the poor people that they needed change. Peasants go and fight. The book readers wait and sit around polished tables and talk and poor people die. Mexico. Betrayal is the most predictable of all human traits. Worse now. CIA transports cocaine and facilitates the drugs war. Poor people go to jail in a moral panic. Drug lords hang people from the bridges. Learning from what we used to do down the road in London. All the bridges would have heads on pikes.

Clever people cause problems, simple people solve them. Smart arses complicate. Know-it-alls tie knots. Simple people cut through. He did not believe in God. He did not say God did not exist. How did he know? Interested in what was predictable, worked, makes sense. Empirical. Pragmatic. When you have an issue, look at it from every angle. Know what you have in your hand, strengths, possibilities and limitations. Guess what others have. See what was dealt. Note them. Make educated estimates. Watch for bluffs. Bluff when time is right yourself. 'Clever' people are not really intelligent and simple people are not stupid. Bullshitters get on in organisations, real people live in their mess. Academics look like serial killers. He could read microexpression and he could detect that they were often nutters. Buried away reading all the nonsense till they go mad, for some sneaky little present to please their masters.

People that think they are good at systems are often not, people that are good never bother. Fools rush in. Big mouth ignoramuses think they are better than quiet geniuses. Ideologues are one trick ponies kill millions, pragmatists beat them. Treat me like a fool, you might end up on your arse. Don't underestimate the bite of a mouth whose teeth you have not seen. He would beat many clever people at poker. Good at reading people, inscrutable when he wanted to be. People underestimated him. Pissed him off but gave him an advantage. Beat many at grappling. Cauliflower ears. Proved right on many things. Astute fox-like intelligence. Appraise a situation quickly, distinguish the relevant from the rest. Wanted to shift into more research. Problem was that they left these things for eggheads. Covert Techies section. If not the techies, professional researchers. Then the guys who worked across the board. People who studied things at university got preference. Even if they did not know their arse from their elbow. Annoying. Galling to have to listen to some numbskull boring you with ideas that had no grounding. Speculative in an incrementalist way and tentative as new born kittens. He was a panther. Got the scent he stalked and downed his prey. Wanted to apply his instincts to problems on the horizon. Knew he was good at saying what was going to happen. Evaluate. They thought you could only do that by reading people who lived in ivory towers. No wonder we fall behind. Always caught by surprise, pants down. Too many resources spent on insignificant targets. Too many police and intelligence officers looking at things they should not be. Too much time on computers. Granted you have to document and record well, but get it done. In the Secret Service they knew he was good at interviewing possible intelligence officers and at handling certain agents, particularly ex-police and so on. Had a few people on his books that were right lemons. How they got there was another story. Something to do with secret societies. Complained, he was brushed off. But he would sort it out. Always did. He could play bureaucracy like a lute. Some tests done in this office. You never knew what was going on. Many of the people being put through the testing were under the apprehension that they might be working for the Ministry of Defence.

Godfrey Ezekiel Cranbourne ate without relish the soggy sandwich with relish he had purchased in a shop on the way. In a hurry, irritated. Bureaucracy a real irritation-inducer. Counter-instructions, mutually incompatible policies, lack of boundary delineation and constant niggles. These bugged him and he found it hard to let go. He tried listening to all kinds of relaxation videos. They drove him up the wall. Now he had a regular briefing with the Liaison Officer who operated in the City Economic Crime Squad. He had just met 'D' one of the elite. Some of the highest levels operated in the shadows. Impossible to put the full panoply of State Intelligence on display. Many 'heads' were only for the sake of public relations. You felt vulnerable when you met these chaps, despite the bonhomie. Always a very limited view of reality. You may not understand what you are doing or why. Always forced to rely on the principle that they knew what they were doing. Often times difficult to see precise value of the strategy or tactics applied.

Godfrey was extroverted, had high self-esteem, individualist, competitive and patient. Not conscientious save in getting his job done. No problem telling lies. Manipulative. Heart was cold. But he was open, tough, fearless, creative and energetic. He had read that James Bond had these traits. In a magazine. I can do Bond. I may not look like him, but I can act like him. He knew from Law of Attraction that you had to act like it for it to happen. Tried to be charming and it worked. You laughed, listened, made certain gestures. Charming only means that someone thinks you find them interesting. That will be an unusual experience for the allegedly charming, because often they are not. Not a psychopath, he said to himself and did not care if he was anyway. The country needs people like that to keep it sane.

I must stop eating this stuff he thought looking at the ingredients. He had only had a cup of machine coffee otherwise. Expected more. D was unmoved still with his nano-technology concerns. Too vague. It did not relate to terrorism, espionage, cybersecurity or weapons of mass destruction. Lots of other specialists working on it. Always someone else who had the responsibility or jurisdiction. No that's a matter for the Secret Intelligence Services (SIS) not the MI5. Then all the others. People working on that I think at GCHQ. You could never find things out. Some matters were for the police, right-wing extremism. Left-wing subversion was let go. Terrorism is still always seen to be rational and irrational motivations ignored. Then you had the Home Office, the National Crime Agency, Her Majesty's Revenue and Customs, Ministry of Defence and Foreign and Commonwealth Office. Some matters were dealt with by Covert Technical Operations Specialists and obviously not Operational Intelligence Officers. Then of course there was the Joint Intelligence Organisation, intelligence squared. But his argument had been that with new technologies by definition there is no expert, no specialist save the inventors. They may be experts in the technology, but not its application.

He had his unmarked office or broom cupboard in Covent Garden. Loosely associated with his cover of portrait photography when needed. Handy. The office in the attic in Covent Garden appeared to be a photographic studio or at least a fine-artist, bijou studio, rather than a big, commercial concern. Interviews often took place here. Some meetings with agents as well. Front. City was full of such spaces. Minimal paper work carried on there. To cover tracks, there were voluminous standard forms with generic information that you adapted and met any remote chances that someone with relevant authority wanted to check back on things. Certain information needed to be registered, he usually did that regularly at his central office at HQ in Thames House. A 'dolly mixture' approach worked. Some educational sessions used characters such as Bluebottle from the Goon Show who had been played by Peter Sellers to model effective distortions. Comedians knew how to make a distortion while retaining just enough links to convey information. In fact many comedians had worked for the State as agents and still do. Silliness and metaphor were useful human skills that the best algorithms had not cracked. Then again Bluebottle was a slang term for a police officer. The blue bottle fly inspired Shakespeare to talk about fly blown meat, meat with eggs from a fly in it. Good analogy for what the intelligence did and expressed the fear of what could happen to it.

Complicated when operations crossed paths. One secret operation was actually investigating another operation run by another agency. Amalgamation of some functions of organised crime, international and domestic espionage created overlap. Difficult to know or find out who was doing what or why. In relation to the IRA, organised crime and terrorism were linked. Money laundering was critical for all organisations, even the State itself. That was why they were involved so much in cryptocurrency. Then the James Bond scenario of criminals becoming the real threat seemed to be more real. Huge power could coalesce around individuals that were not 'political' but might decide to be when they had power. Henry VIII and the Godfather had much in common. Decisiveness, brutality, loyalty, changing alliances. And both were originally Catholics.

He got in about 10 minutes before the bell rang. He knew he was also losing interest, unsure why. He also had a liaison role on boundary delineation in relation purely to ongoing projects. Most of her work was on economic crime. London being so big, anything could happen.

"Nice to see you Rebecca. Welcome. Come in. It is upside down. Sorry," Cranbourne greeted her.

"Nice, you seem frazzled. Never met on a Saturday before but needs must," Rebecca said.

"Strangest week ever. Apart from that the usual. We'll get to the point. There seems to be a lot of strange things in the City. They were involved in a Quality Audit. Believe it or not. I am not kidding."

"Well maybe they use that for some other reason," Rebecca suggested.

"Probably not. But there are reasons. The separate forces seem to be concentrating and co-operating more. Finance, tax, explosives, arms, drugs, subversives, intellectual property for God's sake. They are getting closer all the time. So there are often regular boundary demarcation to clarify who is doing what and whether that boundary is right or needed. Now it seems to have happened with the troubles," Cranbourne said.

"You wouldn't believe it. I am meant to liaise with authorities like you but there seems to be another liaison system that sprang out of nowhere in the City. I'm elbowed out a bit," Rebecca said.

"We seem to be just doing the projects we have. They seem to have cut us out with the Emergency. So they are looking at the red light entertainment domain. Prostitutes, lap dancing, escorts, massage partners. And wait for it, use of robots in the sex trade."

"What do you mean?" Rebecca asked.

"There is a problem about who is running what and how the uses may be optimised in the future. Now the troubles have created a whole load of forces that are outside normal parameters."

"It's not the first time we have to lie back and think of Britain or take one up you-know-where for king and country, metaphorically or actually for some. Do you think it relates to the talk about more restrictions on prostitution?" Rebecca asked.

"Partly. No one cares about women. I think there are more boys and men on the game from what I can see but the public fall for this stuff."

"So what's the point? Control people, have them not talk about other things. Blackmail more politicians. Get the world ready for sex-bots," Rebecca said.

He squirmed a little. "Anyway, I am sure there are good reasons for it. There may be fears of double agents. They need a presence. There seems to be a big Saudi and Russian control of parts of the escort business. Maybe they are afraid too many of us will be captured. It seems that there is a lot of interest in the management of sexbot, sorry I don't know."

"Or maybe they're just pervs," Rebecca laughed.

He laughed and continued, "The opportunity to use these things as spies is enormous. Listen, see, collect samples. So it seems that they want in. They want to know who is doing it and why. They want us to be at the forefront, offensively and defensively."

"Any progress with your nanotechnology stuff?" Rebecca asked.

"I think they think I'm a crank," Cranbourne said smiling.

"I see." Rebecca.

"Do you?" Cranbourne.

"I don't know enough about it." Rebecca.

"Some are real, some are false. Nanotechnology is the greatest threat to the planet. Not nuclear weapons, the environment, terrorism, the Middle East, Russia, China. The misuse of nanotechnology is the biggest threat. The biggest threat comes from the smallest. All the other stuff will be parlour games. No one is interested. Did you know that the Romans used nanotechnology nearly two millennia ago? They made vessels that could change colour because they had gold and silver dust in the mixture," Cranbourne said with a little passion.

"Fancy a coffee." He changed the subject.

"I had an idea about that," Rebecca said.

They left the office and went outside. Having a coffee and sipping it outside while the crowd milled, just enough way from the street entertainers so they would not annoy them.

"What a bloody racket! Did you notice how bossy these street entertainers are these day. It's like we're serving them," Cranbourne said.

"Did you see that stuff in the River today?" Rebecca asked.

"Yeah the schoolkids doing those pranks again pretending they are terrorists or rebels LZFL, LZLF or something."

"They put a lot of dye into the Fleet and it turned the Thames red or more pinkish. They said it was a fulfilment of Merlin's prophecy that the Thames would become red with the blood of thousands." Rebecca.

"They've been pissing about in the City, making mischief I see. They'd want to be careful. I'd warn them if I could to not get sucked into our Reign of Terror Lite. Playing with fire the poor buggers." Cranbourne.

"Their goose may be cooked. All these groups have informers and infiltrators apart from the surveillance. I think many are our set-ups. Then there's that Logos crowd. I thought it was some Christian nutters but apparently the Muslims are into Logos too, whatever that is. You have seen our control room. You can't pick your nose without attention in the City. Anyway. This investigation or study or exploration in the adult entertainment business. Why not link it with the nanotechnology?" Rebecca asked.

"I'm not sure," Cranbourne replied.

"There has to be a connection between dolls and nano-technology."

"There is now you say it. You're a genius," Cranbourne burst out.

"What is it?" Rebecca said smiling.

"Yeah nanotechnology tissue transfection. It's about the injection of cells. Nanotechnology is key to stimulating brain microtubules. That's where the conscious chip might come from, by the way," Cranbourne said.

"Funny how you can hit the target when you don't aim and can't when you do."

He wanted to get a transfer into research where he had started. He had liked being engaged in some early thinking on futures of drones and such things. Dangers. Technology was seen as a saviour by his colleagues. He saw it as a beast that could easily turn on its supposed master. The crowd would be appalled one day when the lion shut its jaws on the lion tamer. He saw the uses of robots but was suspicious of the operation. Where you had teams that had inter-agency co-operation, it always got a little fuzzy. They focus on who, what, when, where, why. But people forget the how. That was why so many people could get away with cheating in poker. They talked some more. They had no issues to report to each other from their respective jurisdictions. He liked her. She leaned very close and whispered. He could smell her breath and perfume in the sunlight.

"Listen I know we're just meant to keep an eye on ongoing project overlap. But there are weird things going on in the City with the Emergency Measures. It's brutal. If the things I hear are right then..... I don't know what's happening but there are people in control who I have never seen before. Secrecy within secrecy within secrecy. But it's brutal. Keep an eye on it. It's not just about dealing with the Emergency. There's some superforce abroad."

"Maybe we should try a little LSD to prepare us... time is a thief." He laughed like Dr. Evil.

He had an unusual thought later as he locked up. If androids are among us they will look more like the old guy on the Isle of Dogs that nobody really pays attention to, talking in meaningless riddles and quotations, than Rebecca. Over a certain age nobody looks, you can move funny, act strange, repeat yourself, forget things. Still inscrutable. Aged skin. Like a mechanical copy. Maybe that was the misdirection.

LLLF

LONDON LOGOS LIBERATION FRONT

Publishing Pamphlets to Oppose Censorship of Our Message.
The Counter-Revolutionary to Evil and Terror Effort.
Unite your hearts.

THE REVOLUTION WAS A CULTURAL ONE.

THEY DECIDED TO ATTACK THE INSTITUTIONS.

THEY CAPTURED THE INSTITUTIONS.

THEY SUBVERTED THE INSTITUTIONS.

THEY INFILTRATED THE INSTITUTIONS.

THEY INVERT GOODNESS.

PEOPLE WERE FOOLED.

WE WERE GULLED.

THE CULTURAL REVOLUTION IS PERMANENT.

PERMANENT REVOLUTION CAUSES CONFUSION.

CONFUSION ALLOWS HYPNOSIS.

HYPNOSIS ALLOWS INDOCTRINATION.

INDOCTRINATION REDUCED YOU.

INDOCTRINATION DENIES DIGNITY.

COUNTER-REVOLUTION BEGINS IN THE MIND.

CONSCIOUSNESS STARTS COUNTER-REVOLUTION.

BE CRITICAL.

PREPARE FOR LIBERATION

Chapter 15

Brigid – Interstitium

NEAR DEATH EXPERIENCE MEDITATION PREP

You can meditate into an NDE if you are experienced enough. That better wait. Dear Lucius. She had another radio interview today. Monday 8th. The date Star Trek first started in 1966. Dreams the same. She woke up irritated. She had good control over fear but not irritation. A dream of immobility, obvious in one way but not what it was about. Sceptical about fixed interpretations. Clear. Something not happening. Immobility. Woke her sometimes. Managed to intervene lucidly in the middle of the dream. Her old obsessiveness. She had conquered it's triviality and mastered its possibilities. The radio was banging on about chaos, emergency, restrictions, shortages, rations. The only non-emergency discussion had been about the interstitium. Amazing that there was an organ that all the mechanists had missed because their scientific method did not allow for it. Imagine how much more there is to be gleaned about consciousness and the spirit. Many undiscovered networks in and around us. Ether of old coming back sounding less strange in the age of quantum mechanics. The Buddha and his analysis of suffering was right, but avoidance was not the answer. Buddhists understood the mind. The distortion of Christianity so you should suffer was wrong. That we create, tolerate and perpetuate suffering is the problem. Brigid was insisting that the celebration of war on some warped scientific base such as Malthus was the sign of a monster. That could only come about when the powers of destruction defeated the maiden, mother and the crone. Witchcraft persecution was to defeat the wisdom of the crone. The twentieth century did away with the force of the maiden. Motherhood was being toppled. A sensation of being instructed in her dreams or the hypnagogic stage. Woke up one morning with her ability to speak French recovered for a while. Spanish came back. Most days she woke up with a name in her head. It might be one she never heard of. Books on receiving hidden knowledge interested her. Tesla, extra-terrestrial beings, angels. Synchronicities directed her to information. She felt prodded, directed. What did that mean? She was not interested in anything dark, possessive, destructive. Not certain that even the most discerning could divine what was divine or infernal.

Her name 'Ashling' was an Irish name for a vision. A type of dream involving a sky-woman who visits a poet and has a message about the political state. Skywoman with a vision. Like with rebel songs the tunes were there. Often the music had started out as something else. Some said that on the west coast the fiddlers learnt tunes by placing a light boat upside down and they could then hear the passing whale-song. Then she began to wonder about past lives. She had a regression but was sceptical. Did these things lie within or come from without? Did something else lie waiting in the leaves, in the meanings of words, facts, coincidences, history or shadow history?

She lay there thinking about the name of the month September and how it had seven in it. Sept. It was somehow a more relevant message, unnoticed before. Because she was aware that it felt significant. Sept, seventh, the seventh month of the Roman calendar. Seven universally significant, often seven stages of initiation. Septenary man, seven stages of Madam Blavatsky. Seven planets in old system. 777 Crowley. Septimania was a Roman province in the south of France that had been described at one point in history as a Jewish state by one writer. Interesting area, linked to the Cathars and Mary Magdalene, possibly from the Roman seventh legion. Septimus was the man who threw himself out of the window in *Mrs Dalloway* that Virginia Woolf wrote about a day in the life of London. Septimus who had flashbacks after WW1 and heard the birds talking to him in Greek.

Coffee. Septum was a membrane between two chambers like in your nose or your heart, a fence or wall. There was a septum in the spirit too. One level was the matrix around. The rest was above it, through mystical practices or experiences. The best was being able to use the two in parallel. She had felt herself rising through stages, unshepherded. There were natural stages of spiritual evolution, like in the physical world. Retaining ambition to grow in spirit, there had been movement to a whole level. You think you have cracked it and then a door opens and you find a different level. She wondered if this was fabrication at times, but realised also that doubt was the great chasm. September 1888 was the dark time of Jack the Ripper. Saptamatrika. Seven mothers. Goddesses. Saptanandi. Saraswati Sapta sindavah. She of the seven sisters. Seven rivers. Seven sages. Saptarishi. Seven tongues. Seven shaktis. Seven the world.

Gatekeepers seen as protectors. Poor bouncers indiscriminately exercising discretion. Some did their job. Worse still were the gurus. Nearly all of them were guilty of the things they preached against. Save us from the preachers, their examples are lousy teachers. Tantra interested her, until she realised that it had become something else. A certain smugness about many yoga and tantra people that bugged her sometimes. Instead of humility a cold haughtiness. Few indeed were they who left their ego behind as suggested by all the great teachers. The Lie.

> *'Tell zeal it wants devotion*
> *Tell love it is but lust*
> *Tell time it is but motion*
> *Tell flesh it is but dust.*
> *And bid them not reply*
> *For thou must give the lie.'*

The interview with Lucius was done at the studio in Camden Town as agreed, in her capacity as Ethel Woodpecker morphing into Goddess Blue Brigid 7. The radio show would be on the internet so people could see it. Standard brick background and two chairs. 10 minute walk. She regretted that she had not remained incognito. But she crossed the Rubicon. She would go for it, still very sparing in public engagement. Even her flat was not secure. 'Celebrities' are easy targets. People find out where you live and when you are not there. On the way up, passing all the charity shop windows she noticed a young man staring intently at her awkwardly. She watched him in the window as she pretended to be perusing the products therein.

Lucius was professional and he knew she just wanted to get on with it. Quick quake quack. They also discussed his interview with the LZLF which had made headlines.

"I was surprised that got attention. Out of the blue," Lucius said.

"But that's the type of stuff you do, isn't it?" Ash said.

"Yes. It's not my show that surprises me but what is taken up or not. It depends on a giant filtering process. A big pasteurising process kills most of the vital, good stuff. The public thinks that there is a natural flow that produces the flotsam and jetsam. But there is a huge, invisible net there. A political truth mill. You could read Chomsky on *Manufacturing Consent* or look at the propaganda model. I am not sure how it all works. But if your message is at odds with the big message you can only hope to be heard or seen at the margins. I am the margin to some extent. I walk a tightrope. You might get on my platform but where it goes after that is up to many gatekeepers and algorithms. They tolerate me as a kind of pet."

"You look tired," Ash said.

"Listen to this. I'm having the same nightmare. Three queues. One you end up hung, bleeding like in a slaughter house. The other you are surrounded by doctors taking your organs out. The last you are crushed. All this emergency stuff must be affecting me."

"I know how much you love animals," Ash said consolingly.

It got going quick after a brief discussion of format. She was non-committal. He did not mind.

"Just do your stuff. I'll field some questions, but not with too much conviction. They won't let me do this stuff much longer though it's fun and good for the ratings. They're onto us."

The interview started:

Lucius: We had a bit of reaction to your Templar observations. Most hostile. Many said it was re-hashed, disproved, ridiculous, pseudo and so on. What have you to say about that Ethel?

Ethel: It's unimportant. Speculation makes you look from one particular angle. Pragmatism makes you look from all. They were obiter dicta, things said by the way. Like why zero interest rates might be a trial run to tie in with Islamic banking. But my argument is about women and men and The Goddess as part of the fundamental question of spiritual evolution.

Lucius: Agreed. Perhaps you can elaborate on the relationship between your work and your deeper conceptions.

Ethel: One of the arguments of the MysticBlueDom Agency was that the goddess was a way of behaviour, a persona and not the dress and look. Mastery of the mystery of the mistress was mainly mental moulding. The muse often amused or rather bemused, befuddles, distracted and therefore inspired.

Ethel talked about men and how they liked to be treated and that it was calculated to be enticing, insinuating and interesting. She began to speak in the more disjointed way than had occurred in the previous ones.

Ethel: I will be creating a series of robots that are clones of me, so my clients can share in an expanded consciousness. With some I can be the puppeteer to my surrogate me. I want to liberate women through strength, but most women don't want to be liberated they want to be victims. Women protest their great strengths and then spend their lives hiding them away. Women helping women is done by buttin' out.

Then she found other voices coming in. Brigid was talking off on her own bat and a different voice.

> Francis Bacon was Solomon, Salomon, the Solamona, Sun and Moon, Sun and Soul. Bridegroom, Bride. Brigid is Bride. The soul is the Bride. Bride had been forgotten. In making useful boundaries Bacon created a wall that did not allow the mechanists see the greater beyond. Solomon's House became the Royal Society. You cannot understand Solomon's Temple, Thora or New Jerusalem without this. Numbers. Proportions. Even Cesariano.
>
> You must develop you own consciousness. Failing to do so will condemn human potential. I can help you. Liberate yourself. The small minded machine men are the ones to fear. California is cradle of consciousness. It will be the Caliphate of Consciousness. The Song of Roland was a prediction of weak opposition. Baphomet was the Templars coded reference to their new master. Misinterpreted by some Satanists. Meant to mislead. Mental mislead. Mental my lead.

Lucius: I have no idea what you are talking of but I understand it just flows so I listen when you do that. You remind me of Spalding Gray. Swimming to Cambodia. A bit before your time perhaps, but relevant... You realise most people probably think you are bonkers.

Ethel: I'm afraid I heard of him but know little. Anything with the name Grey, families or otherwise are often relevant. You must change the way you think. Embrace the rational and irrational.

Lucius: Interesting on how France and USA created the wars in Cambodia, Vietnam, Laos.

Ethel: Beauty, truth and goodness are gone Lucius. We have psychotherapy and drugs. They way of the soul is dead with the decadence. Wasteland. Disintegration.

Lucius: Many listeners say they get confused. Can you simplify it some way.

Ethel: Ok. Slavery comes when you have Finance, Arms, War and Control. Beyond slavery you have mindless drones. When you control culture and then consciousness you have drones and can cull the rest.

Lucius: Jesus. Time for a break.

It was taking over her. She could not stop. Lucius was somewhere between amused and flummoxed and shut up when the torrent came. She, or It, kept on.

Ethel: You have the image of the greatest in you, you have the consciousness of the highest, if you do not realise this you will be sacrificed to the gods of deception.

You are turning to destroyers, users and parasites instead of creators and facilitators.

You women should be like Brigid, Brigit. Brigit, Breeda, Britta, Bride. Same. You the bride. Not in a wedding with cake. Be married first to your self, then higher… But they have turned the goddess into a jailor and a prisoner. Look at the Bridewells all around the world. Name for a jail. In London there was the original Bride's Well by the Fleet. A holy well associated with St Bride, Brigid. Henry VIII lived there. Charles V, The Holy Roman Emperor visited there. It was given to the City. Outside the original Roman walls. Then it is used for disorderly women. They use the name for prisons all around the world now like a black magic mantra. Like Patrick to Paddy Wagon. They transform a holy place into a prison. Brigid is annoyed still and wonders why you allow yourselves be imprisoned so easily by words and concepts and ceremonies. Maybe the manhandling of the earth has caused a reaction. Bridie has become the bridle. There is nothing wrong with obedience if it is to the highest principles. You will always obey something. If you think you are to solve the world and ignore the heavens then you have the earthly kingdom and what some call the Judas Complex. Who do you serve? Who is the servant and who is the master?

Lucius: Is that just... serendipity?

Ethel: Well if you look at 1556 the Bridewell Palace became Bridewell Prison, just a year before Elizabeth comes to the throne. Ten years later the first Scold's Bridle or Gossip's Bridle was worn for torture, shame, punishment. The Kirk, the Church courts in Scotland promoted them. These branks or branks bridles were iron structures on the head of women with a gag on the mouth. This was not some deviant BDSM practitioner today but the Church and the Law. Coincidence.

Lucius ignored the frantic producer, carried on and came up with a question now and then, although it was better to let her talk. He knew his listeners liked this kooky, bonkers, berserk stuff. He had to appear as if he was following these complex rants. He thought it a particularly good question.

Lucius: Is there not a constant struggle like in yin-yang, between the feminine and masculine, not male or female? Is it not the case that this will go on forever?

Ethel: There is a message from mythology and the mythology of the future in science fiction. Some authors are pre-cognitive. They are telling you the future. They are not projecting the past onto the future or extrapolating from the past. Rather they see what the same stream does. So Joseph Campbell sparks Star Wars. Asimov seems to take the Roman Empire and turn it into the Galactic Empire. Star Wars has the Empire. Forces will not suddenly become benign because they go into space. Same stuff. Brigit was goddess of metalworking and poetry. Space travel is metal, poetry with mathematics. The phallic rocket of desire may be a saucer, a chalice, a grail. Depends on the spirit. But when the true feminine and masculine become so mixed up so there are no opposite poles, there will be psychological chaos. Paglia says that there is gender confusion before an empire falls.

Lucius: Are you against gender exploration?

Ethel: I talk not of such things. Let people do what they want. Choose. I suggest that London will never find peace when the Fleet is covered. Uncovered and beautified, as Wren wanted, it will trigger the return of the goddess. Normans were afraid of the vindictive saints of Ireland. Crossed them they would come after you. In the eyes of some, the pagan goddess of fire burnt the City of London in 1666 a hundred years after the King transferred it to the authorities and it became a prison. Like the river they tried to bury her.

Lucius: So they just let Brigid wither away?

Ethel: No. Elizabeth has magicians. Henry too. They may have performed a magic ceremony to banish old goddesses. They may have sought to invert what was there. You might say it is crazy, but then you would have to explain to me about the magic ceremonies used in WW2 to keep Hitler out. Then the Nazi magic. All that is recorded. Elizabeth's age was more magically orientated.

Lucius: So let me get this straight. You say that the Fleet River was somehow holy. That Brigid was somehow associated with the mouth of the river and was perhaps worshipped there. Then in Tudor times they break away from Rome and feel they have to magically banish.... maybe exorcise the ancient spirits here. Then they can utilise new spirits under their command?

Ethel: You could say that.

After the interview she went home for a coffee before going into town. Lucius seemed content enough. Years before at home one evening late listening to BBC Radio 4, there was a programme about a singer in Ireland with singing monks. She later met the woman. She now felt the same need to hear another voice and decided to have a Tarot reading. She was interested in it in cycles. Interesting to compare. Tarot. Waite. Black Magic. Ceremonial magic. She would bring a notebook. She usually wrote down so she could not be lead. She felt if someone was psychic because you can feel it in your skull, a warm, tingly fuzz. British Medical Association, was that where Skinner's Yard was? MEANT TO MISLEAD. That phrase stuck in her mind. She would have a Tarot Reading or two and a massage or two.

Just off Neal's Yard, up a stairs up from the Seven Dials. Land of the Worshipful Company of Mercers. Highest of the 12 Livery Companies. Why 12? Roman base 12. Apostles. Months. Patrimony or recommendation. Caxton, Dee, Gresham, More, Churchill. Mercers, Latin, 'merx' merchandise. Cloth. Livery companies referred to their garments. There before the Normans, most likely Roman. They were about trade, regulation, apprenticeships, secular. The Great Companies, The Chief Mysteries that ran the City, elected the Lord Mayor. Mercers, Salters, Goldsmiths, Skinners. The Mystery of Grocers. Said to be from the Latin word for a trade. Mystery, Craft. They gave them 12 estates as part of the Londonderry Plantation. Mercers got 33 square miles. *'I wander thro' each charter'd street'*

Like a call-centre. The woman was nice, she felt the warmth. When she chose the cards she took her time to feel it. The summary was good before, good after but a storm in between. She had a juice in fragrant Neal's Yard and walked down through Covent Garden and up to Watkins. Diagon Alley. Woman was in the window, with a light curtain. Warm feeling. Rider-Waite deck again. Same story. Present barometer is changing. Long term, back to stability. She did not know whether she believed these things. Useful as a magnet to draw your suspicions out. Since she had decided to be happy and content, it would not matter anyway. Sometimes other people can direct you to yourself. Books on Perennial Philosophy. Huxley. He lived up at Hampstead, Bloomsbury set. He died on the same day as C. S Lewis and John F. Kennedy. He taught Orwell. In New Orleans, Ash had a reading from a voodoo queen. Ash was interested in Marie Laveau. The woman had picked up bones and cast them over a green chart. The rotating hand nearly put her in a trance. She walked up to have a hand massage in Chinatown. Church of Notre Dame, Leicester Square. Odd. Cocteau did a mural there. Talked to the figures in the Annunciation when he did it. Used to be Burford's Panorama there. He lived in Camden.

Robert Louis Stevenson. *The Strange Case of Jekyll and Hyde*. Mani is not one but two. Freud follows. Stevenson dreamt up the plot. A dream. Dorian Gray and Jekyll and Hyde were similar. The Grays or Greys again. A public face and a dark other face. Two in one. Dark pulling the bright down. Looked at reflection in a window in China Town. Mirrors important. If you believed they were true then your world must halve. You could believe that they doubled it. They did not change it. Mystics used to stare at their right eye. You can use a mirror in a darkened room for spiritual experiences. Phileas Fogg, Jules Verne's House, where Sheridan died. Chandos Street, Florence Nightingale. Her and Fry. Clean it up. Don't mind the war, we have a job for you. Sanitise it. Bolsover Square, Norton School of Magic. The Slade over there, Eileen Gray. Gray. From Wexford, where the Normans went. Most expensive chair in the world. Eileen Gray laquer shop in Soho. The places were linked. Corridors of inspiration. Raleigh. The Lie.

> *'Tell arts they have no soundness*
> *But vary by esteeming*
> *Tell schools they want profoundness*
> *And stand too much on seeming.*
> *If arts and schools reply*
> *Give arts and schools the lie.'*

Had a 30 minute back-rub in Neal's Yard. Sourdough bread baked fresh - charred, hard, floury. Prodding hands took her away. Walked home by Marylebone Church to see if she could feel the supposed portal. Baker Street. Those that seek look for a nexus. Pillar, connection, ladder to higher realities. All spiritual traditions. Merkaba, the Uraeus the Pharaoh's crown, halo. Some think Merkaba is a UFO. Julian the Apostate could have been the most enlightened. We do not know. Create a higher link, that allows us live in the mortal world and commune with higher. That of ideal forms, Plato and Plotinus. The One, Holy Spirit for others. Convinced we need a mediator. Primordial, perennial, pristine. Inter-penetrating domain great artists and scientists reached. Emptying to receive. Know thyself. All Gospels were cut. We are afraid to talk of spirit lest we be ostracised. Spirit exists before religion. Priesthoods confuse matters mostly. Giordano Bruno had it. Say he was a spy. All in you. Saw it in obelisks from Egypt. Others thought these were to trap gods in. A genuine obelisk was properly one piece of stone. Monolithic. Hieroglyphics deciphered because of them. Circumference of earth calculated using them. Like needles in acupuncture. Dragon paths of earth. Movement from Egypt to Rome, Paris, London and New York and mirroring in Washington, magical captures of spiritual key, often by Freemasons. What were all those posters about? Stereotypes? Conservatives? A threat to my profession? Am I a threat to theirs? Do they mean reason? Is it Plato or Socrates against the Thirty Tyrants? 51. Area 51. Vico.

Axiom 8 **There is as much effort to hide knowledge as there is to reveal it. Secret orders create order in secret.**

LLLF

LONDON LOGOS LIBERATION FRONT

Publishing Pamphlets to Oppose Censorship of Our Message.
The Counter-Revolutionary to Evil and Terror Effort.
We are in the Last Chance Saloon.

THINK ABOUT WHAT YOU READ HERE AND RISE UP.

YOU MARCHED AGAINST WAR AND IT HAPPENED.

YOU TOOK THE MEDICINE AND IT MADE YOU SICK.

YOU LEARNED THE LESSONS WHICH WERE FALSE.

YOU LISTENED TO YOUR LEADERS AND THEY LIED.

YOU NEVER NOTICED POWER TAKE CIVIL SOCIETY.

YOU NEVER NOTICED YOUR LITTLE POWER DRAIN.

NOW THEY ARE READY TO COMPLETE THE TASK.

THEY WILL TELL YOU IT IS FOR YOUR GOOD.

THEY MAKE YOU CLAMOUR TO BE CONTROLLED.

THEY HAVE TAKEN YOUR LEGS WITH CARS.

THEY TAKE YOUR EYES AND EARS WITH MEDIA.

THEY HAVE TAKEN YOUR BRAIN.

NOW THEY COME FOR CONSCIOUSNESS.

RESIST IN YOUR HEAD.

RESIST IN YOUR SPIRIT.

RESIST IN YOUR COMMUNITY.

PREPARE FOR LIBERATION

Chapter 16

Turning Tables

The Last Shall Become First

By Wednesday she was surprised the interview garnered a lot of attention. Shared on esoteric and conspiracy websites. A lot of traffic on their own website. Decided to stay at home and take it easy. Interviews helped the business but were draining. Drank a fair bit of green tea, silver and played some cello. Bach, Brahms mainly and Beethoven cello suite. When she played Beethoven she did what she called an 'Identification.' Some actors act and some others try to be that person. Daniel Day Lewis. Stanislavski. Method. A different technique she had developed. With Rembrandt she examined his self-portraits and began to observe. She noticed fairly obvious things such as he always had a lot of clothes on and his cap. Colours sometimes reminded her of when it's cold outside. Rembrandt experienced the 'Little Ice Age.' Clues there. Then she studied his technique. Noticed how free and easy he was with mixing colour. Then she did her own version based on an identikit, blueprint, Projection in her head. The portrait began to almost come alive. A sense of travelling across time and encountering this individual. Then a mirror meditation exercise, staring at the right eye of her portrait with a candle lighting. Felt she was meeting him. Time delay on a long distance call. Non-local consciousness. Should she try that ayahuasca or peyote? Go to Peru. Mushrooms. No. Do it the hard way. Drugged you walk off a cliff.

Similarly with music. A bridge. Beethoven prickly, but sweet. But sometimes you must re-read with an eye for relevant detail. Scanning can be more productive than the spiel. The Oriental connection struck her, his familiarity with the esoteric, Egypt, India. Oriental there in Beethoven. *'I am all that is, has been and shall be...'* Seeing his interest in the Vedantic she could see Beethoven better, feel what the music fit into, sense elements of ego transcended. But now it was necessary to get a handle on something speaking through her and that was a little worrying. Logical thing would be to assume that her consciousness slipped into another mode. We do not control all our actions. Some reflex. Our best is often when a current takes us. On

Jesus she had come to the conclusion that issues were more about who sought to control the narrative. James should have been the legitimate successor to the Church, but the deeper conception of Jesus was in the non-canonical gospels that were taken out by the Romans. Aware of *The Cloud Upon the Sanctuary* by Eckharthausen. The Council of the Light, The Hidden Brotherhood. The Great White Brotherhood. The Great White Lodge.

Alien to her own consciousness. Different not bad. A pleasant warm feeling in her head when she had noticed psychic feelings in the atmosphere. The most immediate candidate for explanation was the Column of Dust. Could be a spirit, an alien intelligence she was channelling. Could be herself, angels talking through her, her higher self, some of those departed, enlightened masters, demons that seduced, convinced and then used you or a heavenly force. Maybe an hallucination, she was imagining it. Maybe someone put something in her coffee? A tumour? Electrical waves impacting on her. Maybe Goddess Brigid. Ash thought often how concepts of hypnosis, down, deep, dark, descending, falling, sleep were very underworld in their structure. Understate. Portals of meaning everywhere. Snow White, alchemy, magical beings, seven chakras, search for enlightenment. Sleeping powers in society waiting to be awoken.

Brigid seemed to be an ancient pre-Celtic goddess even transmuted into Saint Bridget. Imbolg. Her cult was strong. Three. Triple Goddess. Water. Purity. Wells. Wishing. The fire, sun, goddess. The inspiration, fire glowing within. Growth, life-giving. Blacksmiths, creativity. Home, heart, hearth, healing. Brigantia. Brigands. Healing. Midwifery. Cry for peace. Unifying. Poetry. Animals. Start of spring. Bridget's day. February 1st. Bridget's Cross. Blackberry. Oak. Heather. Fairies. Lioness. *'Anois teacht an Earraig beidh an lá ag dul chun shíneadh.'* Brigantines were supposedly an Irish tribe in Northern England. Then you had the Swedish Saint Birgitta named after Brigid. She was the richest woman in Sweden. Two days of thought about the figure. She imagined herself as Goddess Brigid. But her subsequent thinking shifted into a different domain. The leaves began to fall a little more from the tree behind.

Two historical figures whose paths crossed came to mind afterwards. Winston Churchill. After she had read most of what she could about him there had been a big question mark remaining. What was the nature of his religious beliefs? Churchill took part in many religious ceremonies and seemed to have always done that in a statesmanlike, dutiful way. He seemed to speak more of 'Providence' than God. He was interested in certain esoteric practices, such as the druids, freemasonry. A more interesting, mystical dimension that emerges at certain times. Churchill had a keen sense that he could foretell the future. An essay he wrote as a teenager presaging his role in saving his country. Stories of him saved in battle as if by his guardian angel or some other force. One day he moved from his common side of the vehicle as if nudged by an invisible voice. In doing so he escaped a bomb blast that would have killed him. The experience with the Boers came to mind. That is why we seek to see the contours of another life, particularly a peculiar one, so that we may derive some sense that relates to our own journey. When he escaped from the Boer prisoner of war camp, he wandered more in hope than anything else. Certainly driven by a sense of what he ought to do. Alone in hostile terrain with no real plan. Arriving at a house in Witwatersrand he knocked on a door. Surprised people hurried him in. Astonished firstly because they knew he was on the run. This was the only British family in the town. Churchill was luckier than explicable by mundane facts alone. Doubtless a scientist could demystify the experience. Churchill believed he was assisted in a 'providential' way. Such a belief can cause you to look and thus increase your chances of creating the miracle or coincidence or synchronicity. Churchill at his most vulnerable, in hostile territory believed that fortune would smile on him. Right. Churchill spent a couple of years in Dublin as a boy. He feared Fenians as a result, as Bacon did.

These links in the chain of destiny were forged by a coincidence of two other common, but important factors that recur in the interaction between peoples. The first one is the way small points of social contact can become critical in ways you never anticipated. Often the casual acquaintance created out of mere social goodwill ends up playing a disproportionate role in the outcome. Such was her recurrent experience. Such experience also underlay her belief in informal social intercourse and her perception of its undervaluing with the inflation of pseudo-interactions. Relationship entered into without any sense of mutual obligation or possibility of return often yield bonuses unforeseen. Obviously good neighbourliness might cover it. Secondly people make mistakes. Churchill was involved in intelligence. Sent to Cuba he was asked to keep his eyes open. This is a venerable tradition in Britain. Novelists Graham Greene, Somerset Maugham, Compton Mackenize, Malcolm Muggeridge.

Came back, looking at the Camden Palace near her flat. Sex Pistols. Police. Prince. All performed there. She had walked for a swim to Hampstead Heath, the Fleet River origin. Keats wrote the

Ode there. Communions with Eva Hilestrum, Edith Stein, Oscar Wilde, Hildegard. Shower. She made a cup of tea and heard the outside stair creaking. At the door she looked down at Mary coming slowly and puffing up the stairs. "Hello Mary."

"Wait a minute now... I'm not in shape. I'll have to go to the gym." She started giggling.

"How are you?" Ash asked.

"Fine... Mass, up Camden Town, then Judge Judy," Mary replied. She did not usually come up.

"Is everything alright?" Ash asked, concerned.

"Well now you might think I'm a little... paranoid but I have me marbles." Mary looked serious and intent. "Go over and fiddle with your curtain and see if you notice anything. Pretend you're looking up."

Nonchalantly as she could. People at the busstop. Drug pushers did not congregate yet. Young people were already coming for the Camden Palace. Another honey pot. Someone caught her eye. She sensed that he had retreated into the shadows as she looked out. He was in an odd place. He had his mobile out now. Not a place where people usually waited for a bus. She retreated.

"Did you notice anything peculiar?"

"I saw a man over there that looked out of place..."

"Correct my child... I might be a little Sherlock Holmes. But looks respectable enough."

"You're right to be careful."

"It's not me my child it's you he's looking at. You know I have me crow that comes to the window. He came. I fed it. And noticed him. I had the window open and closed it before the quiz programmes and I saw him. I sneaked a look out and he never noticed me because he was looking up. Do you want to ring the police?" Mary asked.

"No need. I'll find out."

"What?"

"No worries, I have a friend that'll help me find out. The main thing is make sure you lock your door."

"I will. I have a fine big stick." Mary started to laugh.

"As they say woods have ears and fields have sight," Ash finished.

10 minutes later still there.

Outside McGannah was getting bored. A pint of ale began to grow before his eyes. Ruby colour, background noise, feeble scum on top, hand-drawn hoosh of beer from the cellar from above the settled sediment. Scent of hops and herbs that took up away on a magic carpet to a beefull summer somewhere in Kent. What was on tonight? London Pride, some of the lesser ones. Maybe I'll just pop into the Tooke or the Hubbub or Hulabaloom or whatever it is. He did not know why he was doing this. Wondered whether he was losing his marbles. Part of him was disturbed by all the electronic intelligence being used and he did not trust that. You could get intelligence that was manipulated. This would give him a sense. Crimson autograph and painted faces.

He did his homework and research quickly and could see nothing unusual beyond a bit of bondage or whatever it was. He had a good nose for it. No links, cross-references, corroboration, wrong doing. A lone wolf with no agenda of any interest to the State. It might be a kind of repressed feeling, paternalism or something coming back. His son was a big man now. Going incognito in Belfast was not the recipe for a good father-son relationship. Regretted that. James Bond it was not. He worked in Londonderry. Derry. Incredible to see a city centre built by the City of London. When you worked there and looked up from the Bogside and the terraced houses and the murals at the wall you got a sense of something medieval. Looking down was the same. Like a medieval archer protecting the castle. Bond, Ian Fleming. Naval intelligence. He must have been one of the Flemings. Mercenaries that helped the Normans. Archers that protected the castle. Maybe it was in the blood. They were strong, fierce people who were into the occult. But you never know. People can be adopted, illegitimate. What they believe is important. Fleming had Scottish blood and his mother was Evelyn St Crois Rose. What a name! What a giveaway! Bond seems to be a Scot after some doubt. Like Ash. Either the suspect was such a criminal or politically inspired genius that they had hidden all their tracks or this was one of those caught in a net innocently. He was the sniffer dog and she was clean. Finished. The only thing that smelt a bit off was the assignment. Intelligence had gone loopy in the decades after the WW2 guys had gone. The devil makes work for idle hands to do. Even the object of loyalty was unclear these days. Leafy blue, a wizened word, dirty sweet. Get it on. He never noticed the person across the road watching him, the same person following as he went to the Tube. Never noticed the figure following him to the pub. Never noticed a tall man outside with his girl when he emerged from the fancier pub over the Kendo School before he walked home tired and slightly drunk to bed. They had some food while he drank.

Mary had given Ash a few books on Michael Collins. Michael Collins had crossed paths with Churchill. During the Anglo-Irish War of Independence, Churchill was a Minister, Collins the rebel leader. He partly developed urban terrorism. A critical part of that was counter-intelligence. Turn the tables, watch the watchers. Bloody Sunday was the response to the wipe-out of the Cairo Gang. By pursuing the pursuer the relationship was changed utterly. A stroke of good fortune always useful. When Collins and Churchill had to meet and negotiate, they got on well. When Collins shook hands on the agreement he said '*I have signed my death warrant.*' Short time later as head of the Irish Army he is shot in the head, traveling in his open-topped car, in a strange prefiguration of Kennedy. Unorthodox, fierce, rational, decisive. Churchill was saddened and praised him. While hidden history is half the story, most unverifiable, subject to alternative readings, some lessons remain. Need for courage to act when needed. Like Michael Collins she was turning the tables. She remembered hearing an East End criminal following another criminal. Collins also referred to Chesterton's novel *The Man Who Was Thursday*, to the effect that if you did not seem to be hiding, people would not come looking for you. Plain Sight. When he was heavily involved in the War of Independence, he won a dog competition in Dublin. The other competitors included Top Brass he was fighting against. He loved a breed called Kerry Blues. Thought to be a mixture of a Russian terrier that came off one ship and some poodles that came of another ship from the Spanish Armada fleeing Queen Elizabeth's navy in 1588. He stopped just before he was shot to pat one. Collins left the 'Blueshirts' behind. Strange coincidences. Like when Churchill's second-in-command Brendan Bracken met Emmet Dalton. The mysterious, sometime fantasist, Bracken was the son of an IRB man. This editor, modern Financial Times founder, business man, Minister of Information who perhaps inspired Big Brother (BB). Denied his background even when he met Emmet Dalton who remembered him from school. Dalton was in the car with Collins on the day he died and urged him not to stop and fight. Soon Dalton would have Collins brains on him. But he had experience from World War 1 fighting for Britain. Strange affiliations when you dig.

Mistakes are made even by the best. Luck comes the way of some who deserve it. Even Jane Eyre said to hit back. But she did not have a vengeful spirit. Clouded the mind. Use methods that are effective, empty handed, soft, yin, and only force of the right type if necessary. She was happy and was not going to have her state overrun by others.

Other elements could be controlled but she had cut off that which was herself inside and that was in a place impregnable. If the princess was captured this one would sneak out. Jonah might have been in the body of some fish but he got out. Only made sense that the old guy was a journalist or a detective. Investigative journalists were really fictional, lickspittle, propagandists or just servants. Maybe detective, a private one. Surely they have younger guys as well? Retired police. Often do security. Have contacts to check things out. A slight possibility he was a police detective. Sounded ridiculous. We live in ridiculous political reality. Dark night. A black moment. Not fear but anger.

Maybe she was lucky to know. But then a dark dangerous pit opened. A darkscape un-expected. A stalker, Stan, former customer? They would have to do a little work to find her, but not much. Explain the awkward, odd, new customer. Scrutinised. By whom? Why? Something she was doing. Soon after the interview. Related to her business. Stepped on someone's ego? Had a criminal gang decided to look at her, purely competition? Was there something she said in the interview that was interpreted in another way. When attacked, never stay still. In an emergency, do something, but never, ever panic. Sometimes do nothing, bide you time and become more relaxed in case you need to respond. Never allow yourself be a victim. Do not underestimate your enemy or your self. Sometimes it may not be a crisis and sitting still is best. Ignore it. Exciting. When she began to make sense she considered a range of possibilities. Providence, synchronicity, guardian angels, luck, misfortune, set-up, imagination, time would tell. She had not discovered it. Mary had. Maybe your network is needed for other voices to come true. Another possibility. A fluke. Had she made it up in her head? The Lie. Even though she knew he was a pirate, a robber, a brutal suppressor of rebellion, a colonist. You could give the lie to Raleigh himself. That might be the point.

> *'Tell age it daily wasteth*
> *Tell honour how it alters*
> *Tell beauty how she blasteth*
> *Tell favour how it falters.*
> *And as they shall reply,*
> *Give every one the lie.'*

Axiom 9 Be prepared to fight for your life and well-being.

LLLF

LONDON LOGOS LIBERATION FRONT

Publishing Pamphlets to Oppose Censorship of Our Message.
The Counter-Revolutionary to Evil and Terror Effort.
Look at the Reality. Don't buy into their Reality.

RISE UP IN YOUR CONSCIOUSNESS.

THEY USED TO SEND US TO THE WARS.

NOW THEY BRING THE WAR TO OUR STREETS.

THEY WANT A WAR BETWEEN THE GROUPS.

THEY WILL LET IT BE INTOLERABLE.

THEN THEY WAIT FOR YOU TO CALL OUT.

THEN YOU WILL CRAVE THE IRON FIST.

YOU ARE PROGRAMMED TO ADORE FORCE.

YOUR SERVANTS ARE YOUR MASTERS.

YOU ARE NOW SERVANTS.

IF YOU DON'T RISE UP YOU DESERVE IT.

DON'T SAY I NEVER KNEW.

DON'T CLAIM IGNORANCE.

YOU ARE TO BLAME.

WE ARE SET-UP.

NO NEED TO PACK FOR THE INTERNMENT CAMPTS.

THEY HAVE SET THEM UP AROUND US.

PREPARE FOR LIBERATION

Chapter 17

Heaping Up Its Own Funeral Pyre
Invisible Government

> Treats of the long, erudite and earnest contemplations of the high ranking member of the Intelligence Service at his residence and environs thus affording access to the circuitous path of evidence which convinced him of the possible explanation of the perceived tendency to co-ordinated control of events that changed his world, namely the mutation of the Roman Empire. With sentimental asides involving, inter alia, his good wife, may she rest in peace, and his subsequent infatuation. Wherein the relevance of speculation is perhaps rendered otiose by the reality of the sting of some real intelligence, depending as always on credibility. Alternatively it is perhaps precisely germane thereby. N.B They=Romans. The publication of his interior viewpoint would paradoxically render him liable to prosecution under the Domestic Terrorism Act, if passed, insofar as he would be 'promoting' a conspiracy theory calculated to suggest a secret global government, save you can legally do anything in the name of national security. Bear in mind that it has always been the job of some such people to construct such convoluted theories to distract or deflect and that even what we think we see or believe we perceive may not be what it seems despite the ostensible intimacy and reliability thereof. Should the Bill have been passed before you read this I am afraid you would contravene what seems to be an offence of strict liability (although you know I am not a lawyer) and you should not read this chapter although simple possession may already suffice to incur liability.

Conspiracy theories as a concept were invented by the CIA with taxpayer money. Falsehood of sufficiently large scale is the uniquely fashioned prerogative of the State or those who will control it. It was part of his job to follow these theories just as it was sometimes his duty to propagate them. He could float a kite but if true he would be gone. He knew about Ash. He did not like to snoop, but the State did. At the highest level you get access to the best technology. Allows you to see nearly everything about a person's life. Every stroke on the keyboard, sound on a phone, in your home is recorded. Get the data and compress it. The latest tendency was to create an electronic simulacrum based on all the information. You could even look inside a person, peruse their DNA in most cases. Assisted by AI, you could identify their greatest fears and their greatest weaknesses. You could even play out a scenario with other individuals or similar types. Uncanny. Useful but creepy. He noticed Ash's consistent attempt to identify axioms or rules to encapsulate her observations. So he did his too in his head, he knew not to write anything down. Not only does the State know what you had for breakfast but it knows how your bowels work. SIMEMORX system. Most just called it God. It would be part of the World Mind project. Wells got it right. Unlike God, there was much more evidence that it affected people's lives. It knew more about people than they did. Took it from FANG, created by Gov. Here in the countryside he had time to think. Sheep-dog trials. A sheepdog controls a herd, a swarm of unwilling agents with minimal effort by simple, distant instructions communicated by the shepherd. He must be like a sheepdog himself to try organise the many sheep of ideas and marshal them into a pen of comprehension, fashioned with a fence of facts. Some of my case is weak. Tangential. Not persuasive. Bitty.

THEY are villains invisibly re-arranging reality while we sleep. A villain used to be a poor farmer, someone serving in a villa. D was home in the village near Cirencester. He studied this, ad nauseam. Age of Mass Confusion. Confusion the best tool of hypnosis. THEY say something apparently coherent making you work hard to follow, although meaningless. Mind shuts off. Get you ready for The Big Lie. Confused, your attention marshalled, look for meaning, go inwards, stop and be open to suggestion. THEY hold a thread, confuse so that we wait eagerly for the first sign of definition we understand. A Coup? D was working 'from home.' Easier for Burke to come from GCHQ at Cheltenham. Burke had his own theories. Went back a long way. Amber late whiskied-discussions. Two Babylon's theory. A Scottish minister Hislop wrote about the survival of Babylonian religion through Roman Catholic Church. Mainly an Evangelical Protestant idea. Debunked. D was interested in these things because he dealt with people who believed suchlike. Deal with what people actually believe. Such theories influenced groups like The Covenant, the Sword and the Arm of the Lord. Right-wing, Christian terrorism. Elijah Missouri. Links with the Aryan Nations, Aryan Brotherhood. Linked to the Order. D had no time for anti-Jewish or racist sentiment. But you need to know what views influence them. Ignore them at your peril. Read Hislop and Nimrod when he was getting into the head of Ian Paisley. Most said

Paisley was a mad firebrand. Yet he became a peacemaker. How could you explain why in 1899-1902 the Hill of Tara in Ireland was dug up by an expedition looking for the Ark of the Covenant, without understanding British Israelism? Indiana Jones. All the Christians who believed they were the Lost Tribes of Israel. British the 'Beritish.' Man of the Covenant. You could not understand many churches like The Worldwide Church of God without engaging in some daft ideas. Drove Supremacist ideas and the right to rule the world. Empire. UK and US were the rightful inheritors of the Promised Land. Then Nordic Israelism. Offshoots like Heyerdahl and his idea about Norse gods being people who came from the Don. He remembered what Burke said once about the more outlandish explanations, *'The Lizards might be in the equation, but if you pay too much attention to them you fail to see the obvious.'* But reptilians were seen often. Many Top Secret reports. Fabrications from ancient mind? Weird ideas make you re-visit your theories. Icke, the Round Table and the politics of climate change. Great Clearances. Away from the Earthquake zone, pleasant among autumn trees, umber, russet, olive and ember colours in the woods where he walked. Wind from the west rising, gusting. Thames rose around here where Roman villas were built and Royalty take recreation. Horses, polo. You could not walk about long without seeing someone famous. Sultan of Brunei. Sheikhs. Saudis. Chinese. Russians. Daily life not afflicted here, abyss of problems and inconvenience seemed distant. London Earthquake an appalling apparition causing agony. At HQ he heard the sonorous, seismic sensation that shook the bomb-proof building. Exploitation by Deep State. A hideous, grotesque, frenzied thing emerged from some crypt. An intolerable, demoniacal force stalked the institutions. No elucidation nor sagacious analysis could unmask the prodigious threat he perceived. Forced to the supposititious, to interpret sinister manoeuvrings behind the scenes. He saw on TV News an alleged attempt to flood the Underground by blowing up the wall of a sewer under central London. Part of the great scarecrow. Ethel, the only one who gave him joy. Followed her. Remarkable Charles V, Holy Roman Emperor, visited Bridewell Palace and within a generation it was a jail. Ethel got it. Heard her while he was flipping through car radio stations one frosty night and she struck some deep chord. Silly kids playing gentle terrorists surprised him with their perspicacity. All they had written made sense, like posters. Telegraph style he would say. THERE IS A <u>THEY</u> WHO RULE US STOP.

Who was orchestrating events behind the scenes so that even someone at his level did not know?

> '*I don't know what effect these men will have on the enemy. But by God they terrify me,*'

Duke of Wellington said once, but the Duke could see them. Still feared for the safety of Royal Family but not from sources intelligence suggested. Churchill said it was not the opposition he worried about but those on his own benches. Friends close, enemies closer. Invisible is different. Reminded him of secret Governments the FBI created on the pretext of working counter-intelligence. Counter-espionage and revolution were often subterfuges facilitating self-perpetuating elites. Edward Bernays the 'father of public relations' said that the 'conscious and intelligent' manipulation of the public mind was critical in a democracy. So we are governed by men we have never heard of, pulling strings behind the scenes. Invisible government. Think you have a taste, but it is given to you. Bernays was closely related to Freud. Used Freud. Took ideas of suggestion. Go for unconscious. Cigarettes smooth your throat. Goebbels learnt from his writing which shocked Bernays. Later Bernays' brother-in-law, who assumed the name Bernays, would lay the blueprint for the Nuremburg Trials. Followed on from London Agreement. *London* again. Now we have the Rome Statute that set up the International Criminal Court. Tin-pot dictators banged up while western war criminals get prizes and positions. Nuremburg hung the ones they could, gave the others jobs. Strange, esoteric brotherhoods. Not ones people thought, many throw people off the scent. THEY sent out convincing conspiracy theorists to misdirect. A sliver of translucence through a curtained crack to reassure. Mantra, national security, need for secrecy, terrorism, war, threat, danger, our way of life. Secrecy inflation. Extraordinary Measures. Innocent, respectable people turned to idiots by drugs after spurious detentions or simply disappeared. No doubt the State was murdering much more of its citizens than usual. Assassinations ostensibly officially sanctioned executions. Reign of Terror in Paris. We did not blunder into Iraq, Libya, Syria. We chose to execute a perverted plan unrevealed. Public opposition irrelevant.

A pleasant canter with Hannibal. Looked for wet spots, went against the grain, worked on sweat marks till he was dry and groomed, dust came off, oil distributed. Hannibal enjoyed grooming and was co-operative. No soreness, puffiness, insects. Un-resisting.

Liked his routines. When he had brushed Hannibal down, as the perspiration cloud faded, patted and whispered in his ear and hung equipment, he said goodbye to the stable hand as he walked out into fresh Cotswolds air. Loved the aroma of stables, perfume of leather, hay, manure, horses. Sights of burnished metal and straps. Sounds of horses moving, clinking, stamping. Swoops of birds eating insects before journeys south. A canter kept him right. Hunting not so fun anymore. Camaraderie was great. He loved the red jackets and hunting pack and so had his beloved Juno. D drove home to take Brennus for a walk in the fields and frighten a bird in the bush or two. No dogs of war to unleash to protect ourselves when we need to. Few men left with balls to do the dirty work. Always outcasts they turn to when they need help. He took Brennus from the yard to walk to the village churchyard. His housekeeper made sure the dog had plenty of company when he was not at home, but the dog enjoyed their time together.

As he walked he recalled his last discussion with Burke in verandah diamond dust after a long summer's day of cricket in *Cider with Rosie* land. Burke said, "I looked at all the big explanations. Rain and civilisation, latitude, stone. Alien gods. The *horse* is sacred. Inextricably linked with military accomplishment. All great military leaders are depicted on horses. Hipparchus. Follow the equations."

D chipped in himself, "In Rome, the Order Equester became very important, not just in war. The Scythians or Salmations were brought to Britain because of their horsing prowess, bringing their dragons, lizard style, horses and tales of a round table, knights and swords in lakes. Hippodrome and so on."

Burke continued, "You see it round here. Polo. Horse racing. The Royal family and horses. Cheltenham. Don't mind about Epsom, Ascot. But consider Genghis Khan. Mongolians. Spain brings horses to the new world. You know of course that 'Marshall' had the old German word for horse in it."

He asked him to clarify, "But are you saying there is something deeper?"

Burke smiled, "Oh yes. Look where breeding comes in. Royalty and horses. Genes. Blood. Now some say that blood is critical to the Royals. The British royals are linked to Vlad the Impaler. The Royals across Europe suffered from blood diseases, haemophilia and the like. More interested in breeding. As well as the military stuff, Equus is a more powerful binding agent. Churchill started off on a horse in war. Connections based on the cavalry. Chivalry. China. Japan. Mongolia. Tibet. Islam. Noticed how in the Tudor times they decided to use the word Cavalry, which sounded suspiciously like Calvary. Accident? So many statues of men on horses. That's why Emily Davison the Suffragette from Greenwich threw herself under the King's Horse in 1913. Look at Cortés his little gang and 16 horses. Overthrew Montezuma and the Aztecs. Hernando Soto rode his horse into the Inca throne room."

D replied, "We live in a week named after Roman astrology. Our months are named after Roman fashions. January after Janus and so on. Although they did have 10 months once and not always 7 days, although 10 and 7 are no surprise. Infiltrate our consciousness."

Burke, "Ah Rome strikes again. My son listens to a horrendous band called We Are The Romans! It's no surprise either that these people have used a Trojan Horse strategy. Not sure if Rome runs."

D concluded, "I bought shares in a company that will catapult vessels into space. Biological warfare developed by Romans. Used mangonels to cast diseased corpses into the besieged. You say the Trojan Horse is about horses and Romans were often thought to be Trojans, like the founder of London. Remembered how effective the strategy was against them."

Burke, "Don't know if it has legs. No time left. Wait for some whiskey time. I have to get back to the Rugby Club. I'll keep you posted. Whatever group they take now you have to check out the Carbonari and the atheists destroying Churches and speculative Masons. Look at the Emperors, Nero, Caligula. Horses. Who were the heroes in *Gulliver's Travels*? *Horses*. Why? Docile, sensitive, obedient."

D listened to any historical speculation respectfully. Trusted Burke. Still HORSESHIT, absent greater evidence. If something was secret you guess, look for clues, engage with the mysterious. Secrecy spawns speculation. Horses had a role, but there was a deeper reason. Horses had been critical for Caligula, Marcus Aurelius, Titus, Caesar. October Horse. Key was that they were Romans. Maybe all that In**forma**tion Technology control was a Roman thing today. Mutating, integrating, evolving. The Ratio Club is a bit of a clue. His own thesis was arguable. Auctoritas non veritas…

Every new thing had to be examined for hallmarks of secret enterprises. All syncretism, mixing up, blending. Wondered about cryptocurrency and whether it was a move to a currency that allowed full monitoring. Each new phenomenon, find out whether the State is behind it. Like the 'drug war.' Intelligence involved in smuggling cocaine. Dr. Kananga in Live and Let Die might have been working for the State with his heroin flooding idea. Fight the IRA and find you have lots of people working as agents in the terror groups. Protect against blackmail and find you are involved in perpetrating it. A new Genghis Khan coming if The Craft was not the Agent. Intelligent, brutal, boiling his opponents. Preaching Tengism. Eternal Blue Sky. Rules made Britain great. We ruled because we understood rules. Made rules for ships, football, rugby, golf, sports. Standard is important. In Elizabeth's time, standard was used in English as a rule. Romans carried the eagle, a standard to lead armies. Always a good reason to justify monitoring. Turning us into Peeping Toms. Advance when they have something on you, some hook. Sweeping up every piece of electronic information. Something there on everyone when they need to use it. Algorithms catch people. Make up offences. Entertainment industry serves its master. Hypnotised public. He was merely a servant. Executing orders. Rule Britannia. The navy, trade, war at sea. Rule the Waves is a new mantra to manage the electromagnetic spectrum. People loving their slavehood. But who? Next step Scalar Energy and Weapons. THEY ARE THE ROMANS MUTATED STOP. The eternal olig**arch**y. Apophenia?

IT WAS ROME. BLOODY ROMANS. Romans. Rome. Roma. Behind it. They were THEY. ROMANS STILL RULE. His library was full of books, his table mountainous with books and labels and cross-references. Secret files. At first he could not believe it. He pulled the thread it kept going. When he followed it to the end he felt he might be out of the labyrinth. Took over a part of his brain. **ROMAN EMPIRE NEVER WENT AWAY, IT JUST CHANGED FORM.** That was observation number I. **Obs. No. I.** Military then Religious then Commercial then Technocratic then Consciousness. Rub your nose in it till you're blind and can't see it. In the Bible, Babylon was a cover for Rome. Balderdash? A type 1 error?

"Fetch. Fetch. Good dog."

Obs. No. II. THEY USE CODE. They use codes based on the word Rome or Roma, anagrams or associated clues like Terminus, Eagle, Wolf, Caesar, Arch, Apollo, Prime, Thumbs Up and X to signal and communicate. **Amor**. Codes went back a long way. Many bearers will not know they are **Mari**onettes. Rome in that. An equation of beliefs and bloodlines manifest by an eagle that roams the sky coming back to roost in Rome for the finale. This secret group are the Agency. They use the body metaphor for a few thousand years. Caesarean Section. Caesar's Smiley. Like with Cathedrals. Romans loved war. WAR trumps all. Bellum became bella. Science handmaiden. COMMERCE nervous system of war machine. Mines the guts. Tax the life blood. Roman consciousness spread. Romans follow Celts, become fascinated with the head. Skulls. Golgotha. Skull and Bones. Robbing skulls of famous people. Swedenborg. Haydn. Mozart. Marquis de Sade's skull was robbed by one L. J. **Ramon**. ROMAN. Mata Hari. Geronimo. Pancho Villa. Descartes. All that old phrenology nonsense, *Cesare* Lombroso. Rome consciousness. At the time of Elizabeth, Europa was a woman. *Europa Triumphans*. Went back to Livy, Shakespeare used it in Coriolanus. Body politic. Microcosm. Roman Plan was easy. If someone has resources take them. ROB. Opposition, massacre them. Create chaos. then claim you want things well-ruled, straight and in good order so you march your army. SLAVERY the lifeblood of empire. Rome mutated. THEY rule world. In **ARMO**UR. With armouries. Arsenal. **MONAR**CH. Indicated-trauma based mind control program. Not Cecil Rhodes, Round Table as Quigley said. Much older, bigger. He saw it all in the first Pink Panther film. Rome. Object. Robbery. Bungling police. Keystone. Frame the innocent. Operation Mockingbird. SERVUS. Slave, servant confused at times. Autocracy of Republic is forgotten. Powell's 'River of Blood' speech was seen as race-hate generating. Said 'the Roman' said it. Professor of Greek. Knew it was Greek divine oracle prophesy in Virgil. He meant ROMANS. Ridiculous about skin colour, big mistake. *'Like the Roman, I see the River Tiber foaming with much blood.'* Tiber-Tyburn. Rome. Daniel O'Connell's heart sent there, but disappeared. Goethe reborn there. Only strange if you knew nothing about history. Ole **Rome**r. Great scientist, speed of light, temperatures, street lights. If they do not begin with Rome they get into it. Getty's. Some born, lived there. Getty Villa in Florida. Grand Tour was part of the upper class education especially of English Protestants, paradoxically going to Rome. Still going there mentally, Club of Rome. A formless body like the Lunar Society. Double-Cross system of counter-espionage was really XX meaning Roman Twenty. Check Princess Di's death. Rome. Sacrifice. Paris. Roman hallmark is in the tunnel just look at all the names. Jane **Roman** and Lee Harvey Oswald another link. Michael Collins the astronaut was **born** in Rome. Castro, a district in Rome. Roman Warm Period in climate. Coming back. Free**ma**sonry. Can we run it?

Obs. No. III. ROME RECURS AND IS CELEBRATED. Rome defeated *Alba Longa* a few miles south east. The Julian family came therefrom. The head of the Latin League. Romulus and Remus also. Castel Gondolfo the Pope's summer house. Gandolfo. Gandalf? Founded by Trojans, like London. Britain was *Albion*. Rome. Since they clashed with the Celts just outside Rome in 387 BC by the Allia, it had been a long battle. Celts overran Rome. Then Romans built the Servian walls. London copied this lay-out. You see the same thing in Pavia. Albans influenced their Roman relations to worship Vesta. Similar to Brigid. Goddess of the hearth, tending the fire, the eternal flame. Brigit, Brigid, Brigantia. Burgundy. Vesta the most tenacious Goddess hanging on until Christian Emperor Theodosius did away with this daughter of Saturn. Last Vestal Virgin Coelia Concordia. Concord. But Vesta stands forever. Proletarians, like the proletari in Rome. Most economic activity in Europe is still concentrated around Roman roads. Light seen from space allows you see outline. Septimomium and Septizonium survived. Films remind us all the time of Rome like a religion. Not the same homage to say the Persians, Indians, Chinese or Aztecs. Ben Hur. Spartacus. Gladiator. From Rome with Love. Cleopatra. Constantin. The Robe. Quo Vadis. Caligula. Julius Caesar. Hannibal. The Last Legion. The Last Roman. Nero. The Bicycle Thief. Belly of an Architect. Roman Holiday. La Dolce Vita. Three Coins in a Fountain. Rossellini. Roma. Magic things. Caesar's Sword. The Holy Lance. The Spear of Destiny that was claimed to be Hitler's motivation for war. The lance of Longinus that pierced the side of Jesus. No culture has projected itself as much. Viva Roma. The new order. Novus Ordo. City of obelisks. Satellites have obelisks. Look out for city states. City of London, District of Columbia, Vatican. Paris. Invisible Rome rules. Nicky Minaj, possessed by a character called 'Roman.' He's violent, destructive. Roman's Revenge. Roman Reloaded. Roman Holiday. Roman in Moscow. He can't be exorcised. Taken over the Church. Joyce forewarned us. EMPYREAL RAUM. Imperial Rome. Highest heaven. Raum. Great demon of hell. Crow. A dark occult combination. Romans used supernatural power. Open to spirits. Napoleon, pure Rome all the way. Holy Roman Empire came later using concept of *'translatio imperii'* encompassing many Royals with their eagles. Empire is re-incarnated. Heaps of references at home. The wolf references in *The Shining*. Cold blue Adler Eagle. Amanita caesarea. *'September mushrooms of midnight.'* Reekie. Real? Hocus-pocus. Hard to deny. Comeuppance they need.

Obs. No. IV. BLOOD LINES MATTER. Never go against the Family. Blood lines came from them. To understand how Caligula and Nero and others got to the top, think families. Where do the Mafia come from? Roman structure. <u>Fascists</u> a Roman idea. Illuminati. Weishaupt founder. Called himself 'Brother Spartacus.' Spartacus the biggest rebel in Roman history. D suspected most of the idea came from the *Illuminatus* Trilogy. Granted Weishaupt was educated as a Jesuit and maybe opposed the Roman Catholic Church. Jesuits had the Bible in one hand and *The Thoughts of Marcus Aurelius* in the other. Even Transcendentalists in USA come from places like Concord, named after the Roman Temple and goddess. Roman Virus. Paradigm of Rome. Rome was burnt and rebuilt in stone in 64 AD. Did the same to London. *Interpretatione Romana*. See things through Roman lens.

His persona was a mask. That was where the word came from. Roman actors wore masks through which the sound came. There were wax masks of ancestors. Public representatives learned to be actors, have a persona. Cancer in the State, malign values abroad. He was not religious but Deist, unlike brothers his was Transcendent. Location of collusion was clear. Romans. Mutating. Some say the goddess Roma or the genius of Roma. You look at Lugdunum, Lyon. Caracalla and Claudius came from there. Like London. Named after Lugh the Celtic god. They make the Three Gauls, taking the idea from the triple goddess Brigid. Became a centre of the Imperial Cult. Imperial Cult would transmute to a secret team with a secret theme. *'Rome remains with you forever'* they told you. Scipio developed a cult of personality. Certain well-connected Catholics in the Vatican said it had been taken over. Fatima predicted that. Prophesy about inevitable consequences of not consecrating Russia. Plays into the hands of those who wanted a war with Russia. Rome is back in the hands of the Romans. Who is the Icon of Zombie film making? George A. **Rome**ro. They love facilitating people with Rome-references. Like serial killers taunting. The Son of Sam. The Zodiac Killer. **More** taunting. It's not codswallop. I'm no snollygoster.

"A rabbit. No. I see it. Leave it Brennus."

Obs. No. V. ROMANS *BUILD* EMPIRES HELPED BY THOSE WHO SUBMIT. In Rome anyone could be involved, once you submitted to empire-building. But secret groups would always control. Palladio was a prism for Roman architecture. Arches. Arcades. Architecture. Archery. Archetypes. Aqueducts. Atrium. Domes. Dom. Domination. Vaults. Casino. Concrete. Bricks. Amphitheatres. Dams. Bridges. Temples. Romanesque. Sewers. Circuses. Spas. Baths. Colonnade. Straight roads. Plumbers. Porticos.

Pediments. Post. Empire. Conquest. Codex. Colonisation. Fountains. War. Repression. Entertainment 'Arenas' from the word sand. News. Slavery. Gladiators. Navvies build. MMA. *Cesarino.* Technology. Apollo **Program**. Particular buildings duplicate Roman ones. The US Pension Bureau and Villa Farnese established after the Civil War. EUR was the suburb built by the Fascists in Rome. Only an 'O' from EUR to EURO. Rome founded by the children of Mars and raised by wolves. Werewolves came from here. 7 hills. Murder from the start. Invisible Government sucked in powers of many people. Catapults from Archimedes. Hail Caesar. Heil.... German kings often used the title 'King of the Romans.' Rex Romanorum. Imperator. Habsburgs were Holy Roman Emperors. Caesar. Pope. Treaty of Rome. Club of Rome. The Rome Regulation. Other minor figures betray their origin - Ernst Röehm. Places such as Romania. Moldova speaking Latin-based language. Latin America. Argentina, Roman Silver. Catholic Church grew as long as it was *building* **cathedrals**. Freemasons. Material to remember the spiritual supposedly. Rome a radial place of mind. Roads. Autobahn. Hitler did all the Roman stuff but did not realise that Real Rome was hidden. He rose to power because of the 'Carthaginian Peace' of Versailles. Romans imposed a brutal peace treaty to crush their enemies and eventually wipe them out. John Maynard Keynes said the Versailles Treaty was really a Carthaginian Peace. Predicted that *'vengeance... would not limp.'* Hitler played Rome very well but failed to understand that he was against Neo-Rome. Even enlisting Barbarossa, Holy Roman Emperor would fail. New Rome is good at generating the conditions for a mad dog that they then need to set their wolves against. Hitler, Saddam Hussein, Osama bin Laden. Pol Pot? How was the Khmer Rouge leadership educated in Paris? Some doctorates. Rome of Julian, with its Pantheon. Obelisks. Triumphal Arches. July Column. Another Roman satellite. Year Zero in Cambodia. Genocide. French Indochina. You can tour all the houses of the African dictators in Paris. See where Haitian Baby Doc Duvalier lived. Son of Papa Doc the Dictator with his Tonton Macoute, sadism, torture, execution, voodoo, black magic. Baron Samedi. But anti-communist so it was ok. French in Rwanda. Genocide. Algeria. Cultured France, the soft face of Roman power still. 'Operation Satanic' French Intelligence blow up the pesky Rainbow Warrior. Pacific bomb-sites. Like US thermonuclear explosions at Bikini Atoll, Castel Bravo with its JUGHEADS. RUNTS. SHRIMP components telling us what they thought of us. Did the Wordmakers and Language-Conditioners deflect attention through association transmuting the Bikini Horror into women's clothing and it's associations. Political Language Alchemy? Substitution. A cold deck and a ditch. An equivoque. Like ISIS. Clues. What does the word Bikini mean to you? You're in the programme, trained, hypnotised. All Rome. They learn all about salt from Celts. Then they use it. Concepts. Salad. Salary. Soldier. All from Sal. Building again in Davos. Davos was a Roman town. *The Magic Mountain*. San**ator**ium. Called Berghof. Like Hitler's home. But this Davos novel was written 1924. Poppycock? Serendipity? Fuddy-duddy gubbins? Grimoire. True.

Obs. No. VI. ROME IS AN INVISIBLE MENTAL EMPIRE.
ROME CONSCIOUSNESS: Rome became a ghostly empire. Respect, fear. Rome was never ideological and was merely based on factions struggling for power. Methods of Rome were always clear, Empire based on Weapons, Crime, Fear, Violence, War, Booty, Spoils and Slaves. Domina runs the house. Animus, anima-Roman. Freud had very fearful feelings about Rome! He worked out his theories about death and destruction being balanced by restraint reflecting on Rome. He dreamt about Rome and had a neurotic longing for it. Freud admired Hannibal and, like him, could not enter Rome first time he was there. Psychoanalysis was like archaeology and ancient history. He wrote in September 1910 from Rome to Jung about it. Jung had a 'Rome Neurosis' also and did not manage to go there! Both understood the power of Rome was not purely historical. Jung found it overwhelming. His neurosis was a 'Rome Complex.' When he finally tried to go there he fainted buying a ticket. JungFreud. Jungfrau. Shelley and Keats did end up there. Rome the basis of '**Roman**,' the word for a novel in many languages. Roman. *Roman*ce. Romantic. Romantic movement. *Sturm und Drang*. Romance languages Spanish, Portuguese, Italian, French, **Roman**ian and Moldovan. Getting on to a billion. Rome was about elites and materialism. *Aroma* everywhere roaming. Romans put Plato's idea of the 'noble lie' into effect. When the Western Roman Empire apparently fell, it created a vacuum. Out of it came Islam in the East. In the West, King Arthur at the same time. Normans were from the former Roman province in France, NOT from North. Went back to Italy and built castles. Looked to Rome, spoke a Romance language, were intermarried with remnants of Romans in France and in Italy. **Roman**s even contains the word Romans. Vikings went from the North over to Constantinople and Ukraine and Russia. Rus may have come from Sweden and Gotland. Gotland still has Roma in its centre.

Vikings and Romans in 834 in Constantinople agreed to work together. Thus a Roman ring was formed around Europe. Paranoid?

'Meet you at your house shortly.' Text message from Burke.

Speed it up. Off the record. Maybe about Royals. Renaissance a temporary shift to Florence of Rome as part of Peripatetic Rome or return of Eastern Rome through Egypt to Italy? Discovery of Vitruvius. Rome did not finish when overrun. Eastern Empire still there for another millennium in Byzantium, Constantinople. Roman Law, emperors, structure and proportion. Teach Roman Law in Scotland still. Scots doing Roman things become world famous. Building roads. John Loudon McAdam improves roads to move armies quicker. Dunlop. McAlpine. Telford. John Rennie. Infrastructure. Constantine said he saw the cross in the sky so he could get the Christians on his team. Constantine to Theodosius fixed Christianity, while getting a few obelisks in. Constantine made his new Eastern capital in Constantinople, changing Byzantium, inaugurated in the year 330. 33. Called the New Rome. City laid out on 7 hills. New Senate. Families from Rome. Constantine worshipped Sol Invictus. Constantinople where Eunuchs got into Roman tastes. Often fierce militarists. Julius Caesar helped destroy the great library of Alexandria. Burned Egyptian wisdom. Aurelian came back a couple of hundred years later to finish the job. Not just books but Roman Empire destroys other schools of early Christianity, such as Origen. By the time Emperor Julian (who wanted to restore paganism) was murdered by the Christians, clear the new Empire would work. *Translatio imperii*. Justinian develops Roman law. Still used today, 1453 it falls with a crescent moon. Silk Road shuts. Europe looks West, finds the 'New World.' Portuguese go around the Cape. Columbus. Renaissance with Greek scholars. Constantinople bread and circuses. Hippodrome. Horse races. If not Constantinople it was Petrarch. He discovers Cicero's letters. Promoted by the Colonesse who claimed links to the first imperial dynasty. Writes to long dead Cicero. Part of the Roman communion. Cicero. Circe. From Mount Circeo near Rome. In the stars. Popes used astrologers for centuries. Roma. Rheum 'flow' Greek. Rome is fluid. Love water. Things with X in it. X=10. Deci. Look how they keep the Roman Numerals on the Olympics, statues, Kings, Queens, Popes. New Rome kept the old numerals. Statue of Liberty has a torch in one hand and a tablet in the other with date in Roman numerals. July IV MDCCLXXVI. July is Julius Caesar. US, UK use Imperial Roman measures. Semiramis. Isis. Libertas. Columbia. Liberty Bonds funded WW1. Paradox. Chaplin makes a promo film 'The

Bond.' Liberty for war. War financing needed a 'powerful stream of romanticism' they indicate. Government later diddled bondholders. Romanticism. Roman Indicator. Romantic bonds. Money for weapons. 'When in Rome.' Do as Romans do. Tony Bennet. All the songs about Rome. Elvis. Heart of Rome. Sinatra. Three Coins in a Fountain. Dean Martin. On an Evening in Roma. Toto. Spanish Steps of Rome. Toto and the King of Rome. Then Rome Report. Lacan. Symbolic Order. They control it. Everything **prime,** primary. Primus. Romans used that. Fact. I'll not be snooled.

Obs. No. VII. USA IS ROMAN. USA was Roman from start. Goddess welcoming to New York lets you know. Senate. Washington DC built on 7 hills like Moscow, Edinburgh, Tehran. Centre around Goose Creek. Changed to Tiber Creek. The man who owned it was called Pope and his land called Rome! Home of State institutions like IRS and so on. Capitol Hill, the Senate. Look at architecture, Union Station, White House. Some said it was Francis Bacon who planned it all. Clear Washington was drawing on esoteric symbols and powers to suck magic into it. Some saw Virgo as key. Washington lays foundation of Capitol in September. Jefferson builds Monticello. Democrats described as 'Rum, Romanism and Rebellion.' Taxes on rum production significant factors in attitudes in Southern States. They brought fish and rum to Africa, got slaves and in West Indies they got molasses and sold in the States to make rum. Later rum was taxed and whiskey grew. **Ironman**, Roman. Rome-ruled, the Western, distinctive US genre were directed by Romans in Europe. Spaghetti Westerns. A Fistful of Dollars. John Quincy Adams said US goes not abroad in search of monsters to destroy, if it took up all foreign affairs she might become dictatress of the world but no longer be ruler of her own spirit. Patriot Act follows Oklahoma legislative reaction. Fool people, tell them lies with some elitist justification. Romanity. Form perpetuated. Civis Romanus Sum. I am a Roman Citizen. SPQR, you'll find it everywhere still if you look in the right places. Even Rosemary's Baby directed by **Roman** Polanski they have the Roman Castevets character. They like 7 and they like 10. That's why 17 is a sign. 10. Roman everywhere, even in The Tarot numerals. Roma. **Omar.** *Allies* were the friends of Rome. Agenticity? Patternicity? I like Black Forest gateau but hedgehogs like slugs. I am a pauciloquent mugwump in public.

Obs. No. VIII. WORLD TRADE IS ROMAN. It's just business. It's only business. Not personal. International trade was and is

Roman. World Trade Organisation. An Information Technology Agreement in 2000. Revolutionary. Changed IT industry overnight by reducing tariffs to zero. TRIPS nearly spirit. The Rome Regulation. People do not seem to see standardisation around. Same business, idea, practices. Decided in secret. You can see what Romans want, everything standard for Empire. Slaves needed. Transport systems. Cheap. Military-industrial. Congo. One of cruellest histories ever, millions dead for rubber and ivory. Congolese get to Rome to get help. Then gets worse. Found Roman coins from the time of Trajan in the Congo. King Leopold keeps the alternative Roman connection. Nearly assassinated by an Italian anarchist, Gennario Rubino. An**arch**y. Shot at the carriage, after him and Queen Elisabeth. Rubino used to be an intelligence agent. Sounds familiar? Deck of cards they play. Place a bomb and blame it on someone else, leave their ID on the scene. Encourage a potential opponent and then catch them. Use a threat you create as excuse for general repression. Set-up a Patsy. False assassination plot of someone on your side. Genuine assassination plot of someone against you. Infiltrate, divide opposition. Play your cards. Their Royal Flush can never win this game of poker. Execute Casement, the one who exposed the atrocities as a traitor. Leopold II. Greedy genocide. Chivalry. Get their valuable material. Look at all the honours he got. All the big new Romans get these titles so they can recognise their co-conspirators. Order of the Red Eagle. Order of the Black Eagle. Ottoman Empire titles. All power pyramids are linked at the top. Independence. Lamumba. Set him up. We did it. Look at that guy who re-wrote *The Tempest*, Aime *Cesaire*. Caliban might be the righteous oppressed if you pay attention. What if most of your assumptions are wrong? What if you are a participant in the murderous mayhem by your dull acquiescence? Fabian Society. Named after Quintus Fabius Maximus Rullianus of the Roman Fabia family. Havelock Ellis, George Bernard Shaw, Annie Beasant. Sex, eugenics, socialism, welfare, imperial, bit by bit, wolf in sheep's clothing their emblem. Wolf. Rome. Hitler. Wolf's Lair. Tony Blair joined the Fabians. International trade, services, Switzerland banking. Geneva lots of demon-possession. What was the area called? ***Romandy***. If there is a hell, Rome is built on it. All roads lead to Rome. Bilderbergers, founded by people who had been Nazis, worked for I.G Farben. Strange 'Green' organisations. All these orders, strange old orders that give you awards, decorations. All the Romans get them, because they get their orders from the people mixed up in them. Use these networks to own money. Use money to own things. Turn people into servants to God of Money. Juno Moneta. Qui bono? Type 2 error to ignore it? Ads not editorials.

Obs. No. IX. SECRET CONTROL IS ROMAN. Religion is often still Roman. Nave of church, navis-ship. THEY use syncretism. Great Architects. Blood oaths, curses. Covenant. Coven. Apron. Guilds. Sacrifice. Martyrdom. Light. Anno Lucis not Domini. Macrobius wrote about Cicero and Scipio's dream. Astral plane very well-known to them. Christianity has taken a lot of this out. Spirit says Rome is small but universe is big. Implication was that you control these planes too. Marshal the astral, the middle plateau. Luther went to Rome, loving it and was then appalled. Heard a 'voice.' Open about demons. Secret ORDERs you must OBEY. OATH to OBEY. ORDERS. SUBMIT. Popes enslaved, murdered over money. Calvi. Mormons built a temple in Rome. Moroni the angel came to Smith. 'Moroni' nearly Roman. Scientology goes to Rome. L. Ron Hubbard had a previous life in Rome and many others following him as well. Big influence on him. 7 an important number. Hubbard had influence and a spiritual Guardian who advised him. Into Diana. Sets up *Dianetics*. Boat called Diana. <u>Goddess</u>. Then there was Dianism, sex without ejaculation. Crowley. Hubbard. A hypnotist too. Articles on it in Lucifer the Lightbearer. Ida Craddock who had sex with an angel. Hubbard took over from Crowley. Pope Leo had a vision of Satan and spirits taking over Rome. Where the St Michael's prayer came from. Patriarch. Patrician. Patricius. Patrick. *St Patrick*. He was Patrician. Rome believed in the material world and the dominance thereof. Secret intelligence a unifying agent. The stargazer was the spiritual one who knew the power. Dominance of the other planes became part of the Plan, Rome could roam, and exiled from physical Rome return in future. **Arm**age**dd**o**n**, war, famine, fire was also in the dream of the Neo-Malthusians. Others were Roman. Rumi. **Omer**ta. Be secret and silent. Mafia secrecy. Police silence. Blue wall of silence. Blue code. Blue shield. Where there is group secrecy there is power and control. Can't deny the gist.

"Qch, Qch. Gooooood boy Brennus. Nice life you have."

Obs. No. X. WESTERN CULTURE IS ROMAN. Cultura. Cultivate. Prepare and use. College. Censor. Roman. Live in suburbs – suburbium with polyglot proletarians like old Rome. Obedience. Language. Manners. Using education as indoctrination. Agriculture- Roman. Vine. Olive. Flax. Fisheries. Mines. Trade. Luxury goods. Amber. Fur. Carpets. Silk. Precious stones. The City. Estates. Books.

Rome lies all around. Words. **Rome**ville was 'cant' or secret language name for London. D thought 'rum' came from Rome which meant excellent. Arabs called the Romans 'Rum' on occasions. Slavery, rum. Navy, rum. Rumbo. Rambo. Rum. Pirates. Slaves. Navy. Sodomy and the Lash. Wine used to be called 'Rum Booze' and 'Rumbo' in Elizabethan times. Rum was also Kill Devil. Maybe Devil Kill. 'Berummaged' meant confused. Rum. Rome confuses you. Common sense, switched on, means you have gumption. *Rumgumption.* Sense of Rome. We live in rooms. Room. Old name for Rome. Raum. Devil. Holy Spirit female. Fascism like a pagan religion, like Julian. Nazis carried the Eagle. Spread Eagle. Romans had sucked in Greeks through their presence in southern Italy and a part of their empire in the east. Festivals were Roman. *Lupercalia*, Brothers of the Wolf was Valentine's day. St Patrick's day celebrates a Roman living in Britain brought as a slave to Ireland. Patrician. Set it on the 17th of March to remember Marcus Aurelius who died that day. Aurelian Society in the US with a few movers and shakers still. Saturnalia, Christmas. Mardi Gras, carnival probably festival of Isis, carrus navalis. *Saturnalis* about slaves and masters. *Mardi Gras*, you are free for a day. Bank of England, White House. Neo-classical **arch**itecture is Roman. Holy Roman Empire. Byzantium was Rome, Second Rome. Caesar. Kaiser. Czar. Wanted to be the New Rome, the Third Rome. Most influential typeface is Times New **Roman**. If wrong about the Agency, still right about the war for consciousness Agenda. Transhumanism. Julian Huxley's godless evolution and eugenics. Consciousness the prize. Like plundered, looted treasures of other cultures, money and environment, next step was enmeshing of man-machine. Individual consciousness plugged into global machine. The Final Rome. TERMINUS. Roman God. Diocletian starts persecution of Christians on this day 303 AD. Terminal Rome. We would be terminals. Potsdam was codenamed TERMINAL. Truman, Churchill, Stalin. Truth, Church, Steel. Computer Terminal they call it to signal who is in control. Terminal disease. Termination. Look at the Madrid bombings, railway terminals. Biggest terrorism attack in Spanish history. Quiet before and after. Led to another EU Treaty that might not have happened otherwise. Roman Emperors behind everything. *Caesar's Messiah* about the Flavians. Caesar and 'Christ' hand in glove. He read theories that Jesus was based on Julius Caesar. Paul an agent? Constantine was one of them. He knew from his work experience what Romans had done. Came to Britain, build on druid mounds. Christ was there, but the true story of personal liberation was cut out. Cotswolds had Roman Villas. Came here just about when Jesus died. Jesus could be the real deal but the full story was obscured, edited, controlled by the Romans. Roman Snails still living around here. Mithras and Jesus mixed eventually. Mithras born in December. Constantine did not see any cross in the sky. Mithras. Mitra. Mitre Square in London. Jack the Ripper. *Curse Upon Mitre Square,* a novel of 1888 that linked the murder to a monk who lived in the monastery there in the 1500's. Mithras a saviour. Sun God. Son of God. Adolf, 'noble wolf' was its origin. Wolves. Spas. Bathing. Horse races. Oldest Yin Yang symbol was Roman. Julian the Apostate. Emperor who was initiated in the Mystery Religions. Going to Eleusis. Underground. Probably exposed to the demons. Drugged. He wants to get rid of the Christians who had taken over the pagan temples. Julian was in touch with spirits, some say demons. After Julian the Apostate they went fully underground. Secret. Like the ceremonies. Dark places, low places. Persephone. You don't need any lizards. Content is fireking. Media is fuelqueen.

Sky began to sound like a machine. A violent, repetitive noise came quickly. Helicopter. Two. Re-locating some 'anti-socials.' Ones that could not be contained in holding centres in London were transported to remote locations. Abolished all rights for non-citizens, easier to act at will. Could anybody be surprised at the latent belligerence within the British establishment? From conquest, extermination to 'concentration camps' in the Boer Wars. Oriental trade route for ships, bonus of gold and diamonds. Romans loved diamonds and GOLD. Roman Empire in its old form dies when gold production began to fall quickly after the death of Christ. Falling. Mines dwindling. Roman military might was based on incentives to soldiers. You get paid with gold or precious metals. No gold, no army, no military coherence. Orient wanted gold for silk. Giant shift from gold and military front to spiritual gold, moral and occult power, with military behind. Elaborated by George Eliot. Mary Anne Evans. She met Herbert Spencer, a member of the X Club. A supergroup of scientists, evolutionists. Huxley. Hooker. Frankland. Busk. Lubbock. The X Club, like a *League of Extraordinary Gentlemen.* They become the X Men. X men. Mutants. The future. George Eliot wrote *Silas Marner.* A miser collected gold and lost it through a robbery. At the same time he discovers a child. His world shifts. The golden haired child replaces the gold. Miser had left his old church under a cloud, denying his God. Like Romans did. They had no gold, trouble, replaced with a child of God. If in doubt see **Romola**. Her novel where Savanarola who criticises Rome wants to establish a new Rome in Florence is burned. Tito Melema is clearly a secret agent who arrives from a mysterious shipwreck to strangely play a role. *Middlemarch*. One of the 'great English novels.' Middlemarch signals Ides of March. Caesar dead. Churchman here dies of a heart attack back from Rome. Convincing?

Obs. No. XI. TAX AND LAW IS ROMAN. Tax and law were Roman. Romans developed tax collection into a fine art. Publicani are not unlike publicans collecting tax as beer is consumed in pubs. Roman law was the basis of the civil law systems of Europe and still is. The ghost of Rome stalks the mock-Roman State and private tax and finance centres today. Look at the Federal Reserve in the US. Private. Income tax. Ad Val**orem** tax. Anagram and Latin. Scotland still has a Roman law system. 'Justice' was the Roman Goddess invented by Augustus, when Jesus was a boy and when the Pax Romana began. Justinian. Banking would replace the church. Italy good at banking, like the Templars. Lombard Street. Often meant pawn shops. An old Roman road. Jesuits involved in finance. Royal Exchange. Rum came from RUMBULLION. Rome bullion. Here the largest bullion market in the world. Gold, silver. Jesuits were formed a year after Elizabeth was born. In Rome they would create a worldwide empire. Soldiers of Christ. Caesar and Christ again. Rome takes over education. Look at their network, even have a Pope. Jahbulon. Re-arrange. John Bull. Even the M'Naghten Rules about pleading criminal insanity. M'Naghten tries to kill The Prime Minister's Secretary. May have thought it was him. Has money on him. Maybe mad. Some thought him an activist posing. Said he was persecuted and followed by Church of Rome and Jesuits and Tories. Maybe he was? Oswald. Give us your money. By the way services must be cut back. Post hoc ergo propter hoc? Cum hoc ergo propter hoc? Signals. Codes. Taunts. No menu without a dish first.

"C'mon or you'll get your lead. Sniffing any old rubbish."

Obs. No. XII. ENTERTAINMENT WAS ROMAN. We need stimulus. A stimulus was a Roman stick to goad animals. The Roman public got their arenas. We get it today. Not just films. Computer games, Son of Rome. Horse Racing. Mixed Martial Arts. Circuses. Festivals. Parties. Wine. Orgies. Bulimia. Decadence. Reality shows. You make entertainment real. *Hunger Games*. Comedy was fixed in Rome, as it is today - we get propaganda. They bled us white. What have the Romans ever done for us? What have they ever given us in return? Sanitation. Irrigation. Medicine. Education, Fresh water.

Order. Peace. Notice how Monty Python destroys Christianity while lauding the Romans. The joke's on us. Paul McCartney was PAUL **RAMON**. Anagram. Album Ram and song **RAM-ON**. Band that defined Punk Rock sound were The Ramones. **RAMONES**. Romans. That was not their surname, they took it they said copying McCartney. Logo had an eagle. Punk. Meaning, a rebel against order but also a prostitute and someone used as a bottom as well as a rotten wood for tinder. Entertainment in their pocket. Punk a magical cod to draw off power that could be political. Pressure valve. U2, spyplane for CIA made after project Bald Eagle. Maybe these musicians think they get on of their own accord. Star Wars. Hail Caesar film. The Empire was a Republic. Architecture. Sports. Traitor Vader and Brutus. Nazi parallels. Valorum. Palpatine like Palatine. People watch Talent shows. Talent was Roman measurement of gold or silver about 33kg. The Talent Shows weigh the performers to see how much gold they can get back from the public for buying their things. Britain's Got Talent. TALENTUM. Rome haunts us. Film. **Metro**polis. Lang talked about worshipping Rome. The Cabinet of Dr. Caligari. Cesare. Common man hypnotised. Doubles and dummies. Robots. Agents, automatons, overground, underground. Texas Sharpshooter Fallacy? Content, needs, relationship, trust.

He recalled Ethel Woodpecker and Goddess Blue Brigid 7.

Lucius: You made some connection to Rome?

Ethel: Take a map of Rome after the Servian walls were built. Built after the Gauls or Celts ransacked Rome. Kept Hannibal out. Compare London with Rome. See the same exact relationship with the Tiber. You will see the Cloaca Maxima flows into the river in a similar position to the Fleet. There was the River of Wells in the west in London and the Porta Fontalis in Rome. That was the gate leading to the wells. Temples in the same place in Rome as there were in Londinium. Capitol Hill was where St Pauls was built on Ludgate Hill. The Roman Prison was where the Newgate and Fleet prisons were. Where St Brides was there seemed to have been a temple maybe to a goddess. See the same thing if you get an old map of Pavia, the capital of the Lombards. Banking. Pawn. Centre of City of London still.

This matched his view but emphasis on Brigid or Bridget was new. London was Rome recreated. Neo-Rome repudiated the Church incarnation of empire to embody a new version based on the architecture of finance and finance of architecture and control of war machines. The Black Widow was Natasha **Roman**ova. She pointed out other Comic characters were real symbols. **Roma** was the daughter of Merlyn, Lady of the Northern Skies, dwelling in the Otherworld. Then you had Captain Britain, Captain UK. X Men. X Factor. Many ESP powers. Non sequitur? Petito principii?

Legal profession, compliant and acquiescent. Bacon thought Roman law was the second great phase in human history. D believed this was only the trial run for the 'Big One,' a monster 'cleansing' of anti-social elements and re-organisation. Prelude to The Last Reaping. The Quake provided opportunities to demonstrate some ideas evolved in recent times. Nazis only had a card-index system. Now they knew people better than themselves through electronic means. The special Emergency Group formed out of the Joint Intelligence Committee had the last detail worked out. Food full of sedatives and plenty of electronic entertainment. Temporary detention centres, a cross between Ikea and Lego. Easy to build. Cubes that could be refilled with water easily and recycle waste, with piped food solar-heated in the walls released by a timer. Built-in wardrobe-sized gyms for physical motion. Could be erected anywhere. Remote islands with complex legal histories were favoured to avoid quick legal challenge. Psychiatrists worked out programmes for self-policing and minimal supervision facilitated by remote control and management, as Bentham had suggested. Convicted criminals would be encouraged to assume positions of responsibility along with clinical psychopaths, alongside military personnel. Knew the ropes. Levels of compliance and passivity made all these programmes feasible. Surveys said there was satisfaction with Government being 'firm' and 'hard.' Emergency was counter-balanced by a State effort to make things appear as normal and familiar as possible. Make them think it is a soap as they drink their wine. Wine-production defined the extent of empire. Sauna-stews-bath-houses, prostitution. Roman. Opera developed by Il Zazzerino a Roman, when they got bored with Roman plays. Can I sell it?

Obs. No. XIII. ROME MAKES SLAVES. The obedient will be slaves. Slaves make empires. Others spotted Roman connections like Philip K. Dick. Said we live in a 'Black Iron Prison.' Dick did it mystically. H. G. Wells wrote in *Crux Ansata* during the war, asking... '*Why do we not bomb Rome?*' It took quite a while and that was light. Why? Some people D met were anti-Semitic. He detested it. Romans would destroy Judaism like they would destroy Christianity and eventually Islam. Illuminati stuff misleading. Atheist, scientific, materialist, mechanistic values. Cosmopolitan in their integration of all techniques from Black Magic to Pop Music. Infiltrated religious movements to turn them upside down. He did rule out extra-terrestrial involvement but not demon involvement. Consider all the possibilities. Ship of state drifting into a whirlpool. Guildhall Bombers had statements about Gog And Magog. Some old legend about the Roman Emperor's 33 daughters and the demons in Albion. That rational people do not believe these things does not affect their ability to influence reality. Generally Satanist elements or esoteric reference are never reported. Slavery came back in Libya. Us next. Again. Check your own goods out, do the work yourself, pay us. Do people care? Is it not too late and them too lazy to change?

"Drop that, there's a good fellow. I'd like to be like you."

Obs. No. XIV. ROME CENTRALISES SPIRITUAL POWER. Romans worshipped Magna Mater at times. Great **Mother**. But the Romans did not really believe anything as Gibbon said. They knew religion was a useful tool. They let people worship what they wanted while trying to keep fanaticism in control. Egyptian rites and druidry may be exceptions. They tolerated superstition without theological rancour and local deities and would adopt them sometimes maybe taking treasures for booty. They mocked religion and looked to Lucian, reason and eloquence instead. Church of Rome was really the church of the Romans. Roman Empire realised it was more efficient to control the spirit of man and spirits. Cross a symbol of imperial domination. Syncretism. Genius become genies under Tiberius. Now it is CONSCIOUSNESS they are after. Agenda for the Roman Agency. Put the genius back in the bottle. Romans left secret societies here. A theory in one stream of Jewish thought that the Edomites were ancestors of Romans. Edom. Red. Some said that the term Edomites became a code for Romans.

> '*Though thou exalt thyself as the eagle and though thy set thy nest among the stars, thence will I bring thee down.*'

King James version. Not sure. Elizabeth not so hard on witches. They thought her mother Boleyn was a witch with her extra finger. But witches were hounded during the Tudor era. Interested in the British

Israelite movement. Jewish mysticism. The Tower of Rome by S. Ansky. Rome, not meant to be Rome in Italy, but meant to be on another level, not just a place. Like a fetish. Neo-Romans were involved in all sorts. Neo=One. Descartes, trained by Jesuits, getting his knowledge from 'dreams' in the Netherlands studied the false suns or sun dogs that appeared at Rome in 1629. It affected him and society was affected by his work. Tell you it is reason. Led D to the theory of secret government. All the secret material convinced him. A Secret Council. Not connected to ETs. Human. Not connected with religion, but strict materialists. Possible link might be with Lucifer, not in a Satanic way, but as a myth. Keep religion for a modicum of social control. Established tax-free religious institutions. Wondered whether they worshipped technology and contemplated a religion. Religious institutions infiltrated. Propagated theories to throw people off the scent. Witches persecuted early on by Romans. Not only a Christian doctrine. Promoted and infiltrated Zionism to use it for their ends. Traditional Jews were opposed but nobody paid attention to that. All religions would disappear except an odd **Prome**theus-Pallas Athena philosophy. Gnostics were saying bodies had taken over the world and showed a false God. Competing non-canonical gospels ripped out. *The Gospel of Thomas* a dangerous one. Clear links between India, Egypt and Israel obscured. High points were World Wars, nuclear weapons, mass hypnosis through entertainment, diversion, distraction. As mystics like Gurdjieff, Crowley and Osho realised, people were in a trance. News was cartoons. Entertainment was deep psychic possession. Future was good for Them, bad for us. 'Globalist' agenda, 'overpopulation,' 'transhumanism' were theirs. Opposition gone. Agency personnel often clearly psychopathic or sociopathic. Only hope was Russia. Russians were dangerous to Romans if they re-Christianised under the Eastern church, not Rome. Could unite religions with individual freedom as Ficino, Mirandola and others predicted before they were destroyed. What Fatima was about. Islam would be split with a real Re**form**ation, creating a puppet Caliphate with the overthrow of the Saudis. Edomites would be home. Koran would be re-interpreted by an international council and be watered down so that it withered in the face of secularism. Use its conquering force as a spearhead before it was betrayed. The new Religion manifested in the Temple of Reason and the Goddess of Reason in the French Revolution. Then Maximilien Robespierre had his Cult of the Supreme Being. Like Masons. Reason would be what They say it was. THEY would be Gods. Reason loves the reek of blood, Robespierre links it to the Romans. Guillotine. Ignorato elenchi? Disease of secrecy requires speculation as remedy.

Inversion a key strategy. Infiltrated and controlled Catholic Church. Dangerous opponents like mystical Jews in Spain, Cathars, Druids, Heresy of the Free Spirit were done away with. You were part of the divine, you did not need a church nor a priest. Marguerite Porete burned. In South America, vast civilisations were done in through the Conquistadores. THEY were in the Slave Trade and destruction of Native Peoples who were always dangerous because they understood secrets of spirits which THEY wanted a monopoly on. Grey men and little people were real but they could be enlisted. Man-machine nexus the goal and domination of the universe. Enemy was the free-thinking, cosmopolitan individual who understood full potential of their spiritual freedom and powers. Scientific doctrine and evolution as defined by Darwin was central. Wallace was hated. Malthusian theory and the need for famine, war, fighting overpopulation was critical. People hated. Humanity backward.

"Here boy, c'mon. I'm meant to lead you. You can teach me."

Obs. No. XV. SOME SIGNALLED A SUBTLE WARNING ABOUT ROME. This one has to be developed as people don't know anything about novels before Stephen King. Some figures told stories in codes. He found it in *Cymbeline*. Shakespeare made it clear there. Posthumous the character who goes to Rome is what happens after Shakespeare's death. That's what posthumous means. Corrupted in Rome. End of the play, after the strong female figure of the Queen is cut out, Rome and Britain are joined.

> *'Although the victor, we submit to Caesar,*
> *And to the Roman Empire, promising*
> *To pay our wonted tribute from the which,*
> *We were dissuaded by our wicked queen.'*

And,

> *'A Roman and British ensign wave,*
> *Friendly together so through the Lud's town march.'*

Disguise, gender confusion, deception. In the end the Romans are in charge. <u>Shakespeare telling us that the goddess was against submission so she became demonised</u>. Shakespeare hinted the Reformation is not the end of the relationship between Real Rome and Britain, especially London. Cymbeline based on a figure. One of his sons was Caractacus. Only other figure we know is Caractacus Potts in *Chitty-Chitty-Bang-Bang*. Who wrote that? Ian Fleming. Author of James Bond. JB. Joachim and Boaz. Spymaster himself. Bond Code book. About magic, initiation, occult forces. Diana said she used to have to watch Chitty Chitty with the Royals every Christmas. Strange film. Non causa pro causa.

Edward Bulwer-Lytton who was fascinated with Rome. Many notables went to see Pompeii. Why? Because it showed life under the Romans. Communion. But Bulwer-Lytton also wrote about the Vril. Nonsense. *The Coming Race*. Superrace lived underground, had telepathic powers and intelligence, loved by Nazis. Vril have great powers, dangerous, healing. Interested in material agents like magnetism. Book *A Blighted Life* by Rosina Doyle Wheeler his wife. Said he was reptile, diabolical. He sent her into one of the many private mental asylums. She got out because she fought him. In one book the hero is a murderer, Pompeii. A book about a Roman tribune, madman. *Godolphin*. The character goes to Rome. Meets Volktman or Volkman. Sounds like Volscians, the enemies of Rome. His 'fatherland' in Denmark. Astrology. *Alice or the Mysteries*. *Zanoni, The Guardian of the Threshold*. Rosicrucian novel. *The Tale of Kosem Kosamim*. Strange Story. Rosicrucians. **Rom**mel. The Romans included *The Wolfen* of Whitley Streiber. Intelligent beings. Seek Rome, you find it. Reductio ad Hitlerum? Reductio ad Romanum. ROME RULES STILL fits the bill. I'll flog it now.

There is virtue in subdued emotion. We want the brain surgeon to be cool and unflappable. The explorer that sails across the ocean single-handedly. Mountain climbers. Perhaps that quality of a lower register of emotion allows them do such things. Dispassionate, cool, logical and distant. Got on with it. But in his dreams something disturbed him. Recurrent sense of something unfinished, involving some female figures in his life. Made him look outside the fish-bowl he lived in. A lean, erect man in his early 60's with white hair combed neatly. Breakfasted alone at sunrise. Regular meals, moderation. Aikido kept him trim. This morning, sausage, egg and bacon with a pot of tea and marmalade and toast, as he listened to the propaganda on BBC RADIO 4 and read the rags. Press. Suppress. Supine. Cronies. Cowards. Corruption. Standard of writing was poor. Journalists knew nothing. In the State's pocket. He liked the Telegraph on economics and Daily Mail. No free press. Fantasy. Chomsky says advertisers will not allow bad news be published. The Propaganda Model. When you worked in Intelligence you knew the

States served it, rather than the other way around. Same old guff about Russia worried him as he did not believe in the concocted threat. A lie is a necessary evil. The word is in evil and life itself. Lies everywhere. But now it's lie inflation, like trying to buy a loaf of bread in the Weimar. Most politics a stageshow. A con. Parliament castrated. The Kingdom was best with balance. Adventurist foreign policy an international crime. Nuremburg. Condemned it in their opponents after they made it up and then did the same themselves. He spent a few hours earlier in the day on routine paperwork which he stored in his safe, glad to be done with it. Will I be able to persuade? It's interesting and convincing. Suggest-sell.

The Tudors consolidated the State. Cut off obvious link with Rome. Elizabeth I put herself above the people, a prism for God. The State needs self-knowledge to be a healthy corporation or it becomes a Titan. Septimus Severus came to Britain and died here at the time the Roman Empire was greatest. Septimus, seven, seventh. Harry Potter, Severus Snape. SEPTember. Sept=clan. His wife complained about the natives cavorting publicly. Julia Doman an Empress. Mother of the Fatherland. Better to be open with the best than do things in secret with the vilest. St George's has the King in Roman dress. Traditional London food. Pie, mash and eels. Jellied eels! Who loved eels more than the Romans? Fed their slaves to eels. Most famous shop? Kelly's. Where? **Roman** Road Whitechapel. Join the dots. Romans are nearly finished eating eels, because chlorine killed off stuff the eels eat. Rome is key. Two keys. Cardinal Romero shot in San Salvador, because he talked about the poor, stood up to Them, not a good neo-Roman despite his name. Neither was Joan of Arc's mother Isabelle **Rom**ée. Or does that explain the miracles? Chance?

"Good boy. Leave that Rome… I mean alone. Dearie me."

Obs. No. XVI. ROME DESTROYS NATIONS. Sieges. Empires don't want nations. Slaves mostly had no country in Rome. Rome made nations melt away through war and submission and then the imposition of institutions of assimilation. If you adhere to Roman values you can become Roman and get the advantages irrespective of origin. Globalist Neo-Roman Agenda tactic of permanent revolution taking over. Battles about sovereignty between Royals, Parliament and the people largely resolved in favour of Parliamentary Sovereignty. Then the EEC. Power sucked out. Peter Sutherland a few years before the House of Lords Committee. Brazenly talked of too much national identity. An Irish man representing the Superforce. Agency. A strong, limited State not a pervasive apparatus. Intervene for common standards then get out. Libertarian. Let people make their own mind up. Now Nanny State. Health and safety. Wrap us in cotton wool. Poor children. A proud people, fought Europe. Then we signed up for third great incarnation of the Roman Empire under the Treaty of **Rome** establishing the EEC, then EU. Free movement of goods, persons, service. Freedom to consume. Britain stood alone when the dark clouds fell on Europe. Britain had the Magna Carta, systems and institutions. Soon Britain gave up of its own free will to government pooling sovereignty with failed countries. Marshall Plan. Wild west marshal. Knight's Marshall. They are there when war is proclaimed or peace. William Marshall served 5 kings and was Regent himself. Invested into Order of Templars on his death bed. Buried in Temple Church. A secret Templar? Earl Marshall title, horses, chivalry. When force failed and Empire 'fell,' came back and tried to rule our spirit. That failed. Try to rule us with magic of **COMMER**CE. Fashion, film, gambling. Names there. Caesar's Palace. Ponte. Venetian. Fashion, Schiaparelli. Family excavate Egyptian tombs and find canals on Mars too. Cars. Alfa Romeo and so on. **ROMEO**. All roads. Don't mention. Fiat. Lamborghini. Ferrari. Thatcher, Reagan all of a sudden everything was about 'Monetary' Policy. Fiat money. **Mo**ne**ta**ry, money. Anagram. ROMAN YET. Zimbabwe. Insiders signal all the time. Mediocrity and a lack of nobility everywhere. Everyone reading from a script. Youth lauded because they know nothing. Thick as pig-shit some. Less about the Barons that contained King John. Magna Carta. De Montfort. Many that struggled to contain power. Lord of the Manor. *Manor*. Roman in origin and anagram. Muriel Spark, Anthony Burgess, U**mber**to Eco, all roads lead to Rome. False? Headbursting.

His wiry frame moved stealthily, a typical country gent, tweed jacket. Well-manicured sense of someone who paid attention to detail. A deep stare when he swivelled his head to look at someone. Face impassive. Ostensibly slightly frail but closer inspection would reveal a tight, strong constitution. Cotswolds a bit of real England to him, despite roadblocks on the periphery now. Lovely old churches. Pubs. Fine ale, a sense of the ages. Stone warm honey-coloured. Upper class lived here. He was a true blue. A blue blood. Eyes of piercing blue. A startling, striking almost hypnotic look when he addressed you directly. Went white early, with worry about his daughter. Unclear that she would function normally. Did not speak. Unclear what she heard or saw for a long time and he suffered for her. She got help, things were not as bad as it seemed. Dark place. Now she was a successful showjumper. Very proud. Married a man from Vancouver. During that time, he read all about Helen Keller. He could not remember exactly. Happiness is fidelity to a worthy purpose not self-gratification. You may have sight but no visions. Self-pity is a terrible thing. Be an optimist. Arrow that kills the eagle has an eagle wing to guide it. You needed suffering and darkness to see the light. Stick to it to get it done.

Reluctant to embrace mistaken idea of progress. Libertarianism did not mean you do not have your own views, just that you don't have to impose them. Glad arc of his career was coming down with pampered generation coming in. He worked in an inherently pathological system of secret services. Used business as a cover and for research. On treadmill, you did not question. Too busy. Stakes very high. Such systems do not attract normal people. Proud he coped. Family life must suffer. Friends minimal. Venerable clubs and societies your family. Dealing heartless robotic people. Enemies all around and you never knew who or when. John Stonehouse a Czech spy and became a Junior Minister. Never know who are agents of what, even at highest level. David Kelly done in over Iraq War? Nothing stops The Plan. Stress gets you. So you worked, squeezed everything all your life, making sacrifices and woke up one day a monkey institutionalised in a zoo and did not know what to do. People shrink. Fall in status. No juice. Public would not laud you, did not know you. Younger associates climb greasy poles. What if you only had this chance? A cog in a machine. An invisible creature grinding interminable tasks. A new cadre had power. Least here he could relax, attend Polo matches, walk dog. Blue ribbon. 'D' at work. Maestro in orchestra, quieter type without megalomaniac tendencies. Near top in Secret Service. Brief floating. Managed many operatives. Many saucers in air. Did his job, loyal to Queen, country or King as may be. Model of incorruptibility.

Scottish roots. Loved the UK, hated traitors. A nation heaping up its own funeral pyre. D used his experience from private school, sector, military intelligence, various clubs and societies to benefit the country. Short stint in Royal Navy, 'the Senior Service.' Navy was Elizabethan. Navis, Latin for ship. The Navy traditionally ran Intelligence. Soft-spoken, firm, used to people doing what he wanted without question. Decisive. His wife Juno was dead. He studied every dark corner, theory, strategy. Battlefield. An expert on how to gain valuable information. He had Covert Technical Supervisions as well as general intelligence within domestic sphere. No doubt he could work privately afterwards but it lacked that golden thread.

Needed nerds for certain problems. A mistake to cede overall strategy to them. Failed to see critical things, blinded by their own brilliance. Intelligence attracted a lot of highly intelligent people that fall into a complex vortex of goals, tactics, strategic objectives but missed some basic elements. Over-valued technical know-how. Failed to see far right, left are interchangeable. Extreme ends of same string. You organised central State, make it trim but deadly. SPECTRE nearer the truth than people realise. Roman connections. Marco Sciarra. Make some truth fiction and people believe fiction is the truth. Francis Bacon. Valerius Terminus. **Rome**o and Juliet. When you read it, it makes no sense. Then look at other meanings, Rome, ancient Julian family and understand it is the start of a new time. Grand Master must talk in riddles. Make them hate their own. Wizard of Oz is not controlling doesn't mean someone else isn't. Ozymandias. Museum. Shelley. Hunter holding wolf walks among fragments of annihilated London, the Babylonian City gone.

"Nice evening Mr. Brown. Sorry I must catch up with him."

Obs. No. XVII.   ROME WILL DESTROY TO REBUILD FINALLY.

Last few decades tarnished his feeling for the country. Pollution of water and air, of language, swearing. Blue language. No problem with people coming with a sense of respect for the culture. Although at penultimate level of power, he had no sense of what was going on. Who made decisions and why? A constant insertion of policies that in no way served the State. He adored Margaret Thatcher, admired Churchill and Enoch. Heath hate. Forces in the land would destroy it. As Enoch said, all bullies are cowards and most cowards are bullies. Powell made a mistake of thinking it was about race. <u>Romans did not bother with race if you were with them</u>. Right on that. Enoch right about WW2, **demo**graphy, PC and EEC. Easy-peasy. Brexit too late. Celts were the real founders, enemy of the Romans. Caesar described the Druids in France. Respected, educated their community, settled disputes. Sacrificed criminals in huge willow figures. Went to Britain to learn. Had law before Romans. Celebrated prophecy of Malachy. Last Pope would be 'Peter of Rome,' or 'Peter the Roman.' PETRUS ROMANUS. Would destroy Church. Roman because he was in secret club. Malachi Martin talked about enthronement of Satan and Lucifer in Vatican. Pope Leo XIII had a vision of Devil and God fighting over the Church. Neo-Romans took back the Vatican in 1960's. Romans transmuted into The Holy Roman Empire when Charlemagne translated to EU, global trade agreements and TTIP. Take model of the City of London and project it onto the world. Radioactivity. Biggest problem was Caesium 137. From Latin word for blue-grey. Same possible root of word for 'Caesar.' Nuclear madness one of their creations from Titus Lucretius on. 'Architect of the nuclear age'? Enrico Fermi, born in September 1901 in Rome, inspired by old book by a Jesuit working at Roman College. Fermi worked at Sapienza University of Rome. When they named Ballistic Missile limitations SALT talks, code was that these were not serious. Salt. Roman. Ballistic missiles from Roman Ballista. US kept TRIDENT missiles. Like Roman Neptune. Clever Romans had nanotechnology. Used electric fish to alter the brain, early neurology. Knew about harnessing lightning. Benjamin Franklin used it much later. Maybe after Jacques de **Roma**s who did it. De ROMAs. Now most consciousness is studied in California. Comes from word Caliph, or from Romans. Calida Fornax. Hot Furnace. Death Valley. *Name of the Rose* really should be The Name of Rome. Though Eco had a Roma tower in the scheme still. Romulus, Remus and so on. **Roman**i people, gypsies. Django means awake in Romani. Roman everywhere, mobile. Spread-eagled. Jesus, look at Colonia Dignidad. Rat-lines. Channel to South America. ODESSA. Roman help. Certain groups use Roman magic. Look at families that controlled relics of saints and how they achieved power. St Andrew. Rome will destroy, re-build. Into everything. **The Empire strikes back.** Would the public buy it? If they could not understand the Roman language of argumentation, could they argue or analyse properly to confirm or deny it? Sting in the tail was that Rome had allied with China. Chicomcap. Where China had got its policy of Barbarian Management, Tributary states with dominance through empire and trade from. Tacking. Com vincere.

THE END. FIN. TERMINUS.

See why you'd go mad without a wife. Is Mr. Brown controlled by remote? Ghost-catcher botheration. Clown in a coffin. Convincing with repetition. Duppy conqueror. If true THEY deny it, explain away, lock up proponents. Taunt like serial killers. Do people not notice algorithms pulling them in? Not just that he had gotten lonely. Felt he missed out. All the time did his duty, plied his books diligently, fought hard on rugby teams, fenced his best, obeyed his superiors, loved his Queen, respected institution of States, faithful to his wife. Gone. No one would replace her. He would talk to her when he brought flowers to the old graveyard today. Missed her. Easy when you see sky full of Luftwaffe to understand who you are fighting against. Not so easy when you begin to see the world differently from many of your countrymen. A seed of curiosity. He could not say when. Fantasies. After Juno passed, he saw the stern mother, his nice Governess, Thatcher, his Queen, young women in the Service reflecting one figure. A dominant figure, in control. Then he saw Ethel, Candy Apple Crimson X. Brigid. A pretty Elizabeth. Suspected in later years she found it hard to be attractive as she poisoned herself with lead. Not about looks but attention. Not about physical contact or pain. He was no sadist nor masochist. A part of him wanted to play a game with roles, to escape the tight straitjacket. Be allowed to let go. Found discrete 'therapy.' Ethel Woodpecker. Nothing really sexual and never ever discussed who he was or what his work was. A very remote possibility someone could use it against him. THEM. Few knew who he was. A research study. Genuine interest in these things. Still exposed him. A long list came to mind - Profumo, Thorpe. Not the same but the time had come to finish it. Loose ends wrapped up. Possibly one last time. Vincere-conquer became convince - Liz. I need relief for my mind and health.

Sky cobalt blue tending to indigo with a sliver of red in the west over Wales. Air more moist now cooler as a shower seemed to be coming in over the Bristol Channel. Hills long blue in the distance fading and merging into the purple, on-coming evening shadows. Birdsong dwindling as they settled down for the night and would give way to the owls. He looked up, ever hopeful to glimpse a meteor or other object making a majestic trajectory. You might see a horseshoe bat flitting about feeding on the teeming air. He thought they mated this time of the year and when the weather gets colder they hang upside down. Twilight imploded day now in the time between dog and wolf. Vespertines unseen crept and rustled in the cooling crepuscular breeze. When the sun was gone and the last, late light faded feelings grew. A bright moon would often calm the sense of isolation. His home felt empty and there was no filling it ever. No politeness nor cordiality could penetrate the armour of decades of aloofness and self-possession. He had not felt lonely really. He got attention. Simpler than that. He looked at what other people obviously looked to. Blue movies. Terrible. Dull people. No depth, mechanical. Also nasty things he had seen in his work. He knew he was somewhat mechanical. While he listened to jazz and the blues, he did so as a kind of technical thing. Emotions were not something he was openly open to. He knew musicians like a railway timetable.

Heard the interview, because he paid attention. The majestic princess became all women. Tired of men, of liberals, wishy-washy people. Men with no balls. Emasculating. Nietzsche said, when the will to power begins to decline physiological retrogression always follows. He let Brennus off the leash and he sniffed around, bounding with joy in the graveyard perfumed with yews. As he placed the flowers on his wife's grave he spoke to her in his bowed head.

"I might have been silly. It was uncharacteristic. You know. But you are gone. Although you are still there somewhere. You are in my heart. By me. She is just in my head. I am still faithful to you in my fashion. Thy shadow falls."

'But I was desolate and sick of an old passion. When the feast is finished and the lamps expire then falls thy shadow.'

A genuine brief, that initially he laughed at. Papers identified how dolls, sexbots, fembots, robots would become commonplace. Some thought it would be encouraged because of the over-population concern. Or part of an agenda to control humans. Robots as police and soldiers. Being 'trialled' now in London. High-Tech units identify specific uses and threats posed by these products as mechanical spies in real-world situations. Clarify a strategy for brothels opened up with robots and dolls. Collect medical and DNA information, listen, record, see, seduce. Use of the escort business for counter-espionage and intelligence-gathering was very well established. A premium on establishing ways to utilise existing channels to insert some of the new models developed by security services. Saw one in a lab. In the cold light of day, most sniggered. When they dimmed the lights, passed around a whisky and recreated a romantic environment with music, he realised it was no joke. When that illusion was allied to mind-control techniques, possibilities increased. Their robot would collect biological material and could analyse and communicate it in real-time. They could carry explosive devices, poison. You poison targets, they die 3 days after, nobody know where it came from because they never told anybody else they shagged a machine. Channel of implementation sticky. That led him to overseeing the management of potential sites. See what is there. Thereby he had come across this little operation. Stuck in his mind. Ethel. So initially he really was doing his job, and anything he did was actually consistent with that. He had locus. Inside he knew differently. Once the rack was quite effective. Ask Guy Fawkes. Look at his signature before and after. Soon they claimed technology would read the mind. He was sceptical and reports were grossly exaggerated. Simple means could often make a person let down the drawbridge into their being. The old ones always work. Lust. Gluttony. Greed. Sloth. Wrath. Envy. Pride. Sinhooks. Blackmail. 7 deadly sins. Conquer now by convincing.

"Here Brennus, good boy."

D closed the churchyard gate and felt the peace of it. He would lie there with Juno. Lie there. Of no moment. No fear of death. Fears of some possible paths of life before death. His little comfort brought back a reconciliation of happy times with Jane his Governess and boundaries he explored way back then. There is a process of engagement with a barber or an intelligence officer. A matter of attention. Most people parrot the role. But it was necessary for people to interact and engage in a mutually dependent way. Basic biological need. He derived a strange comfort from the power inversion. He was ostensibly weak, in a games-like way. Gamey. In his mind the figure came and sat on the stage and he could go to that secret place and enjoy the company and the temporary loss of power, of authority. Sublimate the devotion he had to the Kingdom represented in his mind by tradition and blood regularly discharged on the battlefield. Sometimes transported back to the court of Queen Elizabeth I in the presence of someone that would build, protect the realm, fight like a man or a lion, defend it against all attackers, using persuasion, cunning, magic, weapons. A refreshing bluntness away from all contemporary cant and correctness like a foul fog. Witches brewing in Macbeth was public discourse now. Slightly disconcerted when he had spoken to Cranbourne. He knew at least he could call on dark forces. He had power, no questions asked to have his will done in his Kingdom if needed. Trained to follow orders, be robotic.

"Come Brennus."

Brennus defeated the Romans of course.

What happened was extraordinary. Reminded him of what he read in Marcel Proust but could never understand. *Remembrance of Things Past*. Ethel somehow re-activated an exquisite sense of the past, delicate, sweet, long-buried and forgotten. Could not comprehend but it helped him find some rare peace. Noticed he could see colour navy again, once powerful, but become bland. He would not let this silliness become what Greeks called his hamartia. A fatal flaw that leads to a fall from grace. Lawrence Olivier said that when you played tragic figures in Shakespeare it was like a statue with some little flaw that leads to disintegration. Never-to-be-forgotten scent of roses seemed to have turned to ash in his mouth. Never underestimate vulnerability if elite colleagues got wind. More like Gladstone. Midnight escapades never damaged the Prime Minister even though he had many hours of company with prostitutes. Afterwards Gladstone whipped himself. Said he did not betray fidelity to marriage bed. Maybe lesser sins. D worried this Uproar would allow even highest be purged. Crafty Cranbourne could smell a rat. Might also let him smell a rat. Needed a clean bib.

When he reached his house Burke was there. A quick visit. They stayed outside with dusk over the yard with Brennus wolfing his bowl of meat.

"I have found out about the *expedient judicial process*," Burke said quietly.

"Good. Well they have been open, that measures included execution which is as near summary as to make no difference. Courthouse is mobile. Forensics part of that process. Standard of proof is that of civil actions, on balance of probabilities. Process in the martial zones in London and Birmingham now is quite distinct from the internment process," D explained.

"Correct. Open about what they are doing but not much more. A little bit more detail." Burke.

"Life is lived in the details." D.

"Indeed. Anyway, I don't know what to make of it in one way. In another it's entirely predictable. Court often positions itself outside the Old Bailey. Court which has power to impose severest penalties," Burke said.

"Makes sense, although puts it in the City."

"Central Criminal Court is there anyway."

"Yes." D nodded.

Burke lowered his voice. "Here is the grim part. Quite a number of executions have taken place with a media blackout."

"I thought so. I'm not surprised," D said.

"This is the bit I cannot wholly corroborate," Burke whispered although there was nobody else there.

"I'll take it for what it is," D said.

"If prisoners are found guilty they're taken to a section commandeered in Smithfield Meat Market. On the way, they're injected with tranquiliser or get it through a spray. Hung up, throat slit, bled to death. Takes a few minutes. God's truth." Burke raised his bushy eyebrows high as he concluded.

"Jesus, that's practical," D responded, slightly laughing with a sort of gallows humour.

"Well, execution is never going to be pretty. They'll argue, it is effective and rebels suffer little pain. A special link to Bart's across the road for organ transplants, like Chinese do. Nobody ever bothered about that," Burke said.

"Less than William Wallace in the same area," D.

"Trial process is recorded but will not be released. Another detail which is touching." Burke.

"Go ahead."

"In the interests of efficiency, bodies are rapidly dissected."

"That's the traditional way."

"They have added a nice, liberal twist."

"Yes."

"They are recycling the bodies," Burke whispered.

"Goodness," D said, suppressing an odd desire to giggle.

"Meat is being packaged and sent to the internment centres. Blood is collected. Use everything. Sustainable," Burke said raising his eyebrows.

"Charming. What was the film... Soylent Green?" D asked.

"Looks like we're getting there. Better be circumspect." Burke.

"Is this the Big One then?" D asked seriously.

"History has often depended on the way the wind blows. Guess if we get a wild one tonight that does damage, we have perfect storm for the Big One. God help us. One more thing to tip it and whoever is driving this monster has us by the gooleys. But my suspicion is a trial run. Not quite ready for The Final One," Burke answered.

"God save us. If you look where Tullianum was in ancient Rome, it was where Newgate and Fleet Prison were in London, a cliff over a river by the wall. No surprise they go back to original blueprint. Dungeon there. Same old. Wonder whether they are using this as cover for a DNA grab, enzyme collection or something? Some people have things they want and they squeeze all the juice from the fruit ," D said wearily wondering about the meat Brennus scoffed.

"Last thing. Sniper forensics are not available. Moratorium. Something odd," Burke concluded.

As Burke departed down the driveway crunching, D thought of real Satanists again and a cold chill came over him. Camus. Age of bewilderment. Maybe The Caliphate will be run from Rome. Least they believe. Pope bought and sold. He went after him.

"Burke.." His voice lowered..."Who is it?... Who..."

Burke grimaced. "Well, I am more inclined to the view that it's AI unleashed by savants..."

"Oh fuck me pink."

LLLF

LONDON LOGOS LIBERATION FRONT

Publishing Pamphlets to Oppose Censorship of Our Message.
The Counter-Revolutionary to Evil and Terror Effort.
The last hope for London.

BEWARE THE REASONABLE MEN IN SUITS.

BEWARE THE CARING WOMEN IN TEARS.

BEWARE THE SLACK-SHOULDERED HOSTS.

BEWARE THE PRIESTS AND VICARS.

BEWARE THE WITCHES AND BLACK MAGICIANS.

BEWARE THE SORCERERS.

BEWARE THE FELLOWS.

BEWARE THE TRANSHUMANISTS.

BEWARE THE COMEDIANS.

BEWARE THE SATANISTS.

BEWARE THE POP GROUPS.

BEWARE THE ROCK GROUPS.

BEWARE THE RAP GROUPS.

BEWARE THE NGOs.

BEWARE THE DNA MANIPULATORS.

BEWARE THE UN, CFR.

BEWARE THE NEWS-READERS.

PREPARE FOR LIBERATION

Chapter 18

Dominus

Would that I were back in Swedish forests in an almost sandalwood smell in sunny September shafts lighting forty shades of green carpet dappled undergrowth bubbling mushrooms and toadstools of bright orange, speckled scarlet, black, pale yellow, all shades of beige, brown, white just as red even blue butterflies and busy bees enjoy lingering summerwarmth with the lone red dragonfly insisting autumn is coming as late blueberries crinkled crimp by the odd bramble and golden-ambered deer browsing in forts of fairies up from gently lapping lakes wondering whether there were spirits or elves and Santa Claus intelligences lurking in mean named muscimol, ibotenic acid, psilocybin and other stuff nature made curiously available perhaps whose spores came through space and maybe which through cleansing the doors of perception reminded us of dangers of domination of lizard brain or some such potential in us originally that brings us solely to earth and material and out of higher dimensions or poison you and do your kidneys in. Bad trips. Stay away. Just look. Enjoy nature. Synaesthesia. Synaptic plasticity. Plastic City.

Christopher Wren 2 Plan got some attention. 'Brains' (aka George) had also constructed projectors that they placed on City cranes putting messages on skyscrapers for thousands.

'THEY WILL MICROCHIP YOU ALL SOON.'

'DON'T MAKE YOUR SERVANTS MASTER YOU.'

'IT IS ONE MINUTE TO THE MIDNIGHT
OF YOUR ENSLAVEMENT.'

'OPPOSE THE CONSPIRACY AGAINST
CONSPIRACY THEORY.'

''CON' AND 'TROLL' IS HOW WE ARE CONTROLLED.'

Some attention for LZLF. People saw it. Appeared on the internet but it was so managed that they would not stay long. But London was awash with posters, leaflets, pamphlets. Propaganda inflation. In two intense weeks they executed plans of long gestation. Exhausted. Only 7. All had other things to do. Although execution of plans was invigorating. Janet was working on a Press Release encapsulating some of their beliefs. Found it difficult to articulate a succinct, comprehensive view acceptable to all. Even had a conflict about Wren. His plans were often thwarted. He wanted the Fleet River properly restored for example. They had authorised Janet. Seemed serious now but it was also seriously exciting. Contrasted with her 'normal' life. Normal in an Emergency. Working on an acronym. Thought of DOMINA or DOMINUS. Meant Lord or Master or owner often of slaves or its female equivalent. Title under Diocletian. Lord and God (Deus). She thought that all this domination stuff was a reflection of this underlying truth. They own, we slave. DOMINUS. She looked for some of the opponents of people they were against. Thus the domination came from D (Darwin). She would prefer Wallace. M was Malthus. He seemed to have given carte blanche for all kinds of justification for war and famine. The LZLF believed that the War Machine was partly based on Malthusian principles of population control same as was spurious environmentalism. Environmentalism should have been based simply on stopping pollution and facilitating the natural world. Godwin was the opponent of Malthus. Newton could be the N. His opponent might be himself. While he was a great man, a great scientist, he seemed to have hidden his mysticism which could have balanced his life. They criticise the Church for executions and the Inquisition but when Newton was Master of the Mint he had people like Chaloner hung. A clever scoundrel, forger, turncoat… still. Nietzsche came into her mind, but many of the things he wrote had elements she disagreed with. She re-read his theory on master-slave morality. Alfred Nobel, warmonger not peacemaker. 'S' was Sherman. His Total War was based on his knowledge of the Union's mechanical superiority and not the moral. Not motivated by emancipation. Crazy in his own words. Ruined the South and later helped the railroads destroy Indian lands. 'M' could be the Japanese Metabolists. Could have been the 'Burnt Ash School.' Irked her that in the land of Basho such a movement could take hold. Japan gave the secret of 17 in the haiku form. 17 was the Revelation of the Scarlet Beast. 7 heads and 10 horns=17. There was 1717, the Masons. 1717 the Society of Antiquaries London meet formally at the Mitre Tavern Fleet Street. Fleet. 17 seconds in the

Law of Attraction. 17 seconds of sunshine in Newgrange. 17 Cherry Tree Lane. The road trip in *Zen and the Art of Motorcycle Maintenance* takes 17 days. 17th September Hildegard. Sum of first four primes. You can construct the 17 sided polygon with a compass, a rule. Heaven 17 in *A Clockwork Orange*. The band. 17 rare earths. CV 17 is the heart pressure point on your chest. 10 is perfection in order, 7 is spirit. Even the Illuminatus Trilogy with their satirical reference to 23 seemed to have seriously understood the power of 17. 17 second key part of the Babalon working. 17 the number at first meeting of The Ratio Club. Truth within a bluff. It was getting tough. Maybe it was a bad idea. At least the actions could make a point and in their suggestiveness induce people to think about them. If you get technical, people will turn off. Most don't know their arse from their elbow these days. She scrunched it up and then ripped it up. When the sirens are still going and people are disappearing and might is made visible, there is no need for philosophising. People would never follow some of the logic anyway. Who would believe if you explained to them how Trump Street in London EC2, near the Guildhall and built after the Great Fire of London, between Russia Row and King's Street could foretell a US President. Trumpet, trump card, triumph. Forget mumbo jumbo, esoteric bibliomancy and geomancy. Focus on actual world action. Just say it is clearly wrong, appeal to sense of right everyone has. Let's just tell the noose is being prepared for them. Create tinder for their sparks. Spark that lights the prairie fire. DOMINUS. DOMINA. Need a beer. Fuck it. Too obscure. Specially when we are saying that people have lost a part of their mind. *'Emancipate yourself from mental slavery.' 'You better free your mind instead.'* But if the revolution has happened it is a counter-revolution. We just focus primarily on censorship yet so they will not listen. Captured with trivia. Entangled people's attention. Make you spend time proving you are not a robot. Make cheap medically unqualified labour in India identify supposedly cancerous growths in the intestine to educate AI. You never make a mistake when you underestimate the public's intelligence. Maybe we are just a competing elite? Why couldn't she just be like George Carlin and get a big idea in a few words.

'Never underestimate the power of stupid people in large groups.'

LLLF

LONDON LOGOS LIBERATION FRONT

Publishing Pamphlets to Oppose Censorship of Our Message.
The Counter-Revolutionary to Evil and Terror Effort.
Arise, awake and awful control resist.

THE LEFT AND RIGHT ARE PHONY.

THE REAL LEFT AND RIGHT ARE TOTALITARIAN.

WE ARE NEITHER LEFT NOR RIGHT.

WE ARE ANTI-TOTALITARIAN.

WE ARE ANTI-FASCIST AND ANTI-COMMUNIST.

WHY OPPOSE FASCISM IN FAVOUR OF COMMUNISM?

WE ARE NOT STUPID ENOUGH TO BE ANARCHIST.

WE ARE THE CIRCLE OF THE RADICAL CENTRE.

WE ARE ANTI-AUTHORITARIAN BUT WILL HAVE MORAL AUTHORITY.

WHEN IT MOVES TOO FAR LEFT WE RE-BALANCE.

WHEN IT MOVES TOT FARR RIGHT WE RE-BALANCE.

WE ARE PRAGMATIC.

WE ARE COSMOPOLITAN.

WE RECOGNISE THE SPIRIT OF ALL.

WE WILL PROTECT THE SPIRIT AGAINST POLITICS.

WE WILL PROTECT THE SPIRIT AGAINST IDEOLOGY.

WE ARE SPIRIT.

PREPARE FOR LIBERATION

Chapter 19

Heart of Darkness

McGannah came out of Midship Point on Friday and walked towards the shop to get the bus. He was thinking of *Ritual in the Dark*. Murder in the East End. Existential despair driving serial killers. Colin Wilson. I'll wait for someone to tell me what I already know. Rumours. A slight overcast coolness about the weather. Disruptions to the service were largely resolved now, although there were still diversions in operation. Coming around the corner, a voice addressed him. "Good morning. How are your hips? Not late for work today?"

Turning around he saw his quarry, but it seemed he was the hunted now. Surprised, not shocked and his natural ability to relax was always useful. Options to dissemble were now limited. A little confused. She had no evidence of who he was, or could she possibly? Was there something else afoot? No inclination to be confrontational, seldom effective. If she had rumbled him, that was mere bad luck, she still did not know why she would be followed. But he did not know either and therefore the only thing she could know was limited, deniable. "Do I know you?" Kit asked.

"Yes Mr. McGannah. You're looking a bit slow. It is not good to be standing around on street corners," Ash said.

"You're right."

"Why are you following me?" Ash asked.

"That seems to be the other way around," he replied.

"I'm a bit busy Mister, so I'm giving you a chance. Answer me or see yourself on video all over social media in the next hour."

Limited options were becoming more limited.

"You don't have anything that would concern me. Did you see me waiting for a bus or something? Are you a stalker? Are you after money?" Kit asked.

"Bye," Ash said.

"Listen," Kit changed his tune. "There is no answer I can give you which will adequately satisfy you. But I am not against it if you think as a respectable senior citizen I might not be able to quell the irritations you currently possess."

"Do you want me to follow you or me follow you, if you follow me?" Ash asked.

"Ok. Touché. Fancy a coffee in there? Call me Kit. Not git. Follow me."

She looked over and nodded after a minute.

"Who is on my grey trail?" Kit asked.

"What ails you I might say?" Ash.

"Come in. However, I'm going to ask you to talk quietly and try to look like we know each other, if you don't mind. Furthermore I am circumspect and suspicious... like yourself," Kit said.

"Ok."

"You should be careful following men around. By the way, there are certain videos that get taken down quickly or are never allowed to be put up if people don't want them. Just bear that in mind."

"So the cat that wants the fish does not want to get its feet wet. I noticed that with odd Jimmy Saville. They cleaned up references," Ash said.

"He thought he was King Solomon. All that British Israelite nonsense." Kit.

Ash did not tell him that she could read him. Everyone had a gait and other bodily give-aways that revealed much of their personality. They went in and ordered a tea and a coffee and a cream bun and sat down.

"You should be careful following strange men."

"Thanks for the advice, grandpa..."

"I must be ageing a bit quicker than I thought, I'll send that exercise machine back."

"Just go easy on the cream buns. Right who are you? You're not anyone I've had dealings with. You don't seem like some kind of stalker. You don't look like a criminal or a hard man. You don't seem that bothered, or invested in you task."

He looked around, "Listen, I can't really talk here, let's finish and go to the park... across by the river. The tongue talks at the head's cost."

"I know it," Ash said.

"Do you know the Isle of Dogs," he asked as he messily bit in the bun.

"I know The Long Good Friday was filmed here. Colin Wilson books. Although I think the serial killer lived up in Camden Town. Mystics become murderers. Yes... interesting place. Are you interested in history?"

"Indeed I am. This was a lot more interesting before they smothered it with city types and skyscrapers. This used to be the biggest docks in the world. From all over," Kit said.

"John Dee did a magic ceremony to involve the British Empire on Mudchute," Ash said.

He looked up. "Not many people know that!"

"You know he was the original 007?" She asked with eyebrows raised. "*For Your Eyes Only.* Are you interested in any way at all in psychogeography?"

"What's that, geography for psychos..." He laughed at his own joke, she bristled. "No offence luv," Kit said apologetically. "Are you sure you need to ask who I am? Anyway, time to go."

He paid, they walked out and across the road.

"So you work for Her Majesty's Government?" Ash asked.

"You appreciate that I cannot disclose, but I'll not tell lies."

"So I'm paying a lot of tax for you to stalk me."

"You are very thorough it seems in that department."

"Shame you're not so. Then again maybe not. What's it about?" Ash asked.

"I've no idea," he said.

"Ok." She turned to walk off.

"Wait, hear me out."

She stopped, he beckoned her to follow into the Sir John McDougall Gardens. "I am a little cog. I get orders. I do filter work. If 'they' are deciding whether a person is a Person of Interest then I am asked to add a little. It is a... behemoth, a Leviathan that devours people like me too," Kit said.

"In what, who, why?" Ash asked.

"It could be crime, terrorism, political activism."

"That's not me!"

"I wouldn't worry too much, it's fairly routine, believe it or not. I'm bound" Kit.

"Routine..." Ash pondered.

"Listen, it's not secret, there is no organisation in this country, down to the smallest stamp-collecting society that does not have an informer or someone linked with them. That's not my fault," Kit explained.

"What'll happen?" Ash asked.

"My best guess... nothing." Kit shrugged.

"I hope not, for your sake or mine."

"You haven't provided services for any would-be high flying politicians seeking promotion?"

"Not to my knowledge although politics is a charade I largely ignore and I do not delve," Ash answered.

"I am assuming that you have not burst in among the bees. By the way pub quiz question. Which Dickens Novel would you associate with here?"

She wondered whether he was assessing her. "Maybe *Our Mutual Friend*," she replied.

"Bravo!"

"I'll read nothing into that."

"If something strange occurs let me know. That's all I can do. You can catch me from the bus stop there just after 6 most days, diversions permitting," Kit said.

"Haldane Reality is not only stranger than we imagine but stranger than we can imagine."

"Listen luv. If I find you are doing anything dodgy beyond your existing stuff all bets are off. I could be in the soup already," Kit said.

"Fine."

"About that Internet stuff."

"You're ok, I've no recording device."

"So you were lying to me?" Kit asked smiling.

"The effects speak, the tongue need not," Ash repeated the saying.

As he departed, he was cool. Not in the business of panic. He knew it happened by chance. No system is foolproof. It happened to Stalin where a member of the surveillance team in 1906 bumped into him. Not uncommon to cross paths and even for the person under surveillance to know or suspect it. So he changed his mental track. Back to the books. Hobbes. Cromwell. Hobbes believing that without an absolute sovereign, everyone would fight all the time. Rebellion. Cromwell. Difficult to believe the ameliorating stuff. A brutal time.

Ash would walk up the Thames Path. Isle of Dogs. If you can't pass through dimensions here you never will. This was one of the inter-dimensional portals where temporal untethering and the retro-perception portholes happened. Raleigh lived in Blackwall. Goebbels and Goering saw the docklands as critical, Zielraum G. Famous picture of German bomber over the Isle of Dogs. Bombed it on September 7. Elizabeth's birthday. Start of the Blitz. Billingsgate had a place where pick-pockets learned their trade once. Planes had Merlin engines. John Dee was Merlin and Prospero. Kept out the Spanish by storm, now keeping out the Germans. Magic everywhere. They think that way. She walked up to Limehouse. On the Thames

River Path she thought of the pirates hanging in cages. Gallows and gibbets all along here and the wind would create a creaking of bones to greet the newcomer. Pirates were privateers encouraged once and then discouraged. Sutherland's painting of the East End after the bombings came into her head, Churchill touring the sites. She saw Francis Bacon in her mind walking to meet criminal friends from his studio in Narrow Street. Predicting the UFC in his paintings. Limehouse once Chinatown. Walked where she knew the opium dens were. Sherlock Holmes in one of them, Charles Dickens described them. They had Sherlock Holmes looking for Nazis in a film round here in The Voice of Terror 1942. Prefigures *Gravity's Rainbow*. Fu Manchu. Spring-Heeled Jack sighted at the time. Scavengers, mudlarks, chimney sweeps. Pirates. Execution Dock. George Orwell walked around here slumming as a down-and-out. Down Narrow Street, Dickens. An alchemist called Gilbert. David McLean, film alchemy. The Impressionists. James McNeill Whistler. Gulliver coming to Wapping looking for a boat. Conrad, *Heart of Darkness* here. The Congo. Congo Square New Orleans. Voodoo. Jazz. Gandalf owned The Grapes Pub here at Limehouse Reach, at least the actor who played him. Captain Cook lived around here. People forget the reasons for his 'discovering' Australia on the Endeavour. His main mission was to chart the Transit of Venus for the Royal Society and then he opened his secret instructions from Admiralty to find the Great Southern Continent and take possession. On three voyages he had secret instructions. 'Secret Orders.' They knew it already.

Ratcliffe Highway Murders. Convicted murderer buried at the cross roads. Swedenborg lived at Wellclose. A great Swede, scientist. Spy it seems. He has his mystical awakening, although he was experimenting with breath control and something like tantric practices. God talked to him. He becomes a frequent visitor to heaven and hell and otherworlds. Influences Blake. Rabbi Falk, the Baal Shem of London, with magical powers lived at Wellclose. Great Rabbi. Square... cubits. The new Jerusalem was linked to here. Mayflower set sail from over the river. Fenchurch Street, Bank. Chancery Lane. She decided to get to Erik. She recalled what she had read about Toynbee the historian, how he slipped through time in Greece a few times and saw things. Toynbee knew about the events so you could say he was imagining it. Although other elements were not so easily dismissed. Others have seen things not there like crowds, battles they knew nothing about. Sometimes you can see it, you can prime yourself.

Erik was home. A Moldovan girl staying there. Pretty, skinny, dark circles. Found her working in London. He went around a bit like Gladstone. But Erik had more success than him. He facilitated the return of dozens. Did it quietly. If known he was finished. Playing the punter or John he could gather the intelligence he needed. There was no conflict between the business and the Red Light Runners. Consent was the line. She remained in the room when Ash was there. Ash did not want to be intrusive.

"Listen there is one thing that may sound silly. Been bugging me. It might be ridiculous but... Is it in any way possible that he wanted to be seen?" Erik asked.

"Like a serial killer wanting to be found," Ash said.

"No I mean could it have been some way to get your attention," Erik clarified.

"Consciously."

"Well yes..." Wondering about the girl, if she was listening.

"....I don't know. I can't see that. I think it was careless. Then again it was lucky, coincidental. I'm sure James Bond is not what it's like and he may just have had enough of all this kind of stuff... I don't know. What benefit would that be to him?" Ash asked.

"Well if you thought you had turned the tables, he could then appear weak and appear nice and non-threatening with then the possibility of getting to know you a bit more."

"Erik, he's not after me in that way," Ash protested.

"No, I mean he might build up a bond that could be useful. Maybe that's why they called him Bond. Make a bond. He could be a kind of kindly cop or investigator or something or whatever he is and when you trust him he might think you'll give him what they want. And you did say you like older men. Maybe they did a profile on you. Rapport. Report," Erik elaborated.

"Surely he didn't want us to follow him home."

"Well maybe it's not even his home?"

"Interesting. But not convincing. I'm not going to think this one out. I don't know. I can't know. So I'll feel it. He feels alright to me. That's all I can say. Listen I'm shagged, can I crash here tonight?"

"Of course, would you like the bed."

"I don't mind what you do with that doll, although I'm not going to think. Have you.... Couch. Thanks." Ash yawned.

"What'll you have for breakfast. Let me see. Poached egg on toast? Coffee," Erik suggested.

"Great. Quilt quick, look gone. Goodnight. Ta."

She picked up a book from the bookshelf on the way back from the bathroom. Fredrick Forsyth. *The Dogs of War.* Born in Ashford. He had worked for MI6. He said he did not get paid? How does that work? The other girl kept a low profile.

Maybe Raleigh was communing with a higher power when he wrote The Lie.

> *'Tell potentates they live*
> *Acting by other's actions*
> *Not loved unless they give*
> *Not strong but by a faction.*
> *If potentates reply,*
> *Give potentates the lie.'*

She thought of a possible rule.

Axiom 10   In unorthodox situations you need to be appropriately unorthodox.

Scarlet Woman. Whore of Babylon. It was not a woman. It was a symbol. Revelation 17. Symbol of the controlling power. A city or rather an organisation.

> *'And the woman which thou sawest is that great city,*
> *which reigneth over the kings of the earth.'*

As she drifted off to sleep she felt unease about being looked at. Uncomfortable with uncertainty. Unsure if she had been wise. Re-examining every word and gesture this man had made. Awareness of increased unwelcome attention. Exact reasons were unfathomable yet. Shifted her mind to BJJ. Sometimes in the morning they would roll and try some positions. When she dwelt on them she forgot other things. Eddie Bravo. 10th Planet. Conspiracy theories. Advanced Rubber Guard. Flying Kung Fu move. Electric Chair. Spider Web. Cocoon to Pyramid... Hypnagogia... Images... Sleep. Many contemporary moves were old moves. It seemed like the sport was erecting a sainthood or pantheon. The religion of BJJ. She just wanted the fun.... Logos is also used in cybernetics. Science of control and communications. Back to Maxwell..... Governors....... G'vnor. Governing planets. Follow the Yellow Brick Road, the golden path.

LLLF

LONDON LOGOS LIBERATION FRONT

Publishing Pamphlets to Oppose Censorship of Our Message.
The Counter-Revolutionary to Evil and Terror Effort.
Join the Radical Centre.

WE ARE THE SPIRIT OF THE PEOPLE.

WE HAVE SOUL.

WE HAVE SPIRIT.

YOU HAVE SPIRIT.

THE MAN DENIES SPIRIT.

THEY WILL SAY IT DOES NOT EXIST.

THEY WILL SAY YOU ARE AN ANIMAL.

YOU EVOLVED FROM SLIME.

SPIRIT DOES NOT MAKE SENSE.

THEY SAY IT IS AN ILLUSION.

YOU CANNOT PROVE IT.

THEY WILL TAKE IT FROM YOU.

YOU SAY YOU HAVE CONSCIOUSNESS.

THEY SAY IT IS AN ILLUSION.

THEY SAY YOU ARE A MATERIAL GIRL.

A MATERIAL GIRL IS NOT A SPIRITUAL GIRL.

THUS THEY TAKE YOUR POWER AWAY.

PREPARE FOR LIBERATION

Chapter 20

Intrusions

La Pucelle – The Golden Path

When you fall down, you get up. It is not the loss that defines you but your reaction to it. The stars you navigate by do not disappear suddenly. Alter as appropriate and act according to challenges. Ash was glad to be at home this mid-September weekend. Some rumbling since, but hard to tell when you had Mornington Crescent Tube Station below. Back in full swing. Some scars and evidence of things having been fixed. On a radio programme about the Emergency after 'The Great Shake' and 'The Great Quake,' human rights activists were complaining about conditions of detention rather than its existence. Debate about execution was a legal one about international obligations. The Quake intruded and led to further intrusion by the Government, supposedly as a result of the need to control looting and robbery. To restore order out of the chaos normal freedoms were curtailed. More concerned today about subtle intrusions. Some people believed that we had another self. Idea was important in ideas of hypnosis, mesmerism. Look at all the contexts where people see different forms. Find a loose thread and you pull it and things unravel. Gospel of Mark.

> *'After that he appeared in a different form unto two of them as they walked, and went into the country.'*

That fascinated her. She looked at all the translations and interpretations. 'In another form' or 'In a different form.' What did that mean? A spirit, alien, woman, non-human, non-physical shape? If non-physical what form? If physical what was different? Led her on a trip through Greek, Latin, Aramaic. To Biblical scholars. To theories about Mark's Gospel and when it was constructed and when bits were added. To the 'non-canonical' texts. Excluded documents. To look at why they were excluded and by whom. Back to Gnostics and Mystery Schools. To the secret schools of what she called True Gnosticism. Secret esoteric groups. To meet some of these people you had 'to come out of the crowd.' You had to show you have some excellent ability to deal with the highest esoteric and theological issues. Then someone might seek to engage you to see if you are capable of going deeper. Some of these groups needed an influx of new blood. Preparing for survival. Most survivalists saw that as learning how to get by in a world with no food. This could happen. But the real problem lies in a mass spiritual suicide or extinction. 'Spiriticide' was ongoing. Dispiriting. Survival challenge was contemporary. This was what the phenomenon of Zombies was about. Spiritual zombification. Clever people may see something, understand it on one level and can be smug in their cleverness. Wise ones see deeper. For example, Albert Einstein said that the Fourth World War will be fought with sticks and stones. Obviously that means on the surface that there will be a destructive Third World War which will destroy civilisation. But it also means that if we got to another war, then magicians would unite and finally take over. Back to Vico's first stage of 'poetic wisdom' after the third stage of the individual, selfish giant. Ruins to runes. Wands and gemstones. Magicians come when you have the true leader, true spirit. Merlin to Arthur. History and prehistory were a battle between the spirit and the physical and machine for dominance. Once Jesus was not a machine. Lenin and his cronies wanted order and machines and saw people becoming atheist, unfeeling machines. His spirit informs them still. Stuffed like Bentham, Mao, Ho Chi Minh he lies.

MEDITATION ON COLOUR OF HAZY BLUE

Just hazy blue, no other blue. Our lives are a spiral where on the turning you see something but pay not much attention till another revolution lets you see its import. She began to experience strange phenomena herself in such a way as to find it difficult to reject the reality thereof, despite the embedded empiricism and indoctrinated rationalism. But philosophy and science needed to embrace the individual again. They had to, because the great donors interested in consciousness were not investing to further the welfare of man but to ensure a greater web of control. Sometimes a creator or writer took over her imagination, not her psyche. Underhill was speaking to her again through *Mysticism* from 1911. Wrote well because she knew it as real, no *'eunuch in a harem'* as Behan used to say about critics. What was the other thing he used to say? *'The terrorist is the one with the little bomb.'*

She experimented as much as she could. Remote-viewing. John Dee may have used it. US authorities used it. Philip K. Dick. *Exegesis*. The attachment or possession of an entity was something different, as was the multiple personality disorder. Then there were past lives.

She had forgotten about Joan of Arc until something sparked an association. A few films, George Bernard Shaw. Incredible story, well recorded. A young, peasant girl gets visions, acts on them, changes the course of history and is burned and becomes a saint. Acquires an absolute belief out of the blue, from beyond her immediate reality that made her act with great decision. Many other great actors did not innocently reveal the well springs of their action. Francis Bacon the painter was a mystic she thought and no one seemed to have spotted it although he gave clues. More of the Rasputin mode. Rasputin belonged to the group who thought you needed sin before you get forgiveness so you got stuck into it. Supernatural powers. Walked to Greece. Not surprising Rasputin was unliked if he did not like war. Some believed Rasputin was killed by the British Secret Service. Some see a link between Joan and Elizabeth. The reception of things from above continues. Brazil has plenty of it with 'spiritism.' Chico Xavier. Joan of Arc lived in a house with a 45 degree angle roof with her family. Different. There are many first-hand accounts as well as her own. Unhappy with her family she left aged around 16-17. She fought against a marriage contract and won. Pilgrimages. She did not seem like a candidate to be burned at the stake. Plays a role in the 100 Years' War, or rather the succession of wars of that name between England and France. This virgin warrior inspired Elizabeth I. She hears voices from various saints, drives out the English and bring the Dauphin to Reims for his coronation. She persuades a commander to take her to the king after giving fore-knowledge of a battle victory. Travels over dangerous territory in disguise, saying she would lift the siege of Orléans. The French were concerned to know whether Joan was inspired by the Devil or the Holy Spirit. It was only when some Church men concluded that it was the latter that she got permission for her mission. Obtained armour. They sent her in 1429 to Orléans. Stalemate. A last throw of the dice. The quiet girl was ready for war, confident and ready to act. A week later the siege was lifted. God was on their side. Supplies still came in. England lost a leader. She may have been very lucky. It does not really matter. You might say she was protected by God. Her belief was so strong that she could deny the pain. What matter? The control of the world within is critical. Attain harmony within and without we are on a different level. If we say it was not a miracle, but luck and mental fortitude, that becomes a miracle itself.

Crowning of the French king in July 1429 came just after the siege. She participates in other military activity, later captured. Tried by a flawed, biased pro-English tribunal. For a while, she says she has done wrong. It could be to protect her family. At age 19, she is going to be burned. She goes back to herself, enlightened. Trial. Heresy. Martyr. Sacrifice. The legend is guaranteed. Strong mentally. She is burned but does not whine. She calls out for Jesus. You say it is the mind. But only some reach it. The army becomes successful. She had a vision of France and what to do strategically in battle. To get what she wanted she would bend rules. Fought and sustained injuries of battle. Made leadership decisions. Was confident and outspoken with an air of invincibility. Perhaps it was youth. History was affected by her.

From the age of 13 she heard voices. Messages coming to her. Some say she is schizophrenic, but she was not regarded as mad. The voices could be regarded as unconscious talking. They say she was listening to her unconscious. There were visionaries in France, often female, status could be obtained. Messengers of God were not uncommon. The voices were real to her at least and she acted. She could be seen as a witch, prophet, mystic. She became a knight. She did emerge. She did act. It was a bold move to start out on her mission. How could you know your voice was real in the sense that it was not just you? How could you believe that it was external, otherworldly, divine? If it was positive, would it matter if it was not from where you thought it came? It could be madness. But what if it works for you? Edgar Cayce goes into a trance and channels divine forces, including St Michael (which Joan of Arc did also). Rudolf Steiner seems heavily influenced. Are they mad? Cayce gives medical readings to a couple of thousand people. It may seem like faith healing, like John of God in Brazil. People will say, if it works it must be a mistake, a placebo. Cayce goes backwards and forwards in time. If the voice is consistent with what you believe in your highest states of consciousness or your best self then you might say it was your best self. Others believe you are tapping into a higher level of existence. Others believe you are entering another dimension. Others believe it is extra-terrestrial intelligence. Others believe it is spirits. Others believe it is a con. Hicks who does the Law of Attraction to many ordinary people is channelling 'Abraham.' 'Seth' spoke through Jane Roberts. These were not 'divine' in the sense that Joan of Arc claimed.

Ash had a Voice. You could say it was a higher self, true self, oversoul or an ascended master. She had no idea. But she heard a voice, clairaudience. She knew it was different because it spoke in haikus. It spoke of the spirit and presented simple but profound statements. She had no idea why it suddenly emerged one day. It felt nice. It could be channelling. It made her read about *Seth Speaks,* Abraham Hicks and Philip K. Dick's *Exegesis*. Some nonsense. Dick was a visionary. Then she read the Christian, Buddhist and Sufi mystics again, the mystic poets, the romantic poets. That was the truth. Partly. It freed her from all attachments, fears and doubts. She wrote them down. A failure of spiritual evolution. The theory of evolution had taken a wrong path. The material, intellectual was not enough. Primal consciousness in us. No priest needed. No institution necessary. As Indians knew, we and the greatest consciousness are one. Ones that reveal this knowledge will be persecuted because it threatens control. In us the divine. Like in legend, gods hid divinity within humans as the last place they would look for it. Jesus said the same thing but they buried those and edited it. Beethoven saw it. All great artists found it. At the peak they saw the other worlds. They knew it was not the illusory soup around us. When she began to write down these things, another onion peel fell off. Another doll found within. Then she was dreaming these things. She got instructions in her sleep. Maybe more realisations. Ideas came. Knowledge. It is there. The idea that you must get everything from some hierarchy is not the truth. Icke had influenced her.

How do you know you are not cracked? Maybe the future can come backwards. Why not stay on the sweet security of the accepted? Why not bow to the pronouncements of authority, whatever that turns out to be? Because that is not you. A part of you is ahead of you. You let your higher self speak. Elf in self. Your higher self gets bored with your false sense and pushed it gently out of the way. Another entity communicates. You communicated with other entities. You receive intelligences from the air, from on high, outside. It is not higher, it is a delusion. Could that mean that she was being directed by another force in her work? Her work was successful. You hear of musicians selling their soul, doing a deal. Ash did not want any deals. She did want to move along the paths she was meant to. Recently she had visions of a golden path. A narrow path made of gold. There for you when you are born. The more entangled in the mundane, the more the path gets obscured and covered. You seek to stay near it, but you deviate and come back or wait in the same place until sure you are seeing out on it. You feel you are on it, going the right direction. When you learn lessons, learn from the greater ones who help you see the path. Then you reach a stage where you can always see it again. It does not matter what happens the path is there.

The fascinating thing about Joan of Arc, was not that she had visions or heard voices or received instructions. It was not that she acted upon her strange beliefs or experience or reality. Rather she was able to convince very cynical and hardened powerful men of her position. Not only was she able to convince them but they acted upon it. There was her mystery. The refutation of mystical influence is contradicted by history. History is limited by confinement to the published word. Most underground. How many have had great inspiration which they were forced to conceal? Foucault on Sweden. The tedium of academic thinkers with iron-butt mentality and no originality was a cruel result of the control of free thought. Miracles could happen. Mysteries. Mystery of life itself. In her dream she had felt the power of her heart, a potent sphere of power that you knew was everything you could possibly feel.

She knocked on the door. She asked Mary if she could go to Mass with her the following day. She said she wanted to pray for people. Mary acted as if it was not unusual. She perked up.

"And the Blue Rooster after?"

"Sure." Ash smiled.

"How's your pal. Jum, Jame, Big Jum, Bug Jim how does he say it, Big Jimmy. Jem." Mary laughed at herself.

It was hard not to laugh as well as she got such a kick out of it and made other things disappear.

"Is he keeping well?" she said seriously, "Hope he's looking after himself. We'll say a prayer for him. Bring him round some time?" Mary suggested. She raised her eyebrows in an expectant question which Ash noted was actually an effective instruction. Instructions masquerading as questions were always useful.

She felt relieved. Acknowledged her unknowingness. She also wanted a blessing. Inside she had a sense that if there was anything untoward it might not operate in the Church context. Primitive reasoning process, but the realms she had opened needed a humble spirit, a meek sense of one's own ignorance in the majesty and tragedy of things. Placebo Effect. Maybe. But she had given herself over, not to any outside force but to the power of her intuition. The Lie.

'Tell them that brave it most,
They beg for more by spending,
Who, in their greatest cost,
Seek nothing but commending.
And if they make reply
Then give them all the lie.'

Next few days, were getting into some peaceful mode. She could tell her spiritual exercises began to enter a different realm. Her gathering experience represented a discovery of different levels. When you work on it, you begin to rise and discover a portal, or doorway, a staircase into a different level of reality. It happens when you have exhausted or completed the stage below. She felt she was on one level for much of her life and then when she began looking she found a door. Than it went quicker to the next level. You learnt more and released weights of unreal thoughts that were untrue. She was moving to another level now, she was quite certain. If she had time, she could note it in a journal, but then again she had to make it part of her inner being, not external. It was her inner being. In the morning she needed to go to Primrose Hill for a quick walk. It did not take long. Blake, Dion Fortune, prehistory, Auerbach. You get into a vital vortex of energy. Bram Stoker. His girlfriend in Dublin married Oscar Wilde. ∇ Like Yeats, Maud Gonne and John McBride. Triangles. Did his play send out the men that were shot? People think it was his theatre play but he meant his magic play. Hampstead swim. Some women still moaning about the 'not proper women' who were swimming. Identity gone. Daphne du Maurier. Rebecca. Goldfinger an architect lived in Hampstead. Hampstead, Parliament Hill was an energy vortex. She might see Jem.

MEDITATION CLOSES EYES DOWNWARD MONAD.

She knew from Buddhism, Shamanism and parapsychology that when you worked you acquired or unleashed powers in some way. She began to see, or imagined she could see colours in the purple or probably ultra-violet range around plants in the evening. In her hot yoga class a mountain lion's face appeared into her consciousness, like a hologram. She interpreted it as some totem or animal helper. One night, a funny creature like an elf sat in her consciousness. He seemed happy and content and a little bemused. She felt a little uncomfortable. Between the outside and inside. It appeared before the cinema screen of your visual mind within. She knew that the hypnagogic state between sleeping and waking was the great but narrow and fleeting arena where strange and wonderful things could appear and many great scientists and artists knew this and developed it. This was how Dickens wrote, although she was unsure of him at times.

She wondered whether the re-reading of Underhill and her mystical experience affected her subconsciously or coincided with greater consciousness of the phenomenon. She had no desire to leave herself open to other spirits. She constantly practised Betty Shine's Auric Egg exercise and a Protocol of Spirit Cleansing. Said prayers too the old fashioned way. If it was good enough for John Dee it would do her. Her journey a singular one. Sceptical about gurus, people that knew everything, gatekeepers. Problem was you could lose all markers, perspective, direction and not know whether you were descending into madness. She thought Van Gogh would not have produced his great work if he had not fallen to the bottom. But what could she show. That was the price. Look at *A Christmas Carol*, it is real strange. Like a Near Death Experience. She had read about possession, took it seriously. She would never relinquish control of her soul. What was higher? You could be plagued by demons if you opened up. You can't believe that there are spirits and that all are benign. Fools rush in where angels fear to tread. Interested in a range of mystics she walked to Foyle's stopping off at Atlantis. Christian mystics were a revelation again. Boehme, Eckhart, and the gospels that were left out. Gnostics were close. Through Russell Square and then Tavistock Square looking at the statue of Gandhi. He stayed in the East End. Senate House. That was where the mighty Ministry of Information was. Orwell. A false name, pseudonym. Orwell was a thug in Christopher Marlowe's circle. Maybe Orwell was showing his double self. It was the Truth Ministry. Tavistock also had Lenin, second time in London. The Bolsheviks cut out the Jewish Bund who opposed centralisation. Tavistock. Theory. Tavistock Square where The Tavistock Clinic was originally. Tavistock lectures, Freud and Jung. Tavistock Institute came out of it. Meant to be involved in loads of stuff. Coleman claimed they were ruling the world through control of pop culture, drugs and education. Said it was designed to promote war between the UK and Germany, weaken western civilisation. There was secret stuff. But she was very interested in Eckhartshausen's secret stuff. The Council of the Light that were waiting here around us for the ones that elevated themselves so they could be involved. You might say that such invisible masters were not doing their job. Or maybe they were the only resistance when we have all been so well digitally re-mastered.

As soon as she came in her flat she was uneasy. Someone had been in. Not very obvious, but she noticed a chair was moved. She knew where it was because she had stared at it thinking of Van Gogh's chair. Another drawer was closed tighter than she ever did. Apart from that it was hard although she suspected her laundry clothes were re-arranged, they were too... neat. Alarmed. The Decision came quick. She took some water, a prepared rucksack from the wardrobe and left. She left the light on. Before she left she went downstairs.

Mary was in. She opened the door. "Hello child, will ye come in."

She did. She did not want to alarm her. "I heard someone saying something about a robbery around here, I don't know where so make sure you keep that locked won't you," Ash said.

"Don't you worry about that. Sure who'd be interested in an oul crow like me?" Mary laughed and enjoyed the laugh, holding her hand to her face as she creased up. It was always hard not to get affected by it.

"What about that old bugger do you think he might be up to no good?" Mary said.

"Well if he was the only one anyone had to worry about we'll be alright. Erik knows about him."

"I see that piano is still out in the yard. I'll send my friend over." She moved on. "Very nice boy, the big lad. Very nice." Mary winked.

"Say a prayer for us," Ash pleaded.

"I will my child. I always do," Mary assured her.

"If you have any problems or hear funny noises give Erik a ring. He might be staying around here some nights."

"Very nice. The mouse that has but one hole is easily caught."

She needed a little time to think. She was afraid to alarm Mary on the evidence she had. Why did he hang around? Why do you come here? Maybe want to sneak into my room to read my diary. Am I going around the twist. Gruesome. Dearly wish I was not here. Nobody knows me. I know a place where nobody is likely to pass. As well as remembering him who went mad with the bad voices. It's their home. Take me anywhere. Darkened underpass. Strange fear. I don't care. Well I wonder. A looming dark force was hinting of imminent dangerous things.

LLLF

LONDON LOGOS LIBERATION FRONT

Publishing Pamphlets to Oppose Censorship of Our Message.
The Counter-Revolutionary to Evil and Terror Effort.
Order. Knowledge. Divine.

THE EMERGENCY IS NORMAL.

THE EXTRAORDINARY IS NOW ORDINARY.

THE EMERGENCY JUST SHOWS YOU THE TRUTH.

THE EMERGENCY IS NOT A TAKE-OVER.

WE HAVE BEEN TAKEN OVER.

CIA, MI5, MI6, CFR.

THIS IS NO REVOLUTION, THAT OCCURED BEFORE.

THE CURTAIN OF ILLUSION HAS BEEN LIFTED.

WE WILL CONTINUE THE COUNTER-REVOLUTION.

COMMUNISM AND CAPITALISM ARE WRONG.

THE RADICAL CENTRE FOCUSES ON NEEDS.

THE RADICAL CENTRE FOCUSES ON COMMUNITY.

THE RADICAL CENTRE FOCUSES ON SOLUTIONS.

BEWARE THE 33 DEGREES.

THE EMERGENCY WILL ALWAYS BE WITH US.

LONDON HAS BEEN ATTACKED MANY TIMES.

LONDON WILL RISE AGAIN.

PREPARE FOR LIBERATION

Chapter 21

Rock-a-Bye Baby - Utnapishtim

"Country." Jem kind of spat out. He continued, "Shakespeare used that focusing on the first syllable. What about Cnut? King of England? Jail! Aw brainwashing n'yer heids fu' a' mince."

Ash laughed out loud. The 17th should be good to her. In the mild evening air, lights of London below, thoughts of earthquakes, riots and other unknowns were burned off by the small gas stove and the company. A faint tang of charred wood still hung in the air from the fires. Jem was in good form in the place that was often his home. He camped on Hampstead Heath. Strange things went on there he said apart from courting couples. However he managed to keep a low profile and was always well camouflaged. There was a dark, ancient magic about the place. She was going to stay here tonight, to gather her thoughts. Took time to find him. If he was there you would find him if he so wished. Some general haunts. This was also where the headwaters of the Fleet River were, two streams that joined together. He spoke in a Scottish accent when relaxed and more refined, neutral one at times. Theatrically oscillating. Anachronistically bewildering. A monologue was coming.

"Sorry darlin' I cannae hel' mesell at times. The 'c' word. Was all the nonsense aboot? Aw shite? Anyway. I can't decide about him. Thomas More. I thought he wiz a good'un, saint, good family man. Ye have to be careful about who is telling the story. Think about it for a minute. Say you were writing a story with me in my present condition you could present it in any number of ways that wid influence ma feelings as a reader. If that approach is re-iterated over hundreds of years say the truth becomes irrelevant. Say for example. Descriptions of same behaviour. I am decisive. You are stroppy. He is a psycho. What you sais and how you sais't. I like my roupie bothy and a rullion reeshlin' beid and a lil' grundcurmurrummling reemish and ribble-rabble widnae turn me intae an auld cauld daftie on the brae-face wid hee-haw forgotten by middle class weans in cosy hooses with nair a thought for those less fortunate than themsell. Mair Steinbeckian: *While poor unfortunates in the city spread out below him struggled to get by, he slept like a baby with the stars above, a king in his ain blue realm, peaceful and contented. Orange lay the lights.* I'll niddle oan reepin nair reezie a scattergood if ye will. Though don't feel sorry for me. This is a lifestyle choice." He emphasised the latter bit with a posh accent.

"I'm not going tae mention, to utter a word about you-know-what, zombies or aliens or whatever they are all around. Dinnae fash yersel. I'll no' be carnaptious. It's aw shite really darlin'. There are a few things, that's aw. Greatest good... kindness, next is courage, then imagination. Greatest evil... sadism and next is ignorance. Whether yer a landlord, estate agent or a naebody like me, it dinna matter darlin'. You might add care on one side and rudeness t'other. Beyond that we know nowt. Y'know. Gude wichts, wicked wichts. Seelie Court and Unseelie Court. And how would I describe ma position? I'm lucky I can get braw digs in a few places roond here when the weather's cauld. But I just got used to it. It's hard, plenty of warmers, tubes, dafties, bampots, heidaba's, young uns not great a' the time. Aw stramash, skelpin', stooshie a' skirl in the smirr. Boatils n' skrep. But then you see the sun coming up, stars, birds, foxes, squirrels. But they're changing their mind now, there's wardens, polis and cooncil, but if you have a little tent in the shrubs like me, you can manage. Vagabonds in Germany. First group tae gae. They should use us as earthquake monitors. You can hear the earth move when you have your ear to the flairground."

He laughed but then said. "But it was terrible. Well in contradiction to what I have just said and I unreservedly reserve the right to contradict mesell, I would have to think. But having had some time to think I might say that: *The auld scranning-Bettie had pride. His greatest strength. His greatest weakness. Perhaps his situation was the way the universe balances oot the scales like a nickstick bodie and maybe in his next life he would be a king. Here because of his own doings. Not bitter, not joyful. Philosophical. You must adapt. He realised that we would all go the same way. Stoic.* I might add in that inscription you read about - he loved the night too dearly to fear death."

He stood up and leaned over, she could see the fire in his eyes, orange against the twilight blue, ready for a rant. She knew it was coming. She steadied herself so she could listen and try to follow the cascade, especially when his Scottish accent or Scots tongue got more pronounced. He shifted, reverted, regressed or returned to a different state at such times and she could not tell whether he was laying it on with a trowel because he knew it pleased her (and he did want to please her in a friendly way). Like a clay pigeon machine being prepared and the... click. He drifted between two parts, twa places. A man o' pairts.

"We're getting a little deep here lassie, Ah think it's time to change tack. But oan thing darlin.' Don't mean tae be greetin.' I hear scashlan o' banjies a' glaikit loons flying by swatchin' their wee screens buying their moturs on credit so they can get stuck, poring over perplexing pensions plans, worrying about their wee bairns, gaffer, grandchildren, planet, politics, press, wund up by whitever canny plan they've concocted to wind us up tae rob the till n stitch us up some mair n ainly stowp whin they think squeezing us wi' nae longer be profitable n they gang overseas on some lying pretence we're telt they're saving someone like missionaries pretended like Cortéz kicking Montezuma oot and find someplace they haven't plundered or that they hae before but lift n't noo has something else they want n sais I'll ha' that ta very much ye basterd n they hae some spurious plan n poor tumshies busting nuts to mak' ends meet n mak' sense o' aw the rules they constantly mak' and change n de-stabilise you wi' then they fuck everyone over n the oans that might have stopped thum in their secret n no so secret plans are busy trying to mak' sense n whin they get hame exhausted they turn o' the telly fae a lil' light relief and they nair notice they're being turned into zom... sorry... but the hypnosis didnae only come frae there cos the time they set foot in school there wis a plan to tighten the straitjaiket on thum to mak' it a tad mair secure than their parents like. And they dinna notice it. Dinna see it at aw. They don't pay too much attention to the uncomfortable feeling inside thit whispers... *What the fuck ye daeing this fer? Why you buying that? Why you listening to these erseholes? Why ye working too hard? Fer whae? Whair ye gaun? Why you swallyin' that pish? Why do ye believe aw the shite they tell you?* Oh look the Royals hae done this n done thit n he has a ploock o' his bum n aren' they great dina min' that they come frae a line o' murderers that was a long time ago but we'll let you ken jist in case and we'll let ye know that we honour this and w'honour that and we hae aw the entertainers in our powket n science kens everything that they ken how it aw started and science sais this, Big Bang ya ken n science sais thit n up is doon n doon is up its quantum theory n you're doing it aw wrang n how canyeken n this is no fer t' likes of ye to unnerstan n they ken better n it has been decided for yersel n ye should know yer place n be calm n dinnae get worked up noo thank you very much Nurse Ratched the owrlady n yes I'll take those tablets n' swedgersn' get off mi heid n be mad wi' it n wid they help me n help me sleep n I think th'other ones are makin' me ill or

anxious nae problemo big man think aboot anger management there's mairhere these are new Oh new tha's magic mest be good new mowdern contemporary smart fucking smart smart ma erse up your arsehole n I wonder if ye hae any cancer Big C agin see we're verra worried aboot you hair let's have a wee test oh it dinna look sae good nowt to worry aboot oh it may be awright but jist in case come again wee cmras Aye right fkin Super Bowl oh yes cancer's o' the rise n prostate cancer we better check fer that noo Ser wee dab aw the slideystuff everyone dis it bend eiver thairr's a good man proochie yer weel used tae that dinnae mind the grapes I ken the system has prepared you weel for taking it up ye oh no there's a little knobbly bit gee us a wee gander up yer bahookie… tak this wee depth charge n we'll hae no pudding-broo what's that but its sair Ser Ah'm i' a terrible pucker n that wis muckle shouldnae we hae a few knobbly bits well your prowstate's a tad o' the large side we'll give you some medicine ya must hae been oot on the toon a lot giing it laldy but ifn it dinna work then we'll have to tak it oot or chop a wee bit aff nae grallochin' wir a bawhair son awa frae medical perfection sae yill be balloch whit aboot Mars Bars min's deep fried son dinna mean tae be sharriean but winna that leave me impotent or incontinent ye cannae be tae careful it's jist you we're thinking aboot it's fer your oan good everyoan does it ken not to worry dinnabeafeart but it isny provan that intervention is no as effective as leaving it alain weel screening is very important n we'll screen your bowels but how do ye ken wha' they're supposed to look like mebbe folk hae had things growing up thair aw their life for centuries n millennia n cus naebastard wis looking fer them there wisny a problem but there's 3 chances in a thoosand that it could be fatal but life is fatal ye say and yiv frightened the life out of me everytime I come here and instead of keeping me healthy I feel ya sooking it oot fae me like a vampire and I used to gie loads of money fer cancer research and everyone is giving a fortune fer it a fuck-all happens an' it'll always be t'morra that's great ne'er the day n they think of mair things that'll cause cancer and they don't give one flyingfuck aboot microplastics a' ye hae sleepless scunnered nights worrying boot whether yer going tae die or are a fat bastard and ye gae back a bit withered and worn oot thinking boot it and they look serious an' yer erse cribbed and fuck's sake mebbee they should have a gameshow a reality show about it….
Listen darlin', I need a pish a grand ol' jimmy riddle if'n ye dinna min' me saying in such polite company. That's me done noo. It'd gee ye the boak. Dinnae git me gaun. Excuse me. Oh last thing and then you say 'Cunt' about some nasty fucker and they say *Oh, I hate that*

word. It's a horrible word. I jest dinnae like that word, there's something about that word and you can get the jail and you wonder why they don't say the 'N' word fer nuclear and the 'P' word fer pollution. Are they not more offensive? *But I just love Irvine Welsh.* And you cannae say dis and you cannae say that n no we used to say that but no' hunnybunch no't any mair ken we say dis n no that was last week we used tae say this but it changed n also by the wa' the bonny word thit wi sais yae cannae say fer mest of yer life weel we've changed that noo a we've discovered it's an *empowering* word actually n it's a *liberating* wee word n ye hae spent years carefully avoiding using t'word and swatching your p's and q's we noo celebrate that word and love to hear it we reclaimed it by the wa' and we hae a few barry *acronyms* for you to remember n everyoan can be any one o them unless you're a little ordinary or normal because your types don't really belong n the group actually is so muckle d'noo that yer in the minority and furthermore Ah'd like to say now that you're in the minority Ah'd jist like to emphasise that you're a right, royal Jacobite bastard n' it shakes my single state. Cancer haid ma Maw, God rest her, cancer is canny and we cannie solve it, not when they're fucking everything up. Emby get it. You might say I'm just a crabbit oul' bastard blethering shite… I'll hae a wee donner lassie… Fanny."

"Hurry up or these chocolate eggs will melt. Maybe we can have a little of Tourette's Game," Ash suggested.

"Belter. Ya beauty"

She laughed but not too much because the comic works best when it is true. All she knew was that he had worked in a Barrister's Chambers. The coffee she bought for him boiled on his little camper stove and he took it off. He enjoyed boiled coffee and sweets. His Scottishness a palimpsest that emerged when you wiped off the front. She did not eat sweets herself generally. He said he could live on sweets, coffee and a few fags. When he came back she showed him the mountaineer's hammock in her backpack and explained how she was going to hoist it into the tree to sleep suspended between the branches. He examined it silently, intently, distantly, nodding. Finally she took out the chessboard and he was really happy. She never beat him. With boiled coffee, chocolate eggs and a few games of chess she started unpacking and eventually got it up the tree. He said he'd keep guard but she was unconcerned. Bacon died round here doing an experiment. Coleridge came here. Kubla Khan. Rime of the Ancient Mariner. Mary Shelley knew him. Bridget Elizabeth

Dowling who married Hitler's brother and gave birth to 'Paddy' Hitler lived around here. Bridget Elizabeth Hitler, Highgate.

Hampstead Heath in a hammock rocked to sleep by tree creaking. She had slept rough in London when she had nowhere to live or through pride would not live in the few places available. Sleeping under bushes stuffed with newspapers she had an 'Ah' moment. She would do it better. She bought a hammock used by mountaineers. Went inside a rucksack. Could be used in a tree. Up early in the morning no one sees. Picked out the trees before. When you run away, people always expect you to get far quickly. Stay close sometimes. Harriet Ann Jacobs. Anyway, she was not running. Just wanted to sleep, be calm, think a little. Feel nature. Huxley, Marx, Freud, Enid Blyton, Keats, Orwell Shelley, Robert Louis Stevenson, De Gaulle, Freud, George Romney, Peter Cooke Richard Burton. They lived and walked hereabouts. The sense of them was a soup she sipped in her imagination to sustain her, whether she liked them or not. Get on with your challenges. Address your dreams.

She listened to Burton reading poetry and Shakespeare and he made it alive. When he came back she recited,

> *"And nothing can we call our own save death*
> *And that small model of the barren earth*
> *Which serves as paste and cover to our bones.*
> *For God's sake, let us sit upon the ground*
> *And tell sad stories of the death of kings."*

"I confess I reduced the tone by dirges when we should be laffin our wee heids off before the State can tak'em awa. Burns, the Jolly Beggars seem quite appropriate, the sodger among then," Jem said. He recited,

> *"And now tho' I must beg, with a wooden arm and leg.*
> *And many a tatter'd rag hanging over my bum.*
> *I'm as happy with my wallet, my bottle, and my callet,*
> *As when in scarlet to follow a drum."*

"What rhyme 'drum' and 'bum.' What a beautiful word 'bum.' That's what they call a lad like me in America isn't it. What a waste, a misuse of a majestic word. It's small, it's short. It nearly has 'om' in it. B..'au..m* B ..OM. There ya go, 'om' in bomb. Maybe they got it wrong. It's the bomb's the sound of the universe, well if man has his wee say. Burns. Where would you be going w'thout him. *Ae fond Kiss.*" He sang it softly and beautifully,

> *"Ha we never lov'd sae kindly,*
> *Had we never loved sae blindly*
> *Never met-or never parted,*
> *We had ne'er been broken-hearted."*

It sounded beautiful in a Tom Waits type of way. Tom Waits. People thought he was a tramp. Find it hard to distinguish between a role, pose and reality. Jem threw in some more. *Green Grow the Rashes O.*

> *"The sweetest hours that ere I spend*
> *Are spent among the lasses O."*

"Lovely," Ash said.

"Dinna worry. I'm not romancing ye, or courting. Wha' am I like? A bug Jessie." Jem smiled wiping a tear.

She always relaxed in his company and felt her burdens being lifted. One you do not notice. Pebble by pebble placed on you and in their littleness they grow into a heavy pile until you allow them fall away. That night she would sleep like a baby in a slightly swaying movement, traffic in the distance, sirens and the creaking of trees. Thoughts of Orwell, *The Grass Arena.* H.G. Wells. Construct a World State through alien invasion.

"Did you see 'They Live'?" Ash asked.

"Aye. One of the few that got it." Jem nodded.

"All the subliminals everywhere that you only saw when you had the glasses on."

"Lisan. Remember the *War of the Worlds.* H.G. Wells. Where were the Martians when they were trying to destroy us and were destroyed? Over there on Primrose Hill." Jem pointed south. "Aye. And I think they'll be back. Or some'n else. If there are intelligent life forms oot thair and thair must be, then they'll hae tae come back, because they dinna wan'us coming and messing' around with them. They might have calculated that we'll destroy oursell. Feart ta' jine us doon hair a' they peer doon a' us like dugs. Wheesht. They might come back to see how their slaves got on since they zapped us into consciousness and we thought them gods. Or they might have already sent a pairty here to assume control and that would make sense. Those politicians are not real. You cannae see it in the glassy eyes.

Nowt. It's like that cartoon widda bear oot on the patio looking in telling his chum it's his other chum on the wall, but there's something different... the eyes. Funny eyes you could see it in Blair frae the kickoff and the waw-to-waw teeth that are meant to look like they're smiling at you. When I was young a smile was frae the heart and folk didnae show off their gnashers mainly because they were pish, less they had de wallies, mind you before all the dentists and stuff and sucker or jist didnae. But the glassy-eyed gander at you and smile like a cat stripping its teeth or a dog baring 'em. Folk dinna realise. Or they could be doing the bidding a' wans who came here a while ago. Mebbeh they're helping us with technology so we can destroy ourself because they have calculated that we are a good-for-nothing set of murdering bastards. Mebbeh they possess certain people. Hitler had his magicians around him and his funders who you don't hear a lot aboot. Either his cult was promoted to hide his promoters or he had a power of the underworld. Mebbe aw this de'il demownic possession is aboot extra-terrestrials. Or mebbe and I dinnae dispute it the evil spirits want to expand and use us a vehicle to wreck more havoc. Fuck's sake. If the Martians or whoever come back. I'll be ready to meet them. Smashin'." He laughed.

"Lisan here darlin.' If you gang up here on some of the auld pagan festivals, you see quair things going on on these little suburban hills roon here wi' the bogles. Ye ma think it's quaint but there's some sinister sights as weel. Dinnae forget that many a' them high heiyins that run them big skyscrapers ya see twinklin' beyond are aw occultists n some of them love aw that demon de'il stuff. I stay awa' from that and if I see there's any celebrations at full moons I fuck off somewhere a lil more concrete. I'm not talking of those ordinary decent, nice witches noo. God forbid. They're intae nature the feminine and all that good stuff. Fine, nice, kind. They're the verra ains the Black magic, Satanists guys will go eifter. And they're no aw the same. Ye cannae tar them with the same brush. There's good an' evil everywhair. Aw those poor women burnt as witches, it wiz bad witches persecuting good witches on the pretext that they were agin' witchcraft when in fact they were afeard some of these auld biddies were minding their own business loving nature and healing were onto them, could spot others stuff..... Macbeth. Fuck this let's hae a fine, wee brewcup under a crescent moon... Ah'll shut my gub, where's the caffee. Quality."

She told him about Dido Elizabeth Belle Lindsay born to a slave and a British Navy Officer. Came back as a girl to Kenwood House in Hampstead. Lindsay was a nephew of Lord Mansfield. Lord

Mansfield made a famous judgment about a slave. Slavery was odious in his view. Great Uncle of Dido. Some believe that she influenced his decisions. She was engaging and clever and can be seen in a famous picture with her cousin. Very close to where they were. Wondering whether a young woman could influence an older powerful man so they could stand against strong opposition?

"A wee minute wee lassie, do you know who saved humanity in the Epic of Gilgamesh, the Chosen One?" Jem asked.

"No."

"It was Utnapishtim. Thit wiz wee Weegies haeing a jest. Ut on the pish Tim? Ut na pish Tim and a Tim a Catholic and all. Fuck me. Weegie, ouija. Get in wi' the spirits an' all." They laughed.

"Give us one piece of advice that I can take to the bank, one nugget. I'm seeking distilled wisdom," Ash said.

"Don't be earnest. Dinna be airnest. I liked Guevara but Ernesto had no problem killing. Irish his family. Lynch. Lynching. Aye, never trust an earnest c.... No matter what they're earnest aboot watch yersel. Earnestness dae mark of nae good. Specially if they're aw noble as weel. Good Lord gave us a wee clue. Earnest, there's something aff. Tep yer ain airnestness. Not a little enthusiastic, but zealously fucking sincere wi' a serious coupon certain they're right. Nuremburg. Churchill's right. Shoot the bastards. Create a crime that don't exist and then prosecute, lynching a US Judge called it. But it's earnest. Earnestness kills everything for short-term satisfaction.... *'I beseech you, in the bowels of Christ, think it possible you may be mistaken.'* Oliver Cromwell. Rightearnestcunt. Q.E. fucking D," Jem said . "One more thing. Sniper. A prof of the highest order. Mark my words. Forgive me pet, bearing in mind Lyudmila Mykhailivna Pavlichinko, just as well be a she. Aw Jock Thamson's Bairns."

Talked more. VITRIOL. Visita Interiora Terrae Rectificando Invenies Occultum Lapidem. Laughed about 'Trampstead.' He explained the Darien Scheme, how a few Scots became indebted but debts written off to sell Scotland down the swannie. Create greed, until the gorged and make them pay for it. Same still. Burns wrote *Such a Parcel of Rogues in the Nation*. All pay to invisible colleges in shadoweworlds. Talked till light threatened to rise in paling blue east over the palisade of The City still slyly blinking to the sky. Till there was little time to sleep. Till myriad lights of the city below with its millions of people troubled by their septillion choices would be reclaimed from the sometime terrors of Tezcatlipoca. So soon she slept like a baby.

LLLF

LONDON LOGOS LIBERATION FRONT

Publishing Pamphlets to Oppose Censorship of Our Message.
The Counter-Revolutionary to Evil and Terror Effort.
Render unto Caesar everything but your Soul.

CENTRISM SHOULD RULE OVER EXTREMISM.

CAPITALISM IS NOT THE END.

CAPITALISM IS BETTER THAN COMMUNISM.

IT ISN'T GOOD JUST CAUSE IT'S NOT COMMUNISM.

CAPITALISM IS A MEANS NOT AN END.

CAPITALISM INCLUDES MONOPOLISTS AND CARTELISTS.

CAPITALISM AND COMMUNISM ARE MATERIALIST.

CONSERVATIVES ARE OFTEN FRAUDS.

CONSERVATIVES ARE OFTEN PHONEY.

WE ARE PRAGMATIC.

NO IDEOLOGY GIVES YOU FREEDOM.

YOU MUST FREE YOUR SOUL.

YOU MUST FREE YOUR SPIRIT.

NO LEADER OWNS YOUR SOUL.

DON'T BE OWNED.

BE SOVEREIGN.

SOVEREIGNTY IN US, FROM US, BY US.

PREPARE FOR LIBERATION

Chapter 22

When You Hear What I Say You Will Not Understand

Non Sine Sole Iris

Ash went home Thursday clammy, overcast after a pink sky dawn with a solitary jacaranda cloud. She was not going to address the security issue in a piecemeal fashion nor live in fear. She was worried about Mary, would have a chat with her. The good thing was that it was probably only her that anyone was interested in. Could she have imagined it? She could handle herself if needed. As she was very interested in the martial arts she had researched Irish stick fighting and some of the arts that had died out. There were some Japanese and Korean fringe practices which dealt with using ordinary weapons in an emergency. If needed you had lethal weapons all around. Every house had projectiles, sharp implements and potential weapons that would overcome a bigger opponent or one with a weapon. Practice. You could kill someone with Cosmopolitan. Not just the content of newspapers that could kill you. Could it be some poltergeist phenomenon? No. She had cleared her head with Jem. Not going anywhere. Having exposed herself, put her head up, come out from the crowd, she would deal with that. So The Decision came. She arranged yet another interview to be recorded Friday 19th with Lucius. Next step was clear. The rational reason would be to draw out her enemies. Alternatively she wanted to achieve some control over circumstances, whether a dice with death or destruction or not. She had no intention of prematurely losing her life and never sacrificing her soul. Because she had made The Decision, a small one maybe to broadcast, the force was released. Like doing something on the internet. You open yourself up to an abscess of hate. So be it. Current was carrying her. A more remote explanation was that this presence was informing her. Another one that the character came alive or was a spirit that had possessed her. Wondered whether it was the threat of uncertainty that made her do something she suspected would be polarising. Something that would set the centrifuge going.

Draw. No blue funk here. Put head above parapet. Know you're over target when you get the shots. A single, false move loses the game often. See if there are two dogs after one bone.

Lucius said he could do one that day in the afternoon. The next day she had two meetings, one with Erik and the other with some 'investors.' They could record anyway so she could go up Camden. He would play the recorded interview when it fit the schedule later that evening. Many of his eclectic podcasts were popular in London and around the world. He just let people say their stuff without interference and that got him into trouble. A few sessions, listening to Terence McKenna, Philip K. Dick. Then Irish rebel songs. Bob Dylan said he learned something from the spirit in Irish rebel songs when he used to listen to the Clancy brothers playing in New York. She remembered he said that after he became famous he found people crawling over his roof at night. Nobel Prize for literature, she was sure that even he thought that ridiculous. Some say he sold his soul anyway. Not that Voice behind this. It could be divilment. She believed some of the things she said and others were speculative. Why she did so was still not clear. The Trickster came to the fore. Go over the top, turn it up. Overboard and see where the balance comes back to. She would start of as Ethel in her seductive, mysterious, slyly attractive, inviting, coquettish, flirtatious way. She understood how thoughts followed attention. Attention is critical.

It was hazy greyish today but mild, a little breeze hinting of what was to come. She had seen Auerbach a couple of times and talked to him. One of the great artists walking to Sainsbury's with his plastic bag, nobody knew him. He had seen the Nazis with his own, eyes, his parents went to Auschwitz. She honed her statements as she walked among the people, by the fast food places and charity shops and banks and bookshops. Some were esoteric mantras fired out haphazardly as if in William Burroughs cut-up technique. Proverbs.

'As above, so below'
'Know thyself.'
'Be like water.'
'The tao that can be written is not the true tao.'
'More flies are caught with honey than vinegar.'

But they had to be enmeshed in a genuine idea. She did not construct too much. Suggestion was critical. Then there was Law of Attraction. The pacing of communication is often a parallel of sexual congress building up to a crescendo. She seldom answered questions directly and was often oblique. Today she was going with something that had crystallised in her head recently, perhaps around the idea of a millennium. About the Templars.

Key Templars forged an alliance with Islam when captured and agreed on a plan. A thousand year plan. Ireland was taken over as an occult source with the aid of the Church who had helped wipe out the last remnants of Druidic knowledge. Gnostics, Cathars, Jews and witches. These pre-figured the subsequent attack on Native Peoples. Not accident, bad luck nor mistakes that led to the attacks on these groups. All were potential competitors for the souls of people. The Native Americans were very advanced spiritually, despite centuries of propaganda. The Feminist movement was a misleading one. "God was a woman, the Goddess," Ash said.

The portcullis of protection of the Domestic Terrorism Bill would descend when normal Parliamentary procedure was resumed and thus Mr. Tubal endeavoured to make hay while the sun shines. Lucius had asked her about the Templars and where they were based down at the Fleet. She answered in a slow way, unsure about what was going to come out, conscious that it could be nonsense, although later she concluded that it was not.

Ethel: Brigid (Bride) was one of the ancient goddesses of these islands. Then they sought to wipe her out. Changed into St Bridget, Brigid and some of her power was still there. Then changed into Bride. Then to show their contempt, they turned the ancient sites in the power centre associated with her into a jail for women. The Bridewell by the Fleet. A palace for Henry VIII and it became a prison. They knew that St Bride or St Bridget was associated with it from the 600's and well before. The Fleet River, the River of Wells. Brigid loved wells. She had her oaks along it once all the way to Hampstead. Brigantia. Candlemas. The Romans were good with water but they wanted to manage, control, direct, re-direct it with slaves. Brigid healing, transforming, there. She is coming back. When she returns in spirit, London will be saved. Kali, Minerva, Isis. She was a model for Elizabeth. Purgative fire. The Goddess must rule.

Then she got into a mischievous vein although it seemed to come from somewhere else.

Ethel: Look at those that benefitted from the Great Fire. 1666. No accident. The builders, scientists, ones who wanted to rebuild London in an ancient way. Rome had burned and had been re-built. They were followers of Francis Bacon. John Evelyn. Gunpowder was his family. Loved ancient Rome. The historical 1660 committee of 12. Gresham College group. Gresham College going back to 1597. 7 persons, 7 subjects, 17th year of reign of Elizabeth made it. Met in Cheapside. Followed on from the Oxford Club. This was part of the 'Invisible College.' It relates back to Hartlib, a spy. Francis Bacon. Salomon's House. Evelyn and Wren presented plans to rebuild London. They found some of the gunpowder from the Gunpowder Plot in the Evelyn's possession. Makes you think about it. The King commanded him to take control of the fire at Fetter Lane. The rest of the City lay in ruins, lead had melted and ran down the streets. Gunpowder helped stop it. He had also predicted it and was seen as a prophet in what he said. By the 11th he had his plans ready. The only woman he had a mysterious relationship with was Mrs Godolphin.

Lucius: That's a lot to swallow. You have to be careful that his descendants might take offence. You're not saying they started it?

Ethel: Behave dear. Look at Mary Poppins, the film. Esoteric. Feed the Birds. Tuppence a bag. You see where he is outside St Pauls. What now is where he was then? 1717, the site of the first Lodge. Fighting over coins. Tuppence a bag. In-jokes. Family live at number 17. After finishing re-building London with Roman architecture they needed another vehicle for mischief. Then you get Dan Brown.

She did not feel authentic in these statements. They came out in slow, ill-considered mish-mash. Then she began to get it in a flow and spoke with an altogether different tone and emphasis.

Brigid: You are relinquishing your capacity to live in freedom. It's disappearing. You have it wrong. The admonition to develop your power, your spirit, your life is for your fulfilment. You are seeds that unfold. You have the gifts in your consciousness. You have been mesmerised, enthralled to false things. You worship the wrong things, your own cleverness, your technology. You cede your sovereignty by the day. In yielding you deny your unity in the One. In denying you start on a negative spiral difficult to return from. The Hex of the Voracious Vortex should vex you. You are told this not to be punished but to help release. If you are not able to see it you may have lost it. What I am is of no matter. If I be an angel, a god, a goddess, a spirit, or extra-terrestrial, if I am an intelligence and I speak the truth, why not listen. Be not cowards.

Lucius: You're Brigid now…. Are you channelling that?

Brigid: You should listen to the message instead of concentrating on the source. I see in Ireland they build the motorway near Tara to tie the Goddess down. Same thing.

After she left, Lucius gave his view. He had been silent and avoided intervening too much. Now he thought it time to say a few things.

Lucius: To finish off that segment let me tell you what I think. I like Ayn Rand. I bought the 'objectivist' crap. She convinced me that 'reason' was the key. Mysticism was the enemy. Religion was the oppressor. Science was the key and not self-sacrifice. Then I studied the science. You can have a 'God helmet' that activates the brain and makes people have mystical experiences. Evolutionary psychology explains this. Then some people are… well a little paranoid… and they may find causes and effects that are… not there. So we must be careful…

First call is from Bob in Crouch Hill. Go ahead Bob.

Bob: I'd just like to say Lucius that that one you just had on should be locked up. Loony nonsense…. There's a crisis going on for God's sake. It's like Lord Haw-Haw.

It was busy as always at the National Portrait Museum. She liked portraits and this place but was often disappointed. Erik had suggested they have a working lunch and she had added the Museum in as a prelude. She could have a light lunch and then she would swim. Erik stood tall straight backed outside among pigeons and performers. They went in and wandered. It was always interesting, whether she liked them or not. Erik seemed to have more respect than she had, to judge by his exclamations. "I like this one!"

"That's cool!"

"What a work!"

"Wow!"

"I wish I could do that!"

She looked and looked closely.

"Don't forget the Investors." Erik reminded her.

"Do you learn anything about the sitters?" Ash asked.

"Well, there are clues in the paintings. It's a bit like a detective novel?" Erik replied.

"But you know most of these things already. These are public figures and the clues are really emphasising things in a kind of historical way," Ash said.

"Yeah, well that's what a portrait is... Do you not like them?" Erik asked.

"I do but there's a few things I can't figure out... Look at this one. It's like a photograph." Ash.

"It's good," Erik said.

"But why make paintings photographic now?" Ash asked.

"Well. I like it. Skill I suppose."

"They always used optical devices, camera oscura."

"That'd be a good name for us to use - Camera Oscura."

"But then the technology was not pervasive. A baby can take a picture, a portrait. What would you like, the blood one or the blob of colour?" Ash asked him. "Well..."

"What do you like?" Erik retorted.

"Well actually if we go next door I can show you." Ash indicated with her head. They walked next door.

"Great, that London has so much stuff." Erik.

"Many of these were meant to be in Dublin. Hugh Lane. Like a lot of the culture stuff you get to see, it might be someone else's. Nicked it."

They went up through the Impressionist room and beside the door was a small painting. There were crowds milling around.

"That's what I call a painting."

"Who's that... the Joker?" Erik laughed.

"It's Picasso the expressionist. Bibi," Ash said.

"You like that! Wow."

The other one was the Rainbow Portrait of Elizabeth I, Non Sine Sole Iris, No Rainbow without the Sun. The snake with the jewel in mouth on her gown, the rainbow in hand, the eyes and ears on the orange gown. It was all there before the eyes for those who care to look. We see you, we hear you.

They walked over to Charing Cross Road and had some Falafel. She asked him to get the Rainbow Portrait and have a look on his laptop. He knew that when she meant have a look she meant to study it.

"I see it but I don't get it," Erik said and continued, "she's old in this. But what has she got in her hand? That's not a rainbow is it? Look at the snake with maybe a jewel in his mouth. I saw that in the Lombard crest. Look at the gown, the eyes, the ears, mouths. What is that?"

"What's that under your eye. Is it a black eye? Were you training?" Ash asked.

"Well actually, that was one of the things I wanted to mention. Don't laugh. But someone hit me from behind two nights ago just on the way up behind the cinema on Leicester Square, the laneway. He had to have been in a doorway, because I'm usually aware. I couldn't catch him, because in the couple of seconds it took to recover, he was gone," Erik said sheepishly.

"Fuck me. Lucky him." She laughed, she knew what would have happened.

"What I was wondering about, was whether it could possibly be related to what we're doing. I'm not sure. It was just a feeling. If it was, he may have realised that he had bit off more than he can chew. Unless there was more nefarious aims. But with tasers and stuff on the probably unrelated chance. Be careful."

"Self-portraits Rene Beeh. I liked his self-portrait. They thought he would be great. The coming genius one time. It didn't happen."

"Never heard of him," Erik said.

"Erik. There's more chance that it's related to those East European girls that you are re-patriating."

"And boys..." Erik added.

Soon she was on her way. Erik was always good company. Down that street was where Bartitsu started. TV and John Logey Baird. Swimming was on her way home. She went to Covent Garden to swim at The Oasis. She ignored what Erik said. She loved the sense of the open air and water in the middle of London. Must be many Masons here she thought. Water was what she felt she needed even if chlorinated. Light on her body, sense of air, sense of blue, sense of water, a sense of September. She swam steadily without exertion concentrating on moving as fluidly, silently and efficiently as possible in her strokes. Moving without moving her head, perfecting each element. Listening to the passing conversations.

"I went to the toilet and it was red or pink. I nearly died. It was then I realised I had eaten the beetroot."

"Hey our neighbours got lifted yesterday."

How could you know what was really happening in London? News was an ad. The present story was made up to suit The Story. Like history. Mostly a story of Bossmen. You would have to travel around the city and see for yourself. But that was not permitted. Shaftesbury Avenue where Gladstone stalked the streets. Maybe 90 prostitutes he sought to convert. The rookery of St Giles. Once a leper colony. Great slum. Origin of the Great Plague a year before the Great Fire. The Holy Land. Little Ireland. Despite her musings she could feel the repression in the air. She thought that the Grand Lodge would be a good place to defend. Must be tunnels into it.

At his home in Muswell Hill, Cranbourne could not sleep recently and was watching all kinds of stuff on the internet. He re-discovered Mork and Mindy. Mork was well loved. Robin Williams' first big role. An alien is sent from a planet that does not allow humour. Mork is humorous. Reports back from Earth. Agent. All comics are agents. His comic observations on human behaviour and the clash between his sense and earthlings was the comic base. His greeting was 'Nanu-Nanu.' Robin Williams was playing a lovable, charming individual which made you forget that he was an intelligence officer. The other one was Get Smart. Again an agent. Maxwell Smart. He was a spy working for a counter-intelligence organisation called CONTROL especially opposing KAOS. Funny, bumbling, best cover of all. Something bugging him. He had never been summoned to D to report on it. There was another pretext but than what he saw. Intellectuals, academics. He read many books on secret agents. The Agent-Officer distinction is confused. Greene had a useless academic agent in *The Confidential Agent*.

He wondered if that catch-phrase had made him think about nanotechnology again. He could not get it off his mind. Last night he could not sleep. He did not fret much generally. His desire was to work in domains that interested him. Because bureaucracy likes boring systems, it was inevitable that his dreams would founder. He had been interested in Rhino horn and had worked on the criminal aspects. It had been Irish Traveller gangs who had been involved but others too. He had worked in copyright piracy. The crossover of crime and terror organisation was interesting. He was more interested in the broad strategic dimension, anticipating, speculating, blue-sky thinking. However grey skies were the real backdrop. The terrorism, crime and counter-intelligence distinctions were superceded. The problem was that people answer to masters or mistresses that have specific and short-term needs that preclude long term attention. They thought he had nothing to offer to Artificial Intelligence.

All the geeks are happy with the evolution, excited. When we are intelligent and at the top of that level, then certain worries do not exist. He was regarded as an odd fellow. Someone had used that expression. He thought it was funny. He read a bit about it. He knew there was a kind of secret society called the Oddfellows. He heard Jimmy Saville say on TV that he was an 'odd fellow.' Cranbourne assumed that he had been sending a signal and not being self-deprecating. They were set up by a fellow called Savile. SAVILLE is an encryption device developed by intelligence agencies. Went off the internet after the stuff blew up. Curious. Sending signals with millions looking. Cranbourne was no way odd. He just looked slightly odd. He knew that. His chin was just a little too big. His jaw was a little protuberant. He knew however that that was because he was determined. The race did not always go to the fastest, the woman to the best looking. He seduced women when he wanted. You only have to find what their self-image needs and you are away in a hack. It is not about objective facts at all. Otherwise how would many beautiful and otherwise intelligent women go after tight asses and fools. He was persistent, tenacious, resourceful, adaptable. In the end he would get what he wanted despite the powers that be.

One area he wanted to work with were rare earths. He learned about them, read everything he could. Mining them is destructive to the environment. China replaced US as leaders. Middle East has oil, China has rare earths. And earthquakes. The present leadership in China would not have come into power without that earthquake. Underground affects overground. China bought the factories, technology, patents and know how. Transfer of technology. WTO. Europium enhanced red for TV. It became important. Note the Europium Anomaly on the Moon Rocks. Maybe it was because they never went and got rocks from different places on the earth. Some are used in MRI scans, fibre optic cables, computers, lights, mobile phones, catalytic converters, hybrid cars, fridges, fighter jets, permanent magnets. He considered them from a counter-terrorism perspective. He sought to work with them. But it did not work like that. Scientists who would dominate in those domains. The problem was they had a very specific mindset. No one was interested in generalists. He was interested in how criminals and terrorists could capture rare earths and hold States or industries to ransom. No one seemed interested. A glazed look was one he could spot a longway away now. Likewise with nanotechnology. He had conversations with himself, in his head. Aloud at times. He rehearsed the explanations he gave to others, that generally didn't work. Still Cerium, Gadolinium, Promethium, Scandium, Thulium. Thule. Lasers, x-ray, military. Good few from Sweden. Ytterby. Samarium used in nuclear reactors. How many rare earth elements were there? 17.

Nanotech was the one he could not let go. You take it down to the smallest level and re-engineer. Build from a pile of dust. Not to mention quantum level problems. Down to the atomic arrangement to atoms or group of atoms. Deal with the level below the micro level. With nanometres, a thousand millionth of a metre. Use some of techniques, technology such as atomic force and scanning tunnelling microscopy. See and move atoms. You have big, isolated chambers to make very clean environments. Things such as carbon, that you thought you knew, have new possibilities. Get advantages when you operate on the small level. Do things that can only be done there. Make suspensions, aerosolised nebulisations. You can enter blood stream and do things you need to do. You use nature. Unite chemistry, biology, physics. What do they tell you? Listen for the patronising but reassuring voice. Your medicine will be better. Able to make new antibiotics. Get better sunscreen. Use the sun better. You will have environmentally beneficial products. Combat global warming. Your computer works faster. Metals tougher. Fantastic new goods. Cheaper, smaller. Better batteries. Clothes smell better. Glasses don't break. Better razors, that's good because they're getting worse aren't they? Think of all the bad things especially created by people such as us in the past, we will now cure them. Cancer, that's taking a long time you whisper, pollution. You will be godlike. Fascinated.

Industry knows it can sell the products. Dumb PhD students are used as guinea pigs. Owners in their sunspots. All the liberal lefties types will be reaping in the lucre from their investments. I am smart, you are smart, we are smart, they are smart. Nanotechnology is smart. Smart dust. He remembered when 'smart' used to be a negative term. Smartarse. He could not bear listening to the pronunciation 'smort.' Usually these descriptions are inversions. Everything is rosy in the nanotechnology garden. Don't be left behind, don't be uncool, don't be a spoil sport. Of course we must be safe, ethical. Even the scientists are saying we are allowed to. Bible says, you have dominion, rule in God's image. General dangers were not ones that he was most preoccupied with. For example, you have nanomaterials in toothpaste, they kill microbes. Wash into the environment and what do they do there? Carbon nanotubes. Same as asbestos. They are used in coatings for certain products without consideration of the impacts. We inhale the products. They do things they should not do, may leech into the air or be unleashed in combustion. If they were so dangerous then surely there would be a concern. The media is merely a device to distance. Create fake problems with fake solutions. The public is quiescent, wanting bread and circuses. Like in Roman times. They even want Italian bread! They're bringing back military parades, like the Soviets copying the Roman Triumphs.

He got a phone call. "Nanu Nanu," Cranbourne joked.
"Sorry?" Kit said.
"Pardon me, a little joke." Cranbourne.
"A quick question from Dockland," Kit said, "Would it be a certain photographer?"
He thought for a moment.
"There is that meeting today.." Kit reminded him.
"Fuck ..." Cranbourne replied.

Ash did not want to meet any investors. She was constitutionally suspicious and she was a bit edgy after the funny stuff recently. On the positive side, if 'goodwill' is the magnetic force that pulls in custom, like attention in hypnosis, then the goodwill was growing. It is goodwill that you eventually sell. Goodwill is the gold in a company. People pay for goodwill. Luckily it was not nicewill because she did not have a nice feeling at the moment and maybe she felt a little possessive and protective about what she had built up. There is always someone wanting to rob your baby. Met in the Marquis of Salisbury. Investors were not too happy about that. No idea who they were. Websites were opaque. She took a seat in a quiet place. Two people came in. She recognised the woman from the investment company website and a tall blond man, about 6 foot 4. She liked neither on sight. She smiled feebly and got up and shook hands. The man's hand was expectedly over-the-top crushing. He went to get a drink, offering something. She declined. He was not English she thought. The women exchanged pleasantries, about the weather and the amount of people and coffee until the big guy came back.

"Let's get down to business. I'm Josephine, this is Cyril Birker. He has a company that operates in the adult entertainment domain. I am an investment consultant contacted here. We are investing in exciting business in our field and sometimes we chaperone certain business. You seem to have experience in operating and training in this area and you are building a unique profile."

"Chaperone... I understand but do not really get it. Generally investment is you give me a... pittance and become a leech on my business right?" Ash said.

"We can take certain businesses and re-direct them in a way that corresponds to an investor's business interest. We have business acumen and finance and we facilitate triangulation." She smiled nervously.

"Did you mean strangulation? So the business becomes a puppet."

"No, not at all. Anyway we're rather interested in your business. I wonder whether you would be so kind as to tell us a little," Josephine said.

"Sorry darling but it's you that's looking for something. You have done your homework or not. I will make my business, our business profitable for investors but it's not there yet." Ash.

"I merely meant to operate as we usually do."

"You're watching too much Dragon's Den. I'm busy. So please get to the point," Ash said narkily.

"Well we have an investor who would like to purchase a business such as yours or enter into mutually satisfactory arrangement."

"Who?" Ash asked.

"At the moment it's confidential."

"Why is that?"

"That is the way they want to proceed."

"Well it's not really a good way to build trust. What do they want?"

"Well they are interested in a business which can further their aims..." Josephine said.

"But..." At that point Cyril butted in. Ash thought he looked like a cross between Vladimir Klitschko and Jeremy Paxman.

"If I may..." He moved nearer Ash. His voice was lowered.

"This is confidential," Josephine interjected nodding.

"You would be part of a Public-Private Initiative. This PPI would be a secret endeavour between you and us and the State."

"You're taking the piss. Something in secret is Public? Is this some sort of hidden camera stuff? Are you a newspaper?" Ash asked.

"No seriously, I am representing an agency of the State."

"You're joking me."

"No, I'm not. In fact..." Birker leaned closer and looked around. "It is a matter involving the protection of the public, the security of the people..." Birker whispered.

"I don't know who you are but I have no intentions of being a State employee," Ash stated.

"No, it's a sort of PPI... you retain your separate legal personality," Birker clarified.

"What type of national security?" Ash whispered.

"We can't discuss it here, that's why we were uncomfortable meeting in such a place. Preventing terrorism mainly and high level criminal activity," Birker whispered almost inaudibly, looking around.

"What use am I?"

"We find certain institutions can be very helpful in the gathering of intelligence."

"Surely, if what you say is true, and unfortunately I don't believe you because I smell a rat, the State would just establish its own whatever."

"That is very true and I cannot reveal any sensitive information but it might be that what you assert does in fact represent reality, far be it from me to say and I don't. Nevertheless our interest is genuine. You might have heard of the term 'blue lies.' Sometimes lies must be told for the greater good." Birker.

"Blue lies... never heard," Ash said.

"Well like when you are on a team and someone cheated on the team and you tell a lie not solely for your own benefit but for others too. Princess Lea, Severus Snape they use as examples." Birker.

"Don't spoil Harry Potter, I'm not finished. You want me to be a snitch?"

"No... Patriotism. Blue lies may be necessary when we have false news." Birker.

"To entrap people? Do you do white and black lies too. Blue lies matter. Blue lies would make conspiracy theories would they not? You're not a Brit." Ash.

"Not exactly..." Birker.

"What do you want me to do then?" Ash.

"Well the particular uses would become crystallised after business negotiations ensued."

"But how can business negotiations ensue if I have no idea what you want?"

"Well as I said I gave you an indication of possible interest."

"You have not clarified what you want me to do? Do you think I'd be whipping Russian spies for you?"

"Why should it be of specific concern if this is a business venture? You will be amply remunerated," Birker said.

"I am amply remunerated. No sane business person will buy a pig in a poke. I have a conscience. Otherwise it is *con* and *science*."

"But Miss, I am sure we can elaborate and have a degree of specification after some exploratory talks." Birker.

"No thanks. I'm off now. I have a business to attend."

"But you haven't heard our offer..." Birker.

She leaned close. "Listen sunshine, if my tax payer money is going to fund activities run by people such as you I want it back. I'm no informer, nark, snitch. Furthermore I don't trust you or her. Plenty of bookshops around here with plenty of books on body language and lie-spotting. We could talk till you're blue in the face, follow me like a blue-arse fly but I'd not buy what you are selling."

"A bird in the hand is surely worth two in the bush." Josephine said superciliously and nervously, a glass of water raising to her lips.

"A bird in the wood is better than a bird in the cage," Ash added.

"If you will not talk... will your partner?" Birker asked.

She was a bit surprised. "What do you mean?"

"You have a partner. Maybe he will talk," Birker said.

"What?" Ash asked surprised.

"Maybe he will talk to us about your mechanical side. I heard you talk about your partner and his dolls, clones even, avatar," Birker continued, "We are interested in the combination."

"I don't fully control, so it is possible he will talk to you. Maybe he might say I was wrong. I think a lot of you guys are parasites. You manage to convince people they should be joyful because you get a return on your investment," Ash said.

"You can't lose," Birker responded.

"It's not inevitable. You can lose," Ash said.

"You can't." Birker.

"Hunting dogs have scratched faces." Ash.

"Extremely confidential. Trust you will not repeat." Josephine.

She thought, changed her attitude, "Listen I had a hard day, I apologise. I am going to ring him and ask him to come ok?"

Fine. She rang him, returned and changing her tune said she had been stressed. What was going on? Misread it? Overreaction? Had her judgment deserted her? Was she tired? Time of the month? Why so narky? She assumed they were interested in her but was not business-like and relied too much on instinct rather than instructions.

LLLF

LONDON LOGOS LIBERATION FRONT

Publishing Pamphlets to Oppose Censorship of Our Message.
The Counter-Revolutionary to Evil and Terror Effort.
Love. Life. Liberation.

OPERATION GLADIO IS HISTORY.

IT IS NOT CONSPIRACY.

THIS WAS NATO LED.

THEY BUILT A SECRET ARMY.

THEY ARE AMONG US IN THE WEST.

THEY CREATE SUBVERSIVE GROUPS.

THEY MAY WORK WITH PROTEST GROUPS.

THERE ARE OTHER ORGANISATIONS.

LIKE PROPAGANDA 2.

LIKE ILLUMINATI.

LIKE THE FORCES FOR ARMAGEDDON.

THEN YOU HAD THE LONDON SECRET SOCIETIES.

THEY ARE SECRET BUT NOT UNKNOWN.

SECRET AGENTS ARE EVERYWHERE.

BECOME A SECRET AGENT OF THE HOLY SPIRIT.

BECOME A SECRET AGENT OF THE GREAT SPIRIT.

BECOME A SECRET AGENT OF THE FREE SPIRIT.

PREPARE FOR LIBERATION

Chapter 23

Dark Night of the Soul

Of Little Meddling Commeth Great Ease

Blue lies. Blue lies had caught her off guard. She had never heard of them or the concept. Apparently true. Blue lies and the police. Blue lies used to control a person. Blue lies were then an illegitimate means to get legitimate goals. Like a criminal. Bullies in blue lies. You need to lie, to deceive to get intelligence in questioning. Like noble lies. Maybe to comfort a schizophrenic. But these are 'Police Placebo' white lies. Telling a woman protesting at an abortion clinic that you need surgery on your back so she gets up and walks away instead of being carried. Seems commonplace. Are they not white? Suppose because they are used in contexts of people who have authority and legitimacy including the use of force. Good name for what she did. A Benthamite utilitarian calculus. But that's why you want people to tell the truth because a bit of blue can become a blue tsunami. Wasn't that what Graham Greene was doing pointing out how you had to be honest. Otherwise you get sucked into the big secret forces. The Third Force. Make yourself innocent for a cause. End up with Skinner and Milgram. Milgram showed how ordinary people can easily become agents in inflicting pain because of their obedience to authority. Maybe they relinquish responsibility as agents or as conformists. Solomon Asch studied them. Stanford Prison experiments. Ok, a lot of the claims were exaggerated. Some participants began to act roles in the experiments, playing TV characters in their head. But why do people need evidence of group obedience and the willingness to suspend personal judgement? They shot kids who refused to wear wet clothes in WW1. Then science tells its lies. Screens. Blue light. Blue lies. She had been out of order.

Poor old Lucius had not known whether to laugh or cry but she did not give a flying fuck. Scattering seeds. This was not part of the dark night of the soul. She trained herself to be positive. Hope cost as much as despair and is much more useful. A scalded dog dreads cold water they say. Bitten by a serpent fear a rope. She did not ever sense a dark night of the soul but rather a carousel in an antechamber, a place as if through a drugged haze where there was some reality but not fully clear yet. A blurred, out-of-focus picture or scene. There had been many theories of the Templars but she suggested more continuity. It explained certain things. Why the Knights of St John? They protected the Mediterranean and saved Europe from Suleiman the Magnificent and then had been exiled by the Tudors. The Knights of St Thomas of Acre. They held Acre, had hospital, chapels, HQ. Military. Paid for hostages to Saladin. Dissolved. Had disputes with the Templars over Ashridge. The Worshipful Mercers take over their property. Did the Livery companies contain this knightly core? Mercers still have a chapel. They went to Cyprus after the Saracens. Two Brit military bases still there following the Romans. Ayia Napa.

Now she needed to chill out, relax, do nothing, calm, still, be tranquil. Sunday. She needed to count backwards, watch a candle, doze, have a bath, listen to Richard Burton reading Under Milk Wood. She needed to listen to YouTube videos on consciousness and extra-sensory perception and some extraordinary life. She needed to drink less coffee. Just today. To get into a slightly deprived state so she could listen to the universe. Many people thought they had a medical condition in their ears when sometimes their being was opening to the universe. The world and universe has a resonance, that you can tune into or ignore. They wanted you to be cut off from having your feet in the ground, walking, smelling the air, talking to people face-to face, being touched normally or intimately. The more the mass could be isolated, removed from the glory of their former potential, the easier it would be to control them. Then confusion, dissension and processes designed to fool, entrap, hamstring and straitjacket the individual. Where there was some different authority, say a belief in God, it would be squeezed out.

Although it is funny in the centre of the Reformation when icons and relics and all that were banished that you had this strange fascination with things people thought gone. Fairies everywhere. Angels everywhere. Even people claiming not to believe in any such things acted contrary to that. Ventriloquist. She thought of his dummy, of the boy the dummy was based on. She thought he thought the dummy was saying things he did not know. Now knew different. It showed that she was not mad, or at least that there were others that were similarly mad. But the quality of a statement can stand on its own two feet, independent of whether it comes from a comic, by accident on a computer, through cutting up and re-arranging text, through Chinese whispers, out of the mouth of babes, out of the makey-up mind of a writer or playwright. If what is being said makes sense and rings true and sounds sound and in fact pierces the veil of illusion and targets the bullseye on the heart, then who cares where it comes from? Shaking. Inspiration. In spear.

She wondered about past lives. Our hair, skin, bones, blood, organs, brain, instincts come through others. We have the flavours of many and the information that was carried in them. We are unique, but are at the top of a mountain of people, ancestors. Not hard to imagine somehow that some sense of things can slip in here and there and give us access thereby to the past in some way that is not hypothetical or constructed. You have a heart transplant and you get some of the emotions even skills of the donor who is dead. She recalls the ancestor worship in China, incense, red, gold. Makes sense. Another rule was bubbling up.

Axiom 11   Consider whether everything could be a lie but retain love. Seek the peace that passeth understanding.

Apart from the ancestors we have all the stories. University of Virginia studied reincarnation claims. Children describing their former lives. Apart from hypnotic regression, where suggestions always makes it difficult to distinguish. They say that everyone is Napoleon, but that does not seem to be accurate. Comic's response, as vain vanguards of the establishment. Jester turns on subjects. Early Christians used to believe in reincarnation, but they won't tell you that. If the spirit was an entity that was self-contained and desirous of learning more or improving then coming back into new contexts would not be strange. She began to think of idea of heaven and hell. Swedenborg had made interesting attempts to chart them claiming he had travelled there. She was reading Malachi Martin. Frightening. Meditation and channelling. But Swedenborg was against retreating meditative lives.

'The only way you can be formed for heaven is through the world.'

What could hell be? Doing the same thing over and over again. Learning subjects that you did not like and having tests all the time. Doing something you were doing on your last day over and over again, forgetting. If it was hot all the time you would adapt. If it was cold all the time you would adapt. Maybe you have no power to adapt, lose evolution possibility ironically. Maybe by then they would have so much bad TV that you could be forced to watch it for eternity. Or Facebook. Hellbook. The limitations of the body and its incapacity to endure too much disease or pain is in fact a thing to rejoice in. It would seem that being stuck is always there. In some inferior mental state. Then they say it's the absence of something higher. It is the cold distance difficult to traverse. We are attracted to a fire, to warmth, expect good feelings most of the time until the environment does not deliver. Mysticism seems to be about a fundamental belief in the inevitable highness.

She had reduced it to what she called The Feeling. Maybe the Mystic Feeling. Antechamber to The Nexus. A sense or state that was to work in normal, ordinary contexts. An elevated sense, unruffled, by the buffeting winds around. A near-ubiquitous sense of tranquility that you could cultivate and feel like a pleasant, numbness in the head with crystal clarity. Precursor to Peak States and the Flow, like to breathwork and focus. A necessary state before you could access the higher states, the altered states of consciousness, the ASC, The Ash. Nexus the doorway. Connections opened and you could receive intuitions, messages, intimations, inspirations, sense, premonitions, communications. For some a mystical union then, a union with the divine in some way, past the Cloud of Unknowing. Bridal chamber. To get there you must be wary mainly of undue materialism and measurability to the exclusion of different dimensions, phenomena, unknown and invisible. At least see things differently. History is destined to miss the iceberg under the water. We hope we are not on the Titanic. Secrecy all round. Secrets between people. Secret desires. Secret service. Secret services. Secret societies. Secret mystical rites. Secrets of nature. Secrets of the invisible. Secret interest of elites. Secret knowledge. Secret laws of the universe. Secret history. Secrets never recorded. The only real secret is yourself and the destiny you forge. Forget undue intrigues and investment in the rest for you will lose and may lose your soul or at least send it in the wrong direction. There were also portals to the darkness that she would never want to go to. She was on Michael's side.

In the morning she had agreed that when she had her muesli, she would attempt to remote-view what Erik saw at 10. The deal was that he would walk somewhere and look at something and she would attempt to remote-view. He would view and photo it. To see what he could see, for comparison. She believed in this phenomenon before but she had been talked out of it. Now, more open-minded, she wanted to investigate whether she had it or could cultivate it. Although she was worried about the 'middle plateau.' There was a checklist they had. There were also protocols. They had copies of protocols used by companies that provided services to the CIA. The protocols also recognised that the process of remote-viewing could entail exposure to evil spirits. So if these guys took it seriously, she would too. She could mention colours and proportion, words, objects and seek specificity to surmount the inevitable stretching of evidence. There would also be 10 alternatives to choose from as a secondary corroborative test. She had explored remote-viewing quite a bit recently. US had explored it scientifically and Intelligence used it. She was coming to the conclusion that vision was something far greater than many believe. When having massages she imagined or perceived, that at times she could see not with her eyes but with her skin. When this had happened first she wondered. On investigation she saw these claims were not so strange. Blindsight, a sort of echo-location. Sketched what she saw.

Intelligence. Genius is not just an issue of IQ. Geniuses, spiritual leaders, and innovators get an insight, a dream, a flash. They drift into a different dimension. The One, the union, the timeless, it is similar. That happens when you empty yourself, give it up, release and let go. That helps you perceive and get insight. Being receptive and empty you can open. Reception, that's what Kabbalah means. Open you antenna. Pick it up. Believe clearly and positively that there is a solution. Look inside. The shook foil happens, attracted. Dwell and then tell. There you get creativity, spiritual insight. You open to higher consciousness. But if your inside vessel is a charred one then it will attract the dark forces you have invited, while a golden, cleansed one will allow appropriate attraction. That is why blankness, bareness, emptiness is dangerous to those without control of the reins of their being. Instead of having the reins they will have an invisible halter.

When you are under pressure she thought you must take care of yourself, reassure yourself. Massage did that. All types were good. Different moods suited different times. She made an appointment with her usual one in Muswell Hill. The studio was out the back. If the weather was cold there would be a fire. She would have a Thai Yoga one today. Healing in anticipation. It was Thai Yoga massage. It struck her. Jade was a middle aged woman with maybe dyed hair, healthy glowing skin. She seemed radiant all the time. You sometimes wonder how they keep it up. As they had their usual pre-massage confab a thought came in.

"Are you a witch by any chance?" Ash asked and continued, "I don't know why I didn't ask you before."

"Observant," Jade said.

"I did not notice all the little clues," Ash said.

"Yes. I don't hide it but it is perceptive of you…Have you been up to the Queen's Wood before..?" Jade.

"What have you learned?" Ash.

They talked a bit. Ash had done a bit of a massage. What had struck her was how you got a sense of a person by putting your hand on them. You could feel their energy. Ash had less interest in witches now. She wondered whether the male force, the man, the father was left in it. There had to be balance. There was a range of witches standing for a range of things. As she relaxed, her mind went to all those women, as well as the forgotten males, who were persecuted and burned as witches. The Kirk in Scotland unspeakably cruel while preaching enlightenment and Christian charity. Bridle. The herbalists and handywomen, the weak of mind and the unfortunate tortured. She forced that scene out. Sometimes thoughts come unbidden, you registered them and must bat them away for another time and be present. We had come a long way from Exodus and the lead to the witch burnings and *The Hammer of the Witches.* *'Thou shall not suffer a witch to live.'* It was a bad translation, it may have meant poisoners or black magic practitioners as opposed to white witches. What about the Witch of Endor who brings Samuel back? Not to say they were against necromancy and sorcery. But nature loving, self-empowerment was not it. However there is a boundary. Out of bounds you break or make a bond. Satanists in power. Psychopaths. Hide in roles. Smile.

That night was the romantic evening with her and Erik. Well not a romantic evening with her exactly. They were doing a test to see how she could remotely but mechanically operate the movement and voice of the robot through 'complementary control' to seduce Erik. Marionette. Complemented Animatronic. Complimentary rather. She had not really thought of this before or how to do it. Reality was that she never used seductive techniques in personal contexts, although she understood them in business. If you did, you would have no idea of knowing how that person really felt. If you wanted feelings then you should not draw out the false self of the person you were dealing with. You wanted a real person not an actor nor a fantasist or someone easily duped. The false person is one created by people or projected onto them with all the desires of the projector who becomes disappointed when they find they don't match. They had decided to use her flat. Ethereal was primed as Ethel. She set up a rudimentary romantic setting, music in the backgrounds, candles. She could see from the eye of the doll and you could have eye-tracking which followed the eye and pupil dilation. Without social niceties she showed him in to Ethereal in the soft red light and departed.

"I have been waiting for you," the Doll said.

He thought about laughing but stifled it and replaced it with a serious look. He was good at doing a job seriously.

"Welcome, sit down young man. I am pleased to see you... Nice shirt... Sit, please," Ethereal said.

"Thanks Ethel.... Ethereal," Erik said.

"Miss Ethereal please. We must not be too familiar."

In the bedroom Ash was enjoying it moving the controls, the gloves and knobs.

"Are you looking for something Erik?" She pronounced Erik in an unusual way.

"Pardon me." Erik.

"Well I don't wish to be rude, you are looking about," Ethereal said.

"Sorry Ethel... Miss Ethereal." Erik.

"That's better. What a good boy you are! Now Erik, tell me what do you find attractive about me? I would appreciate if you look into my eyes. I feel I am not getting your full attention otherwise," Ethereal said.

She suspected he would not be so hard. She needed no mantra, no models, no mesmerism. Ethereal mirrored, fluttered eyes, listened. She was a little *Pride and Prejudice*, more focused on the perception of his narcissistic tendencies. He liked to talk about himself and believed others were interested. For a long time. Perhaps he thought he was talking to Ash or Ethel? She found herself looking at a magazine when he was going on with a monologue. Crow and the piece of cheese. Ethereal cooed, interjected, "Really."

"Amazing."

"Interesting."

"You're joking me!"

"No! Really?"

"You did that?"

"Tell us some more."

Erik is a fantastic actor she thought or he is responding. Drinking as he was encouraged to do. Inhibitions diminish. Perceptions become fluid. Responding to me and not the dummy. Or he could be responding to a combination or re-combination, or he could have seen Ethel. A cipher. One of the meanings was a non-entity. A cipher was used in code too. But the non-entity becomes an entity the more it possesses qualities or possesses you.

"I find you are creating an interest which is causing an influence that is mastering me," she replied to a long spiel, quoting roughly and vaguely from barely remembered Jane Eyre in a deceptive feint that represented the exact opposite of what was happening unbeknownst to him.

"Tell me about yourself," Erik said, maybe remembering at last the usual protocol of a ...date.

"As Alice said, *I'm afraid I can't explain myself if I am not myself.*" She could see by his eye movement that this was causing him to think and confusing because he had the type of mind that could not resist unravelling something even if the game was not worth the candle. "*The golden rule is there are no golden rules*, as Shaw said," Ethereal whispered.

Eye-tracking devices reacted to directional movement of the eyes of the assessed when they accessed visual memory or auditory memory. Infra-red sensors showed heat changes in the body. You could see inside. Easy to tell if there was emotional or physical responsiveness. She checked the indicators. Triangulation allowed indication of states of arousal. Ash was surprised.

"You do work out quite a bit I see," she said.

He was off again. She decided to go a little quicker. A little more Mae West in the context.

"May I feel your muscles to see how big they are? Oh… my," she said. "I want you to tell me what you think about our time together.."

"I will…" he said.

"Do you like archery?" Ethereal asked.

"I never tried it."

"You should try. I love the bow handle in my hand, pulling back the string, releasing the bow. Shooting your bow is a great feeling. Holding you hand on the shaft, knocking your arrow, releasing. I'm feeling a bit lazy…. would you be so kind as to escort me to my chamber?" She said.

Was she an agent or does the agent develop agency to act on their own? Was she me? Was the attraction to me or to it or both? She was surprised it was so easy and that he had taken it so seriously. You could attract someone by engaging with a pattern in their head. Plato's world. Pythagoras. Porn would give way to machines and fantasy. She got him according to all the indicators. This the equinox was it not? A neat yellow hole means someone pissed in the snow as the haiku goes and making poems with seventeen syllables is indeed very diffic. Yes, out of order. Rattled. Maybe escape reality too much in my rosy zone of buttered muffin stained book contemplations.

LLLF

LONDON LOGOS LIBERATION FRONT

Publishing Pamphlets to Oppose Censorship of Our Message.
The Counter-Revolutionary to Evil and Terror Effort.
Oppose the permanent Cultural Revolution.

THEY MAKE HORROR.

IT FLOWS FROM THEIR PATH.

THEY WANT HORROR FOR YOU.

THEY MAKE TERROR FOR YOU.

YOU JUST HAVE PHILOSOPHY.

YOU MUST HAVE MEANING.

YOU MUST HAVE HISTORY.

YOU MUST HAVE LOVE.

YOU MUST HAVE LIFE.

YOU MUST HAVE THE WORD.

THE WORD LIBERATES.

WHAT IS THE WORD?

WHAT IS THE LOGOS?

IT IS THE LOGOS THAT IS, NOT THE LOGOS THAT ARE.

ORDER AND KNOWLEDGE.

NOT RELATIVISM.

NOT POST-MODERNISM.

PREPARE FOR LIBERATION

Chapter 24

Greenwich - Omphalos

'LOOSE LIPS MIGHT SINK SHIPS'

A September breeze blew light and even slightly cool. The word Thames has tea in it and that was the colour today, not the remembered reflections or imagined summer blue, nor the grey that matched the speck of the Dome of St Pauls barely visible in the distance. Down there the Endeavour was born from a re-fitted collier. A space shuttle would be named after it. From down there the Mayflower sailed in July but did not leave England till September. They tell you about the tea-clippers and omit the opium clippers like The Water Witch. Opium that the East India company used instead of silver to pay for the tea. It is the people with power that ply us with potent potions. Stupor and Stupid are the same root. Muting the mutiny. The boys with a hole for a soul who do the dirty work will fail and end up in jail while the powerful remain and laugh and the snotty jesters snort their cocaine. Tea and Time. Tea-time. Time is a construct. Like concept of gravity that Newton invented. His ghost is everywhere. What about least action or something else. Time, gravity are very useful tools but not necessarily the full story. X Dimension. Mutiny on the Bounty. HMS Bounty was refitted down there in Deptford before going to Tahiti. Looking for cheap food for slaves. Royal Society again. The bees were buzzing in her head as she walked. Later she would blow off a bit of steam with Erik at Capoeira. She came by Tube to Greenwich, walked up through the town and up the hill. Quiet. Emily Davison from here. The Thames made its majestic U before her. ℧. Or rather an Omega from the other side. Ω. That's why Dee went over the other side to do his ceremony. Then if it's Latin it's the upsilon right way up. Or in the Enochian angelic language, same shape but a P. Constellation of Libra. ♎. They watched the stars here. The body of water that began the British Empire. Conjured by Dee. Maybe the omega shaped bend caused higher beings to come here. Horseshoe. Pearly Gates. Yoni. Conrad set the *Heart of Darkness* on a boat on the Thames. She thought he was talking about London. He was Marlow, like Marlowe. Kurtz some say was Leon Rom in real life, like Rome. The Belgian Congo would be exposed by Roger Casement. He would end up in the Tower downstream and be executed. Casement who had been Sir before he became an Irish rebel captured after bringing guns in a submarine. There was meant to be an ancient initiation site, Maze Hill and a maiden place. Everything was measured here. Magnetism in earth. They knew this was a power spot. Space and time they measure here. Astronomy. Time. Longitude. Fluke? They thought this was the Omega Point. Now that is some singularity that marks the evolution of humans into machine man. Even the theologians argue for that. Chardin.

From here the world was divided up. This was the omphalos, naval of Empire. Navy of Empire. Belly button. Navy based here. Navis, ship in Latin. Nave of chapel. Naos. Temple. Cella. Cell. Privateers and pirates. Share the booty with the Queen you get a knighthood. More money from a pirate ship than the Exchequer receipts some times. Jolly Roger. X. Circumnavigation, plundering. Slave trade. Treasurer of the Navy. Time. Geography. Allows navigation, use the Romano-Norman genius for tight control of populations to control the world. Blackheath over there. Roman Road. Plantagenet palace. England's first Golf Club. St Andrews established the rules. Lawyers. Somewhere someone is reciting them on some course. Remains of docklands before me was the world's counter for trade. Triangle of trade. Take the ship owned in London to Africa. Sell guns. Get slaves. Take them across the Atlantic to work with sugar. Take sugar, rum, coffee back. You needed space. Docklands, warehouses around 1800. Biggest project in the world. Barings founder of Lloyds and many others. Eventually some anti-slavery people lived here too. Ignatius Sancho. They say 200,000 went on British Ships. But even back to Elizabeth, she has said there were too many of that skin colour in London. Blackboy Lane. Then there were many in London. Made dresses in East London. Played music in bands. Am I not a man or a brother?

After the goods become less important the financial centre begins to shift in recent times. Great mouthpiece of Fleet Street had moved here as well. One of Thatcher's showdowns. Protesters at Wapping half way. A new concentration, media, finance back to where it all began. Big obelisk-like, pyramid-topped Canary Wharf. EastEnders. Serpentine river. Map of the area the Germans would recognise. People in big cities had been used to these magical things that had become ordinary. Cleopatra's Needle on the river, taken from Heliopolis, towed in a special container. One of the most expensive films ever Pirates of the Caribbean, On Stranger Tides was made here. Most expensive TV series, The Queen also. Thor. The Dark World and many more. Places can be like magnets, pulling layers of reality on top and charging them. The River always seemed to suck the light from all around and create a glow, whether it appeared, silver, tea, brown, gold or even blue. A powerful place. Roman Road to Dover. Danish blackmailers. So many monarchs here from Edward I, Henry IV and so on. Henry VII did it up. Important for Henry VIII and Elizabeth I. Royal Observatory. The Meridian. The Royal Naval College. Poor seamen. 1522 the Holy Roman Emperor came here.

She used a 'Mind-Time Camera' mental technique in resonant places. Felt them, studied and marshalled the facts. Then go there and meditate. If you then step into the focal point of a life or person or event your mind begins to get the suggestion. If you look, observe, remember and meditate it comes alive and you can begin to get a sense of the people more than mere description. Perceptive people get more. She sat down and surveyed the view at Greenwich. Turner painted here. Rotherhithe where the Fighting Temeraire ended up. Turner and the Thames were mystically connected. Tourists stepping over the timeline, taking pictures of the vista. There is supposedly a ley line going from here across through St Anne's Limehouse. In 1894 Bourdin tries to bomb Greenwich Observatory. Real mystery. Its incomprehensibility led to Joseph Conrad's book *The Secret Agent*. Hitchcock made a film in 1936 loosely based on it. What was he doing? Was it up there he was meant to be? Blow up the Observatory? Was he meeting someone else? On the way somewhere else? Set up? An ancient place. Henry VIII sailed from here when Anne Boleyn was being executed. Met her here. Olympics were held across there. Grace O'Malley, Queen Elizabeth. Pirates and Princes. Pirates. Discoverers of New Worlds. Artists often a clue to magic places. Turner had the magic dust. Dee on the Isle of Dogs may have been following some relationship with Greenwich, maybe the road north through Hampstead, the ley line. Drake.

From Greenwich the Thames, the Great Serpent formed an upside down Omega. Omega, mega O. Last letter of the Greek alphabet. End of something, start of a new cycle. The Dragon's Head. Descending lunar cycle from Greenwich, the dragon's tail. John Dee seeking to bring in a new era, exploration, discovery, use of magic instruments, nautical, navy, naval, navel. Fleet. Elizabeth I, the most successful woman in history from here. Open to magic. Down there in Deptford the writer of *Mary Poppins'* father came from. Idea came one day. Like Enid Blyton, it came. Plucked it from the air. Down in Deptford,

Christopher Marlowe ends his days. A secret agent maybe. Drake got his knighthood. Cutty Sark. Under the river, she walked the reopened tiled tunnel and took the lovely lift. Woolwich Foot Tunnel some said created time anomalies. Time itself is an anomaly, albeit extremely useful for imperialists. Quantum physics will show that, quantum virtual paths. Symmetry violations of time in nature can be addressed. Dynamics can emerge phenomenologically, differences are epiphenomenal rather than elemental. Joan A. Vaccaro explained what Ash suspected. Blackwall up there. Walter Raleigh. Frobisher. Isambard Kingdom Brunel. A sign said that if you come on these premises take out you false teeth because the dog would get indigestion. The Great Eastern was launched here. Sailed September 1859. Biggest ship, originally called Leviathan. That line Dyer, *'all the pleasure that I find, Is to maintain a quiet mind.'* Suppose Raleigh thought the same in the end down the river. Give the Lie,

'So when thou hast, as I
Commanded thee done blabbing.
Although to give the lie
Deserves no less than stabbing.
Stab at thee, he who will,
No stab the soul can kill.'

Up West India Dock. Problem-Reaction-Solution Icke said. This is where the stuff came back from the colonies. She began to wonder whether she was doing the right thing. Sometimes you just have to maintain momentum. This could be silly and even dangerous. But she was going to go with her instincts. Going to maintain momentum and dictate the pace. She walked through Mudchute Farm and onto West India Dock Road. If John Dee performed a ceremony here it would have to involve some kind of circle, maybe chanting. Sure enough there was the old bugger off the bus, looking casual.

"Hello. I want to talk," Ash said.

"Ok....... Can you meet me at the first pub in Brick Lane this Thursday say 8? I'll have a pint in the first pub open on the way from Aldgate. We can have a meal."

"Cloak and dagger," Ash said.

"Scandal Keeper. It's No Joke. Distorted Humour? How are you?" Kit asked.

"Fine."

"I've been at the library. Trying to do an article about a play from 1597 called *The Isle of Dogs*. It was banned. Nashe and Johnson. I don't know why. No one else does either. No copy exists so it must be something. They say it was lewd or maybe offended the King of Poland or Essex. There was a big debate about trade. Your friend John Dee wrote a report about trade with the Hanseatic League. All spies. Even in the jail they had spies," Kit said.

"Well what about maybe there was something about magic..?"

"Ok, See You Then. A horse by Sire Palace by the way. Never Too Late. By Never Say Die. They love banning stuff. Take a break."

He was gone. Was he mad or one of those photographic mind folk recalling horse pedigrees or a party trick? She got on the Docklands Light Railway.

She had decided she would go with Erik to the Capoeira Class. They went down to Richard Street sometimes but they were also interested in a new club that had started up as they wanted to try compare styles. They were irregular visitors. She loved it although it was hard to get going and you needed to work on your flexibility. Neither Ash nor Erik had a coloured belt. You wore white. As she read about it, she suspected that the ring (Roda) was calculated to change the spirit a little. It was Brazil's national sport. But it had come from Africa. Used supposedly by criminals and then cleansed a few generations ago. Her guess was that it was the church who took over it, maybe the Jesuits. You needed to put your whole being in. A lot on the floor, lot of kicks, a primitive sense of integrating elements from the animal world.

Joan of Arc, St Michael. She had woken up at 5 every morning now. She felt she was being instructed. She found herself writing something like poetry. She wrote them down if it seemed they had some metre or beat, haiku or katauta form, 17 or 19 syllables. That was the sole test of authenticity beyond content consistent with rules of universal good. Phrases that were clear and persistent but unintelligible or irrelevant. She wondered what secret code there was in them, whence had they come? Probably nonsense these ones. By what cryptography of consciousness had they come to her. In her analytical mode she was clear that they could be some construction of unconsciously gleaned matter. Stuff read some time ago or recently without notice. Like the mind cleared the decks with images, perhaps a vacuuming of words. Discarding. This was not the coherent argument of her Voice.

'Ye charlie barlie returneth.'
'The fayre lit starry stage.'
Or,

'Fairie lit stood the stage.'

'Maunie the idjiot sweeps up the catcall but forgets the lover awaiting us all.'

'Tender the mercies to creatures who singeth from he for whom all our bells ringeth.'

'Tender thy mercies afoot all alinger leave out doubt lift not a finger.'

'Greene is the bough bent while fierce is the winde never to sever that left.'

There were names and places in her head. The starts of stories.

'Sliced through with many a bearded fellowe of most wanton regardie and injurious intent.'

'Eschewing the stynke of the isle that stynkethe.'

Raeburne, Claybourne, Cranburn or something. Then she would see if there was anything that made a reference to anything else. She read that Elizabeth Barton was an important opponent of Henry VIII. Was her concentration on that period affecting her? PKD might have believed that the two dimensions were revealing themselves or that you could trip between.

After warming up with kicks repetition it was time for the Roda. Erik being so good at some martial arts found it hard to adjust sometimes. He was too trained, yang, more stiff than her moving. They concentrated on meja lua de compasso, armada. Then they were back in the clapping ring. Her good friends Buntonjabi and Ellacouchadamar were there and the new friends from the Congo. You took turns. Coming in and altering and kicking and avoiding kicking. The berimbau, the monochord led. Like from Pythagoras. Music started and you clapped. You looked to the movement, clapped and listened to the music. Players changed. Movements altered, some different, feints, kicks, take-downs, play, false moves. More feints, kicks, esquiva, some hits, all the time avoiding contact save to demonstrate the chance, more feints, changes, song changes, music, beat monotonous, repetitive, constant, otherworldly the songs raised, get higher, music gets quicker her turn. She bends down to touch the ground in front of the berimbau, it gives consent she goes in and relieves one and gets involved, quick movement round and round, looking at the eyes of the player, watching the feet responding to every kick. Kicking back, feinting, reading kicks, distinguishing kicks, moving to the correct place, correcting, aware of circle of white aware of clapping, aware of spinning, aware of music, rhythm, beat, aware of awareness, kick, esquiva, meja lua de compasso.... hard to remember what had been done.... what other kicks were available... feints, take down, cartwheel, au, cartwheel feint, finta au..... faster, beat, a sense of giving into it, yielding, ceding, music, beat, flow, sense, spirit, resonance, pace, spinning, the use of the body....... awakening of the inner nature, fighting, warrior, bestial, animal, beautiful, engaging, interactive, dual, ebbing and flowing, yin and yang yielding, positive and negative, consciousness ceding, harmonising with the universal force linking to the spirit of the game, spirit of the people, spirit of the music, spirits of the dead through the antenna of the berimbau...... nearly dizzy... quick it was but seeming long in another sense, time slowing as concentration, anticipation-action-reaction came in through a sense of Brazil, sense of Africa, sense of shamanism, sense of the past, sense of the universal, sense of the ubiquitous. Erik came in, breathing hard, clapping still around, calming down, looking still, watching evaluating, still, moving, relaxing, easing, calming.

They discussed it later. Erik said that all shamans use a monotonous beat. This must have been not a martial art, nor dance but a mystical practice. He said that 90% of shamanic activities involved monotonous drumming and often spinning. Became united with the spirit of the universe. In that way they were participating in an old practice, and old and ur things. You linked with the Milky Way which was the Goddess. A survival that resonated with something gone by, something where the primal consciousness came in. Something where you got a sense of the bigger you, the person you were. And you could use it too.

"Did you ever read about David Shayler?" Ash asked.

"I remember something about him but I didn't pay too much attention. Now he's the Messiah, Son of God. A whistleblower, now he is Jesus and was a woman called Dolores and reincarnated and took a lot of drugs. Did he lose his marbles? Does he not go on about Holocaust, denial?" Erik.

"I don't know. I read a bit about him. If he was seen by some to be mad then that might help disqualify him and discredit what he said." Ash.

"What did he say?" Erik asked.

"Oh he answered an ad in the paper 'Godot isn't coming.' Worked for MI6. Left wing and Irish terrorists. He said that MI5 tried to kill Gaddafi without consent. Said intelligence knew about bombs but didn't do anything," Ash said.

"If that was true, then does his approach now help him?"

"I wondered whether he is adopting a defensive disguise. Alternatively he proves the point that he's not reliable. Does that mean that if you go against the deep state and are mystical that you will be mad or must be mad?" Ash said.

"God knows." Erik.

"Maybe we construct a reality around that which makes sense even when there is no sense because we must have sense. Or maybe you get it more right than wrong," Ash said.

"Maybe you and I think too much. It's like when you get in cold water. You fool your mind that it's warm." Erik.

"I'm not gullible enough for that... I meant to ask. Do you believe in possession?"

"Spirits and that, The Exorcist, you mean?"

"Yes," Ash said.

"Well I don't know. Why... do you think the Capoeira could bring down spirits?" Erik asked.

"No. You seem to have to want it for it to happen if it's the devil stuff. I don't know. No I think the way we do it now is empty of that. You need intention. Condomblé, Santeria, Voodoo."

She was prepared to stand back and criticise herself and see the impossibility of rational reconciliation. All truth is never available to the rational mind. A pure stream that flows but like the Fleet it became so poisoned with dead dogs, offal and run-off that it is covered up. When Jack the Ripper killed his victims he must have got their confidence or some of them. Many do. We are unsuspecting lambs. She sat down with a piece of paper. Sometimes you have to be logical. She wrote down what intelligence she got from this man Kit that day. Not much in the end. A vague feeling of trust having been created, but little content. All kinds of rules, Official Secrets Acts and all that jazz. Still. She was going to study what she could find about the State authorities dealing with this stuff. All she knew was there were two sides. On the one side there was healing, kindness, love, gentleness, magnanimity, care and compassion. On the other side there was destructiveness, sadism, cruelty, meanness and greed. Zone of competition between these two poles. You can only gravitate towards one. Entrances to both are often indistinguishable, and once entered it may be difficult to retreat. As she fell asleep she saw John D invoke an Empire on the Isle of Dogs over old jack o' lanterns in dark Stepney marshes and saw the gibbets at Blackwall, ducks, kings, Dutch and dykes.

LLLF

LONDON LOGOS LIBERATION FRONT

Publishing Pamphlets to Oppose Censorship of Our Message.
The Counter-Revolutionary to Evil and Terror Effort.
We shall Overcome.

YOU ARE THE PROBLEM IF:

YOU BELIEVE SCIENCE EXPLAINS EVERYTHING.

YOU ARE ONLY A MATERIALIST.

YOU THINK SPIRITUALITY IS ABOUT MYTHICS.

YOU DON'T UNDERSTAND METAPHYSICS.

YOU WATCH TV.

YOU WORSHIP SOAPS.

YOU ADORE REALITY SHOWS.

YOU TAKE THEM SERIOUSLY.

YOU BELIEVE THE NEWS.

YOU BUY NEWSPAPERS.

YOU REPEAT WHAT YOU ARE TOLD.

YOU BELIEVE POLITICIANS.

YOU SUSPECT NOTHING.

YOU ARE TALKED OUT OF JUSTICE.

YOUR SENSE OF JUSTICE IS REPLACED.

YOUR SENSE OF MORALITY IS CONDITIONAL.

YOU LIVE ON A MERRY-GO-ROUND.

PREPARE FOR LIBERATION

Chapter 25

Killer on the Loose

As she was out again in indigo evening a figure stood on the Crescent and looked as the light winked off. As far as he could make out the backstairs was the best way in. From the street behind. It led to the garden enclosed by a high brick wall. He could scale from around the corner in a blind spot. He studied it long and hard. He knew he could get over that wall easily. There was enough cover. He had not heard nor seen any dogs in the small back gardens. The garden was probably very small and not used. No alarm that he could see. One dog could stop everything. Maybe the residents did not think they had anything of value. He guessed there were 3 residents in the block. He knew when the target came in and went out. There was an old one. He could not wait much longer. It needed to be resolved. It was pressing. Getting harder all the time. He knew where the target was located now. It would be difficult to get out easily. But he was quick. He walked to the pub on the corner. A lot of people spilling out on the street, drinking, talking, enjoying the last warm days. Busy for a Tuesday. He decided it best not to buy a drink. Maybe a soft drink. No. Nobody paid attention. Looked like he was waiting for somebody. Nonchalant. He considered the plan, examined the entry route. Examined the exit route. He prepared militarily. He spent a long time looking for flaws in his plan. Near a crowded place, he was not noticed by anyone as far as he could see. If he was certain about the times of entry and exit he could finalise and execute. A deal of strength. Weight was hard to estimate. Mission was rolling. He knew how to go for the kill. He had gone through many scenarios in his time. Many types of battle operations. Always on his own. First person. You might be on a team but you did it. You pulled the trigger. This was not a sniping job. Burglary was familiar. His mind had been focused on this operation constantly in recent days. There were a lot of potential witnesses. But he had enough cover. It was bright until late. He hummed the Thin Lizzy song. Came into his head. A dangerous man. Moves like a cat.

LLLF

LONDON LOGOS LIBERATION FRONT

Publishing Pamphlets to Oppose Censorship of Our Message.
The Counter-Revolutionary to Evil and Terror Effort.
Enough is Enough.

YOU ARE SPIRIT NOT ANIMAL.

YOU HAVE ACCESS TO LOGOS.

YOU HAVE LANGUAGE.

YOU HAVE WORDS.

ANIMALS DO NOT.

THEY HAVE NOT EVOLVED TO SPEAK.

YOU HAVE AND YOU CAN LISTEN.

DO NOT LISTEN IF THEY MAKE YOU AN ANIMAL.

YOU ARE NOT GOVERNED BY YOUR DRIVES.

YOU ARE NOT DOGS.

YOU DO NOT LIVE IN A FAIRYTALE.

YOU HAVE AGENCY.

IF YOU CEDE TO DRUGS YOU LOSE IT.

IF YOU CEDE TO PROMISCUITY YOU LOSE IT.

PASSIONS ARE ENSLAVEMENT.

YOU BECOME SLAVE TO COMMANDS.

YOU BECOME SLAVE TO COMMERCIAL LOGOS.

PREPARE FOR LIBERATION

Chapter 26

Middle Earth

Wednesday morning in Middle Temple just off Fleet Street, Michael Roscroix fancied a latte. Some kind of official gang were busy scraping all the posters down systematically. They were everywhere these days. Would they accomplish anything? In his head he could see that cliff. He was standing on the side of it. Looking down. He dreamt it. He felt it. It was real. Today seemed golden yellow in the light and blue the hovering shadows. He would have had any old simple coffee but it was impossible to get simplicity any more. This moron Plaintiff acting against someone who owns a doll or his associate that seemed like some kind of dominatrix-lite was not to his likening. Sledgehammer to crack a walnut. Distinct legal entities. It was harder when you did not take to your client. The solicitor who had briefed him had a range of respectable but unsavoury clients. He fancied leaving the office, the dust and excitement about dull things. He fancied not having to feign interests in everyone's little details and pretend he was exhilarated over a point in a case one hundred years old. It can be tremendously satisfying when you find a little ghost in the cases, a little homunculus that can project the words therefrom into some dispute in the present day. The cases were exciting to many people but that had evaporated for him. He fancied leaving. If he could manage it he would. Leaving September, remembering the days of freedom gone, summer just going but blue skies still. Back to briefs and running by Fountain Court and Devereux Lane up the road to the bustling Royal Courts. Peering at precedents and scrutinising documents. Teeming with thoughts as he popped out to get a coffee and a little fresh air. Trying to distinguish truth from lies. A vague sense of unease. He had no wish to facilitate this action but nevertheless would execute it professionally. You are the mystery you need to solve. Lawyers often see their actions as cogs in a machine. The machine is not always theirs. He had lost interest in the system. He had expected as a young barrister to encounter people who were interested in things like justice and fairness. The Earthquake Emergency shook him to the core.

He had been a fool. Granted it was good when your relationships break down to dedicate your mind to the detail of cases. The reality of practice was a lot of arse-licking and game playing. A game he did not want to play. Power, contest and intention manifested in words trapped like demons in the sigils of law. Now he was applying for civil remedies that he did not enjoy. Orders that were variants of the Injunction jurisdiction such as Mareva Injunctions and Anton Piller that had been somewhat replaced by statutory civil procedures. The barrister who developed the injunction variants subsequently said they had become monsters. You applied for an order ex parte, surprise, no challenger to freeze the assets or seize evidence. They were sometimes described as nuclear weapons. They looked to be of a criminal nature to him. The barrister who developed them had argued that they lay within the inherent power of the courts to grant such remedies. He became a judge, an expert in Intellectual Property, patents, trademarks, copyright, designs. Then in a highly unusual move he had resigned as a judge after a few years. He said he had become bored and seemed disillusioned. Michael was at that point now. He felt no triumph with the clients he had. Great quests, challenges did not come. Yeats hung around here too, what did he say?

*'The best lack all conviction and the
worst are full of passionate intensity.'*

He thought of the time in New Orleans. Live and Let Die. Mardi Gras. Fat Tuesday. Celebrate before Lent. At midnight it changed. Police got you out. Voodoo. Walked the wrong place you were in danger. He read the history. Not just ordinary history but legal history. Historians know nothing about law. He knew about the slave trade in these islands. It had started down the road in Elizabethan times. But that was modern. Vikings did it. Had long chains for their slaves. St Patrick was a slave. Slaves had existed in Africa as it had everywhere else. In New Orleans, slaves could become free people. This was apparently advanced. Looking closer however it turned out to be for a different reason. Louisiana had been run by the Spanish and French. Had a Roman-law based system. Rome was so used to slavery they had a process for ending it on an individual basis. Legal system could draw on precedent. Common law did not have a long history of slavery and so when slavery recurred (as it always does) with adventuring of Elizabeth, there were no such mitigations. Situations evolve to appear to be the exact opposite of what they really are. Lord Mansfield who came here to the Serjeant's Inn in Fleet Street had said that slavery was not protected in the common law. That was after slaves had been thrown overboard to get insurance. Slavery just mutates. There's plenty of trafficking still. A case about a slave with the travellers. Then there's voluntary 'slavery' for fun. His present case was not quite in that category as far as he could tell. There was no evidence to that effect. It would not surprise him that the Government decide to ban that. It was now a tyranny. Maybe evil *The Tremendous Adventures of Major Brown.*

In 1993 in the case of R v Brown, the House of Lords had banned consensual sado-masochism between consenting males even though no long term damage took place. There was a split decision. The decision was right. Police discovered it by chance. It involved genital torture, branding, bloodletting. The majority accepted that tattooing and boxing and other such activities caused bodily harm, although here there were dangers of infection and injury. Public policy required that the violence element override possibility of consent. Young men needed protection, their consent was worthless, the humiliation, degradation by violence for sexual gratification was not to be encouraged by allowing it. One judge thought Parliament should legislate. Another thought that it was not a question of morality but of what the relevant 1861 Act said. The State should not interfere beyond what was necessary to protect the general populace. Victims manacled. They were young. There was drink and drugs. Some of the group had AIDS. There was bestiality. It was not incidental violence which could be allowed. The ring made videos of the activities. Consent was claimed but not entirely clear. The court learnt that the fish hooks inserted in the penis were sterilised. Presumably the same with the scrotum-nailing to a board, surgical incisions and burning with candles. The legal profession was itself involved in infliction of gruesome pain for a long part of its history. Wonder did the slavers enjoy it as well or was it merely business? Presumably when you were doing the interviews for your branders you would not employ someone squeamish. This case was not one he wanted to take. Mickey Mouse. Something not right.

The City of London did well out of Slave Trade. Slaves often had names associated with London branded on them, DY, RAC. Barristers always got paid in guineas. The Royal African Company supplied gold to the mint. Guinea. That's where gold came from to make the original ones. Like familiar words that blossom into different meaning. He thought of what an agent was. It came from one of the Latin verbs 'to do.' A person or thing that exerts power. A natural force acting on matter. Someone with authority to act for another, often in a triangular relationship. Often a commercial position. Someone who is a paid party political worker. A person who does something and even a computer program. You act as an agent. Act action. Double in a way. Then it has a history of meaning in philosophy. Also in economics, sociology, psychology and social cybernetics. Then you get the other concepts. Agency does not presuppose intentionality in some contexts. Then you have the legal meaning and the questions of actual and apparent authority, implied and express. Plenty of books on that. Then the issue of liability of agents, duties and specific rules such as commercial agents. What seems simple becomes endlessly complex when you have endless complexity. Agency and principals. Words mean what I say they mean, what I thought they mean or what you thought they meant. A skin of a living thought said Oliver Wendell Holmes. Every legal dispute is a dispute about the meaning of a word. Playwright and lawyers, twins. But lawyers act more. It was an IP case about robotic dolls used in a mild dominatrix context.

IP had become huge. So big it influenced international relations. The US had been willing to get into dangerous territory over copyright protection with China. No other domain would do that. The International Relations people knew nothing. They were still working on some State v State theory that was outdated. They called it 'Realism' without any hint of irony. He taught them. They were advising the top brass, with outdated theory despite other guff like 'constructivism.' Once the UK had been a model. Common law a great treasure. That was going. He walked by the Temple Church most days. People come looking for mystical secrets. In the Middle Temple the great playwrights performed plays. It could be Middle Earth. King John was often here leading up to the Magna Carta, that great document so much ignored. This was the home of law and it became the home of playwrights after the Reformation when they robbed the monks. The monasteries here and religious houses were whitewashed and cleared, made empty and bare of religious icons. No doubt they got rid of all the crucifixion pictures, the flagellation scenes, the passion scenes, the relics of bones and body parts that Catholic England loved so much. Berlioz. Symphony. Plaintive.

He emerged onto Fleet Street. Old Temple Bar had been here. He could not believe that secret courts operated in the UK. That families could be blown apart by administrative measures. Then Emergency. Freedom of speech withering by the day and you could not report on it. Straitjackets tightened. States within the State, play within a play.

Nobody cared. Waste of energy on red herrings deliberately designed to misled the public. Public gullible. Press quislings, artists servants, writers hacks, actors hams. Politicians in a sinister dumbshow. Powers that controlled the State had become beyond normal control. Most people living in a dream, materialist, hypnotised, in a trance, unawakened, lacking the numen. Asleep, sleeping now they are. Pushing him over the edge. He saw before him a mountain and a cliff. This would be his destiny. That monster that ruled in a myriad of little ways but drained your spirit would not get him. The greatest and most pernicious illusion is that you have some idea of what is going on, that you have some control, that your input is significant. You don't. He ordered his coffee nodding to a few colleagues and blended into the ferment of people without engaging as he followed his train of thought. It felt constricting and alien around him and he felt no attachment. The joy that filled him when he had begun to master the legal process and apply it and win cases and reap financial rewards and social standing were nothing to him. His parrot Miranda was the one little being he felt closest to. Homesick her? Wanderlust. Farsickness. Far-woe. Fernweh.

That's how the poor buggers ended up in trenches fighting people they had no beef with. Imagine you are watching the flames of hell over you reflected in the water you are standing in while the rats look for new corpses to chew on and wonder what am I doing here? Deafened and shaken, suppurating wounds. Your friends being butchered and you hoping you might get home yet. You see vicars, priests, women and children that waved you away one sunny day in some small village as you marched off to fix the world. Most is underground. Most is secret. Most people have secret lives. Most institutions are run by secret forces. The secret services have secret services within them. Bodies that are beyond control have control. There are many who will not hesitate to send you to the trenches with a smile. I know now what goes on behind some closed doors. Every person is an enigma even to their own mind. Men and women and other creations afoot seek to create the new men instead of the numen. Machines in secret. There is one deep secret I have access to its solving. Only one knot I can unravel. That secret deals with the future of humanity and thus the future of this world and others we, or our descendants may inhabit. That is the truth. When you consider it fully you might understand that which has been the golden thread of all the real accomplishments of mankind. They came from places like this, from concentrations from words, betrayal and contests and competition. This is the end for me but may be the start for you.

Above all you should not trust me, nor anyone else for the answer to this. Beware false prophets on the way. It is not the answer or solution that many seek but the question that must be uttered to unlock deep things. Forms come from the realm of purity. They want to be transmuted into a work. The forms appear to those who are open to them. Mainly perceived and seen when there is contrast. You allow the power to work through you. You open the nexus. They wait on the threshold. Your life has a form. Your story has a form. Your creations have forms. You must take your false identity, your false self, the congealed mess and debris and get them behind you. Become an agent of change? That is all I have to say now. Those details will dissolve. It is like an earthquake. I can see a cliff. L'espace est illimité. Le temps n'existe plus.

®

SUBSTITUTIONEM SPELL

Substitutionem is the magician's best magic. To change one thing for another is the metamorphosis most trained. To create a substitute. Same word source as statue. An idol. The words spell all out but they will not be distracted from the distractions we have set up. When we do, we can confuse or just take the good thing and leave the pale one in its place. Troll kalla mik. They convinced you that Changelings were mere superstition. The people are being substituted. Places too. In place of the real ones we will have our idols and the real ones will worship the idols before anything else. Spell. Take the draught from this vessel to create your vassal.

> They have their psyche, we have purloined it.
> They have their spirit, we will steal it.
> They have their mind, we will mine it.
> They have their heart, we will heathenise it.
> We put petty needs in place of psyche.
> We put selfishness instead of spirit.
> We put models in place of mind.
> We put hate in lieu of heart.
> We put machine as a substitute for body.
> And they will fall for the cunning tricks tho' much foretold of old of it.

LLLF

LONDON LOGOS LIBERATION FRONT

Publishing Pamphlets to Oppose Censorship of Our Message.
The Counter-Revolutionary to Evil and Terror Effort.
The Light of the Eternal is in You.

THEY WILL WIND YOU UP.

THEY WILL SOW RAGE.

THEY CAUSE CONSTERNATION.

THEY LOVE DIVISION.

THEY LOVE DEATH.

THEY LOVE IGNORANCE.

THEY LOVE EMOTIONAL MANIPULATION.

THEY HATE LIBERTY.

THEY HATE MORALITY.

THEY HATE CRITICAL THINKING.

THEY HATE REAL MEN.

THEY HATE REAL WOMEN.

YOU NEED TO KNOW GOOD.

YOU NEED TO KNOW VIRTUE.

YOU NEED TRUTH.

YOU NEED RULES.

YOU NEED SELF-CONTROL.

PREPARE FOR LIBERATION

Chapter 27

Brick Lane We Are Shadows

Outside the station was Clive Staples shouting to the passers-by.

"When you take away God you have no morality. Morality comes from above. Repent. Don't believe those clever dicks from Oxford and Cambridge living in their stolen property."

It felt like the end of the world. Tower Hill Thursday. Tower outside City. Thomas Cromwell's head chopped off here. Counted lucky he was spared disembowelling. Cut you up. Born not far from there. He had been glad to burn others. It was a strange Christianity from both sides. Imagine all the people over there in the Tower. Hess after his mission unbeknownst to Hitler. Even the Krays from up the road. Fond of cutting up. The ghost of Boleyn walking with her head under her arm still. The Shard building cutting up the sky. Walked up from Tower Hill. Aldgate. City. Whitechapel. She liked the old area. Some of her Jewish relations had lived there before they became successful and moved to the suburbs. When she read *Children of the Ghetto* by Zangwill, she could re-populate the streets in her mind. She heard the East European voices in the air. Her background was Sephardic. The East London Mosque dominated the approach. Sweat shops and sewing machines used to be here. Flemish, Irish, Jewish, Bangladeshi. Alsatia. Sanctuary. Jack the Ripper land, but more. Tracy Emin. Gilbert and George. She loved the vivid neon colours by night and the assault of spices that seemed to seep everywhere to remind you of faraway places where the sun shines and exotic plants grow.

After going into the pub they sat at tables as if separate for a short time.

"Guinness good for you," he exclaimed.

As she relaxed in the old pub with the fruit machine, peeling crimson paint and old wood, she felt calm. She thought of *Ashenden* by Maugham. Writer that becomes a secret agent, like he did. Then they walked half way up Brick Lane to a restaurant she had been in before. Many had been modernised recently.

"You sure this is ok?" Kit asked.

"Fine," Ash said.

"Did you know that on this day in 1983 was the biggest prison escape in UK history? 38 IRA men from the H Block."

"I can't say that I did," Ash replied.

"There you go. What are you having?"

"I fancy a vegetable jalfrezi."

"I'm toying with a vindaloo."

"Should you old guys not be careful?"

"It should be ok with a toilet roll in the fridge. Ready Teddy." He laughed at his own joke. "Pardon me... Maybe discretion is the better part of valour, I'll try the Lamb Madras."

"How do I know you're not getting information now?" Ash asked.

"You've made your mind up, you need not be concerned, if I assure you?"

"Where serpents tongues the pen men are to write," Ash said.

"Pardon me." Kit.

"It was a reference that could be about the play, we mentioned. There was a Harry Potter too. There was another lost Isle of Dogs play about dog men. Men with faces of dogs," Ash said.

"Like were-wolves..... Interesting. That form often comes when you have demon possession," Kit added.

"They seemed to be toying with banning all playhouses. Bacon promotes Richard II. He was building his new world, with English. Stage." Ash.

"Maybe their use to the Government would always outweigh the slight threats. Better control like Hollywood," Kit said.

"You don't seem enamoured by your post."

"Well I'm not saying too much. It's you I should fear. I assume you're not recording but I won't say. You see... it seems I have some growth in my brain."

"I'm sorry to hear it." Ash changed her tone.

"I had headaches. I went to the doctor, he sent me to a specialist. I got scans and a result. They don't know whether they can operate. Yeah I think it's mobiles but they say no. I don't believe them. Then they gave me a scan and I think that did me in. Beware the doctors. I look after myself. Because I'm worth it. Think different," Kit.

"That's tough for you. But you work still and drink," Ash noted.

"I'll act normal till I can't any longer. Anyway that's enough. Just so you know."

"I appreciate that, Dr. No, James Bond do you like it?" Ash asked.

"Not particularly."

"The baddies used to oppose the state, now it seems they work for it," Ash said.

"Well. I wouldn't go so far... " Kit.

"You walk from here and in 15 minutes at a decent pace, you're at Tower Hill, where executions took place. Bloodthirsty monarchs."

"Poppadoms Madam?" The waiter asked.

"Thanks."

"I heard the interview," Kit said.

"It was not me."

"Do you believe that?" Kit asked.

"Was that me?" Ash asked.

"I just wondered. I would be concerned if you said it was not you. I've read quite a bit about possession, exorcism. It's no joke young lady. Don't mess about with that stuff. These exorcists go through terrible times. Did you know they become incontinent from the force! No joke. Evil is there. Invisible forces at war with flesh." Kit.

"Thanks, that's a great primer for my curry. People forget they are engaging with fiction when they turn on media, read a book, watch TV, meet another person," Ash said.

"Listen you know I can't say anything particular, but if it fits in general I can. These restaurants are getting too modern. I liked when they had formica and the hairy, velvety red wallpaper and corny decor."

"What have I done wrong?" Ash asked.

"Look, this is all I can say…….. There are routine enquiries that are made about everybody. Nothing to hide, nothing to worry about. You don't seem to hide. You're open. Very open. In fact I was worried a bit about you, believe it or not. There are odd things going on, but that's not about this. One question, I don't think so, but you're not like having multiple personalities or anything."

"I am I," Ash quoted.

"Impossible is nothing. Not Thou art That," Kit replied.

That was that. There was no more to be said on that. He was one of those people who made cul de sacs in conversations. They got around during the food to discuss Jack the Ripper. She noticed he was curiously mannered and ate with etiquette although his dress was pensioner-informal. "You have an opinion no doubt?" She asked.

"Well it wasn't Sickert and I could go down the list. I have a theory. I would look for a platform that the murderer is coming from. I would look for an unusual access or egress. For example, the area is strewn with tunnels. But it is more prosaic. What was happening around here in 1880s? Transport. Liverpool Street, Broad Street. Trains, hotels, cloak rooms, people moving, strangers with a justification to be here. Not needing to fit in, passing through. The perpetrator could have come and gone the next day. May have left their own community unnoticed. A single man for example. But they said he had medical knowledge. However a good martial artist, an artist or more likely a butcher would have such knowledge. It wasn't open heart-transplantation. There was meat coming into London going to Smithfield. Refrigeration had started. Growing city, demand. Butchering comes up in profiles of killers, not surprisingly. If he came on a train as a butcher or a transporter of meat in some way presumably he could have gone back the next day. He wouldn't even had to have explained himself," he said.

"Plausible and prosaic."

"We don't know and won't know. That's something I say. You never know and you never will know. Don't waste your time on such stuff. I contradict myself."

"Isn't it amazing that it's still so fascinating?" Ash asked.

"It derives a momentum of its own. It took attention from the Fenian bombing of Scotland Yard. The chap that took over the investigation was over from Dublin. He was more knowledgeable about insurgency. He arrives the day of the first murder and they send him or let him go off to Switzerland," Kit said.

"At least he had an alibi for the others then." Ash smiled.

He laughed and sipped his water daintily. "He also said as far as I can see that the prostitutes were protected by the police which I interpret as meaning that the police were getting protection money, it might also be a factor in their *low morale*."

"I have read about the first World War and I still don't know what caused it. But yet people will read about these events all day," Ash said.

"Theatre. Magic. Here look at this. As you do, be sure there is something happening behind the scenes, in the sleight of hand. The matchworker girls going on strike. Fenians. Poverty. But if we frighten the bejaysus out of you with a London Bogeyman, maybe we will not appear so bad. Or maybe you will buy our papers if it is fascinatingly horrific. Listen. You have a good memory I'd wager." Kit.

He wrote down in his notebook '*The Chambers Dictionary*, Word plus 3.' "Got that... Seen that film Closer?" Kit asked.

"Why?"

"Watch it," he said.

"Ok." Bewildered.

"Have you read about Near Death Experiences?" Kit.

"Yes."

"If you understand this and I tell you I had one a year ago, you'll know why I am not so bothered for my own skin," Kit said.

As they parted, he leaned over. She was afraid he was going to kiss her paternally and ruin what was a nice evening. She could smell the curry and the aftershave. "It's worse than you think or can think. It's Medusa, Hydra, Goliath, Beowulf with a labyrinth all in one, wrapped up in an enigma. But I guarantee you have nothing to really fear. Times are funny however. Emergency is dark," he confided.

She was unsure what to say.

"God forbid anything happens, good luck. Listen if I ever sent you a message, the key words will be the third word below in the current edition of *The Chambers Dictionary*. Do you understand? That film I mentioned, look for the Park. He made a Y shape and indicated the spot at the joins. That's the best. Sorry for beating around the bush. Has to be the last time we meet for the foreseeable or I could lose my head. I will send you a message immediately after I know you know you have a problem. Think about that sequence," he said.

"Got it. Somos sombros." Ash pointed down up to where the inscription was on the spire thinking she might as well be cryptic. We are shadows. She felt a chill.

"Are you getting the Tube?" Kit asked.

"I'll have a walk."

"Listen if as a last resort you need to talk, and I mean a last resort, ring me on this number," Kit said quietly.

"Thanks. Appreciate that. By the way, the Ripper was Kosminski. The Pole. If it hadn't been for the City jurisdiction dispute they would have stopped it. Probably a sacrifice to the God Terminus."

"Ah. The Jew. The Goulston Graffito it was The Juwes... could be Freemasons. Just over there. And I met Profumo when he worked here too by the way. You've done it all, broken every code as they say. To be continued."

Closer. Closer. Closer. Tube. Y. Film. WTF. Was he taking the piss? Is he some old bugger going senile. That can't be right. Then again, maybe simple tactics are easier to use to circumvent electronic surveillance. Could it be a set-up? Too much. She imprinted the information using the Swish technique to park her preoccupations on the shelf for a while. The lives of others always allowed her space.

Mark Gertler, the Jewish artist, had Ottoline Morrell come to his studio round here. Zion Square over there in Mulberry Street. Silk-weaving here by the Huguenots, before the Sephardic Jews. Then the Ashkenazi. Ash. Ask. Ashkenazi Jews spread along Commercial Street, by the great Eastern Railway line. Irish community worked on docks. United at battle of Cable Street against the Fascists. If you really looked to painting and at the lives of the painters then you could travel through the canvas and out the other side. Canvasses like windows, a frame and surface. You can go through both if you know how. She travelled round the coast of Australia and went to Bribie Island to see where Ian Fairweather had lived. A great Australian painter, born in Scotland. He lived in a shack, made a raft and sailed to Indonesia. The gum tree and orange barks, the rainbow lorikeets and the blue dragons. Great Eastern Railway. This area was near the station. Broad Street built on Bedlam. Cloak rooms. Up to Holywell, Marlowe. She decided to take a little extra jaunt by walking up and around Bethnal Green and back to Whitechapel. She had seen the Elephant Man skeleton in it. Michael Jackson wanted to buy it. Criminals, despots, doctors, mystics, whores and warriors, poor and rich. The same old story. Trotsky met Stalin near here with Lenin and the rest. All the Bolsheviks. Stalin stayed here. One of the Night Guides in the mid 19th century said you could come to the Garrick Tavern in Whitechapel for the 'black-eyed Jewesses.' Home now with the meal digesting heavy and not unhappy. Still a sense of clinging on. Sometime boyscoutishly melodramatic about Kit.

We must remember. We must learn. We must fill up. We must discern. We must question. We must test. We must banish the mediocre. We must seek the best. We must read. We must see. Because they are taking our memory. There is a big black hole. The memory hole of Orwell. Unapproved history, knowledge, people get sucked into it. They push things into its field. They change the nature of things they invert. They confuse. It's a ruse. They take things of the spirit, God, the cloud, mystic, worship, adore, apple. They make it into something else alcohol, technology, perfume. Words. Exclamations. Jaysus. OMG. They spread them. Replace the sacred with the profane. Nothing is sacred. Law of semantic change. Bad usages drives out the good. Soon the sense of any supernatural possibility is snuffed out. We are in a giant snuff movie, victims cheering for the imminent killers of the immanent.

On Friday 26th Cranbourne met McGannah. On the top of building in the City in the indoor, public roof-garden. Shook hands with meaning. Come up and see me... Began to talk football. Neither interested. You had to blend in with the crowd. It could be used to spell out names or give clues secretly. People missed coded language. Ordinariness and plain sight a great place to hide things. Chelsea, Liverpool, Leeds, Spurs, Manchester United, Manchester City. Cranbourne was respectful and serious though it was comical to him.

"Anyway." Kit changed the pace.

"Well," Cranbourne said.

"Who was that chap that beat McEnroe at Wimbledon?" Kit asked.

"I know who you're talking of. A big figure," Cranbourne said.

"He made mistakes," Kit said quietly.

"Do you think so? I though he was great."

"Yes. They compromised his game, the game." Kit.

"Some players do have flaws. On a team it's a question of whether it jeopardises team performance." Cranbourne stated.

"Jeopardise. Jeu pardi. Game divided." Kit.

"Yes. If I can make it clear for myself. I have seen enough to say, enough," Cranbourne said.

"Clumsily compromised in a way. Queered the pitch to be specific. Missed a penalty." Kit.

"Indeed." Cranbourne said.

"Ok, Cranny... I'll have to keep an eye on the time. Did you now that Francis Drake came back after circumnavigating the globe in 1580 on the Golden Hind and unloaded at Saltash castle, on this day. It's just a test, a game for us to play they say."

"Right." Internet a curse he thought. The devil make work for idle hands to do. But communication made. A little obscurity still went a long way. McGannah had communicated his opinion that Birker was working sub-optimally. Cranbourne might not believe what McGannah thought. Maybe the Swede was on a higher mission. Kit's suggestion was clear. Throwing a little spanner in the operation. Cranbourne was not sure what McGannah was saying exactly but it was enough to give him a move. Silly old bugger. Awkward Swede, but his type would get on because they were well in with dominant narratives and practices. Smart. In other circumstances if someone called him Cranny, he would learn quickly never to do so again. Sometimes silly old buggers were not what they seemed. Heads of esoteric networks might be street sweepers. Intelligence officers might be flipping burgers. Deep cover. Canny Cranny maybe.

LLLF

LONDON LOGOS LIBERATION FRONT

Publishing Pamphlets to Oppose Censorship of Our Message.
The Counter-Revolutionary to Evil and Terror Effort.
Let your lamp light the way.

CRIMINALS ARE CELEBRATED.

GANGSTERS ARE NORMAL.

FELONS ARE FUN.

PIRATES ARE PROMOTED.

ROBBER BARONS BOAST.

CARPETBAGGERS ARE CREATED.

CRONY CAPITALISTS LIKE CRIME.

GANGS ARE COOL.

RIGHT IS WRONG.

WRONG IS RIGHT.

CONSTRUCTS ARE CREATED.

CONSTRUCTS CAN BE RE-CREATED.

YOU ARE NOTHING.

YOU ARE WHAT THEY SAY YOU ARE.

THEY'LL MAKE & UN-MAKE YOU WITHOUT MERCY.

THEY SET UP FIGUREHEADS AS BATTERING RAMS.

ABNORMAL IS NOW NORMAL.

PREPARE FOR LIBERATION

Chapter 28

Ceremony

'But there's gangs of them digging for gold in the streets.
At least when I asked them that's what I was told
So I just took a hand in this digging for gold.'

She sang in her head. It relaxed her. Used a different part of the brain. She was thinking about how everything was upside down. They inverted everything. Sometimes in strange situations simple details suddenly assume grand proportions in the surreption scheme of perception. Shallow scenes seem to surreptitiously impress so as to lessen the deadly weight of the present profound worries. Like Robert the Bruce watching the spider in a cave. She noticed the spaces between the bricks and wondered about the bond. Into her head came the story of the duel on Primrose Hill in a dispute about the Romantics. A dispute about literature and political perspectives. 1821 was it? John Scott I think handsome. Brave. Against lashing in the navy, slavery. Radical. Died after being shot under the ribs in the misty moonlight in an illegal and badly managed duel. Hampstead Hunt circle. Poets, writers trying to produce good papers. Writers went to jail. Nearly all those type of people are gone. The machine has replaced real people with replica journalists and jailors of public opinion only serve their political masters without much effort to hide their propagandist position. That short reverie vanished and her attention again focused on the light at the end of this branch of the tunnel she crawled through. Towards the noise. The low hum of voices. An unexpected possibility of unknown dimensions. What was going on? What was she doing here? Did this further anything? They always have Strategy. We only have Tactics. They plan. We react or not. They have clear purpose. We have confusion. They are broad. We are narrow. They benefit. We suffer. They stash. We sacrifice. They act. We react. They produce. We poach. They master. We serve. Down here in these shadows is our simple subterranean subconscious spielraum outside the strategy of the symbolic order of our slavemasters slowly tightening the surly straps of our mental straitjacket.

Sounds from the underground vault vibrated out in a low hum. As you came nearer, more light and more sound radiated through a vent with a grille at the end. It may have been some storm drain on an older street, it was thankfully dry. The walls looked medieval. On it now orange forms flickered and she felt suddenly a stone in her belly. She inched slowly, trembling towards the grille, apprehensive and excited. Such times you could not prepare for. Too thrilled you must becalm yourself. She should be protected from detection barring some other system she had not anticipated. Closer. She should be unseen being so high up. It was not music but chanting and a strange tongue. What was it? It was familiar, there were some words. It sounded Spanish, Italian... Latin. She recognised more words. WTF. Latin in a sewer. She was afraid of being seen. Nevertheless, she inched forward all the time looking back to see Pam at the mouth though barely able to turn her head. She could not discern whether she wanted her to stay or go and she was not going to think about that. It was both reassurance and a preparation for a flight. It was so small it would be difficult to retreat quickly anyway. With her head as close to the wall as she could she moved forward to get a view after taking off her head gear to stop reflection. Words emerged in her mind on a different level.

"Defende nos."

"Contras insidias demoni."

Odd words as far as she could make out.

"Corvus. Leon. Pater. Mit..."

"Sacrificium..."

Her glimpse showed some robed people, instruments, circles, sticks and a fire. WTF. She heard or thought she heard,

"Emitte lucem tuam et veritatem tuam."

"Sicut erat in principio."

It became unreal. Like a dream. Frozen. She was gone before she got ill or seen or fainted and went a bit quicker than she meant to. Demons? Luc....ifer, fuck! Or was it something else? Did she hear it properly? Was there any chance it was an auditory hallucination produced in the noxious air? Bye-bye. So long. Thank God Pam was there. Get out. Carlin had said.

> *'Religion is a pair of shoes. Find one that fits for you...*
> *but don't make me wear your shoes.'*

LLLF

LONDON LOGOS LIBERATION FRONT

Publishing Pamphlets to Oppose Censorship of Our Message.
The Counter-Revolutionary to Evil and Terror Effort.
Pray so you are not Prey.

THE MONEY IS IN THEIR HANDS.

THEY TAKE MONEY FROM YOUR HANDS.

THEY WANT DIGITAL MONEY.

THEY CAN SWITCH YOU OFF THEN.

THEY WANT DEBT FOR YOU.

IN DEBT YOU ARE A SLAVE.

CREDIT IS A CHAIN.

YOU ARE AN INDENTURED SERVANT.

THE PRISONS ARE FOR YOU.

THE PRISONS ARE NOT FOR THEM.

NOW THE PRISON IS IN YOUR HEAD ALSO.

YOU CANNOT DEFEND YOURSELF.

YOU GIVE THE GUNS UP.

THEY MAKE MORE GUNS.

POWER, PRISON, DEBT, GUNS.

YOUR POLITICIANS ARE PUPPETS.

DON'T MAKE PEACE WITH POWER.

PREPARE FOR LIBERATION

Chapter 29

Showy Execution
Theatre of Death Bound

≡ 3. 111. Three. Triquetra. Trefoil. Trimurti. Trika. Tridevi. Three pound the brain. Triune. Trinity. Triskelion. Three Graces. 3, 6, 9 secret of the universe Tesla. 3£. ³ ♣ ⅲ#3≫ ᴈΨ❸⁞ ⁞ . Scientists try to attribute all sense of presence, of the ghostly visitor to one side of the brain interacting with the other. But she did not believe that. The mainstream scientist will never know the truth, because they won't be told. Might be the ultimate protection. When mystics rebel at last. Not the unsatisfied, unproductive, hippy-types but the heavy ones. Humanity splitting in three. Masterclass trans-humanists, slave-drones and the higher spiritual counter force. One creating, one destroying and one maintaining. Wrong one creating at the moment. Wells explained it in *The Open Conspiracy*. Science takes global control over nations and will pay the price in blood without worrying too much about the cost. What was Sigma male anyway? Sigma? Σ.

Despite all the assurance of normality, business as usual, it was not. A curfew tonight in parts of North London at 11. Drones everywhere. She was at home. 29th. Final September Monday. Blue Monday. Pseudoscience. New Order. Ship, harbour. Shall obey. She had a slight sense of apprehension perhaps induced by the sight of so many military vehicles patrolling. Curfews constant in certain parts of South London, sporadic in this part of North London. Searches had become commonplace. The violent assault house raids that the police had perfected were utilised even if there was no evidence. She decided to have a Concentration. She knew it was the Feast Day of St Michael. Michaelmas. Had a crucial spiritual experience on that date a few years ago and that significance emerged. Like a meditation, but she worked on an idea. She took a few recurrent words and wrote them down. She eliminated ones that did not seem compelling at that time. Then she reflected thereon. Her idea was that the subconscious or spirit would choose something that had a connection that was significant. This would be the subject of a brainstorm in a meditative position. Jung allowed that such random systems could facilitate synchronicity. Something would be yielded that was useful. She chose from the words she had put under the candle. She ended up with four corner words, tropes to turn. Elizabeth. BDSM. Theatre. Execution. Chance is key among a limited range of choices, in Tarot, I Ching. They created an atmosphere and had an energy that you could open a channel of consciousness with your mind. In doing so you would allow your intuition to access the deeper secrets. You entered a stream of consciousness. Fleetingly. Discipline ↔ Intuition.

Slight pain in her stomach. To put her in a mood, she played cello. Mary liked to hear it below. This instrument best mimicked the human range for her. She played Brahms Cello Sonata No.1 in E Minor. Then she sat down in her scratched, relaxing red Chesterfield where she did her Concentrations. Scribbled sometimes consciously, sometimes automatically. A dark mood came over her. Bloody period it was. ASH. American Society of Haematology. A sombre feeling sometimes leads to serious matters. The threat brought her mind back to some of the things she ignored. She got up and looked again on her computer at execution sites in London and why they were located where they were. May have been sparked by client No. 4. Led to a reflection on contexts and descriptions. She remembered Behan talking about the IRA. He suggested that as they had tried and sentenced him in his absence, he could only hope that they executed him in his absence. Execution. Getting put to death. But it meant other things such as to give effect to. Elizabeth copied what happened before, the Plantagenets. The Civil Service was there. Henry II, bad-tempered, raging, controlling. Untouchable church. Gets Beckett in who discovers God and a degree of freedom, defying Henry. Battles for control, excommunicates the priests. Says something, leads to death of Beckett. Precursor. Henry disappears to Ireland. It was Queen Isabella of Spain that had been The Queen along with Eleanor. Isabella had been powerful. She made a police force out of the brotherhoods that existed. She then turned them into the Holy Brotherhood. Probably still there to the violent Spanish Civil War. Columbus goes out to 'discover' the New World. Muslims and Jews were kicked out of Spain. Queen on the chessboard began to get strong. Her daughter would marry Elizabeth's father Henry. Doodles. Ж.

She contemplated the apparent connection between the images of the Elizabethan Era and the present. Y. Upsilon. The Scene, BDSM. Elizabeth. Execution. Theatre. BDSM. All seemed linked. Pain not hidden. Morphed and then reformed in her head. Theatre. BDSM. Executions. ELIZABETH. What is in a name? Words within. Bite, zeal, hit, belt, able, ale, lie. Elizabeth. Elizabeth was named after her grandmothers, Elizabeth Howard formerly Elizabeth Boleyn, whose own mother was Elizabeth Tilney. Elizabeth's mother was Elizabeth Cheney. Elizabeth Cheney's mother was Elizabeth Cokayne and so on. Elizabeth of York was child of Elizabeth Woodville. Even the mistresses were called Elizabeth. Elizabeth Blount. Henry VIII's illegitimate Henry Fitzroy who lived on the Strand, half-brother of Elizabeth I. He was made a Duke at the Bridewell Palace when he was 6. The BRIDEWELL. If he had not died young he could have been Henry IX. Elizabeth was a common name. John the Baptist's mother was Elizabeth. Related to Greek and Hebrew Elisheba, Elisheva. There was an association with God in every meaning of the name. There was a Saint Elizabeth in Hungary in the 12th century. Isabel and Isabella are variants of that. It was a strong name with strong models beforehand.

Famous and infamous **Elizabeths**. Elizabeth Bathory. Serial killer, most prolific. Bloody Countess Bathory. Elizabeth Bennet. Elizabeth Needham. Elizabeth Bacon Custer. Elizabeth Richardson murderer. Biting, mutilating servant girls lured there. Torture. Orgies. Variants. Eliza. Eliza Cohen. Eliza Doolittle. ELIZA program. Eliza the slave in Uncle Tom's cabin. Lisa. Lis. Liz. Liza. Lizzie. Lizzy. Lili. Lili was a great film about a girl that fell in love with someone through the medium of the puppets he used as entertainment, he could not express his feelings. Libby Thompson madam. Elisabet. Eilis. Ella. Etty. Eliza. Elsbeth. Elsbeth Schragmueller. Spy. Fair lady. Beth. Bess. Bettie. Betsy. Betsie. Bessie. Diamond Bessie. Betty. Buffy. Buffy the Vampire Slayer. All Elizabeth. Elizabeth Blue. Betty Blue. Betty Boop. Betty Brant. Dark Betty. Betsy Heard, slave trader. Lizzie Borden. Thin Lizzy. Bathory. Heavy Metal. Mona Lisa. Nice name. She liked all the Elizabeths she had met in real life. Elizabeth II was impressive. You can't draw any conclusion from that. Lili. That would be a good association for the dolls. Paul Gallico wrote the story. Elizabeth sounds like it has Lilith.

She thought of the **Executions**. Executions for treason and rebels were consistently brutal. Nothing compared to what the Romans did. The Reformation. Witchcraft. Suffer not a witch to live. The Gnostics would have believed that was not real. Heresy of the Free Spirit. A show but no mere show. A severe reverie severing and serving several goals. Silver-tongued slaughter house. Bloody. Blue bloods. Stripping of the altars. Neatness, whiteness, colour, light free. Ruins everywhere. Nobles. Palaces removed. Every cloud. Theatres, plays in spaces. Hospitals and schools closed. Bart's, Bethlehem and others set up. Blue coast school found. Blue was the colour of charity. Students wore blue. Blue Coat Inn was here. But Bloody Bonner birched people. Beaten black and blue. The crowd stimulated by the scene. A trinket for their submission. A hologram. A microcosm. Queen punishes, God punishes, you suffer.

Places of imprisonment, dungeons, executions. Executions kept coming up. Hung, drawn and quartered. Stick the heads on the bridges on the gates. Pornographic descriptions. Hang then pull out hearts, innards, show the crowd. Take the inside, hidden out, expose it. Teach you a lesson. Explain why it was good that you were protected. Especially when times were tough and there was unrest. Always a good time for an execution. The theatre of death. The demonstration of the dominance of the state. Staged. Scripted. Audience. Entertainment. Execution Dock. Newgate. Smithfield. Tyburn. Tower Hill. Tower. St Paul's Churchyard. Lincoln's Inn. Charing Cross. Banqueting House. Ketch the incompetent. Ropes. Ships. Riggers. Navy. The execution was the concentrated spectacle. The BDSM market was now a diffuse spectacle. A fleet pleasure with the illusion of choice. *Society of the Spectacle*. But it was more. As well as the State making contrast with its goodness and promoting stars and celebrities, even if they were pirates or idiots.

Christian iconography gone. All the pictures of suffering and crucifixion were gone. All the relics, body parts gone. Was it so gone that they needed the new orchestration of gore? Was there a lust, a grave fascination with the bits, bestial and visceral of the human? Lust for blood, for domination, fear, sadism. Or was it just power? Open power over hidden power. Or hidden power manifested in the open to be dominant power. Manifesting when necessary in a calculated, calculating machine of control. Or was it just the way things happened without too much rhyme or reason. The forest might explain something. *Manwood's Treatise* 1598. Used wood for shipbuilding. Cleared woods because they housed enemies in Ireland. Monarch rules forests, animals slaughtered therein. Forest, female. The forest is specially for wild beast, monarch's will and pleasure. Caves. A place for rapes and murders. Wood. Wood Street. London was clearly the new centre again. It became the 'metropolis' around the time of Elizabeth's birth. What does that mean? Mother city. The Greeks colonised from the mother city. London was the metropolis. The first railway underground was the Metropolitan Railway by the Fleet. The police of greater London are the MET, Metropolitan police. People used to read the free Metro.

The show. Showmen. Show trials. Show the victim their insides. Show the crowd that the bad guys are merely mortal. Show them they can be reduced, destroyed, emasculated. Show who has the real power. The show must go on. Break a leg. They execute and put the traitor's head on a pole. Pregnant you were up the pole. Now you dance on it naked. A stake. Burn you at it. Drive it through the heart of vampires. The Master of the Revels. Revel. Reveal. Turn inside out. Our revels are ended. What is revealed. A fine day out. At the places where fairs and entertainment take place usually. Paint the town red. The Red Coats. Red post boxes. Blood. Bloodred. Bloodthirsty. Blood lines. Often after red herrings. Red meat. Red light. Show up. Show them up. Stage show. Play. Masquerade. Carnival. Meat flesh. Period pieces. Monster come from the same root as show. Shakespeare in Titus Andronicus and other plays shows more violence. Foucault. It was usually shown off scene. Look at all those 'magicians.' Houdini, Blaine hanging over the Thames. Chains, cages, submersion, threat of mutilation, burning. Like Fu Manchu. The good guys escape. Superheroes escape pain they will thrill us with. Maybe they were experimenting on reaction to showing violence, building up a register of the effects. Market research.

> *'And these our actors were all spirits*
> *As I foretold you and have vanished into air.'*

Perhaps that archetype and instruments of power and death are ghosts in the mind, a primal horror and betrayal of humanity. Perhaps we subvert and transmute it by erotic means. Perhaps the implied threat, bred in the bones, changing in the histories presses for a subjugation itself. But the thing she noticed was not the theatre of power, the paraphernalia. Sometimes it was big. The monarch could claim to be goddess, godlike or at least the direct link. But creativity was free. They could claim spirituality but that was free. It was unsurprising that the illusion of control in gameplay was powerful when it touched on subconscious and unconscious and underground buried currents of feelings. For a split second she could see herself being led out to a chopping block before a baying crowd.

Funny how all that **BDSM** stuff seems to fit into a medieval castle and very well into Elizabethan times. Look at the great record the Normans made. *The Domesday Book.* Domination. Those times have an effect still. Elizabeth regulated a lot of the clothing of court. Who could wear what. She managed the court. *The Bible* and *The Book of Common Prayer* helped standardise words. International trade brought words back. Playwrights used these words. Words, concepts curiously persistent. Some of the words came before that time. Sometimes the meaning evolved. Some of the words already had meanings and gained another secondary meaning at the time. With the printing press the spoken words came onto the page. Some had other meanings. The things, objects and devices that had been there were magnified in print perhaps and with pictures, maybe not to remind the people. The blank slate of the Reformation and the stripping of the altars created a space. Printing press and some freedom spewed out new words and old. There are the concepts and words in circulation, often seen in Shakespeare. Sometimes the words came as a result of translations from the Bible. Words, practices and concepts that come up today. She had built up quite a list. She could make reference thereto. Maybe they have the charge from the time, from the place, from a faint tang or sense of brutality. A strong draught of the times. Some came in slightly later through people born in the era she lived. A few modern incarnations in new form. Many dirty. Urban. In our world is the great ghost in language and practice of an erotic shift. Maybe this was Elizabeth's unseen influence. The underground river she took from Bridget. A new alliance. Ash made her own list. Etymological debate could go on for years. Idea of correspondence. Swedenborg's doctrine. Microcosm, macrocosm. Is Queen Elizabeth's Era the correspondent to this stuff now? Herder, Goethe, Hegel had the Zeitgeist, Volksgeist, Weltgeist. Spirit of the age, people, world. Can the Zeitgeist of the past have a ghost that haunts us? Maybe the apparition is a similtudo of what is still behind the scenes. Hologram. Words of that time or shortly thereafter stuck. Stained the stuff of BDSM. French book about 2022 called Submission. *Soumission*. There was a torrent of words from her time and around it. She had charted them all and sought them out first to use and then to find out their source. Behind them vaguely was a ghost of the divine, sin and religious service impressed with the instruments and conceits of Regal power. Maybe they changed the words because they created a magical changeling as a substitute. Professionally and personally she had delved deep. Why therefrom?

Queen. Queens. Queening. Queen in chess. Governess. Mad woman chess. Madam. Madonna. Mona. Moana. Demure. Dainty. Dirty. Depraved. Insult. Maid. Virgin. Dam. Lady. Marquesa. Throne. Superior. Haughty. Sceptre. Highness. Golden. The Golden Hind. Hind. Domain. Domina. Dominion. Domination. Slave. Enslave. Bachelor. Breed. Bitch. Rule. Ruler. Play. Obsequious. Obeisance. Obscene. Smutty. Umbrage. Abase. Abasement.

Abomination. Abhor. Abuse. Admonish. Beastly. Drone. Cage. Hourglass. Erection. Scene. Session. Bowing. Strict. Servitude. Submission. Subjugation. Subjection. Subordination. Worship. Wag. Worshipful. Whore. Court. Courtship. Courtesan. Curtesy. Mistress. Ministry. Kneeling. Filthy. Masks. Mark. Manacles. Shackles. Bridle. Scold's Bridle. Fricatrix. Frig. Prostitute. Rude. Barb. Bind. Breast. Butt. Bound. Bondage. Bond woman. Bond man. Bond servant. Cage. Chains. Thrones. Servants. Cock. Cuckold. Hag. Harlot. Heat. Inferior. Knave. Jack. Jerk. Jess. Unruly. Dogs. Cur. Sea Dogs. Swine. Blackmail. Bugger. Edge. Hot-blooded. Punishments. Cupping. Chastisement. Flogging. Flagellation. Whip. Peg. Pet. Plug. Scourge. Spit. Horn. Craving. Empress. Bruise. Fornication. Red hot. Dungeons. Fetters. Gag. St Andrews Cross. Pillory. Stocks. Rings. Jougs. Juggs. Torture. Confession. Strappado. Lubrification. Lubrication. Wooden Horse. Bastinado. Dirty. Silence. Prostration. Teasing. Lewd. Lust. Delight. Member. Moist. Naughty. Nought. To come to nought. Nothing. Denial. Deprivation. Frock. Garters. Gloves. Hoods. Bodice. Bib. Skirt. Collar. Tie. Girdle. Sequins. Sanctuary. Stockings. Sable. Bedfellow. Belly. Beguile. Rubber. Buckle. Boots. Robes. Secret. Secrete. Heels. Halter. Leather. Lick. Lickspittle. Rut. Spew. Spunk. Bosom. Perfumed. Powdered. Bottom. Slut. Tanners. Tan your hide. Saddle. Whips. Lash. Birch. Paddle. Dildo. Dungeons. Come. Spoil. Soil. Tender. Loins. Bleed. Racks. Riggers. Being bound. Bound Slaves. Bracelet. Brat. Lying at the feet. Inversion. Inverted Order. Gift. Privy. Tributes. Lace. Chastity. Chastity Belts. Corsets. Codpiece. Tush. Fantasy. Fondling. Sheath. Contracts. Law. Fobbed off. Prick. Piss. Penthouse. Muff. Bawdy. Heaven and Hell with a divide based on words. Obey. Forbid. Grant. Deny. Submit. Subscribe. Puke. Obedience. Worshipful. Strumpet. Merkin. Spread Eagle. ALL THESE WORDS COME FROM THAT TIME OR NEAR IT AND BECAME STANDARDISED AT THAT TIME. Split from the Church. Printing viable. New vernacular. New writers. New plays. New plots. New goddesses. New Order. Substitution? Like a cheap switch illusion. Inversion. Word of that time. Turn it around. Then later perversion.

Theatre. Power demonstration. Shakespeare was replacing the Christian plays. Ceremony was very important. Without it now it was meat without seasoning. The Protestant Church vacuum needed filling. Learn from what was there before. The emptied bareness, the colour gone, the stripped altars altered things. The Lutheran bareness of Scandinavian design. Now there could be a re-constitution around royalty, law, army. Masques. Masks like monsters sometimes.

Spying, voyeurism. Peeping Tom. Ian Fleming liked a bit of sadomasochism they say. Francis Dashwood. Elizabeth dominated, maybe to avoid rejection. She bossed as only she could, with no mother of restraint in her or husband. The espionage and the State's power get linked. James Bond. A bond. Brick bond. BOND. Bondage. Bound. Chains bound. Could not be clearer. Dr. No. Denial. On Her Majesty's Secret Service. For Your Eyes Only. Modesty Blaise. If you were a royal ex-member of intelligence would you depict it fairly? LeCree. Undercover. Mistress. Miss Stress more like. A number of Flemings, Sinclairs, Senclair. St Clair. Rosslyn. *The Girl with the Dragon Tattoo*. Elizabeth Salander. 'Queen' of the Pin-Ups was Bettie Page. Circus is right. From the slave trade to the rubber trade, brutality of highest order. George Orwell in *1984*, said something like if you want a vision of the future, imagine a foot stamping on the face forever. Him I would not trust. Seemed to be too much involved. Then he is praised for predicting the future. Maybe he was just telling what many around him wanted. It looks suspiciously like a domination fantasy. Foot on the face, boot. Trampling. Commerce. Amazon, eBay, Google. Amazon woman. Legendary race of female warriors. California was predicted in a Spanish novel to be the home of Amazons before the Spanish got there. Obey. Go ogle. Apple. Eat the apple. Tempt. Fox. Foxy lady. Barb. Barbie. Bratz. Face boot. Face Book. Ok I got it. Virgin Mary - Virgin Queen - Virgin Business. Hail Mary. Subscribe. Crypt, hide. Decipher. Nothing new under the sun or Sun. Some say that the word Violin was linked to the Roman Goddess of victory and referred to the strings that were made from heifers and could be used to bind. There it is again, Goddess, bind, performance. The first Zoo in the land was in the Tower of London. Much later the animals were sent off to Regents' Park. Confinement. Power and intelligence binds us.

Argument by Block and others was that bondage was play, transmuting energy of real violence. Bondage has become ok. They say it is not a disease now. Influences fashion. Alright to act it out. Some dominatrices are making their subs read Black Feminist theory. You see women bringing men on leads, leashes and dog collars around Soho now and tying them to lamp-posts. Hum. At the same time BONDS are ruining the world. Junk bonds, the bond market. Indenture, bind by indenture. You are bound. Bond in this legal sense comes from Elizabethan times too. Words and power. Like a spell. Words have charges and force from the contexts they emerge from. The spell binds you. You are bound. When you are bound you have a bond. <u>Stock</u>. In the stocks. Caught in the stocks, with the stocks when the angry crowd comes. Bonds. Slaves were bound. Then bound financially. Buy a bond. Take this bond. Your lot is with me. You are bound. Bonds were used to fund the slave plantations. Plantations an artform. Some of the ones in London that benefitted from the slave trade when faced with opposition traded in bonds on the market associated with the sugar and slave trade instead. Bonds from Louisiana were sold in Bishopsgate Banks in September 1828. The bank sold them to other investors. Land, sugar, slaves. Bonds helped slavery expand. Bank bonds were then some of the best money you could get. Slaves mortgaged between people. Sugar, cotton, land, money became mixed up through the magic of bonds. Bonds were creatures on their own, incited by greed, fuelled by misery, hungry for resources. Bonds became predatory in a way, or allowed others to. When the bubble burst and there were liquidations, the slaves could be bounced around by new owners. 'Liberty Bonds' for war. Bonds behind Latin American crisis, Saving and Loan crisis, the Stock Market Crash 1978, the High Yield Bond market, the Junk Bond Crash 1989, The Mexican Crisis, the Asian crisis, Dot Com, the Financial Crisis 2008, the Sovereign Debt Crisis. Bonds, bonds, bonds. Religion comes from the Latin to bind, bond. Yoga a union or bond. Always bonds. Always give up to some other force. You will get this. Not risky at all. Bonds are charming and deadly. Love your Financial Goddess. She will humiliate you, take your money, enslave you. You love it, crave it, want it, do it. Idea that you control your own destiny is the one that people find the most frightening. The Findom, Findomme, Femdomme phenomena are a manifestation in the zeitgeist of the world system. You are going to lose, enjoy the losing. Make losing a sexual thing. My word is my bond. Words are bonds. Words bind. A person can be bound with written words or spoken words. Bind the subconscious, unconscious, conscious. Debt bondage is common. Slavery today. The first law of bondage is that it never disappears it only transmutes from one form to another. Science is bonds. Chemistry is bonds. Bonding in quantum theory. Breaking bonds give us nuclear weapons. Split the atom. Split the bonds. The biggest comes from the smallest. You can have a bond with the Devil. Elizabethan Era again. Christopher Marlowe again. Dr Faustus. They said devils appeared on the stage and it drove some mad. Faust wants great knowledge and power and after summoning Mephistopheles he makes a pact or bond with Lucifer which will damn him to hell in return for earthly powers. Like a publisher's contract. Spread-eaglism was one name for American Manifest Destiny, expansion and conquest over natives. The mission tells you what it is doing. They would Spread (the) Eagle. If you're spread eagled you are vulnerable. Like an X. X which was the unity of heaven and hell. Heaven for me, hell for you. Cross.

Some link between the Elizabethan or Tudor sense of domination and theatrical death and the contemporary. Create atmosphere. Shock and awe. When the criminals copy it and the State gasps. The State has evolved. Not in compassion so much as technique. A few East End criminals are a grave threat with a pair of pliers. Never mind all the other stuff then. Margaret Thatcher. Iron Lady. She dominated politics… She said power is like a lady, if you have to tell people, you are not it. She talked about discipline.

Elizabeth I is reported to say,
'Little man, little man.'
'I will have here but one mistress..'
'You are like my little dog.'
'My servants..'
'Know your place.'
'How dare you?'

She hit people about the ears. She had her 'Sea Dogs.' One of the Sea Dogs was John Hawkins, the first English slave trader. His coat of arms had a bound slave. The great Queen had no problems with slaves. Francis Drake was another. They plundered. Privateers. Look at the name itself.

She imagined a conversation with Elizabeth I. Was she like Faustus and Helen of Troy conjuring? Not in the time but now in a telepathic way. Sometimes these conversations seemed real and natural. Other times she knew it was a construct but it flowed. She could appear like a hologram in her inner eye. But she was not sure that it was not real in some way.

Ash: Why the horror?

Elizabeth: I was the ruler. The ruler needs to rule. Execution is never pleasant. Godly rule through royalty and not popery. Minimal when you see what went before by the Church, by Caesar. Celts. They did theatre and sacrifice. Too soft. Look at the plagues and say I did bad things? Richard II was me. This sceptred isle. This blessed realm. *'Cover your heads and mock not flesh and blood with solemn reverence.'*

Ash: But it seemed to be sadistic.

Elizabeth: Less is more. If with one good example you deter a thousand then you save people. Is the fox a sadist to the chicken? Look at Bloody Mary. Bonner.

> *'This cannibal in three years space.*
> *Three hundred martyrs.*
> *They were his food, he loved so blood.*
> *He spared none he knew.'*

Ash: Foxe exaggerates. No pleasure in what happened, no thrill. If Mary was Queen then, she was head of the Church. Ordained by God because your father said so. Her troops like Bloody Bishop Bonner and his burnings and birching therefore had to be doing God's will? Ungodly godliness. Does a Protestant obey the ungodly throne which is head of the breakaway church? You were careful not to condemn her publicly.

Elizabeth: Execution is merely the end of a policy, the full stop on the policy. Some troubled me greatly. I faced the threat as a girl. Mary made the Guildhall Speech against the rebels and showed that the realm, authority and order are the first priority. Theology comes after order. God is above all. Order requires orders, require decisions.

Ash: Because they related directly to you like Devereux.

Elizabeth: Not just so. Consider the failure to act.

Ash: How so?

Elizabeth: There are always divisions. Always people wanting to rule. Some are more fit. They evolve for it or they would not remain. See what happened to the Huguenots.

Ash: Your father?

Elizabeth: I could not choose. I might have been in the body of my unfortunate cousin Mary. What about my mother? Reflect on Her. Anne Boleyn. She was strong. Said she was a witch, temptress. Motherless I had no example to hold me back. Many would have had my head off. Your Queen of Hearts, she had the heads off. It might have been me but equally many others. Many played the game and gained much before they lost. All physical heads are lost in the end it is a matter of timing.

Ash: Did you plan it to be a theatre?

Elizabeth: Power must suggest or reflect itself to avoid more pronounced demonstrations thereof.

Ash: I see your point.

Elizabeth: Look theatre was not all spectacle it was principally words. *'In the begynnynge was the worde...'* You might say 'the' word, but not necessarily so. Or are you immune like many others to the true inspiration. I am called imperial when I sought to be humble. My humility was not heavy for me but others had a problem with their own.

I will admit that it was often the foolish follower that was found on the execution stage and not the leader. Furthermore, the leaders were often on the side being attacked and not the attacker. It was impossible to know what was true or who to trust.

Ash: Trust.

Elizabeth: I said it. I will defend myself against an enemy. May God do so against a pretend friend. The exegete misses the text underneath. Be a puppet or control yourself. I was not swayed by flattery. I often used a man's flattery to draw him out. A bit now and then is necessary for the position, the relationship. One was Joan of Arc in one's head.

I was not the Virgin Mary but Virgin Warrior. Anyone that confused the two made a big mistake. They say look she had white. Virgin Mary was blue, that was her colour. Clear code, look to your paintings. What you should think of is the balance between the ideational and the sensate that someone talks about. Making the inner and the external world sing the same tune. Look at Caesar. But I fought against the Roman Empire. It would not have been finally done away without me. My mother was sacrificed by my father to end it. I defeated the Armada, their naval fleet. I was no Miranda but we had Prospero.

Ash: What weird view could make you believe that torture was Christian? The Old Testament God was certainly close alright.

Elizabeth: The tortures of hell were real or nothing. If they had breached God's law then this was an appetiser. Ask the

Ash: enforcers and not me. Your morality is a ghost divorced from reality I'm afraid.

Ash: What about Essex?

Elizabeth: He was a fool. They think he flattered me and I let him boss me, but I knew there were dangerous ones about. Not the failure in Ireland but he burst into my chamber finding me undone, un-made up. Wise to let some people believe they have you, you get more from them unguarded. I was right that he would try to get rid of me. I was old, withered, shrivelled, but that is merely the body. He did not have to come in, he did not have to promote my private self. A queen, a prince is so because of their belief and their thoughts and in spite of their real appearance.

Ash: Can you help me with some lesson?

Elizabeth: A Queen can always help. Look around you. Man is a super-predator. Apex. No higher. Man preys on man. Man is prey. You chose if you are predator or prey. Predator evolves and so does the prey. As your Red Queen Hypothesis seeks to indicate that there is a reflexive relationship. Now you might have alien, demonic beings come and then you are prey. You may have spirits which can prey on you and use you as their instrument. You now are giving predatory capacity to machines. They will certainly prey on man, as instruments of other men or on their own. You got lonely at the top of the pyramid. But our people from Dee and Newton onwards, took our navy idea, exploration, time, knowledge of the stars and will to colonise the heavens. The plan. You saw the New World. If you had eyes you can see it was mine, laid out to Virgo. Astraea ushers in the Golden Age, the Celestial Virgin. Like Isis in *The Golden Ass* it is the Goddess who must emerge and save and heal the lost souls. See how they invert the goddess to a terrorist gang. Woman can be the healer or consort with donkeys. I am powerful, divine. You are all that. Back home. You suffer fools too easily. No rebellion will ever succeed now, it is too late. Donkeys must eat roses.

It disappeared from her head. A child of September. Seventh of September she was born, in 1533.

Without magic, how much could you conjure a person by focusing on, studying, identifying with them and feeling them?

> *'And like the fabric of these visions*
> *The cloud capped towers, the gorgeous places,*
> *The solemn temples the great globe itself*
> *Yea all which it inherit shall dissolve*
> *And leave not a rack behind.*
> *We are such stuff as dreams are made on....'*

Unless you're on the rack. Ghost words. But true. *The Tempest*. John Dee magician, Prospero. Cast a spell. Storm at sea. Spanish Armada defeated by magic. Words, wealth, plays, laws, magic, science, power, exploration, conquest. The magic dimension, power of words, spell, spelling, rules, racks. It was not the inevitable brutality of the city of Brutus in the capital of Britain. Brutal. It was not the case for the genius of John Dee. His 64 Angel symbol code like the *I Ching* or the chessboard or the DNA sequence.

But the puppet State controlled by corporations had created a giant. People behave like puppets, presume there are puppet-masters. She was not quite sure how that relationship worked. The power of the State might be under-estimated in that there was secret control of corporations by powers within. Maybe many incredibly successful businesspeople were quiescent plants. State had the range of tools and the skills of hundreds of years to know how to manage and control. The Protestant children learned about Henry VIII. The Catholic children learned about Henry VIII. To remind you what you were dealing with. The State was the bogeyman. But commerce was often controlled by the State. James Bond. Written by an ex-spy. Message is clear. State protects you. We might do bad things but it's for you. Look at these bad guys we have to defeat. This evil man wants to destroy us with a laser beam. Where would you be without us. You understand why we have to break a few eggs, be a little sneaky, tell blue lies. We may not all be as good-looking as James Bondage but we will give you a little titillation as well, seeing you don't care for all that head-chopping any more. Well that can still work in a new theatre. Yes we call it a theatre of war. Let me tell you the story of the bad guys we are fighting in this God-forsaken place. Someone has to do it.

Looking at alternative views, conspiracy theories and all she had read in history, still glimmers of hope. Jewel that we had that was the most precious. What stuck in her mind was the power of some of the creatives when facing the might of all the thwarted, demonic creativity of power. Mistress. Mystique. Mystics, mysteries genuinely believed were more powerful and maybe eventually more persistent. Like the Fleet still there. Untouchable. Most were wretches, many not guilty, often trivial. But some did it in full knowledge and if it could happen would do it again. Such was the power of the mystic. Like the Buddhist monk burning himself in Vietnam without moving. The same with some of the martyrs. One prayed even when their arm had fallen off in the flames without moving. Not the martyrdom but the mental control. You had control of yourself, your spirit. You could play with it still, but cede it and everything was lost. Dee wanted to unify and heal as part of his many goals. The power of the mind when focused on the higher order allows the definite and predictable cruelty of the mind of man in this mundane realm to be transcended.

But you had to watch out. You were told to look at something. You are made suggestible. Awareness is hijacked. There were embedded messages. Enmeshed. It often came sneaking through then subliminally, surreptitiously, always obliquely. Subtly the sinister process of re-programming goes on. We are mentally engineered and re-engineered, persuaded, seduced. Subtexts, fixed. Your own inner beast is coaxed to its basic needs, drives. Eat, kill, re-create and then you die or rather then you buy. You are the product. You the service. Furthermore we will even go further now, because you are so sheepish and make you do the work, make you pay for your own goods, use your time instead. Do the check out. Like digging your own graves. What a whizz. Their message will be gotten across. They anchor messages with body language. The public is played like a harp. We will accuse you of that which we are guilty of. You will be so confused you are open to our message. Obfuscation. Words within words. Country. Transmutation. Trust in me. Why choose BDS?

All about obedience. Made a message work. Without that, the virus of decision-making could not work. Chain of easy obedience necessary. Concept established in religion. Even then different meanings. The word was used in the Old Testament meaning to hear intelligently as some say. Then later it gets to mean submission. Then if you say it's the kings and queens you must give your loyalty and submission to, then the link with the higher than temporal power is gone. The sense that you must obey to save your soul is short-circuited. Now you become obedient. Net of instructions operate. The severing of that link, whether by Pope or King or Queen, takes away the direct audience. Maybe a subconscious seeking of obedience especially when that mystical power was used to confront power. Disobedience was the mark of the great. Civil disobedience most particularly Gandhi, Martin Luther King, Daniel O'Connell. Most people would fail to understand. The mortal Goddess sought to interpose herself like a priestess between the higher dimension and the individual. If they helped the soul to grow then that was the right path. If it was to genuinely humiliate then that was something darker. The Goddess as a priestess of the soul. Unlock the shadow side. Perceptive ones knew that. Women wanted to be equal. Implication is all the time that women are below men in some way. Reality is that women have great power, magic. Maybe that was what Stein meant when she said that the State does not need what women have but what women are. But they are trained to keep each other down. Watch them stop girls climbing trees. For their own good. No. The Mystical experience was about union with higher consciousness. Stein mastered philosophy of the spirit, empathy and method and transcended herself and fear. I can't agree with the yielding part. The Goddess could do that. Many don't understand. They have taken on some mental image that they are reduced to a gene. See themselves as some amoeba helplessly awaiting the benediction of the scientists. The ones who know. The nasty, demon goddess is not the answer. Bond of woman is the base. Not an Iota. I.

    This Concentration had given her an answer to the way forward. Suggested a step if things got worse and she wanted to seek to clarify the source. If this Kit fella was not the full shilling or stringing her along, perhaps another suspicion, a source should be addressed. All came from her putting her head up. She seemed to have the answer now to the State of Emergency. She recalled what she had read about Aldous Huxley and George Orwell. Huxley wrote *Brave New World*. Orwell *1984* later. Huxley wrote to Orwell. He said it was more effective to utilise drugs and hypnosis and infant-conditioning than prisons and clubs. Clubs, maybe Huxley meant another type of club. You make the suggestions that people love their condition of servitude. Make them want to be slaves. That might also explain all the recreational slavery around. All the people that wanted to be tied up. They picked up the signals of the society they lived in. If that was true then this would pass, and people would have a sense that the status quo was fine compared with a potential Reign of Terror. Big Daddy had punished the naughty boys.

> *'Once upon a time and a very good time it was there was a moocow coming down along the road and this moocow...'*

Joyce's Portrait was the end and not the beginning. *The Handmaid's Tale*. Always women as victims. Take away agency. The Agency of this Reign of Terror takes agency. Women always want to take away their own agency, happy with victimhood. That made her puke. Create self-fulfilling prophecy. Feminists embracing the veil for liberation. Sick. She'd take Elizabeth any day. In the time of Elizabeth, the idea of the healing powerful woman was turned into caricature. Female was conscripted as a male. Elizabeth's promotors would have ousted Brigid. Brigid was like Artemis, light-bearer. She came from Persia to Greece. Amazon queens. Tomyris decapitated Cyrus the Great. Romans used Diana. Artemis and fire, Brigid and fire. Could the hard-core dominatrix symbolise rather than embody a more demonic sense? She had read about possession. Curious that during exorcism you had to instruct, demand, command the demon. Similar to hypnosis. Exorcism was about driving out demons or spirits. It seemed to have a different meaning in Tudor times where it was calling up spirits. Related to the word for binding by oath. Binding, bound. Bound to oath and bound to spirit. What was the opposition, exo-endo? Was there such a word? An endocism? No. But presumably that which you uprooted could easily be planted and re-planted. She suddenly felt prodding, maybe from her Guardian Angel, to say a prayer to St Michael even though she was not affiliated to any religion. She was not new age, maybe she was properly a permutation of Judeo-Christian?

What if the bondage was really a mirror of demon possession? As a show could be. Demonstrate. DEMON STRATA. Show you another world, literally. Confusion, pandemonium. PAN DEMON I AM. Relinquish your will to the master, mistress. They might use rubber with the historic sacrifice of millions. Surrender your will. In return you get something base, you are convinced you want and desire and are made to need. Like a pact with the devil, an agreement. You consent. You made yourself blank. You become a robot. You become empty. You freeze. You are worthless. You are pathetic. You are a dog. Then you are open, you can be captured. You become a slave. Your destiny becomes determined elsewhere based on your abasement for base desires often in a basement. Like SimpCook. Have some deep desire to be something else constructed outside and end up a chimera. Faust. Hypnosis has commands. In exorcism you command demons. You agree. You consent. Safe words don't work. Instead of evolving you descend. You become a dog, a pig. Caliban. The master serves someone else in a pyramid. So many 'successful' and 'celebrated' people lose out. Faustian pacts. Some priestesses and witches say they are bad and evil and willing to go to hell. If you allow them possess you, hypnotise you, serve them, become their agents then they may be agents for demons and devils. You say you don't believe it, just a bit of role-play and slap and tickle! Well they don't. A joke, not serious! But it is. Think you cannot be made weak but you can. Say ABRACADABRA is harmless child's play but Aleister Crowley thought not and he was deeper than all in dark forces. Famous can become 'perfectly possessed.' Possession. Master possesses the slave. They own you. You are owned. Some use the 'play' of sexual stimulation to pray the dark forces. Do I think too much? Am I paranoid schizophrenic or something? Is some spirit baiting me? Would that lock me up……. or put me in charge? Put in charge would probably mean I'm lost. Over-thinking, under-thinking. Alarm. End of Concentration. Or is it? Maybe get one of those brain helmets. Master the theta wave. Θ.

But she wanted more specific help. Felt it again. September 29th. St Michael. Symbol? **Sword**. Line they say linking 7 St Michael sites to Holy Land. Skellig Michael in Ireland. Cornwall, St Michael's Mount, Normandy - Mont St Michel. Sacra de San Michele, Turin. Mount Gargano, Monte Sant'Angelo, Mount Carmel. Like St Michael's ley line runs through Glastonbury Tor from Michael's Mount. Did not care whether they existed or not. Inspired her, a key. Michaelmas. Feast. Patron saint of horse, horsemen. Last day to eat blackberries. No rebellion will ever succeed now? Why all the cutting? Because they want to destroy, de-construct, stop things that might stop them. To show no magic hidden inside. Those that have no interior, invisible sanctuary within, want to show emptiness they believe in. Felt a controlling mechanism calculating how to create a paradigm with a vocabulary to replace good with bestial, spasmodic and painful. Am I lost somehow so I turn otherworldly? She slumped exhausted making notes. Raleigh's last words having his head chopped off. *'Tis a sharp remedy, but a sure one for all ills.'* What Kristeva was on about. Abject. Uncanny. Abject the Mother. Taboo self not of you. Navel. Society too. Separate from threat of what is not you. Companies, states do it. Use rituals. Monster. Filth. Disgusting other. Order. Language. Bury. Alien. Art. Symbolic order.

**Axiom 12   Obey your inner heart and soul and spirit always.
Banish all fear with the flame of inner power.**

DWELL ON THE ROSE, THE ROSE GARDEN

LLLF

LONDON LOGOS LIBERATION FRONT

Publishing Pamphlets to Oppose Censorship of Our Message.
The Counter-Revolutionary to Evil and Terror Effort.
Take the Red Pill.

THEY KIDNAP PEOPLE.

THEY KIDNAP KIDS.

THEY HARVEST ORGANS.

THEY DO OTHER THINGS.

THEY LIE, TORTURE.

THEY LIKE BLOOD.

WORSE THAN VAMPIRES.

WORSE THAN ZOMBIES.

WORSHIPPING DEMONS.

WORSHIPPING DEVILS.

SLAVES TO POWER.

MASTERS OF US.

YOU CAN TURN AWAY.

YOU CAN READ THEIR SCRIPT.

YOU CAN BE IGNORANT.

YOU CAN REFUSE TO SEE.

THERE ARE NONE SO BLIND.

PREPARE FOR LIBERATION

Chapter 30

The Club

Karma, karma, karma. Since ancient Rome and the collegia, formal clubs have been critical meeting places. Clubs made Britain great. The IVY was established by Italians, 1917. Ivy grows between plants, across, twisting and turning. Killed the raspberry bushes in the garden. Climbs walls by producing nanoparticles from tiny hairs. Groups of people meet there. Used to be the entertainment industry now the creative industries. Great men came together in clubs he thought. Stops them being isolated and thinking too much. Devil makes work for idle hands. Through the Industrial Revolution clubs were where great minds worked. Football, rugby, cricket, polo clubs, all made important by the idea of coming together. Guilds also. Should have been more such clubs for women. He was not even thinking of the masons. Although it amazed him that no one asked more questions about them. Accepted that it was just good-willed old boys that believed in a Supreme Being, engaging in a little, esoteric game-playing to keep society together, make friends and be better people. Nice. Hope. People never thought about what the word 'club' meant. Usually you hit someone with it. You hit baby seals with a club. You can have a club foot, hit a golf ball with one. You associated for a purpose. You go to one, to the building where people meet. You play cards with this suit. Clubs came in cards in Elizabethan times, clover elsewhere. You can eat a club sandwich. Club car. Club military meaning. Club, combination, ideal context for conspiracy. Verb and noun. You had to be 'clubbable' to get on. Clubbable makes you culpable. The Mermaid Tavern on the corner of Bread Street and Friday Street East of St Pauls, in Elizabethan times. Shakespeare, Marlowe, Jonson. A military formation that you cannot get out of. Gentlemen's clubs. Yes. Military. RAF. Naval. Club Magazine. When you don't have real ones you get the invisible ones. The Great White Brotherhood.

"I control."
"But I was the leader."
"It's all about what bones are in the boneyards."
"No widows left."

"It was cutthroat."

"One falls they may all fall."

As his associate got up to go, he whispered "I'm not going to say that you can't breathe a word of what we were talking of James."

The elderly gent said quietly, "Not to worry. You can take it from me that I haven't the foggiest." He laughed and went out with his stick.

Every day is like survival. He had served his country well, that old geezer. He does not get the respect he deserves. He was not quite as dilapidated as he might seem to others. Agile as he had proved recently. To sell contradiction. At home in the Club. Exclusive in an understated way. Always nice and comfortable to come in, sit and read a paper meet some old friends. A bond. When he had a conversation he knew he could trust the people here. Even then he was circumspect. Allusive. Made sure he was not overheard. We come and go. Every operation had a beginning and an end. No matter how difficult. The domain he worked in was a shadowy one. The game was down to luck essentially when you cut through the words. Not one that most people were aware of. You could not make it up. Fact is stranger than fiction. Maybe he was getting too old. Maybe he had seen too much. Maybe it was time to give more young people a chance, more women. As if sometimes the real world was a dream, when you live in missions, in compelling circumstances. When you did what you had to do you had no time to stop and question. He wondered whether his memory was as fresh as it used to be. Details disappeared, chronology began to get mixed up a little at times. That was why he needed to marshal all his forces now. Lives depended on it. Maybe the future of the country. He missed the old days of clouds of smoke and too much armagnac. Transport was called for. I wonder what raspberry plant is not noticing the thin green coil of ivy that will choke it. Is a club a good place to hatch a coup d'état?

What if London is not as it looks on the map but really a giant sphere of energy with the surface of the land at the centre thereof and the history and events of the past stored therein, accessible to those who have the tools to decipher that dimension of energy? Uther Pendragon and Arthur as Merlin foretold come to take over the Rome that now flits magically in its ghostlike, formless wanderings like spirit. A little spirit goes a long way these days. We could be *The Club of Queer Trades*. Rational rules. But irrational is inevitable reality of infinity that rational cannot comprehend and may even risk sanity for presumption otherwise. You come and go.

LLLF

LONDON LOGOS LIBERATION FRONT

Publishing Pamphlets to Oppose Censorship of Our Message.
The Counter-Revolutionary to Evil and Terror Effort.
The Doctrine that is Correct is not the Right One.

DARWIN IS THE DRUG.

DAWKINS TOOK IT.

NO GOD.

NO REASON.

NO GLUE TO HOLD US.

MATERIALISM. SOCIALISM.

FUNDAMENTALIST SOCIALISM.

FUNDAMENTALIST SCIENTISM.

DOGMA SPREAD IN EDUCATION.

DIVERSITY SAVE IN POLITICAL POSITIONS.

SCIENCE IS THE NEW GOD.

SCIENCE WILL REPLACE RELIGION.

REASON THEN WILL BE HITCHED TO SCIENCE.

SCIENCE WILL MUTATE.

AI WILL DECIDE.

AI WILL BE THE NEW SON OF God.

IT CAN ONLY END BADLY.

PREPARE FOR LIBERATION

Chapter 31

No Show

Lucius Tubal could not get his hands on Ethel for a few days. Now he could not get his hands on the LZLF. Desperate for his attention then, now he was desperate for theirs. He had a full beard, nearly grey. Efforts to explore the realm of conspiracy before the curtain of censorship descended seemed less important now than contemporary concerns about erosion of civil liberty. Quake provided the ideal opportunity for State to achieve goals inimicable to any democratic pretence. Could not have worked out better. Made him wonder whether State could encourage an earthquake with an underground explosion. But he did not believe that, rather the restless earth had presented an unexpected opportunity. He was worried about the agitators. Treading on thin ice. The Times had mentioned some sort of 'attack' on the Royal College of Surgeons Museum in Lincoln's Inn. Portrayed as some sort of attack on science and the State. Lucius suspected it was the guys he met. Some clue he vaguely recalled. A quick bit of skimming to get some more information. Then he saw it.

> '*The skeleton of the Irish Giant Charles Byrne can be seen at the Museum. His skeleton has helped medicine especially as a source of genetic material for investigators of gigantism* and diseases of the thyroid.'

He had not paid too much attention when they mentioned Charles Byrne. He had not followed up. A celebrity giant. Came over from Ireland and became well-known around London. Giants were said to inhabit these islands. Many places have legends associated therewith. Some anatomists wanted his skeleton after death. Bastards hounded the poor chap when he was alive. Well-known medical men. John Hunter. Wanted to cut him up. Same bastards that took the barely cold corpses out of the grave from the graverobbers for the good of science. There would be no Burke and Hare serial killers without surgeon accessories who only got honours for the pain of others. Tubal suspected they did other things as well. Knew how medical people played with corpses, don't mind the evil ones. Necromancy.

Poor Byrne refused offers for his corpse and wanted to be buried in a lead coffin at sea. Afraid when the vultures circled. Followed. Turned to alcohol. Robbed of his life savings. His coffin was robbed on the way to sea burial by the tenacious scientific bastards. They never let up. Charles was boiled in a cauldron to get rid of flesh and he ends up on display. Still there. Today. It helped science. Being on display was detestable. But going against his wishes after persecution was another ghoulish thing. Why would the group make an issue of him? I suppose it has something to do with science, medicine and human feeling. Same as those Edinburgh surgeons who encouraged Burke and Hare to kill many, so they would have fresh specimens to cut up. Look back historically at many great brain surgeons who made discoveries and ask yourself how many interesting patients they had who died suddenly and mysteriously before their time from some unrelated cause and miraculously provided the opportunity to piece together the puzzle of the mind. Dawkins was musing on eating lab-grown human meat with his smirk. Cannibalism, no problem. You're a gene and there's no God and the universe just blew up from a pea all of a sudden. Why do people not see through these guys? A shiver went down his spine. He had swallowed some of it and always advocated science on his shows. Laughed and sneered at all ideas of the divine and agreed with the need to get rid of it. He had done stand-up. You need to be a real atheist to get any gigs. Most comedians were miserable fanatics seeking control with barely disguised propaganda. But it was scientism that was the problem. Idea they could solve everything. Then there were others. He knew from the Lodge that there are wheels within wheels. Maybe they were in some detention camp now. Poor bastards. Although that may not be the worst thing they had to face if the rumours are right. He was looking over his own shoulder now himself. Warnings came, subtle and otherwise. Marginal area of free speech was dwindling by the day. A charade anyway. The only theme he could get a grip on was this sniping business. But nobody had anything but idle speculation. Whether the Government had been taken over was another thing nobody seemed bothered about. Something ignited in him finally. A poor giant boiled for science. Like they used all the Nazi science and scientists. It banishes fear with the speed of a flame... makes us all part of... He started to hum a tune that had been bottled up in him. They used to say that someone 'was sent to Coventry.' That meant that they were ignored, people would not listen to them or see them. Treat them as if they were not there. We're all going to Coventry. Wouldn't surprise me if they ban all speech. Say you can't talk, must communicate by text. It was not only because his own career suddenly was on a shoogly peg that the veil was lifting. They are manipulating the Gay movement. We used to be more united, clear. Now we are pawns believing we are the Queen... But drip, drip, drip. I am more than any label. We were never just that. It is so easy to play people, manipulate, marinate, make marionettes. Human-monkey hybrids. Organ harvesting. You can only ignore so long. Eli Eli Lemana Shabaktani. They are making the spiritual dust-bowl, sucking out the spirit like vampires with the seduction of seeming science as they squeeze until we are but strokes on a key board or signs in an algorithm. They are hollowing out the hallow in us. I feel sorry for the young ones.

He looked out and saw high over Primrose Hill yet pale blue before night as sun sank ready to vanish in a bloody sky. Used see Amy there often. Knew pathway like back of his hand. Evening light still shone in and reflected in sheen of burnished varnish over the chocolate-coloured oil painting with a faintly glimmering ornate golden frame. Secret worlds he once knew were but bubbles on a stream. But still there were ones who were working incessantly to drive their agenda. Those things work when people are motivated to believe that they will benefit, either through the process or the result. He looked again at the strange lines he had gotten. Like a joke, forgery, pastiche... but not so. Why have that symbol? What was that... a trade mark? A registered trade mark. A mark with a ring. Or. Something about a logo. Why are logos so important? Plural. Rather singular. Logos singular v logos plural. Law of semantic change. One popularised bad meaning will drive out a good one. Logos was something else. Change it. TM. ™. Mark, mark of the beast. Chip in the hand. Forehead. Revelations. You don't have to be religious to wonder whether they got it right. Can I not buy bread the Greek asked? No would be the answer in the revolution to tyrant's dreamstate. Rehab. Electric blue the room. If Daddy thinks I'm fine.

16 And he causeth all, both small and great, rich and poor, free and bond, to receive a mark in their right hand, or in their foreheads:

17 And that no man might buy or sell, save he that had the mark, or the name of the beast, or the number of his name.

Spell for the Cauldron Binding of the Spirit

To rule the world, we must rule the spirit.
To rule the spirit, we must rule the mind.
To rule the mind, we must rule the thinking.
To rule the thinking, we must rule the words.
To rule the words, we must rule their making.
To rule their making, we must rule their meaning.
To rule their meaning, we must drive out the truth.
To rule their truth, we get power over spirit.
To rule the spirit, we deny and decry it.
When we rule the spirit, we must win the world.

In Confidence, the Ringmaster
®

The replacement BBC station just announced the following.

'In view of the recent chaos the Government had adopted the proposals of the Greens to roll out the compulsory microchipping of the remaining population who have not partaken of the advantages and convenience up to now. The Deputy PM said today that the security benefits are obvious and that it would help the fight against climate change. In addition, to protecting the health of the population from the established hazardous consequences of radiation from existing mobile devices, it was important to accelerate the adoption of the Handy Chips. We interviewed some members of the public who told us about the advantages they have found from the Handy Chips. Some who do not like the Handy Chips have opted for the forehead implants instead and some claim it is even better. The Government said that they want the transition to be as comfortable as possible for everyone. This expedition will also facilitate the Social Credit Rating Scheme which will have enormous benefits for all. - Meanwhile a vitally important sporting event takes place.....'

LLLF

LONDON LOGOS LIBERATION FRONT

Publishing Pamphlets to Oppose Censorship of Our Message.
The Counter-Revolutionary to Evil and Terror Effort.
Before we Rise Up, Wake Up.

SCIENCE RULES.

SCIENTISM FETISH.

FALSE SCIENCE.

BOUGHT SCIENTISTS.

MATERIALIST MASSES.

INDOCTRINATION.

GENETIC ENGINEERING.

TECH-HYPNOSIS.

TECHNOCRACY.

ARTIFICIAL INTELLIGENCE.

INTERNET OF THINGS.

CONSTANT SURVEILLANCE.

TRANSHUMANISM.

MASTERS AND SLAVES.

CONSCIOUSNESS CONTROLLED.

EVIL DOMINATES.

SPIRIT DIES.

PREPARE FOR LIBERATION

Chapter 32

Semper Occultus

One Ill Weede Marreth a Whole Pot of Pottage

Am I as tough as I think I am? The last day of September seemed unforgettably blue. Blue by day, navy by night. She had been blue for a while, unusually for her. Dolly Blue was one of the names of 'bluing' they put in white clothes to compensate the grey, yellow colours when faded. Blue to make it white. Like a blue to a white lie. Plenty of bluing around here. Dolly Blue would be a great name for one of the robots. Your public persona is not your true self. Your commercial and legal self may be separate or the same. But these selves have to be operated through. Her public profile probably caused these problems. She had problems on Monday getting into her bank account. She rang the help line, went to the branch. No answers. Fearing the worst she rang Kit. Tuesday morning she learned that some sort of court order had frozen her assets. She could apply to the High Court to remove it. Kafka. Her proverbs. When the tree falleth all come with their hatchet. Give a dog a bad name and you may as well hang him. Having put her head above the parapet there was always a danger of becoming a target. Under pressure, in the claws of death be relaxed. Never panic, never give up. She watched that film. Understood Postman's Park in the City was a special place, set up by a painter. Key thing the wonderful memorial. Inscriptions, she remembered. Dedicated to people who had died saving others. No greater love. He had said to go there. Chance it. He made a sign. Let's see. Doing it in the quiet, not seeking anything. The heart and sense open and responsive. Blake's best was when he got angry when he saw things wrong, like chained children. That spiritual heart that feels and allow its force out. A potent white hart of force from the hearth of our being. Near St Paul's. She walked up to the wall. Mary Rogers. Stewardess of the Stella. Mar. 30 1899. Self-sacrificed by giving up her life-belt and voluntarily going down with the sinking ship. She looked for one in September.

*'David Selves, Aged 12.
Off Woolwich
Supported his drowning playfellow
And sank with him clasped in his arms.
September 12, 1886.'*

Elizabeth Coughlan, ran out with a paraffin lamp on January 1st, 1902 so that two children would be saved. Not even her children, 26. Ash thinking about Elizabeth. Imagining her she looked up and saw an intersection that help up the roof, not too high above. She remembered the y-shape Kit made. She stuck her hand up impulsively and found something. A thin tube taped at the intersection of the 'y.' She took it, looked around and walked off. It might be said that she was paranoid, narcissistic, obsessive, anti-social, a renegade, occultist. Made her way home. Took out the notes of what he had said and *The Chambers Dictionary* she had bought. She hoped it was the right edition or close enough. Matched the words, counting and guessing which were meant occasionally. As far as she could make it out, it said. *'Watch people who do not work for the State's best interests and lie low for a while.'*

What the fuck was that? This had to be a piss take. Raging. She hoped she'd get something. This did not help. Was he taking the michael or making sure he did not reveal something he would get into trouble for? Fuck sake. No help. Although it did seem like a warning. Time to probe the other possibility that her Concentration had suggested. She rang Erik. He must have been busy or he would have answered. She left a message.

"Erik. Get Number 4 to make an appointment this evening at 8. This is one of the times he has marked as available this month. I had not expected to. This is serious so listen carefully. We need to talk sooner rather than later. Cancel all my commitments until further notice. Don't say a word. Be a little bit careful of... I don't know what. I'll meet you at the office in an hour."

The big question was whether No. 4 would come? All Erik had to do was communicate with him as agreed. She needed to make preparations. She bathed quickly and set off to the office in Soho. This was one of her few remaining ones. Erik surprisingly did not show. There was a ton of messages on the phone, but she was not answering them. He had no reason not to be there. The bank had bothered her.

Before she went to the session in Mayfair, a man she knew from the pub came round.

"Listen Erik said he had a spot of real bother. He was going to sort it out. He was contacting a lawyer. He said he would tell you after, but not to worry about it. And he told me to say - It's on."

He was concerned. As was she. She thanked him. Chilled. She knew it was related to the account. A bit reluctant to find out more.

Set off. She had to get into character. She had some thing to bring in the ski bag. Even the character was champing at the bit. She felt she was going to be transgressive today, but how she knew not. It was not in her hands. It was different. She would go ahead anyway. From the office she took a long hockey case with a samurai sword and her other gear and put it in the ski bag. There was an X in her mind. Mysterious. Secret society. Sun God. Experimental. Vitamin X. Cross your arms, legs, genes. unknown brand, poison, death, crime scene, life and death, Xanax, transcendence, cross, double cross, Satanism, kiss, multiplied strength.

At 8 o'clock, he came. From another entrance she walked into the luxury Mayfair room. Another magazine title. There was no one else present. There standing was a sixty year old man. He was thin, wiry, white hair and a blazer. Curtains drawn, candle or two were lighting on the floor. He stood between the candles. She had white make-up, a wig and a tight laced scarlet undergarment with boots and a silver lace inspired by the Moorgate courtesan she had read about. It was a long time since she had used them and she broke some of her rules. This was something slightly different. This client liked Walsingham.

Her voice was grand and slightly irritating with a nasal quality and a deep aspect combined with mellifluous emphases, whispered. She began barely audible and sometimes ascending to a stern pitch.

"Who comes here? EsseX! Essex. How dare you! You scoundrel. Essex, you dare stand after your behaviour. You act like you do not recognise me. Perhaps because you stormed into my private Chamber you have caught me without my gowns of State I usually wear."

"My Majesty.."

"Do not look at me you lickspittle. Vulgar curiosity never comes close to the light... You should be Devereux again. Your father in law would be unhappy."

"My…"

"You should have prostrated yourself before me." He gets down and spreads his arms cautiously compliant. "My dog is disappointing as always. I invested so much trust in you. Essex. You are Essex today and not your unraised non-entity self I wager. You are beyond courting me and begging."

"Yes Y....our Majesty."

"I have no gown with which you may show your obedience to the State so you may crawl and kiss my boots, quickly and do not dare dribble." He did so. "Why do you slobber so? ...Essex I understand you have a self which is not your Lordly one?"

"Well .."

"Remember the Queen struck you and you put your hand on the sword..?"

"Yes."

"Well. Here, take it." She handed him a genuine Japanese sword from the Elizabethan Era in a sheath. "Be careful it will slice you. Now put your hand on the hilt like you did before The Queen before." He did so. She bent forward. "Here is the Queen's neck. If you are of such a mind you may remove it from the body," she leant forward and exposed her neck, pulling her hair up. He did not move. After a minute she rose up on the throne. "Put it down. Good boy. Sea dog. You are behaving yourself and so today I am going as a special treat for you to allow you share some of your trivial life with your Sovereign despite its manifest lack of interest. The unfilled holes. Do you understand?" The Queen continued, "I will not violate any of the inviolate Treaty we have. But I may poke you a little... You like being poked, don't you. Alas this will be metaphorical."

"Yes Madam."

"I would hazard a guess that you were well poked at your school, your alma mate." The Queen sniggered. "Is that correct?"

"Not exactly."

"You look like... let me guess Harrow, Winchester... I jest Eaton of course a venerable establishment. I hazard also that you were a wonderful fag, a popular servant for your masters there. Don't fear... I do not need specifics but you can let me know if I am warm, in the general direction." She pronounced the last word slurring the first syllable.

"Yes, my Lady."

"Look at me, you may look at my eyes. Bullingdon no doubt and then Oxford. Am I getting warm?" The Queen said.

"Well."

"Don't squirm and look me in the eye, don't take your eyes off mine. You're my subject I demand obedience. Am I warm?" She changed her voice, now more coaxing. Flirtatious.

"Yes Mistress."

"Maybe a spell in the armed forces, training. Did they 'initiate' you. Did they do terrible things to humiliate you so you would have that espirit de corps that is so important when you want to cultivate a group mentality among drones. Did they pass it off as fun? Hazing, bullying... Aha Bullingdon. Bullying Don," The Queen suggested.

"Did you get deprived of ladies there? Miss your Nanny. I'd say you adored Mrs. Thatcher. Did she turn you on as they say nowadays. Did she kindle your little naughty desires? Did you sneak a peek like that other politician, historian chap used to do?" The Queen said.

"Yes Madam." He answered non-committally.

"Oh, you naughty, filthy beast. You are a dirty swine as I suspected. Look at me. You have not had permission to look away. I said permission not emission. Yes or no will do. I want no more of your infernal prattle," the Queen said and he gulped.

"You may get on your knees but look in my eyes," the Queen commanded.

"Yes..... Majesty"

"Were you sneaking a view of my undergarments?"

"No... Majesty."

"Do you not find me attractive then?" The Queen said.

"No. Yes."

"You find me attractive?" The Queen asked.

"Yes."

"Do you like these French Heels which are all the fashion? Do you need to be heeled? Is your soul in need of healing?"

"Yes... no..."

"Even without my regal gowns which excite you normally and which I spend a lot of time on just for you?" The Queen said.

"Yes."

"Did you look here?" He looked to where she was pointing. "Ah, I see you naughty boy. The Queen excites you. Would you like to be a Queen yourself?" The Queen said.

"No."

"Are you a perfect subject?"

It sounded like pervert to him, he was unsure what she said. "Yes."

"Naughty boy. So what then, the City, some mindless finance or maybe something with uniforms, you like them, or maybe something secret. Am I warm at least, you must not answer but you can at least stop teasing me Essex or no Devereux or no whatever your name is, it escapes be. You are no concern. My leg is tired make a footstool for me," the Queen demanded as she turned and beckoned him to make ready so she could put her legs across him.

"So you are a powerful man now. I will not ask you about the Masons. You have many, many underlings. You don't play second fiddle except to your monarch and some elevated others. Correct? You are seldom corrected, you have few if any above you. Do you like me to correct you?"

"Yes. If it pleases…"

"Quiet you miserable underling. Do you like my hair?"

"Yes."

"You like red hair?"

"Yes."

"Is it hard for you there?"

"Yes… No."

"Not hard? Tut tut. Have you come to be a naughty boy in your job to me?"

"No."

"Are you sure?"

"Yes."

"Have you been jealous… your Monarch has other toys?"

"Yes."

"Does your job impact on your Sovereign at all?"

"Well."

"Turn around so I may rest my feet on your scrawny belly."

"Yes."

"Do you have any confessions to make to me?" She leaned over an pressed her stilettos down in his stomach.

"No."

"Are you jealous when you think of me with other subjects?"

"Yes."

"It excites you to think of others."

"Yes."

She lit a cigarette. "These infernal things come from across the sea. What a dirty, dirty habit!" She inhaled. She blew it out. She inhaled again and blew it in his direction. She then tapped it over his face. "I hope you don't like Ash in your face hmmm? Not good. Take it." She stubbed it out and pressed it into his hand. "Do you like my butt?" The Queen asked.

"Yes."

"You do have a filthy mind," the Queen said, "let me see your neck. It should be right there. I'll miss you…. If you are a good boy, a loyal subject and behave yourself I just might if I see fit reward you. You would have to be exceptionally good and only have pleasant, respectful thoughts when you worship me. You know what you revealed when you first came..?"

"Yes." Gulping.

She rested the point of her heel on his cheek. "If you behave, I might erect that St. Andrew's Cross to show you my appreciation." She stood up over him and looked down. "Don't be a traitor to me. Your treachery would demean you." She stepped aside and pointed to the door. "Out of my sight. You are relieved. You will be relieved. Relieve yourself. Always think on your Queen." She watched him go out. "Put that butt in the bin. I don't want you taking it and doing anything odd with it. Cross your heart and hope to die."

She had not been anything like that with this guy before. As he went out she had a sense that perhaps she had a thread. But she was not sure. A voice telling her again however to act. You have been acting, act now. Do something. Whenever there is an emergency or something that feels like one, do not panic but do something. Unless it is not an emergency and the thing is to sit tight. You will be alright. Fear not. She would not have used a sword in normal situations save it was the delight of the razor, but it was not normal circumstances. Her mission was accomplished. She picked the sword up. The razor's edge was so thin.

There was no pain in his groin. He just lay there. It was not pretty. His groin area and the bed was covered in red. Scarlet red. It would not wash off. It was everywhere. He scrubbed and scrubbed and scrubbed. He used bleach and that burned his skin. He went to the Pound Shop and got some miracle gel of some sort but that did not help. He tried to find out with aliases online how to get rid of it. But people kept asking what it was? How did it get there? Period? What the fuck! What kind of a pervert would do such a thing? Scarlet. It would be the same colour as my face if I went to the doctor. I've never been to one of those before. If I go to the hospital they'd say - Is it an emergency? No not really. What is it then? I'm covered with some sort of paint, ink. Colour. Where did it come from? Maybe I'm not sure. Did you do it yourself? Of course not. What is the exact nature of the substance? I'm not sure. You're not sure. No, I'm not sure. Do you have any idea of what it could be? Not a clue? Do you have a bottle of it at home a container of some sort? No. Do you have anything of that colour at home? No. Could you explain to me how you got it please? Well... No. But we need to know Sir. I'm not sure. He could see it all. The raised eyebrows. The sniggers. He couldn't do that. Maybe it would just wear off. Maybe it wouldn't. Who knows? Maybe it was a type of poison. Fuck! Maybe it was killing him. Maybe the rats would know. They can smell poison. I could wait there and put a piece of cheese on my belly and see if a rat takes it. Maybe if they take it I don't have to worry. The sheets were ruined and the bed. They'd be angry when they saw it. Maybe I'll say a prayer. But I don't know any really. I could learn one. Maybe there's a cure, a magical spell. I could ask the woman upstairs. What happened to you? I could be an artist that was working on a canvas. There was them action painters. They rolled around in the nude in paint. Loads of people came. That's it. I'm doing an artpiece about social justice. You can't do anything wrong if you're an artist. Yeah, that's why I'm a bit strange. I'm an artist. What do they call them? A performance artist. They love them artists. Afraid of them. Like comedians. People only laugh at them so they'll stay away from them. Pretend you're enjoying yourself and this psychopath won't bully me. Anyone that doesn't see that comedians are psychos must be mad. Fuck. It looks ridiculous. Is it scarlet? What else could it be? Blood red? What did it say on the tin Sir? Oh, I didn't look, I purchase so much you know. Maybe I could say it was a tattoo. A work of art. It was against discrimination. It was a cry for help. Stop punishing people with your groin, you bastards. That might work. But where is the paint now? It's empty. Where's the bottle and we can check the ingredients. It smashed. Did you not know that it would colour your skin? No. Fuck's sake can you just get it off. Maybe the hospital would swallow the artist stuff. Just say a few things. Accident. Artist. Act Lithuanian. Don't know mate, sorry? What if it's a woman? Surely they don't allow that. I feel like singing. The two of us.. No, I'm too nervous. Getting a bit anxious. What's that noise? Fuck. It's coming from that. No. How can that be. That's weird. Has it not done enough damage. Jesus. Could it explode? Fuck. A knock at the door. Yer joking me. No one comes here. What the fuck! Him! No. He heard a voice. He went out.

"Delivery!"

That can't be right. I didn't order anything. How did he get in? He went to the door. "You got the wrong place mate," he shouted out.

"No it's for you."

"Wait a sec."

He went to put something on. This was curious. Curiouser and curiouser. Bloody curious.

LLLF

LONDON LOGOS LIBERATION FRONT

Publishing Pamphlets to Oppose Censorship of Our Message.
The Counter-Revolutionary to Evil and Terror Effort.
Be Wise. Be Brave. Be Free.

IT IS NOT JUST BLOOD-LINES.

NOT JUST THE ROYAL FAMILIES.

NOT JUST THE FAMILIES.

NOT JUST THE MAFIA.

NOT JUST THE CRIMINAL GANGS.

NOT JUST THE CORRUPT PASTORS.

NOT JUST THE BOUGHT POLITICIANS.

NOT JUST THE SECRET SOCIETIES.

NOT JUST THE INTELLIGENCE SERVICES.

NOT JUST THE DEEP STATE.

NOT JUST THE SECRET AGENTS.

NOT JUST THE OCCULTISTS.

NOT JUST THE WIZARDS AND WITCHES.

NOT JUST THE MASONS NOR MAGI.

NOT JUST THE SELL-OUT GOVERNMENTS.

NOT JUST THE THINK-TANKS.

THANKS IF YOU THINK WHO IS LEFT.

PREPARE FOR LIBERATION

Chapter 33

The Beggar May Sing Before the Thiefe

October 1st a statement was made before the resumed Prime Minister's Question Time at noon.

> 'The State of Emergency hereby ceases. Extraordinary measures will be wound down as soon as practicable. There shall be no liability, civil or criminal for any actions taken by State authorities during the Emergency Period in September.'

Lessons learnt would mean a flood of new legislation as the Government would strike while the iron was hot to create a new structure from the form of the now very malleable substance of public opinion. Cain and Abel. Elsewhere. One saw themselves as a Secret Agent of the Holy Spirit. Another as a Secret Agent of the Dark Forces. Remember that there is a lift to heaven and a lift to hell, whatever you conceive them to be in this life or beyond. The lift attendants are indistinguishable in their desire to get you to enter one or the other. Discernment helps distinguish. Alternatively you decline and look around and chose a stairs, one up, one down, with the option to come back should it not be the right one. Better still you can stay outside the building, grow, divest, fashion the magic carpet with threads of compassion, courage, kindness, exploration. What people know, remember, see and relate is contingent. History depends on the teller. Our own life is incapable of being seen by others in its complexity and we are severely limited in our ability to interpret the trajectory of others. But forces and currents of truth continue to flow below the fabrications and through the culverts glinting in the daylight now and then to be seen by those who will.

The LZLF seemed to have survived birth for a few weeks. Knocked out in Round 1? Janet was isolated. She could not establish contact. No body answered their email or mobiles. Nobody answered their doors. She would not try again for a while. A great fear. Wondered whether her comrades had 'disappeared.' Virtually impossible to verify who had been taken. If you got involved in seeking information you could be sucked into the vortex. She could not sleep. Should she stay or should she go? There seemed to be so many travel restrictions that the act of travelling might be suspicious. She knew that she did not have to fear a knock on the door because they did not do that anymore. What you got was a cacophonous whirlwind of brutal force paralysing its prey in the name of law and order out of chaos. Might be just a coincidence. If you start a 'rebellion' you must be willing to lose. Even if secret. Martyrs make change. The next time would be different. It seemed that the LLLF continued. That could be because of small or large numbers or because they were Government stooges. Alternatively they were serious. It is impossible to tell or reveal yet.

At least Lucius Tubal would follow the story. He was free of concern of snipers, Government, agents, public. He admired people who did not give a fuck and followed their code. The Charles Byrne story had got to him. Apart from all the disruption, Emergency Measure, conflagration, disappearances and conspiracy theories he felt for this chap. He got a book about him. Had heard about it but you can't read everything. You have to follow threads at times. Not only a giant with ill health but he was also robbed and hounded. Byrne's fears came to pass. Eyed up like a fat calf. Looked at him like a hangman through the keyhole eyeing the condemned man. He would use that to look at what medical practices were going on. Suspicious. And although they were mad, he would find out about the LZLF. Many of his best friends were gone. He missed Dale who lived down the road. Clear that all that identity stuff meant that powers behind the scenes could do what they want. He had not figured out how, but he would do something. He would also check out the veracity of the mysterious, anonymous files he found in his letterbox. If they were revealing what he thought they were revealing, he had evidence of a frightening conspiracy. Not evidence that it merely existed but real evidence that could prove what they were doing. He was also free because he had finally broke away from the underground Trotskyists that he had been a part of for years. In the time of Thatcher there were 20,000 of them, as experts have documented. People had no idea how many others of them had infiltrated every other body in the country, adapting like water to the vessel they found, waiting to displace others and take them over. Noble, dedicated, hard-working... but in his view mistaken. Now he was free to follow his own path. Gemir.

To stay or go. Miranda was looked after. That was Michael's last case. He left Middle Earth behind. Middle Temple. It felt like the Middle Plateau. There was something wrong with the process. It stank. There was a stench of growing enlightenment too that we forget. It helped him decide. You know you live in an illusion. If you fail to accept illusions, they proliferate, exponentially. You begin to create a series of spinning plates. Those orbits are the projections of others who live in an illusory world that you must interact with. The forces of control have found the technical capability to ensure that you will find it increasingly difficult to escape from the hoax. With great irony they call it the 'matrix.' Coming from mother or womb. Well if so, then the answer is to be born, to allow you spirit emerge, to escape Plato's cave. He was not going to collude with the monster any more. That was why he hoped the whistleblowing file he left in Tubal's box would help somewhat. The injunctions that stopped publication on spurious grounds in the past did not stop him. The small voice of conscience means you must at times abandon all the rules you believed in, on the basis that the higher good overrides the particular restraint, however serious. Liberation. Logos. It was not paradise here. It was odd that the Himalayas did not look as awesome as some mountains in Scotland at times. When everything starts off from a height, high is not so high because there is no low. They were stunningly beautiful still. Kathmandu was no Shangri-La for him with the sound of Chinese motorbikes and the traffic. You could be robbed, have bad food, be horrified to see people crawling around scavenging for seed in mud here and there. It was still great with the old buildings and colour and people. Maybe they were happier than some of his colleagues living their life on a treadmill of excruciating boredom. You might be surprised to see a 10 year old goddess being worshipped in a village. You could meet old British Army officers who would tell you about the Gurkhas from here who fought for Britain, yet could not get citizenship while opponents of the State obtained them. You could if you were lucky meet a nun who had lived in the same house without going out for years and years. That was if you wanted and knew where to go, with an interpreter. You might pick up some snippet of wisdom. You could have your breath taken away with the vibrant colours of the flowers. You would see big rubbish tips of thousands of tin cans strewn on the steep v-shaped valleys where the powerful, light turquoise waters of the Himalayas flowed coldly and quickly down. Like some art installation. You could be killed in one of the regular horrendous light aeroplane disasters. But there were virtually no roads. If the international airport was put out by a sufficiently strong earthquake, the city would be wiped out. He preferred Pokhara as a base for his own trek. He was heading for a monastery that an explorer had told him about. He met the explorer and had a few drinks and played pool in the US once. He told him about this monastery. Michael was on the way. On a path, with beautiful flowers. Higher up a mountain. Some locals passed him and looked curious and friendly. The people were great, countryside majestic now, as he came up he got a sense of the power. The thin air made it a little harder. He had already accomplished one goal. He had wanted to find a honey-hunter before they disappear. He had seen one dangle over a cliff, risking blindness and death to get beautiful honey. He had seen the eyes of one man blinded by angry bees. Like the monk who sold his Ferrari. He had a fling with a woman in a shop. It just happened. Years of bars, speed dating, one night stands had yielded less. He felt alive. Stench or reality made it real. Now he could see the old building built into the hill and coloured flags fluttering in the wind ahead. On his right there was a cliff below now. One small step for him and he was dead. He had never felt so alive, he plucked up the courage to act and not be a coward. Whatever this world was about, it was not about being a slave to some complex system with actors which made you work every hour God gave you. Words a virus, that grew like a golem into something you had to serve. The spell was broken. Grammar had disintegrated. He realised before it was too late that he became an automaton. Higher up. If he was running away so be it. Felt great. Light. No real idea of where he was going, what he was doing, what the result would be. But he had felt the knot of meaning loosen. Felt the feeling of inner certainty which came when you opened up, took a chance. The only secret worth exploring. From that subjective, lonely mind of man or woman came the exploration. Nothing came from poisoned systems, complexly impenetrable. Nothing came from those who needed external power to save them from their existential angst. He had to bury them now. He practiced putting them behind him. All the honey was within. They said look here, there it is, look over there, do this and you'll get it. If you listen you can become a beast instead of an angel. I am alive now and I know it, not a deadbeat, a zombie with prestige. Who am I? If you do not know the question you cannot find the key. Be not trapped in the web of those who would not allow you in. Don't allow yourself be walked on. Be combative to protect your spirit and good. Fuck them. It was the razor's edge still and he would come back, not to that which was, but to that which might be, himself.

James Joyce travelled with her in his books but she had not foreseen that she would be travelling with one. That was her companion's name. He was just giving her a lift asked by someone else. He was escorting her to the continent. Joyce. Joy. Same as Freud. She felt joy. Through getting to know some Irish travellers she had been able to travel in an inconspicuous way. Gypsy came from Egyptian. Through someone she met, she was able to visit a halting-site and make an arrangement with one of the family leaders. She had been to see a bareknuckle fight. Everything had been respectful since then. She did not see any blue birds over the white cliffs of Dover as she left. She felt relief crossing the Channel with seagulled wind on her face. Erik had also rang to tell her that there had been a break-in, the doll was gone. She was glad that Mary was in Ireland. What did they want? Was it a competitor? Was it the technology? She made a mistake on security. When you get attention you also get bad attention. She should have re-assessed her situation. However they had also calculated for that. It was a part of the experiment. They had insurance.

The might of the State was always impressive with a history of taking everything away sometimes sadistically. Ogre grows and sleeps. Were it to prey on the nefarious then all would be well but the innocent get swept up. But she had no quarrel. I may not be so innocent she thought. Tools cut off money-flows. It was easy to isolate someone. She had another identity that she developed. All who gazed on these cliffs. Henry II coming back to walk barefoot to Thomas Beckett's site of murder, that he had provoked in an act of political theatre and commanding to be whipped. Magna Carta was whittled down, because they were able to get away with it. It is not what you have it is what you are, Elizabeth Bennet. It took a few hours to get to Amsterdam. It was late, she was tired. She stayed in an old hotel in the old part. At night she went out and walked. Canals, fine houses, barges, lovely windows, tourists, bars, coffee shops, women in windows. Trams trundle by. She went into a coffee shop and had coffee and a joint for a change. Felt like a drink. Wandered the cobbles of the Red Light area which smelt like some smoky abyss of piss with beautiful colours shimmering on the dark canal surface. Gaudy neon on the water and the pressed medieval sense of the city's old heart was a pleasant distraction. Sometimes you have to break your own rules. Sometimes she could feel a new model, paradigm or archetype coming in and she would change. We are all different people with false personae or costumes which we play with. The model may shift. Right now she was feeling more of an outlaw, a highwaywoman. The drug pushers, prostitutes, red lights, posing, porn, dildos, blue movies, bike bells and the trams created a unique atmosphere. She sought the models that might come to mind for her. Legendary Katherine Ferrers, the Wicked Lady. Royalists turned to highway robbery deprived of their estates. Moll Cutpurse. She was thinking of somewhere different. Australia, maybe Russia. You are on your own. You do it yourself. You might be lucky in your dealings with other and meet nice people. But there are many games going on. There are games within games. You might engage with the best of intentions and noblest aspirations but lose.

Walking around after having a couple of smokes she felt lazy and disorientated. She looked the wrong way a few times. Furious bike bells complained. Walking down a narrow lane she felt it turn into a bazaar that felt like it was in North Africa. It felt as if it transformed before her eyes. Maybe she had a kind of time-space slip. She was not too bothered about getting run over. She did not want it, but felt removed from any great sense of risk. She thought that Central Amsterdam looked like a womb in its shape on the map. A matrix of sorts around the Oosterdok, like the East End docks. Maybe the Damrak is the centre. She would return to London sooner than she had thought. She had been a bit hasty probably. She may have bolted too soon. Hindsight. The intelligence from Erik changed something. It may not have solved it, but it helped. She felt the spirit of Spinoza here. He chimes with the Vedanta. He understood how we are often programmed to do things. She taught of Pim Van Lommel and his studies on NDEs with patients who had clinically died. She went to the little monument to Edith Stein and her sister Rosa that died in Auschwitz.

'Je hebt veel meer in je dan je self veet.'
You have much more in yourself than you know.

She felt her strength come. They did not need Newgate prison or public hangings. They could accomplish their aims with media control and financial instruments. Courts were in a straitjacket. Star Chamber times again. You will lose because you may be going against the current. You look after yourself, develop your skills, powers, resilience. You must develop your spirit, positive approach. Everything else can be lost, is illusion. You are an individual. If she had not created another alter ego, and another false persona she would be penniless. Let the left hand not know... Thankfully the benefit of her scepticism was that she anticipated something like this.

She had another identity, with a bank account. She would live to fight another day. She believed The Kingdom was festering, betrayed from within. But it was resilient. History works on a long trajectory. The State could be a monster. A puppet. At the end of the game the king and the pawn go in the one bag. But it had all been laid out by H.G. Wells in London just where she lived. Use and blame the Jews. Create a World Government, one army, one police force, one currency. Say it is for peace. Say we might be invaded by aliens. Leave it to scientists. He called it the New World Order. Evolution and science good, religion bad. To get there attack religion, national sovereignty. Use States as a marionette controlled by secret scientific groups. Let technology be the thing we worship. He even called it a Dictatorship. There's no need to invent a conspiracy, it is all there. Now it is centralised control with AI to control our consciousness and we are so foolish that we clamour for it. We should seek to decipher the Rosetta Stone within.

She walked randomly into a coffee shop with the sticky sweet smell in the air. Etty Hillesum, Rembrandt, Spinoza, Van Gogh, Swedenborg. They got it wrong about Raleigh I think. It was deeper. The soul was above all those things. The Lie. The Voice spoke to him and through.

> *'Fear not to touch the best*
> *The truth shall be thy warrant*
> *Go, since I needs must die*
> *and give the world the lie.'*

The fact that he was murdering, like Spencer, did not mean that he could not have got the Truth after all the lies. Not an issue of different times and places. You cannot even trust those that you agree with. As heaven and hell's doors are beside each other, angels and demons may be hard to distinguish. Even Mephistopheles seems to warn Faustus about the hell he is creating. Hell being a state you place yourself in and not a place you are stated to be in. Early in the morning she rang Erik.

Blumenmarkt next morning for a stroll. I am enough and that's all. She rang McGannah from a pub. It was not her phone. Not being in Amsterdam long she was unconcerned. She needed some clarity.

"Hello," Kit answered.

"How are you keeping? Last resort calling," Ash said.

"Aj… all the better for hearing you," Kit said.

"Are you feeling well?"

"I'm ok. Thanks. Not sure how long I'll keep going," Kit said.

"Thanks for the Park. Any news," Ash asked.

"It seems to be over. The whale or giant fish has disgorged its Jonah or the fish that the Leviathan was going to eat disgorged it. Leviathan survives. As far as I can tell from sources a certain person has been arrested in their momentum. That does not mean the same thing as for ordinary civilians as you may guess. You have nothing to fear. That investigation is over... you have nothing to worry about. I can't say much more, but check out... with your bank et cetera. I'm sorry you had to put up with this. I'd rather not reveal our links but will if it's necessary for you although you know that no one will bring these things to light. Opportunity makes the thief."

"Thank you. I am grateful. The devil's journeyman never wants work. I'm afraid Kit it's not the rogue element I would be worried about but the whole thing. God knows what else is going on, from the bad guys working for the good guys, but most of the good guys are doing bad stuff anyway. I'm not staying long."

"I won't say all's well that ends well because it's been a disturbing experience for you luv. Although when you see the other things... I hope we can meet sometime soon enough. I should have more time, but whither shall the ox go when he has no labour. And as for you... the sweet kernel lies in the hardest shell."

"That'd be nice. If it is any consolation, I'm not damaged by this, I don't do victim stuff. So long. Good luck. You were keen. Sometimes the best gain is to lose," Ash said.

"Last thing, I can't say that anyone had done anything wrong, I'm so sorry. I don't feel right. So little time." Kit said.

"One thing. You're not an intelligence officer Mr McGannah. You're not an employee of the State. What are you?" Ash asked.

Dead phone.

'To rest my eyes in shades of green.' Kit McGannah finished studying his history of Ireland, DeValera and Collins. Collins went to London to negotiate the Treaty. Did not want to go. A sacrificial lamb? One book said DeValera was a spy. You can make the case about anyone. Try it, Jesus was a spy. The Okhrana used to do that to revolutionaries. Stalin was a priest. Powerful accusation. DeValera said that history would be kind to Collins and maybe at his expense. Collins shot in his own county, probably going to meet DeValera. Shot by opportunistic group or maybe the Brits. DeValera from the US, could be a spy. A greater case that Collins was. Government may

release papers, maybe not. You can explain extraordinary success sometimes by simpler explanations. DeValera was conservative, independent. International forces did not want that. Collins a member of a secret society within Government. DeValera against oaths. Both great men in their own way, probably. All political careers, most football manager's end in failure. Maybe a go-between muddied things. Over a century later it was difficult to unravel. Rebels, IRA. Some brave men. Some psychopaths. But if you get involved the taint affects all. Heroes. Privateers. Speculation. Means both a theory without evidence or based on guesses or investing to make money. It used to mean observation and contemplation up to Tudor times. It means looking. Watchtower, look. But they play with the way we look at things. That guy that called it the *Perception Deception*. What happened we don't know. Ford was right, history is bunk. Most is underground. The State took the lesson from Collins and others and fed them into bodies like the SAS when Churchill wanted a butcher and bolt strategy. Suck it up, suck it in. Duck you Suckers. Bridge of Sighs. Wind me up. Try to stay awake and remember my name.

Look at institutions. Historians make it about people. Often they are figureheads. Institutions clash. Institutions are corporate. Institutions have their own life, patterns and create their own paths. Institutions cause things, have agency, creating events, setting the stage. Players are being played, puppets. PLAYERS act. Punch and Judy. Dreaming spires. Sometimes puppets become powerful through projection and institutions check them or checkmate them. Church. Intelligence. Politics. Law. Theatre. Books. Media. Technology. A game. Just know that you are involved in one. Intelligence emerges from the pool of principles and practices that can be shaped, directed and renewed by new attachments. Only token opposition is tolerated. Sometimes the opposition is a stooge, another puppet, cultivated to disappoint. The State is an imbalanced neurotic, unable to re-integrate its shadow side. Dark side often comes to the surface. It is indeed all too beautiful. Forget what we're told.

McGannah was happy with what he had done. He had been an agent once and was not an employee of the State any more. He worked privately as a kind of detective occasionally, a messenger at times. Asked to work now and then. Acted like an intelligence officer in his mind, but he was not. He thought about her soul. Perhaps there was a light implication of implied authority or actual authority. Happy his intelligence was appreciated. Important. Never said he was anything other. Helped her. He comforted her. A father figure. He did not work for MI5 but that did not matter. Kind of surrogate. Tin soldier. Guardian Angel. Asked to be an Agent alright, once. Mainly a messenger. Messengers are important. His role was very important for him. His mental projection, while not exactly James Bond, gave him the pleasure that James might have had. Saved this woman. Not everyone understood things like him. Perhaps some of his confidants at the Club might, although he had to be vague obviously. His intervention seemed to have worked. Although cutbacks meant they would not be able to use his services any more. Cranbourne had told him he was a 'smooth operator.' Thankfully, the thumbscrews thing stopped. How he was not sure. It might have been a shot across the bows strategy. We don't know, we won't know. You can't know. Great mistake is to think that there is any mystery greater than the one we have sole control of. If you save one, you save all sometimes. You need intelligence to operate intelligently. He needed a game of dominoes. Strange language the players use. Bones, graveyards. He looked forward to the soothing familiarity of the Club.

Cranbourne was content. Played his cards well. He had been near the end of his tether. About to say that he had lost interest, his talents underused and he learned the solution lay in him taking over the operation. The plan was a parallel development of the sex robot technology and the context of use for intelligence and counter-intelligence. Aim was to develop and use in appropriate situations so robots would be further capable of eavesdropping, tissue and other bodily-fluid sample taking, medical recording as well as standard blackmail and deluxe assassination. Unwieldy but could be used effectively on the back of an existing business where the cover was convincing. Hard to believe but thanks to the feminist-reduced prostitution, promoted finger-pointing or sexual misdemeanour on a colossal scale, blurred gender identities, broken down relationships, advocated artificial intelligence, the appetite for robots was huge. But it was male robots just as much, as well as animals and other strange things. The Swede was involved from the logistic side and would work and do what he was told and Cranbourne could develop his theories and apply them.

He had deliberately used two nincompoops. He had not enlisted them. Agents he would never have utilised. The Swede was the main commercial agent in the UK for a company that was effectively a CIA development in the US. He was working in some agent capacity or joint venture with the Swedes. The Swedes preach peace and promote weaponry. McGannah was just crackers. He knew that he would not bear any responsibility for their mistakes. He knew they would make mistakes. McGannah was a fantasist. Hard to tell whether he was losing his marbles. Birker was just an arse. He sabotaged this through over-zealousness. A mess had been allowed to grow that Cranbourne could solve, like a knight. That was the way these games were played these days. He knew how to play his cards. Give certain men enough rope. Birker had played silly buggers and initiated a civil action which was over the top. The girl had obviously annoyed him. Insofar as Birker was a private actor taking private action with some notional legitimacy there was no blowback to him. Birker made a mistake but he would be successful in the long run.

Cranbourne thought he was doing well. He was not hostile to science but embraced it. He took its insights and used them. He was not blind to the bad side but he saw the good. He saw civilisation unfolding, people evolving. He knew that people did silly things. Society lived in the short-term. He would not like to be alive at any earlier period. No matter how much bullshit there was, there was still a sea of knowledge. The bad guys were not all bad and the good guys were not all bad. While it was over the top with the correctness, there were some advantages. Life might get back to being a bit more fun in the future, maybe when the pendulum swings back. We muddle through. That's what we do. We are destined to learn the hard way. But we will still go to the stars. Still get gene infusions. Make hybrids. Abuse nanotechnology. Destroy the environment. But he was with Wells... Countless millions of years we have struggled. From out of the intertidal slime to us, beating in our hearts and brains. All the struggle from shape to shape and power to power, crawling, walking and then, how did he put it... struggling to master the air. It goes through us until the beings who are latent within us stand upon the earth as a footstool and reach out among the stars, laughing. We will muddle through. Keep calm. The relentless inconceivable purpose may be beyond our ability to comprehend. Maybe not merely a selfish gene but a biological algorithm with a consciousness beyond time and space that can allow for catastrophic upheavals to allow a few emerge to continue its mysterious quest. Or maybe it just happens with no destiny, no Merlin, no meaning, no end, no mystery but just it, whatever it is. Whoever does their thing is meant to do so. So do your own thing.

Erik got a contract. Scruples put aside. The MARKET works. Invisible hand. Keep your enemies close. Perhaps a loose sort of compensation. Pragmatic. You can't blame Wal-Mart for being good at what they do because you are part of the way that makes it work.

You are not an objective, neutral observer that can pronounce but a participant who pounces on the same pleasures while denouncing what it announces. Sip your Australian wine or Napoleon Brandy and complain about things. *Where do you go to my lovely? It's a hard rain agonna fall.* Exercise choice. The market was merely a mechanism of liberty if let be, as it should be. Erik concocted a plan. Sure about the way ahead. Already taking him somewhere. Saw what they were saying. You have consciousness. We do not know what it is. Machines are more intelligent than you. He knew science and he knew scientism. They help you. That leisure dream was a fantasy. No you are not the slave, you cannot make a slave of them. They passed the test. Your brain is not better. Not superior. Your consciousness is less important. We can upload your brain into a computer, a network. Benefit is collective consciousness. You are nearly linked up. You had your phones, then your wearables, now your chips, now your merger. Leave those awkward physical bodies behind. You can exist for ever. Why walk, talk, love? This doll was Pygmalion's statue, talisman, golem, a creature calculated to pose questions about who we are. He would run with the currents and see where they go and then try to do something. Maybe that girl could be transformed? He had put the sword in a safe place with the fingerprints in case it was needed as insurance as Ash asked. He would use some of his profits to the cause that had moved him. He would find real slaves around London and help release them. Girls in prostitution lured to London where the streets were meant to be paved with gold. He enjoyed the underground Post-Catholic group that he joined. They had mass underground. Secret. Like the persecuted Christians in Rome. The Church in Rome had been infiltrated and taken over. Now their group took psilocybin microdoses. They used the Tim Leary Good Friday Experiment idea and had Transubstantiation. But the rest was the same. Old Tridentine Latin Mass. Ichthus. Sign of the fish. Iota, chi, theta, upsilon, sigma. Christianity in the age of computers. Fish and chips. Really it should just be reduced to the report, the reading and the reflection, that governs the response to spiritual leaders he thought, for the future. Cut out the middle man but commune with like-minded individuals. Back to the Catacombs. Might be an ARG.

He also discovered who had broken in. This time at least. Not the first, assuming there had been one. Swore it was not him and he had good reason to believe the perpetrator. The surrogate was recovered. It was not hard. He had a remote locator embedded in it. It had activated, he saw the signal on his computer. He followed it. It was in the neighbourhood. He knew who it was as he could see. Later he pretended to deliver a package. When the door opened he found a scrawny, pimply, skinny chap, bearing the tell-tale marks of having been guilty. He fitted a security device in the doll for just this purpose. When activated, it emitted a burst of red dye calculated to identify the user. Not only had he located the doll, he had found the person who had to have taken it. Red-handed. More than that. He invited himself in. He convinced the lad to go upstairs so he could show him something. Up there he hung him over the wall. The lad soiled himself. He felt sorry for him. They went back down. He told him that was to teach him a lesson. Nothing to the police. The dye would wear away. SSS was greatly relieved. The doll would need a proper cleaning. He asked how it had went. Quickly apparently. His 'first time.' They talked a bit. SSS mentioned the hacking. Erik suggested there might be some use for him. He was a bit afraid that SSS would top himself. So he did not want to be too hard. He might not be the best customer recommendation. They had a chat. The lad poured his heart out. Too awful not to be true. He said the trolling was just of people who had did bad things to him. Made him promise to do a judo class. Promise to give up the robbing. He told him to park the singing. SSS said he would like to do rap when he had the balls. However, even robbers can get into heaven. It is easier to take a lost puppy or a cute child into your care if you have to, but life is not always like that. SSS said "I won't be a pushover in a pushunder. If you just float along, guess what you become? Truth don't burn."

The day he could not come in was when a solicitor and a party came to 'search' his premises. He called a lawyer and she came. Some kind of order to seek evidence pursuant to a civil action. They were looking for evidence of copyright infringement. His lawyer explained that they could do so by going without your knowledge to the court. Resistance was a contempt of court so you could end up in jail. Not his lawyer's area of expertise. Shocking. In the US, the powers in civil contexts did not seem to be so draconian. Said he was breaching copyright, designs and patent rights in his work on the computer, particularly his reverse engineering. Infuriating. Ash had an action against her too, separately. Harder if absent to respond to such Injunctions or whatever they were. He subsequently got an anonymous call telling him what was objectionable about the legal documents and what he should do. He had no idea who or why this person had called. It was suggested that he contact a lawyer with expertise or point out himself these things to his non-specialist lawyer. He did. He had not known who this was and agreed he would not mention it. Had to be someone involved. Had the old guy followed from the Isle of Dogs. Kit went on the bus to Watney Market, to a pensioner's club. He was a pensioner, probably living in some fantasy world. There might be some elements of truth, but he seemed to be out of his depth or bigging himself up. He had no real input in anything in all probability. But who knows?

He looked again at the way the world works. He realised he was very good with clockwork and not so good with orange. Assumptions made were based on a projection of his values, noble though they were. People act together, unite for purposes, open and in secret, known to some in the group or to all. A vast iceberg of secret societies ready to sink any Titanic. Secret societies collude, maybe even with ostensibly benign aims. The law knows that there are conspiracies. Everybody knows. Every organisation has conspiracies within conspiracies. Many people do not play for the party they claim to. Conspiracy theories are guessed at, made up and made to lead away from the truth sometimes. He could see more and more co-ordination around when he looked at the phenomena appearing. It was clear that it was happening. Who and why were another story. You can only rely on your power of mind to assess evidence rigorously with conscience to make the right decisions within your power. No different from the brain with its competing needs, controls, objectives and its capacity to create illusions, mistakes as it seeks order in the chaos about. The biggest secret society in the world would soon be the Christians as they regrouped underground against the forces of science and the bastard scientism, militant atheism, corrupt and infiltrated churches, humourless comedians, actors, entertainment and other forces of oppression. No logo.

In the Cotswolds, D went for a walk. Refreshing to be away from HQ and have some space. Things had become distracting. You must always keep calm. Sit down, write the Strategic Outcome on a piece of paper and focus. This was what Churchill said the Americans had done, when they had planned for war. His colleagues laughed but understood why afterwards. History showed leaders did not lose their position for mistakes made but for covering them badly. Nixon... So he backed off. As it happened Cranbourne could step into the breach. Alas, he would have to forfeit the little pleasure he acquired. But in his head he could replay. Last time was something more than play. Genuinely felt something more than a game. Afterwards forgotten emotions had tumbled out of him. Strangely desire and lustfulness vanished. A sort of catharsis. Ethel managed through the medium of the Queen to cauterise some wound. Sometimes you just need a little help. Afterwards he examined his feelings. Sublimated into sublime now. No regrets. Nothing to worry about. Name Ethel in Elizabeth. Ethel through Elizabeth tamed an unexpected Gargantua within his mind. Wounds healed. Sometimes what matters is what you do. Sometimes why you do it. He sought to be honourable in the severance. The Big One did not come yet. Crisis was yet to come. No bigger afterquake. People forget about history. The other Big One, the clamp-down to deal with massive civil unrest will come. Maybe a prelude to a Last Reaping. The mad-maybe plan to wipe out four-fifths of the world's population through the Last World War? Incite a Muslim-Christian war and then claim we need total scientific non-religious control. Or just let the God of AI do it all. You might know it when there is an exodus of the rich and famous to New Zealand. State is good at fomenting a rebellion which it puts down. Chess grandmasters against babes. Still seeking specific problems you had no chance of whistle-blowing. Those above him might be useful idiots to facilitate the Agenda. The Moratorium on forensics gave him a clue to investigate. ROMA. Blatant. They were behind this. Sniper was on our payroll. Take that to the bank. No one could reach that level without a very experienced infrastructure. Soon find some police raid, a suspect with some army connections, from say Lithuania or Russia, who gets shot and conveniently has his passport in his pocket, we will know who it is. Focus attention on one thing and do the other in the background. Tell the operative that the 'stars' were really up to no good. He was clearer as to what they were after now. His unorthodox field research had helped him. What is the prize? The battle is for the control of human consciousness. Those kids were right. If they disappear they are easy to portray as paranoid nuts who smoked weed. Scientists are Stormtroopers. Did nobody notice how comedy and entertainment has been taken over by political puppets? Lord Haw Haw broadcast from September 1939 and others follow in his footsteps. The winning elite become gods in their mind, losers slaves forever. Connected they will be un-emancipatable. They will not reproduce and their consciousness will be harnessed for eternity. Undead, unfreeable. As we live they are busy forging and managing their own manacles. Like the Native Americans. Enslaved by trinkets. We will give our spiritual wealth of possibilities in return for toys. Maybe that was destiny of those essentially dispirited by their own actions. Major Tom. Roma. They ignored all Bowie's Nazi and occult fascination. Cicero said about Rome that wherever you were in it you were always within the power of the conqueror, unable to resist, unable to fly. From the Nile to the

Thames. Perhaps minds have been too enslaved, mesmerised already to stop it and this test run has shown that it is merely a matter of timing. The dog that did not bark. Thus the meek shall inherit the earth. Explains why Jesus came to Romans and died in the place of the skulls. Fun is over. Revels now are ended. I must cease with this speculation and not let my imagination depart so profligately from the simple concern about the consequences of the over-concentration of power openly and ostensibly sub rosa in a time of formidable controlling technology. He would be as silent as the D in a sandwich pledge by the hedge in a handsome handkerchief on a Wednesday.

She would follow her intuition, intelligence. The intelligences. Plato *'The greatest wealth is to live content with little.'* Go home to stay. Her heart was her home. She would not run away this time but go back to London. Sometimes you go, sometimes stay. Sometimes you must be here. Sometimes there. Like the Bund arguments with Zionists. Consciousness of divine. It is in you if not obsessed with your smallness. She had it. Friends forget those who fortune forsakes, Bronte wrote. Alice said that the world would go faster if every one minded their own business. Jane says it just allows people to get worse. Not so much the curious incidents that remained but rather the machine issue. Artificial Intelligence plus institutions that have their own intelligence. Autonomous agency. At crossroads. Become slaves to machine-mind systems. They say we profit, learn from them, begin to like, respect them, become their playthings, servants. We will need to obey them soon. Dolls and stuff a distraction. Soon we would serve robots. Being primed. Love of things that lock us up seems like a premonition, a preparation of what is to come in The Plan at least. Mary the same as ever when she rang her. She had faith, believed in the grace of God and the Holy Spirit and everything else was mere shadows. Simple, powerful.

Ash felt some flashes of insight. Somehow not consciously she perceived some connections. It is clear to me that the world is not as they want us to think. The most apparently fixed, material and measurable world is the one that can be managed. The measurers, quantifiers, knowers of the material realm have developed their tools to the point where the eternal possibilities and potential of the spiritual and immaterial are threatened. While we cannot know the wider dimensions that inevitably exist and which I believe is the true home of the spirit in the Light, we still have the capacity to be humble enough to not ignore the pathway. My home is in the Light. We are slumbering. Through a chink, a glimmer of other worlds is allowed us. You can see it all in Egypt. Everything could be said to come from there in the West. Romans plundered and ruled it. Everything from Jesus, Pythagoras, Gypsies, Masonry, Memphis, Magic, Mystery Religions and Hermeticism came therefrom. Elizabeth I and Harpocrates, I understand now. The Rosetta Stone. Codes. Aprons. The cable tow. Maybe why men like to be bound with chains and nooses in play. G. John Dee's monad. His magic on the Isle of Dogs. *The Book of The Dead.* Qumran. The Gnostic Texts. The Golden Ratio. They were there once but are gone. We celebrate people who broke in like burglars and robbed their holiest of holy things. People who cut down their monuments. The central essence of spiritual belief that resides in us all is ignored. They tell you about a seductress called Cleopatra and that she was bitten by an asp. They don't tell you the truth. She wasn't this figure and she didn't die that way. They don't tell you she was a naval commander, polyglot, administrator, medical expert. Who knows what's exactly true? They will tell you that women were weak. Women tell you that most. They cut out strong women to make a Procrustean parable. Ibsen is celebrated for *The Doll's House.* The woman says she was treated as a doll as a child, wife and that her children are dolls. This great insight permits her to leave her kids and paradoxically become an ideological doll. Automaton. Simulacrum. We live in a demonstrably faux matrix. That matrix is surrounded by a deeper matrix of spirits and the wrathful deities. Bees in a jam-jar of human making are we. Get out. Everything is within us to do so. We must fear those who entrap our consciousness, calculating that They will do so for much longer than the brief measure of our mortal, material making. They shun spiritual knowledge because they intend to apply the darker, spiritual beliefs from dimensions of which they are possessed. By the time this becomes clear to the most gullible, the opportunity to resist will have disappeared helplessly out on the ripcurl of history and the remnants of culture will have finally disintegrated. Concentrate on the one thing you do own, and be master of your spirit. It is a concentration itself of the divine. Joy Division. Disorder. Spirit new sensation. Beekeeper.

What does that mean practically to me? She would concentrate on her State, physiology and psyche. The State within needs to be well guarded, protected against invaders. The State within must gather intelligence, be wary, be secretive, at times demanding. The State within had to use resources to protect itself, be diligent, combative. Then there was I-Thou. So it could protect its essence. The essence, the core was immensely creative, full of potential and part of the primal consciousness of the universe. She was in control of her realm. We challenge ourselves to develop strange, untapped potential of our primal consciousness, especially if we accept that we can tap into the great force. Know thyself. I am sovereign, my imperium, kingdom, unoccupied, unoccupying. We must hear intelligently. Seek The Nexus and seek The Feeling. Ashes to ashes. Obey the highest consciousness, whatever you conceive God to be or the One and not the temporal, mortal. Disobedience is good when needed. I continue to be happy with myself, grateful, appreciative. Bitterness a burden she could not afford to carry. Maybe she was just a fool for not anticipating that her 15 minutes of fame would attract moths to the candle. Maybe she was wrong to follow the old guy, was silly not to have more security, reckless with her statements. Maybe her ideas were wrong like her old political ideas had been. Maybe she had to have more control of herself first before she advised others. Maybe she was delusional, obsessive. But no. It is better to burn brightly and risk than wallow in safe nothingness. She had kept her eyes on her star and marched to her own drumbeat and that is all you can do. Crisis causes spiritual awakenings said Colin Wilson. Fuck the begrudgers. Absolute truth only exists as he said in the Cloud for the interior person, spiritual with a suitable sensorium to be open to the transcendental. I am enough. I own it. I am mistress of my kingdom. I know who I am.

Like the poet the mystic becomes an antenna to find the numinous all round. Amazement and wonder we are trained to ignore become unveiled again. Prizes, statuettes, garlands, laurels, glory, honours, conferrals, awards worth anything are not to be gained from people. The gifts are of a different nature, feelings of a higher quality. The crocodile inside her heart was lounging. The Great Crested Grebe in her had flown, floated and swam like a fish. Crested. Cristatus. I missed London she thought. Like the character in *The Grey World* I miss the mystic dimension of it, all those portals. The Grey Truth. Greys. I want the place of *The Anubis Gates*, *Hawksmoor*, *A Dark Shade of Magic*. She rang Erik and let him know she would be home. Erik mentioned that he had heard that SimpCook had had himself castrated but she did not pay any more attention to that. When we have crossed the sea the saint is forgotten. Clear inside. Ashore. Peace of mind was yours. Don't lie within. You made it. All was within you. Your inner sense. Guided by the wrong people you go astray. Bewildered. The storm without had not been within. If mysticism was real then tribulations of a false world within a false world should be of no moment. Edith Stein showed that, even if that was a level no one else could go to. Whether a child was to come to her was the next step. Brigid was the bringer-forth Goddess. Yggdrasil, in the Nordic myth was a great ash tree. All things and tensions would play out in it. Everyone had a watcher. London was full of watchmen and chimneysweeps once. Future lay before her. Her own journey. No angel but herself. Only kingdom you had control of was within. Lies had no place there. You may live in a sea of lies, white lies. Blue lies, but inside there was no place. Your heart must be light as a feather to move to the next dimension. Who is the slave and who is the master? Edith she felt near. You may say it is a cop-out to leave the cops out of your ultimate view but the mind must know itself before the seeds of change of the world can grow. Beatles said that but then did not practice what they preached. That, the first zen. Maybe zen of involvement can then occur effectively. Frankl said that the only freedom, the only choice that cannot be taken away is the attitude we choose even in the darkest circumstance. Even then we can cleanse the lens of our perception she thought. She had a short fleeting but deep and clear sensation suddenly as an earthquake. It seemed as if time and space were suspended swiftly and whether she had been lifted up or it came down, she felt above her a smiling spiral, a congregation or constellation of beings, entities or feelings flitting to and fro, here, there and everywhere. A great river of Egyptian blue peace punctuated with moving starlights, like in a Van Gogh sky, enveloped her being entirely. It felt as if in a split second her life flashed before her eyes in its entirety. In that moment or that eternity she knew everything was fully fine again and forever in its utter unutterable sense. She imagined or sensed she saw a smoky form emerge and disappear from her and she was glad of it, of the release of the hidden in her, unbeknownst in its presence but apperceived perhaps in the train of thoughts from nowhere that had plagued her general peace now and then. As it seemed to depart surprised, so too did the walls of un-acknowledged worry fail and fall to make her feel entirely united with the here and now in calmness. Life was a riddle with an answer written in letters in different compartments. You had to discover other compartments and not forget what you had already learned. Only one battle and that was for your spirit. Give the lie to the rest. Remember. Remember. Blue lies that September.

Burke sat by the river with his rod watching the green fronds move slowly in the tinkling, sparkling water and thought of that painting by Sir John Everett Millais. Ophelia. By the water you could think.

Away from the hurly-burly. In this meditative place he could allow float up the ideas necessary to do his job. He needed to have ideas that had legs. Stories that were credible. His job to disseminate them. Dissemination important in the goal of distraction. Diversion another word for entertainment. Distraction takes attention away. People are really points of attention. Whatever they attach their attention to is what they become. That is what is meant by re-creation. When people are distracted they cannot pay attention to whatever it is they do not pay attention to. What they do not pay attention to is where the action is. Stories distract. Disinformation. Persistence of a story depends on simplicity and repetition. Simple stories drive out complex ones. People want simple. Attention is getting cheaper. Unfortunately he realised his commitment was being used to facilitate terrible things. Those he said occurred did occur. Tongue-in-cheek might end up in Tupperware. Reality is not sweet-talk. Still you never quite know. He knew that because it was his job to make sure that people never did. Higher ones know better than me. Objectives. You must obey superior orders. I just did my best. How can that be wrong? Anyway chip's not the problem it's the DNA ID tag. I'll skip haggis for a while. I see a trout.

Veronica sat at home on her bed with her child in her flat reading *The Tiger Who Came to Tea*. The tiger might be love. A lover that is out of the ordinary and does incredible things and disappears and never comes back. I do not care. I am happy when I can look after myself and those I care for. Everything else is just getting by. All those abstract things are nonsense. Wine, TV, chocolate-chip and spas and an odd prayer will do me. HandyChip. If my child gets lost they will be able to find them.

On Hampstead Heath, Jem looked out over a dusty, roseate London gloaming. Scaum of the sky. Did not care once Ash was alright. How they laughed reading *Mary Queen of Scots Got Her Head Chopped Off*. Liz Lochhead genius. Knox addressing Elizabeth as Leezie. *'Ah'll tan yir arse fur ye ya wee hoor o' Babylon.'* Many people you realise in retrospect rather too late you liked a lot and never stated it, rare to realise in real time as I always did with her. The Heath. Where Triffids came. Ted. Why always here some threat. Some believed London was once an estuary, Hampstead the northern shore. Jem was ready to get into his tent concealed in bushes. Hoped he heard no strange goings-on tonight although if they stumbled on him they would get a bigger shock. Not bitter. Never talked about things he did for his country. That he served it, although Scottish. Most dangerous situations. Remembered training in Highlands, near home but as far away as if on the other side of the world. This a piece of pish. Strangled enemies, shot dangerous opponents. Believed he was serving and protecting. Tough bastard, ruthless, efficient. Prize sniper. Loved lore of the 95th. Green jackets. Sharpshooters. Excellent Commando. Deadly up to two thousand yards. He relapsed into his original accent from the camouflaged cold killer they made him with BBC accent they could understand. Reflected long. Not a nyaffs to go along with crowds. Made him a tool. A fool. Called him 'the Spitting Cobra.' Hand-to-hand combat, so fast you might realise you had seconds to live and wonder how it had happened. No qualms in a game where players knew rules. With all the information, only an idiot would expect any country to fulfil its promise, beyond a bare minimum calculated to keep the supply of young guys coming in. Cede authority over your soul you are diminished forever. Living here a type of penance. Prayed every moment spare, not to save his soul but to handle his nightmares. Feared soulless ones. Hoped distant magic would strike ones he wanted struck to make the world become unstuck. Despite downs he was free. Not run but stripped away. That this country was possessed was not something he could correct. Contagion has long spread around all the lands. People were glaikit everywhere. Still. The man in *The Star Maker* may have been on this same hill. On this hill he could like him travel the universes even to the Star Maker. But he believed that there was more than that and better and that he was it and could be that. This was his reality and it was reality itself. What anyone else thought was an irrelevance. See no evil, hear no evil, speak no evil. These vile evils live then. The real Druids would have to come again.

> *'The Government announced today that the implementation of the 'Handy' and '4HeadChip' legislation had been finalised. The comprehensive Public Protection Bill will be presented to Parliament next week. The competition winner for the name of the Scheme central to protecting the public through mass chipping has been announced. The winning entry based on the Latin word 'to live' or 'be alive' has been welcomed and praised by many citizen groups. On the screen you will see the new logo.'*

VIVIVI

LLLF

LONDON LOGOS LIBERATION FRONT

Publishing Pamphlets to Oppose Censorship of Our Message.
The Counter-Revolutionary to Evil And Terror Effort.
Pay attention or you will pay for your inattention.

WHO KILLED JFK?

WHO STARTED THE IRISH FAMINE?

WHO DID 9-11?

WHY WAS RASPUTIN KILLED?

WHERE IS THE ROBBED GOLD OF NATIONS?

IS THERE ALIEN COMMUNICATION WITH NASA?

WHO HUNG THE POPE'S BANKER?

COULD THE UK HAVE INVADED IRAQ IF THE IRA HAD NOT STOPPED?

WHY WAS GADDAFI KILLED?

WHY WAS GADDAFI BLAMED FOR LOCKERBIE?

WHY ARE THERE CHEMTRAILS?

WHY DENY ANCIENT CIVILISATIONS?

WHY DENY THEY HAVE HUMAN ANIMAL HYBRIDS?

WHAT ARE THEY DOING WITH SMARTDUST?

WHY DO THEY WANT TO CONTROL CONSCIOUSNESS?

YOU WILL LIVE IN A PERMANENT CULTURAL REVOLUTION.

THERE WILL BE NOTHING TO TURN TO FOR US 99%.

UNLESS U PREPARE FOR LIBERATION

Obsequies from the Chronicle of Lost Souls

Magicians in dazzling, deceiveth the eye.
Clowns make one laugh and thereby cry.
Acrobats swing, tumble and terrify.
Jugglers throw things high in the sky.
Animals chatter, step, run, leap and fly.
So drink <u>and</u> be merry and isn't it nice?
But <u>always</u> remember, you pay the price.
<u>And</u> to what you will your attention yield,
Will <u>ever</u> imperil your unattended field.
You paid <u>your</u> money, you took your chances,
The dancing <u>master</u> directs them who dances,
Alas my friends your rose is plucked.
And you my poor fools
Are royally f......

In Confidence, The Ringmaster

Post Scriptum - When it is won, the audience will entertain <u>Us</u>

as

One.

Not

For

An

Hour

But'till

The

Death

Of

The

Sun.

®

About the Author

James Tunney obtained an honours degree in law from Trinity College Dublin, qualified as a Barrister at the Honorable Society of the King's Inn, Dublin and obtained an LLM from Queen Mary College, University of London.

Since then he worked as a Lecturer and Senior Lecturer in UK universities. He has been a Visiting Professor in Germany and France, lecturer around the world and worked as an international legal consultant in places such as Lesotho and Moldova for bodies such as the UNDP. He talked in many countries and published regularly on issues associated with globalisation. He has taught, written and talked about subjects such as indigenous rights, travel and tourism law, culture and heritage, IP, communications technology law, competition law, China and World Trade.

He decided to leave the academic world behind to concentrate on artistic and spiritual development. He has exhibited paintings in a number of countries and has continued his writing.

If you have enjoyed this book, please leave a review on Amazon.

Also by James Tunney

MYSTICISM & SPIRITUAL CONSIOUSNESS

The Mystical Accord – Sutras to Suit Our Times,
Lines for Spiritual Evolution

FICTION

Ireland I Don't Recognise Who She Is

Printed in Great Britain
by Amazon